AirWhisperer

Lorraine Eljuga

Essential Earth

Lorraine Eljuga's website can be visited at http://www.lorraineeljuga.com

This is a work of fiction. Names. All characters, organisations, dialogue are either products of the authors imagination or are used fictitiously, and any resemblance to actual people, living or dead, is coincidental.

First published 2022 Essential Earth Pty Ltd
Copyright © Lorraine Eljuga, 2022

Cover design: Natasha Snow Designs
(https://natashasnow.com/)
Publisher: Essential Earth Pty Ltd
Printed & bound: Ingramspark Australia
ISBN 978-064899-62-1 (Paperback)
ISBN 978-064899-63-8 (eBook)

"Air, I should explain,

becomes wind when it is agitated"

– Lucretius, On the Nature of Things

PROLOGUE

I suppose you could say, I realised I was different the moment I knew I could fly.

I was eleven years old, or thereabouts, and well, it wasn't really flying that first time, it was more like falling with style. I was on the roof of our old house in Blackwater, in northern Australia, escaping Dean and his dumb mates, where they liked nothing more than shoving my head down the outside dunny … just for fun, and … well … I fell. Instead of hitting the ground like I should have, I hovered a foot above the flowerbeds outside our kitchen window …

For

five

whole

seconds

before landing arse first in the dirt.
Was I shocked?

Hell yes!

Was I scared?

Shit no!

And you better believe I raced around the side of the house, climbed up the old lean-to shed like a flat-out goanna, and threw myself off voluntarily.

Childish?

Yeah, that's me in a nutshell.

I jumped off the roof twenty-eight times that morning and thirteen more in the afternoon. The next day was double that, until I finally realised that I wasn't just a punching bag so my big brother could get his kicks and impress his mates … that I was something … well … something kinda *cool*.

Something not of this world.

The power to become invisible came later, along with the other air powers I now take for granted. It was this, that set me on a path of discovery – to find out who I am.

To find River Fulton.

Because what kid, *ever*, can make this claim – I mean, I'm a legend. I'm a freaking superhero.

Years later, and after a lot of poking my nose where it wasn't wanted, I discovered I wasn't Superman, not Ironman or even Spiderman.

I am an Elementar.

I am the AirWhisperer.

Who would've thought?

ONE

FOLLOWING River Fulton has always been easy.

Even in the early days.

Even before we'd formally met.

He had no idea I'd been stalking him, sitting across from him in bars as he picked up the worst, skankiest looking chicks in a ten-kilometre radius, listening in on his wild and disgusting, but mostly downright depressing thoughts.

You see, I had to be certain it was him.

It's not every day you walk up to a complete stranger and tell them they have supernatural powers. He knew he was *different*, as he put it. He knew his overcharged, overactive sex drive wasn't altogether normal, especially when his daily quota of four chicks wasn't met, and he'd be struck down by the most intense agony known to man. Except he didn't know why, or why water was the only thing to slake his desire or offer him comfort. He was green *as*, and had no idea what was really going on. He, like the rest of us, are simply meat suits for the Elementars to hide in.

What kind of wanker would I be if I told him he could summon the power of water. Imagine, if I spilled my guts about how I could fly or hear his deepest, darkest thoughts, or that I was able to turn invisible right there in front of him, let alone command the element of air to do whatever I wanted. From the size of the big fella, he would've smacked me in the chops and left me to the ants.

That was the River I knew back then – thump first, think later. Thanks to Ember, he's a little more civilised these days. The question was … did I want to sport a new black eye every other week?

The short answer was … fuck no!

Instead, I did what any *budding* Superhero would do … I kept it from him until the time was right to break it to him gently. Like Peter Parker's dad says, *with great power, comes great responsibility.*

Finding River Fulton was my sole reason for emigrating to the UK in the first place.

Reckless? It sure was!

So, what was I supposed to do? Ignore my destiny when it came knocking? That's not me at all.

The impulse was strong - the kind of desire that happens of its own accord without any prompting. The compounding ache to find him began to disturb my sleep, screw up my dates, mess with my social life. It came down to one thought …when you know, you know.

In hindsight, I'm convinced this troublesome *calling* was designed to disrupt my life, setting me on a path to find him, which in turn, would lead us to find the others. So, I gently manipulated my parent's brainwaves, courtesy of my superpower, to uproot their lives and move to the other side of the world.

I'm not proud of what I did, but this *thing* is bigger than me, my family, in truth, bigger than all of us. The whole world is relying on me to get the job done.

And I did what I had to do …irrespective of the cost.

Oh, but I paid big time for it.

And still paying for it …every day and every night.

It cost me the lives of my parents.

Not many have a claim to fame for killing their mum and dad, regardless if I was cleared of any wrongdoing. A tragic accident was what was written on their death certificates, but if I hadn't brainwashed them into leaving Australia in the first place, they never would've jumped out of that damn plane … the skydiving disaster of the century. It was the one thing on their bucket list that they wanted to do before leaving their homeland.

Thrill-seeking was my thing; surfing, rock climbing, paragliding, anything that gave me that *rush*. I loved it. With no fear of heights, how could a fourteen-year-old, *not*? Skydiving was different though. It had become more than a hobby after we moved to Kings Beach. It gave me the freedom to be who I really was. I didn't need a parachute but obviously had to wear one for legal reasons, and learnt how to pack shoots.

I cringe at the memory.

Hate the way the guilt still slithers through my veins. My heart falls out of rhythm as I recall that moment Dean and I stepped onto British soil for the first time, almost eighteen months ago … alone and parentless.

I bite down and scold myself for thinking of the past when I should be concentrating on the task at hand.

Following River Fulton.

Again!

Although not in my usual way.

I'm sitting cross-legged, arms folded tightly across my chest, hitching a ride on the bonnet of his flashy red BMW 3 series. Being invisible does have its perks.

It's stupid, I know, but something about this whole scenario brings a smile to my lips that won't leave. I also know he'd be well hacked off to see me sitting on his precious car, messing up that beautifully polished paintwork that he loves to see his reflection in. Not to mention me shadowing his every move, and yet, I can't erase the way his wild eyes said to *get the fuck out of my way or else,* as he left.

He'd stormed out of the house fifteen minutes ago, not telling a soul where he was going, so naturally, me being the curious lad that I am, I had to see what he was up to.

I stare at him through the windscreen.

His eyes are barely open, squinted, focused, not to be messed with. His lips say the same. No music, although his fingers thump out a nameless song against the steering wheel – either that or he wants to punch the shit out of someone.

I try to empathise with him, appreciating that Nereus, the WaterLover Elementar, has been drawn out and imprisoned by Ra-Mon, the creepy immortal inflicting havoc on our world right now. And, that he must be feeling all sorts of ways about that, especially now that his emotions are aligned to a more *human* frequency … I just wish he'd trust me enough to open up, because right now … I smell trouble - the air around him reeks of it, and it has nothing to do with passing the gasworks on Reuben Road.

River takes the next left.

We're heading over to the east side of town which is currently undergoing a suburban facelift. New apartment blocks are replacing the older-style houses, and more trees and parks are springing up all over the joint to entice the upper class back into the area. I don't think it's working. It's still a dump.

I'm positive I know where we're going, having been there a couple of times before, and I'm not stalking him because I don't trust him. I do.

    With

        my

            life.

The problem is … he's taken it upon himself to be the saviour of us all, and if it comes down to it, he will sacrifice himself to save us.

And I'm not okay with that.

River's frown deepens as though he's heard me, but I'm not responsible for the wrinkle on his brow today. *That* is all Iris Perkins – the sexy private investigator River *metaphorically* sold his soul to. I have to admit, the woman is a total MILF and I'd be a liar if I said I hadn't added her to my wank bank. I mean, the woman barks like a chipmunk when she has sex.

Finally, he pulls the car over to the side of the road, a short distance from her apartment block. I re-tighten my scarf and stuff one end back into the neck of my coat before sliding off the hood of his car, even though I'm technically not even touching it. It just feels good to do it. I pull my beanie a little lower so it covers the tips of my ears. On the bright side, at least it isn't raining. Makes my wings wet. In Gloucestershire, it seems to rain almost every day.

River scoots across the street, dodging traffic and ignoring the horns that beep at him. Lush, potted ferns on either side of the elegant entranceway to Iris's apartment block, do little to hide him loitering around that familiar tall, cream building. He peers over his shoulder, not once, but twice, like the total amateur he is … like he's about to rob the place, before slipping around the heavy wooden doors, framed with glass panels and golden handles.

I count to ten.

Now it's my turn.

Still invisible, I wait until the road is clear before jogging over to join him – no point in deliberately juicing up my energy before we start. One power at a time is easy enough to handle …two, and my battery is in the hands of a six-year-old with his first iPad. And that certainly *doesn't* work at three hundred feet in the air, with no jumping castle beneath.

I look up.

Ascending, floating and flying, whatever you want to call it, is easier than closing my eyes. I don't have to think about it.

I simply have to want it, and it's there.

Instantly, I bask in the glory of being weightless. The heavy constraints that come with being human – the everyday worries … the emotional struggles … the guilt, drops away. Becomes obsolete.

I am free.

I am brand new and without any hang-ups.

I can be anyone I want to be.

The temperature changes as I climb higher and higher. That icy edge to the air, chilling me to the bone, has now become a bubble of sunshine around me. My body throbs with pleasure.

One complete sweep of the building is all it takes to locate Iris's apartment. River's thoughts help by drawing me in like a bee to honey. All I can hope for is that he isn't there for sex. I couldn't handle watching that.

Lucky for me, the blinds are open.

There is no sign of Iris parading around in that tight red basque I've seen her do her housework in, bringing a giant sense of relief to my body.

I press my nose as close to the lounge room window without going through it. Part of me wants to slip through the wall so that I'm only depleting one power instead of two, but I can't run the risk of River getting a feel for me being there. It's uncanny how he can pick up on emotions like that, and since we've become closer, that bond between us is tighter than it is with others. I can't take the chance that he'll sense my presence, even this close, I'm risking it. But I can't believe what I'm seeing. Can't believe what I'm hearing. The words in my head are on repeat.

This *can't* be happening.

This *can't* be happening.

This *can't* be happening.

River is consorting with the enemy.

Air rushes out of my lungs in a big hurry, dizziness finding me, spinning me until I think I might throw up. My vision distorts slightly and my fingers seem to freeze

11

to the glass. I unglue them, rub my eyes, seeking to remove this abomination before me.

NO! NO! NO!

This *can't* be happening.

My eyes say YES, deal with it, Skye!

You've been deceived.

You knew you couldn't trust him.

My brain says NO.

He would never do this.

We are brothers!

Ra-Mon's sidekick, the olive-skinned chick from the eerie crypt we flooded back in Chartres only a few days ago, is handing River a glass of wine. The two toast and drink. The young man standing by her side is Salvatore - this dude has more aliases than a secret agent. First, moonlighting as our aloof taxi driver in France. Then, we discovered he was the Roman Commander who murdered Tomas's family, tricking him into an eternity of servitude, and lastly learning his true identity as Horus, son of Osiris and Isis, God and Goddess of the Underworld.

There is no sign of Iris Perkins.

But it's so much worse than afternoon bubbles with old *friends*. The words that float on the airwaves between us, puncture holes the size of shotgun shells into my heart with River saying *he'll do whatever she commands him to do*.

Salvation is lost.

Hope is gone.

We are all doomed to a life of hell on earth.

If we have a life at all.

River glances in my direction as though he knows I'm watching. I never was any good at hiding my emotions. I'm an open book. Pick a chapter, lend me a soft ear, and I will lay bare my innermost thoughts. I hope someday River will be that person too.

I don't need to hear anymore, and the longer I juice up two powers at once, the worse I will feel later. I lower myself to the ground and wait for the turncoat to show himself.

I don't have long to wait.

Ten minutes later, he saunters out the front doors of the hotel, hands in pockets, head down.

'Oi,' I call out.

River turns and I wave at him. He continues on his path until I remember I'm still invisible. I jog up to him and slap him on the shoulder as though he is my button to visibility.

He jumps, although he doesn't seem surprised to see me. 'Do you wanna tell me what the fuck that was all about?' My fists clench and release.

River glares at me, his normally vivid blue eyes now the colour of dishwater. 'You heard for yourself. Why don't you tell me?'

He's in another one of his moods. I honestly don't know how Ember puts up with the grouchy old shit. It takes a lot out of me to remain positive around him - Mr doom and gloom.

'I thought we were in this together – you know, comrades and all that?' I think back to the pact he, Ember and I made on the steps of Chartres Cathedral after almost drowning.

River looks at me, and I know he knows what I'm thinking. 'Yeah, well. That was before,' he says, clicking the alarm to his car. He reaches for the door as I step in front of him.

'Before what? You mean before you jumped ship and decided to slip between the sheets with that fucking Egyptian slut and her son?' I need some anger from him. I need a reaction. Anything? 'Are you doing him, too?'

River glares at me. 'NO! And it's not my frigging choice,' he says, spitting the words in my face. 'I'm fucked if I do and fucked if I don't.' Secrets swim circles in his eyes.

Not good enough for me.

I'm furious we are back to guessing games again. I thought we were past all this, and as much as I hate to keep this party going, I need to push his buttons a little longer to find out what's going on. I waggle my finger at his dick. 'Is that thing between your legs making all the decisions again?'

It works.

His eyes widen as he grabs me by the collar.

'You've got no fucking idea, have you?' I shake my head, preparing my power to block his predictable right hook. 'How long were you spying on me for?'

'Not long,' I say defensively. 'And I wasn't spying.'

'Then what would you call it?' he says.

'I was … window cleaning?' I say with a smirk.

I'm rewarded with his customary scowl and he lets go of my shirt.

'Come on, man. How bad can it be?'

River drops his head and massages the back of his neck. He doesn't look me in the eye when he murmurs, 'I drank her blood.'

The earth suddenly stops spinning. 'You did *what*? I thought you were drinking wine.'

'I didn't know it was *blood*,' he snaps. His face, fifty shades of anger. 'She tricked me, and now I'm bound to do whatever she asks …'

River pauses. His voice softens.

'Just like Tomas. I'm a Bloodslave now. A slave to do her dirty work. Forever!'

A revelation comes to me. River isn't pissed at me, and he isn't in a mood because he feels like it. He's ashamed about being tricked. Embarrassed about having to tell me, and everyone else, he didn't see it coming and he's made a mistake. That's what's crawled up his arse.

'And if you don't do what she …' I begin to say, but River has already pushed me aside and is getting in the car. 'Riv, man,' I call out.

He winds down the window. 'Get in. We need some professional advice on this, and no offence, but I don't think you're particularly qualified.'

I race around the other side of the car and get in. His face is like steel, like ice, like no life ever existed there.

I'm in for a quiet trip home.

TWO

RIVER's house … did I mention it's a bloody mansion?

No way did we have houses like this growing up near Rocky, I mean, Rockhampton. And, I'm not one for poetic imagery either, except to say, it's a humongous, grey stone house with loads of white windows, a long driveway that could fit a whole procession of wedding cars, and more rooms than my entire school. It even has a library – what idiot thinks that's necessary? And, I reckon it's about five times larger than our old house on Curlew Street. I think I dreamt about this house once because it felt so familiar when I dropped in unannounced last month.

Last month …so much has happened since then, including losing Nuria and Nereus to Ra-Mon, the sick and twisted God who wants to take over our world. It's a massive loss, but that won't happen with me.

It can't.

This time, everything depends on *me*, and truth be told, I'm scared shitless, I'll screw it up.

Like I always do.

I never intend to sabotage any strategies ... I mean, it's not like I go out of my way to create mayhem wherever I go. It just seems to follow me.

Mum used to say, I was a magnet for chaos.

And I absolutely am.

In fact, I'm quietly impressed when it *does* go right. I try to stick to the plan, but when things go tits up, I have to think on my feet, and that generally results in me throwing everything into the pot and hoping to hell it turns into beef stew rather than gruel. Lately, I've been chowing down on a lot of gruel.

River opens the front door. The blinding light of crystal chandeliers and polished white floors catch me off-guard.

White, white everywhere.

I've never known a house to look so clean and bright and it takes a couple of seconds to recover. I stumble in behind River, rubbing the blobs out of my eyes with the heel of my hands.

My eyes adjust, taking in the grand staircase fit for a queen. Classy abstract paintings of pink, peach, gold and coral are the only reprieve from the white-panelled walls, and I stare at them until my vision clears. I don't think I will ever be able to enter this house and not be awestruck by its grandeur. I thought his last digs were impressive, but this place takes it to a whole new level. Despite its icy appearance, the house is warm and smells of honey and apples and caramel.

A hulk of a man is there to greet us.

Not Wally.

Mr B.

He usually gives me the heads up via telepathy that he's dropping in, so I'm not the least bit surprised to see him here, especially after River's SOS call. What I'm not used to is the name Mr B, Mr Butcher, or Butch. I realise

17

this is the name River and Em know him by, although it doesn't have the same ring to it that Doc does, short for Empedocles - that's what I've always called him. I miss the old days.

'Right on schedule,' says Doc, glancing over his shoulder at me before going back to inspect the intricate workings of the old grandfather clock in the corner of the room.

'I *might* be, but your batteries need charging, old man,' I say, smirking. 'I barely got that last message.'

That incredible sense of wonder that's always present on his face, fades a little. 'The airwaves are being intercepted, lad,' he replies.

My eyes widen. '*Bugged*? That would account for all the static lately. Who?'

'Need I remind you, that *we* are not the only ones communicating this way.' He pivots to face me.

'*Immortals*,' I say, like I've just sculled a cup of warm cat piss.

Doc straightens a painting that doesn't require any attention before coming back to me. His fist finds the middle of his chest. 'What are you saying … *I'm* immortal?' he says indignantly.

'Yeah, but you're one of the guys.' Doc gives me one of those sly, signature winks of his, making me smile. 'Still, I'd recharge the old canons though. Got to be on top of your game right now,' I add.

Doc raises his scruffy grey eyebrows at me. I much prefer his colourful beach attire and straw hat to his boring grey trousers and dark grey jumper. I glance down expecting to see a pair of thongs on his feet, only to discover a pair of worn tawny-brown shoes with odd laces. As I said, I miss the old days. 'There is nothing wrong with my *canons*, thank you very much. I can hear, talk, feel, see and smell just fine.'

Smell?

My nose picks up something delicious from the kitchen. If Wally isn't playing the perfect role as butler

18

and guardian to River, and now Ember and I, he's in the kitchen, apron on, sleeves neatly rolled to the elbows, creating even more awesomeness, if that's possible. What can I say? The man is an absolute legend.

Wally doesn't materialise in the doorway, tea towel over one shoulder, and not a hair out of place, like I'm expecting, instead I see Ember coming towards us. She offers me an anxious smile although it bursts into a beautiful sunny day when she sees River.

And then it's gone.

'What's wrong?' she asks, stepping closer to take his hand. For the first time ever I watch River draw away from her.

The clues on her face tell a story of pain. Her eyes water a little. Her bottom lip trembles a little more, and what everyone can't hear are the questions piling up in her head asking whether she has done something wrong. Said something wrong.

They are heartbreaking … deafening.

She crosses her hands in front and looks to me, knowing. Knowing she's the book that's just been read. I surrender a soft wink that says so much more than *I'm sorry*.

River clears his throat. 'Is everyone ready for round three?' He beckons us into the lounge room.

This room is more than somewhere to *lounge* … it's art. By day, it's bright and airy and, if I'm honest, a little formal for my liking … like I wouldn't go in there in case I break something, however when night falls, it is transformed into a relaxed, welcoming space with soft lighting, an open fire and warm cosy rugs. I'm not entirely sure River knows how lucky he is.

Ember and I snuggle into the comfy white sofa, Em lifting the burgundy woollen blanket draped over the back, for her feet. Doc takes the matching armchair that Wally normally sits in to read his newspaper. Nobody occupies the second sofa. A vase of gardenias throws a soft scent over the room that Wally must have placed sometime during the day … like I said, the man's blood is worth bottling. The heavy fawn-coloured curtains are closed, standard lamps are on, fire is roaring … all that's missing is an X-box and a bag of Cheezels, and I would be in heaven.

River trails in behind us, his normal confident footsteps unusually slow, his posture in all kinds of misery.

I feel sorry for him.

He takes his normal spot in front of the enormous white fireplace, preparing himself for the onslaught of judgement about to be unleashed on him. I'd love to drown out his thoughts, but they're louder than a North Queensland monsoon on a tin roof.

Doc clears his throat. 'Before we get started, Mr Fulton, I need to bring everyone up to speed with Amun, the AirWhisperer.'

River nods curtly.

Huffs out a breath.

Wipes his forehead with the back of his hand.

And stares into space, his mind the beginning of a jigsaw puzzle without the edges.

Being the closest to the fire, Doc removes his jumper and hangs it off the arm of the chair. His *Life is a Beach* t-shirt suits him far better than the sickly cream shirt he's got on. But hell, I don't have to wear it. The old man leans forwards, elbows digging into his knees, a frown creasing his seriously aged skin. He waits until we are all settled before he begins. 'You know of Amun, yes?' he says, staring directly at me this time.

'You know I do,' I reply with a smirk.

A smile emerges from underneath his messy grey beard. A laugh looks imminent, but he manages to tame it. 'I suppose the cat will be out of the bag sooner or later.'

'What cat?' asks Ember.

River shoots me a look of curiosity.

'That Mr B, aka *Doc,* as I know him, and I, have a history,' I say casually.

The edge of River's mouth turns down, his brow as turbulent as a stormy sea. 'And you didn't think this was important enough to share with us?'

My eyebrows raise. 'To be honest. No. It wasn't.'

'Mr Buchannan's right,' adds Doc. 'It wasn't important, and still isn't, and we are getting off track. Needless to say, we have known each other *a while*.' Apart from the reassuring ticking of the grandfather clock, the room falls into silence. '*Originally*, Amun was created to bring oxygen to the planet and to be a brother for Nereus after Nuria disappeared.'

'Which totally didn't work, I might add,' I blurt out.

Doc disregards me and carries on. 'He is known as the AirWhisperer Elementar, although as time passed, Amun became so much more. He was worshipped by all of mankind. The Greeks equated him with Zeus, and the Romans associated him with Jupiter. The Egyptians, however, gave him the title of "King of the Gods", who they believed, created all things. He was identified as one of the most powerful deities in the universe, second only to Osiris.'

We take turns eyeballing each other. It's not the first time we've heard the name, Osiris, although it is the first time Doc has spoken of him.

River inhales sharply. 'Great!' he mumbles into his chest.

I sense the old man rummaging around inside my head, pulling on my recent memory of Horus, and his nutcase of a mother, Isis, at Iris's apartment.

'And, as you've probably guessed already, Ra-Mon has recruited Isis and Horus to do his dirty work.'

'Yes, we figured that out weeks ago when we were in the crypt,' says River. 'You kind of *get* that impression when you're ambushed.' A dark shadow falls across his face. 'Where were you? We could've done with your help. Perhaps next time, we can get an up-to-date CV on who is after us now.' His mind switches into overdrive again and I get pulled into his thoughts. He consistently berates himself that he didn't fight hard enough to protect Nereus from Ra-Mon, but more so, for allowing Ember to be kidnapped. I jump out of his head, not wanting to get sidetracked again.

'You know I can't intervene,' says Doc.

'And Ra-Mon *can* …' says River, throwing his arms in the air. 'How is *that* fair?'

Doc shakes his head. His palms close together in prayer. 'It isn't,' he answers, 'but when has war ever been fair?'

River shies away from us in disbelief. His legs look like they might crumble and yet his neck and shoulders are as tight and rigid as steel.

'So, there's *three* immortals after us now?' gasps Ember. 'Ra-Mon, Isis *and* Horus?'

'Maybe,' says Doc sullenly.

Em's mind is silent for once. As if she can't bring herself to think about what the future might hold. She looks to River with eyes that could tear down the walls of your soul and shatter you into a million pieces.

River senses her emotional fragility. It's reassuring to know that that part of him still works after Nereus was yanked out. He cups Ember's chin and smooths her cheek with his thumb. 'Don't worry, love. We still have Captain Fantastic over there to save us.'

Ember regards me, an ounce of hope spilling into her wobbly smile. I beam back confidently, like I've got this one in the bag. And yet, all that keeps stacking up in my head is a line from my page in the book, Peri Phuseôs tôn Ontôn – the mystical book that I found back home in Oz. Under the AirWhisperer's heading were the words; *A brother for life, is a life without atonement.*

Doc politely coughs before saying, 'Has Amun contacted you?'

I screw my face up. 'I don't think so. I seem to get more static than anything these days. Although, I do get a random word now and again,' I pause, thinking, 'but I put *that* down to people's thoughts on the outskirts of my radar.'

'Could be,' surmises Doc. 'It could also be Amun trying to get your attention.'

'I kept hearing Nuria call my name,' offers Ember sympathetically. 'Maybe listen out for that.'

'Yeah, right. I can see how that makes sense. To be honest, I've never focused on it. In fact, I've kinda developed a talent for blocking it out.'

River huffs, and Em's eyes do the tiniest of eye rolls.

Immediately, my hackles go up. I take a breath, relax my jaw consciously prying my teeth apart. 'I don't suppose *any* of you have the slightest idea how freaking annoying it is to hear voices 24/7.' I take a second to look at them both. Words tumble out of my mouth without a parachute. 'How utterly mind splitting it is to never have a moment of silence? Never to enjoy the simplicity of no thoughts in your head, especially when they don't belong to you.'

I breathe

and breathe

and breathe.

Large gaps of time-numbing emptiness fills the room. The hush of life halts for three, then four glorious seconds. Even the wind outside surrenders for one beat in time. The clock, it seems, would stop if it was capable of doing so, so that it may also relish in the sound of peace and stillness and quiet. But silence never beckons me. EVER!

I glance up to see everyone staring at me.

'We're sorry for contributing to that,' whispers Em. 'We ...' Remorse floods her face ... knots her hands in her lap.

I feel the fresh sting of guilt. I shouldn't have gone off like that. 'No, I'm sorry. It's not your fault.'

'But we should be more considerate, right, Riv?' Ember says, turning towards River. His face has lost its tightness, the irritation from before wiped clean.

He walks over. Places a firm hand on my shoulder.

'Sorry, brother. Believe it or not, we do understand what you're going through.' I regard him. 'Well, up until recently, I did,' he corrects. 'We *will* try to be more considerate.' He looks to Em and smiles before returning to his spot by the fireplace. His head hangs lowly, hands gripping the mantelpiece, knuckles white, stiffness in his shoulders even a blind man could see.

Knowing Doc and his intense storytelling sessions, we could be in for an all-nighter. I need to lighten the mood …if only to get us through.

'It's honestly not *that* bad. More like a mozzie in your ear all day.' I add. I throw in a laugh for good measure.

Em and River aren't buying it.

'Hmmmm,' Doc says, scratching his beard. As always, his eyes do not give anything away as he skims over us. 'It's as I thought. The Elementars, have been, and still *are*, extremely wary about revealing themselves to anyone. And I don't blame them. There's a lot at stake here. The four have become masters of hide and seek, going undetected since civilization began. And not just to you all, but to Ra-Mon and *myself* too.'

Doc mentioned to me ages ago that we weren't the first humans to be shopping bags for these immortals. 'They've been hopping from person to person, right?'

'Yes. It's a theory I have,' replies Doc. 'They know how important they are to this planet. Avoiding Ra-Mon's radar has become something of an art to them.' Clouds drift across his eyes. His face, a memory of a thousand lifetimes passed. 'This has all happened once before.' Doc lets his words hang for a minute. River and Ember's faces are the same shade of bewilderment. I smirk, having prior knowledge of the story Doc is about to tell. He told me the first time I met him.

'Did you know, that five billion years ago, our moon was once a small planet, with its own atmosphere? It had mountains and lakes and forests … until.'

'Until?' repeats Ember.

'Until it became a science experiment gone wrong. There's nothing left of it now ... as you know. Just a barren rock, suspended in darkness. Too much power in anyone's hands is a recipe for disaster.'

Fear sweeps in, leaving Ember's face grey and lifeless. 'Wow, that's freaking unbelievable. Is that what's going to happen to us?'

'Over my dead body,' I say abruptly. Newfound confidence sneaks in when I'm not paying attention, assuring me victory is possible.

'It's not all bad news though. Look how well you have faired,' Doc continues. 'You have all benefitted greatly from having the Elementars take up residence in your bodies, giving you a taste of the power they hold.'

'Yeah, but what good has it done us?' It isn't hard to miss the sour tinge to River's words. He isn't holding anything back. 'Two of us down, two to go.'

I cringe. *God, I hope I don't topple it in their favour.*

'Sometimes in chess, you need to sacrifice a few pawns, and a castle here and there, for the greater good of the game, Mr Fulton,' says Doc.

It's my turn to get in on the argument. 'But we're not playing chess, old man. And the stakes are much higher than checkmate.'

'Yes. They. Are. Mr Buchannan.'

I glance around the room ... waiting.

Waiting for someone to come up with something positive to say. The small clock on the mantlepiece, just out of reach of River's hand, chimes once.

The first words end up coming from the one person, who appears the frailest but has more guts than anyone I know ... Ember.

She squirms nervously in her seat. 'Nuria was my saviour, and the reason I am sitting here today. We only spoke a few times, and there's not one day that passes I don't miss her strength and encouragement.' She pauses to remove a tear with the back of her hand. 'And even though she's gone, she has left an imprint of her power in me that I thought had completely vanished.' Ember opens the palm of her hand and a flame bursts into life. 'It takes a little more effort, but it's still there. She sometimes visits me in my dreams. Never speaks. Never asks anything of me. Only offers reassurance that all will be well.' Her eyes crinkle as she smiles.

'I found that too,' injects River. He and Ember seem to share a private joke and for a brief moment, he closes his eyes and the sound of the ice maker on the front of the fridge starts depositing chunks of ice onto the floor, much to Wally's cry of *what on earth is .... oh, ha ha, River. You got me*. It's not the kind of adrenaline rush you need, sitting at the table eating a cheese and pickle sandwich and doing a crossword, but it makes Ember giggle. River holds back a tight smile.

'I have to say,' adds Doc, 'I'm thrilled, if not, somewhat surprised you have retained some of their power.'

'So are we,' replies River. 'Nereus and I spoke even less than Ember and Nuria, which is why you need to build better communication skills with Amun, Skye.'

I nod. 'I'm onto it.'

'I recommend you tune in a little harder with Amun and discover his motives or if he has a plan.'

River is back to pacing again, and I know he is impatient to share his news. I'm equally eager to hear what he has to say.

But his stuff will have to wait.

I still have more I need to say. 'When I first discovered the book – Peri Phuseôs tôn Ontôn, I began my own research on Amun. In the beginning, he was known as the God of the air, but he eventually merged with Ra, another God, and ruler of the sun. He then became Amun-Ra, master of the air and sun. His powers doubled, and he became the most powerful God that ever lived.'

'I'm impressed, Mr Buchannan,' says Doc, 'you saved me some time, and passed your history lesson for today.'

I scoff at his joke.

'I'm getting confused,' says Ember. 'I thought there was only one God. The man upstairs who created you and Ra-Mon.'

'We call *him* the Creator, Ember, the Almighty God who created everything ...' He stops to scratch his head. 'As far as other gods go, there are many, and each of them evolved through the false idols that man held in the highest regard. During their reign, they constantly jostled for seniority and domination.'

'So, where are they now?' Ember asks, 'and why don't we hear about them?' Even though the room is at a comfortable temperature, Ember pulls the blankets further up her legs.

'Yeah,' I add, 'when was the last time you heard someone mention they were going down to the beach to pray to Poseidon.' I'm attempting to be humorous but Ember scowls at me for a second before giving me a friendly punch on the arm.

'We do hear about them, Em, although not in the magnitude they were once revered,' explains River. 'They've been lost to memory, right?' He looks to Doc, who nods. 'They're now only fit for stories and movies as if they weren't real in the first place.'

Ember nods. 'Then what happened to *these* "old" gods we're now dealing with?'

'I can answer that,' says Doc, 'a god can only become powerful when it is believed in and prayed to, and I mean, *believed* in by entire civilisations. That is what fuels its power and drives its people. There were Norse gods - Thor, Freya, Loki and Odin, like Mr Buchannan mentioned; Greek gods - Apollo, Zeus, Athena and Hades; Roman gods – Mars, Jupiter, Pluto, Mithras and Isis. Even Aboriginal tribes in Australia have their own deities.' Doc looks at me.

'The Rainbow-Serpent,' I say.

'Correct.'

'Gods are replaced over time, like Buddha, Allah, Krishna and Jehovah. These gods are now worshipped all over the world.'

'And Norse Gods are making a comeback too, I add. 'You see way more Vikings these days than you used to.'

Ember giggles first and then says, 'but, why now? Why us?'

Doc shrugs his hulking shoulders. 'The book Mr Buchannan found, translates to …"On the Nature of Things that exist". The book went missing not long after the earth was created. Now that it's back in circulation, I assume that Ra-Mon has found a loophole.'

'To what?' River and Ember say at the same time.

'To use the Elementars and replace himself as the Creator.'

THREE

THIS is news to me. '*Overthrow* the big man? He's got to have rocks in his head.'

'Can he do that?' asks River.

'Is it possible?' chimes in Ember.

'Once all the Elementars are in his possession, he will have entire control over the book, including fire, water, air and earth, not to mention every human being on the planet, any spirit that has passed over ... *and,* weaker, less influential Gods that have come and gone.'

'Are Horus and Isis aware of this?' I ask. 'I mean, if he's intending on milking their power, then ultimately, it's going to end badly for them.'

Doc shrugs his colossal shoulders. 'Isis will have her own agenda, I imagine.'

'Can't you summon Amun from Skye and then kill him?' Ember asks Doc.

Her words are like glass in my head … have no business being there.

A strand of her coppery hair falls in front of her eyes, and she teases it out of the way. She looks at me with eyes that have a whisper of a thousand apologies behind them. 'That way, Ra-Mon will only have three of the four Elementars.'

'No can do,' says Doc. 'Like I said. I don't have the power to intervene that way. Why do you think Ra-Mon is getting other gods involved? Besides, eliminating Amun won't do the world any favours. No air equals no life.'

I get up and toss another log onto the red coals and sit back down. It's enough time for everyone to take a breath. Let the words sink in. Let reality find a new rhythm …

a true

in the flesh

rhythm.

'How do Isis and Horus fit into this?' asks River.

'Isis was the most powerful goddess in the ancient world and was loved by her people,' explains Doc. 'Ra, the God of the Sun, originally had the greatest power. He was uncaring, and the people suffered greatly during his reign. So, Isis tricked him by mixing some of his saliva with mud to create a poisonous snake that bit him, causing him great suffering which she then offered to cure. He eventually agreed. Isis informed Ra, that for the cure to work, she would have to speak his secret name, which was the source of his power over life and death. Reluctantly, he whispered it to her. When Isis uttered his secret name while performing her magic, Ra was healed. The goddess, Isis, then possessed his powers of life and death, and quickly became the most powerful Egyptian goddess.'

'Ra-Mon wants that ability too, doesn't he?' says Ember, joining the dots. 'Not just the power of the elements. He wants the power over life and death?'

A grave expression drops into Doc's face. 'Yes. It was the one power that wasn't bestowed upon us from the Creator, and one that Ra-Mon has searched an eternity for. My best guess, Ra-Mon and Isis have struck a bargain.'

This is a lot to take in.

'Great,' says River, rubbing small circles into his temples as Ember drops her head in her hands. 'So, let me get this straight - you're saying Amun, the AirWhisperer, was created by God, who then merged with Ra?'

'Yes,' answers Doc bluntly.

'So, that makes Isis equally as powerful?'

'I'm afraid so. Although, because she doesn't have the huge following she used to, that power now has limits.'

Tension fills the air and panic seeps through the cracks of the weary faces around me. It's when words become frozen and a single thought is powerful enough to break the last remaining hope we all cling to. Ember and River try to find comfort in each other's eyes, except they're not fooling anyone. We're pretty much up shit creek without a paddle, and we all know it.

Hell! There's a boatload of trouble coming.

'You four, happen to be the unlucky ones, and if I could be so bold to say, a little dysfunctional too. Perhaps that is the reason why you were chosen.'

'I'm not dysfunctional,' I say, defensively.

'*Really*?' says River. He tilts his head to one side, one eyebrow arched, and stares at me the same way that Ember is staring.

'Maybe dysfunctional isn't quite the right word.' Doc thinks for a few seconds, drumming his sausage-like index finger against his chin. 'How about … *troubled*?'

Ember takes a sip of the drink that Wally had unobtrusively brought in a few minutes ago, and coughs to the point of near choking. She recovers, eyes watering, cheeks flushed. 'Oh my god, that's *exactly* what we are.'

She does have a point. Now that I come to think of it, it probably *was* deliberate. I mean, what better way to hide an immortal than to choose humans who already feel the weight of the world on them. We're dealing with baggage most teens wouldn't have a clue about. We're all processing the death of our parents in some way, although I am the only one actually responsible for killing mine. River never pushed his folks overboard, and Ember never crashed her family car. I did, however, pack my parents parachutes and manipulated their thoughts.

Me.

I am responsible for their deaths.

'I can't help wonder if it was set up this way,' says Doc.

'How do you mean?'

'God works in mysterious ways.'

I watch River raise his eyebrows and Ember purse her lips. 'So, you think he had a hand in choosing where the Elementars go?'

'*Maybe* … perhaps in the beginning …' Doc slips into another one of his long, wayward stares.

'And now …' Ember says. Frustration knots her fingers together again.

'Let's just say, nothing happens by accident.'

I see the faintest of lights shining at the end of a very long and dark corridor. Please let it be hope. Something we can hold on to and work towards.

Hearing his words makes me want to try harder. 'I don't care what it takes, I will finish this.'

'Me too,' says Ember together. River nods aswell.

Doc smiles around the bushiness of his beard, glowing with the kind of pride only a father is capable of. 'I think Ra-Mon drastically underestimates your abilities and comradery, with and *without* these immortals inside you.'

A warmth settles in …nestles into my skin.

River and Ember are feeling it too – that familiar sensation too hard to hold back. It peaks through disruption and pain. Through the wounds, still open and raw. Through the scars that have recently healed or been temporarily buried because they're too hard to say goodbye to.

'Now, what was it you wanted to say, River?' says Doc.

Time passes in held breaths and thrumming hearts. The collection of miniature teapots on the mantlepiece appear and disappear as River paces four steps left and then four steps right.

I wish he would get on with it. 'River, dude. This is killing us. It can't be that bad.'

River stops and rests both hands on the mantlepiece, still unable to face us. He spins one of the teapots quarter of a turn. Ember's eyes find me, her mind silently begging me for answers. I have nothing, and the only thing I can do is shake my head. I only know half of what he has to say. Finally, River slowly turns to face us.

He is worry.

He is pain.

He is victim and hero.

He is sorrow and shame.

He watches with cold eyes as I place my hand in Ember's ... for comfort ... for support, glancing over an act that once upon a time would have turned him inside out with rage and jealousy.

He blurts out in one quick, short sentence.
I drank her blood.

Ember has become an earthquake.

An unsteady, quivering ... *trembling* mess. I'm concerned she may go into shock.

I stroke the back of her hand, but I'm not sure she feels it. Her lips press together, crushing words that beg to be released. Her mind is a battleground of amputated questions and dying explanations.

I look up to hear River say, 'I'm hers now. I belong to Isis. I have to do whatever she commands.'

Doc rises from the chair. Rubs his chin. Huffs out loud. 'This is ...' he pauses, '*unfortunate.*' The corners of

33

his mouth turn down. For someone who should know everything, I'm surprised he didn't see this coming.

'No shit, Batman!' I blurt out.

'But that's not the worst of it.' River's face falls into shadow. I've never seen his eyes so lifeless, his jaw quite so tense as he stares me down. 'I have to hand Skye over to Ra-Mon.'

Something startles Ember back to life and she scares the shit out of me as she jumps up. 'NO!' She looks back at me, then to Doc and then back to River. 'Over my dead body.'

River sniffs. 'I don't *want* to,' he retaliates and not in the nicest of tones. He collects himself and realises whose head he's bitten off. His face softens immediately. 'Somehow, I don't think I get a choice in it. It might just come down to that.'

Ember steps back.

Sits down.

Thoughts stream through her head again.

'You can't …' she says into her hands. Her voice, barely a whisper. 'There has to be a way.'

Doc slowly leans forwards, clasping his big hands in front of him. His brow is creased with worry, and yet a faint smile tickles at the corners of his lips. 'Okay. Let's work this out. Did Iris mention anything about an antidote?'

River nods. 'She waved it in front of my nose before handing it to the other woman for safekeeping.'

'Nephthys?' Doc offers. He releases a sigh.

River shrugs. 'I guess. We weren't introduced. Tall, Egyptian-like, mean eyes.'

'That's her,' says Doc. 'Figures. I had an idea she would bring her sister into this. So, what were Isis's terms?'

River stares at me, not like a brother anymore. Like a passing stranger. 'Skye needs to locate and acquire the Seven Rites of Mithraism to raise Mithras from whatever stone he's hiding under.'

I swallow hard. 'That doesn't sound good.'

'It isn't. Trust me,' replies Doc. 'And I suppose Ra-Mon plans to use Mithras to summon Amun from Skye?'

'Who knows? I think that conversation was above my paid grade,' says River, shrugging his shoulders lethargically. There is something cold in the way he speaks.

Like he doesn't know us.

Doesn't care about us.

'Binding Nuria and Nereus are draining his power,' Doc informs us, scruffing his beard, first one side and then the other. 'He needs another god to combine powers with him.'

'And if he completes this task?' asks Ember anxiously.

'Skye will be stripped of Amun, I will get the antidote, restoring my blood to normal, and Ra-Mon will be one step closer to world domination.'

Again, aloof and robotic.

I want to tell him to snap out of it. It's scaring Em – her thoughts scrambling in a mess of uncertainty. Pain finds its way into her face, pinching her cheeks, haunting her gaze. She stands. 'And what if you *don't* turn Skye in … what then?' The earthquake has returned to her legs.

River takes a long look at Ember and something in his eyes remember feelings they've shared. I sense the shift in his brain. I feel it. He is cast adrift, lost and utterly helpless. 'It means, I will be under an eternity of servitude to her, like Tomas is.'

'*Was*,' I say, correcting him.

'No. *Is*. Isis assured me that Tomas can't be killed. He is immortal, like the rest of them.'

Man, this is a lot to take in. I know this isn't the right time to ask, but I have to know why he hasn't come for us. 'Then where the hell is he? I mean, if he's on our side, and wants to kill Horus, where is he? We could definitely use a bloke like him right now.'

River nods. 'She didn't say, and I didn't ask.'

I sigh, feeling the pressure in my head begin to rise again. There has to be a solution. Even if it's my slapdash, no bullshit, hit-em-in-the-guts solution, it's better than sitting around here with our thumbs up our arse.

Doc is scanning the room for an answer. He won't find it in the fireplace or the floor to ceiling curtains or amongst the tiny teapots. His eyes fall to me and I feel him fumbling around inside my mind again.

He grins.

Perfect, he says inside my head.

He addresses River. 'If Isis wanted to kill you already, she would have done so. The rules haven't changed. Ra-Mon has simply upped the stakes a little, recruiting allies and forcing our hand, which we already knew he was doing.' He cracks his knuckles. 'I say, we give him what he wants. Play into his hands.'

'*What*?' gasps Ember. 'Serve them *both* up on a plate? Are you completely off your trolley?'

I let out a snigger. Glance over at River, who has finally stopped pacing. He now stares intently at Doc, his jaw taking on its normal, less stony appearance. A concentrated focus thing is happening in his eyes, in his mouth. It takes a few moments for him to respond.

'I agree,' says River, rubbing the stubble on his chin. 'What choice do we have?'

I burst out laughing. 'I was joking, old man,' I say, tapping my finger against my temple. 'If you go surfing around in my head, searching for answers, not everything up there has been properly thought out. Some things are better left unsaid.'

'Precisely why it will work, Mr Buchannan.'

I shake my head. 'Dude, I think we can quit the formalities now. This *Mr shit* is a bit old, isn't it? I'm Skye or mate. I don't care which one. I hear Mr Buchannan and I turn around to find my dad.'

'Playing into their hands is suicide though,' mutters Ember, readjusting her position and curling her feet back underneath her. Her body has calmed. I throw an arm

36

across her shoulder and give her a gentle squeeze. I refuse to believe this is a lost cause and that we are walking into a trap.

'We do have a few talents up our sleeves,' I offer. 'I'm still fully powered up – can create whirlwinds, tornadoes and that kind of stuff … and don't forget, we still have the Earth Elementar. Something tells me he'll be awesome in a fight. Maybe he could summon a dragon and rip Ra-Mon's head off, and dump in it, then we can all go back to our fucked up, *dysfunctional* lives.' Doc and I lock eyes.

River smirks and at last, I see that sparkle – that sunshine sneaking through the fog, through the dark and stormy clouds.

'And besides, it isn't *that* hard. All we have to do is complete the seven tasks, grab the antidote, and *before* Mithras can summon Amun, we take him out – dragon-style.' I throw in a karate move at the end for extra effect.

Everyone is gawking at me like I've sworn out loud in church or something. '*Seriously*? How hard can it be?'

Doc rises. His face doesn't give much away, although I can tell he's up for it. 'It's the only plan we've got.'

Ember looks like she's going to chew right through her lip. 'Aren't you some kind of powerful being that can click his fingers and turn the world upside down? Why can't you do something?'

Doc's face is grim. 'For the record, I am helping …'

I scoff. 'Really, like how?'

Doc simply smiles, like he knows something we don't.

Ember isn't buying it for a second. 'Then what good are you?' The fury in her eyes flits in and out in less than a second. She drops her head. I know she didn't mean to say that, as I listen in on her apology being repeated inside her head.

I dig my finger into my temple, trying to ease the pain that's building. Tuning in to too many minds in the same room has its consequences.

I take a breath
　　and another
　　　　and another.
I get to my feet.

Take a couple of steps away, endeavouring to add a little more distance between them and me. When I first found out I could hear peoples thoughts, nine years ago, I thought it was the coolest thing on the planet. My friends were amazed when I passed test after test, from guessing what numbers they were thinking, to full-on sentences. I was like this shiny new toy everyone wanted to borrow. It came in handy with my folks too, not that they gave a shit whether I came in at 10pm or 4am. We had this trust *thing*, that I had no idea why or where they got it from. They were pretty cool, as far as parents went.

The few steps away works wonders, and when my head feels clearer, I make a conscious effort to zone everyone else out … everyone except River. He's eager to get things moving and now that I'm inside his head, I can feel Isis's blood starting to change him.

It's strange.

Not quite him.

At least, not the new him I've come to appreciate since Nereus made his exit. It's like he's really driven, poised and ready to go without thinking of anyone's feelings again and that nothing will get in his way. Nothing and no one. He's almost mechanical and more emotionless. I can't help wonder, now that he and Ember have finally got a good thing going, that it won't throw a spanner in the works. Some part of me likes this new River instead of the *whingy, whiny, I'm all caught up in my feelings,* River.

I make up my mind.

I'm good to go.

'Okay then. Where do we start?'

'It's not quite as straightforward as that. Isis didn't exactly give me a road map directing us what to do first,' says River, running his fingers through his hair.

'Well, what *did* she say?' asks Ember meekly. Her hands twist in her lap.

'Not much. Only that, it all starts with Raven.'

I feel the colour drain out of my body. *It can't be. It just can't be.*

Words jam up in my mouth. I swallow down hard. Feel them settle in the back of my throat.

'Raaa-ven? As in black and featherlike.' The words don't feel like they've come out of my mouth and yet I can taste the fear left on my tongue simply by saying them.

'I guess so. Unless you know anybody by the name of Raven?'

Bile rises in my throat. My body locks into position. The sound of flapping wings and the eerie scratching of claws on windows has me closing my eyes and wanting to wail like a scared kid waking from a night terror. My head breaks rank and shakes vigorously.

'I don't know any *person* ... ' I can't finish the rest of the sentence.

Ember frowns. 'What's wrong with you? What are you scared of?' She gets up and comes towards me, her hand reaching out. I think I feel her touch, but I can't be sure. I glance down, see her hand on my wrist.

I feel nothing.

There's only one word on my mind. One tiny thing I'm afraid of most in this world.

'Ra-ven,' I manage to whisper.

FOUR

BACK in Oz, right about now, you'd find me in one of four places - a walk in the bush to my favourite abseiling spot, surfing or skydiving regardless of what time of day it was, or lounging around a pool with mates, listening to the sweet, sizzling sounds of a BBQ in full swing.

Am I missing home?

Bloody oath I am.

But most of all, I am missing the warm, balmy winds of an Australian summer.

It's the last day of February here, and I never knew I could feel so cold. Cold that grows inside you, day after day, until even your bones scream out for an extra layer of calcium.

Another sharp, icy breeze sweeps in from the open window, ruffling my hair. At least there are a few things in my world I *can* control.

Wind is one of them.

It's as easy as one, two, three.

One thought. One command. And then,

    Stillness

              as though the entire world has stopped

                  to take a breath

                      just because I said so.

Poised, my rifle cocked, I stare through the scope and wait.

For once it hasn't seen me.

This time, I am the hunter, not the hunted. No longer will it stalk me.

A whiff of delight dances over me, tweaking up my lips a little. I reel it in, focus on my breathing, aware of how shallow and relaxed it now is. I feel the steady pulse in my finger against the trigger.

In the distance, in front of an eighty-year-old oak tree, I see it.

A raven.

Not *just* any raven.

My raven.

The raven that has made my life a living hell … haunting my steps … plaguing me with the most horrible dreams as though I've somehow killed its entire family and crunched their bones beneath my boots. If I had to, I could pick it out in a lineup of ravens. Its body is glossier than the common raven, and its feathers - blacker than midnight without a moon. The pair of piercing eyes, green and devious, peer at me like it knows me intimately.

There is hatred in those eyes.

I feel it. And although I can't hear its thoughts, I get the sense that it's biding its time, waiting for me to fall asleep so it can pluck out my eyes one by one with that sharp, tormenting beak. Then, slowly devour me, picking the meat from my bones until they are clean and white.

I shake the darkness from my mind and focus. The bird is oblivious to how close to death it is, and as the sun's first rays bear down on my unsuspecting prey, as the butt of the rifle presses into my shoulder, my finger lightly on

41

the trigger, something shiny on its foot reflects in the lens … momentarily blinding me.

I draw back sharply … blinking, blinking, trying to clear my vision. I raise my head and look across the field.

The raven hasn't moved.

Hasn't noticed my slight movement.

I squint, both furious and curious to see what threw me off, at what otherwise, would have been a kill shot.

Nothing … I see nothing!

Frustration grinds against my teeth.

I resume my position, my eyelashes feathering the edge of the scope before I draw back a little. It now has its back to me, and what was once shiny, no longer is.

All I see is the devil.

All I see is black.

I draw in a breath, ready for the shot and squeeze the trigger slowly.

'I hope you're not planning to use that thing,' calls Ember from the doorway.

A loud crack ricochets around the room and the shot goes way off its mark. The bird flies off but not before turning to give me the once over.

'Fuck,' I mumble under my breath.

Ember invites herself into the room River allocated to me two weeks ago. She hovers over me. 'You shouldn't be using firearms in a residential area,' she says, with a friendly smile, 'it's illegal.'

'And how would you know, Miss *Judge Judy*?'

'Ooh, someone's got their knickers in a knot,' she counters, punching me lightly on the arm. 'And for your information, I *don't*. River told me to come in here and ask you *nicely* to put that thing away.'

I withdraw the rifle from the window, remove the round from the breach and rest the gun against the wall.

'I think you scared the old couple from next door. They thought you were going to use their ducks for target practice. River had to bribe them not to phone the police.'

I return my gaze to the window. My eyes drift across the

fence to where four, white Aylesbury ducks are waddling about the garden, and then back to the oak tree, where my stalker stood only moments before. I was so close to finally being rid of it.

Ember is still talking. 'You know this is England, right? I'm not sure what kind of rules you *have* in Australia, but you can't go off shooting …'

Ember stops short as an exaggerated breath makes it out of my mouth. No words are needed on my behalf for her high-and-mighty look to become soft and apologetic.

Guilt of a new kind smashes into me.

Takes me hostage.

I hate myself a little more for realising she has no idea what that shot meant to me.

She leans in closer, tucking her head into the crook of my neck as she also gazes across the field. 'Sorry,' she murmurs. 'I forget we all have our secrets.' I feel a moment coming on. Her thoughts betray her, telling me she wants to help. Wants to be someone I can lean on, rely on. In a voice so soft and gentle, she asks, 'why do they scare you so much?'

Her hair brushes my cheek.

She smells like vanilla ice cream. I lose myself for a second until she says the worst word in the English language, *raven*.

It's like a bullet to my brain.

Water to my lungs.

My voice wedges in my throat. Imprisoned in a cage, the key yet to be forged. I've never opened up to anyone about it before, and I'm not sure I can now. Fear has found my jaw … closing it, discovered my stomach … churning it … tracked down my breath … trembling it.

I swallow.

I can't breathe.

She slips her hand into mine. 'It's okay,' she says so soothingly it's almost impossible for me not to believe her.

I draw on my strength … locate the little puddle of courage from way down deep and say, 'it's not ravens in general.' My body has become its own state of chaos. 'Just one. That one.' I nod my head in the direction I was aiming for. 'The one you made me miss.' When I realise Ember isn't going to reply, I add, 'it's trying to kill me.'

'A *bird*?' She laughs. '*Are you for real*?' She turns to look at me and the smile dissolves into her lips instantly. 'You're serious, aren't you?'

I finally let out a full breath, the breath that should have been released after shooting that damn bird.

'You know the poem, "The Raven" by Edgar Allan Poe?'

She nods. 'Sure. We did it in English last year. Wasn't that with the raven called Nevermore?'

My body organically stiffens.

The word Nevermore triggers a series of dramatic shut down events in my body that I have no control over.

Saliva dries up.

Blinking stops.

Brain ceases to function.

Sweat gathers in the short hairs at the back of my neck, bringing with it an Antarctic shiver that blows in from the base of my spine, working its way upwards. Goosebumps explode over my back.

'Once upon a midnight dreary …' she begins to say.

'*Enough*,' I snap.

Startled, Ember jumps back.

I can't hear those words … not by anyone.

With her hand over her chest, eyes wide like frisbees, mouth open-ready to say …

'Let me explain,' I say more softly. I lead her over to the bottom of my bed and sit her down. 'The first time I saw the raven, I was ten years old. I didn't think much of it, back then. It looked like your average raven. I even tried to shoe it away with a stone a few times because it wouldn't leave me alone.' Ember is quiet, hands lying relaxed in her lap. I continue. 'It kept coming back, day

44

after day, week after week, peering at me from trees or park benches or tapping at my bedroom window with its black pointy beak.' A shiver runs clean over my body. 'I remember clipping it on the wing once with a pellet gun. Then it disappeared.' I take a breath. 'For three years, I never saw it, until it showed up on my thirteenth birthday, swooping me on my way home from school, almost taking my eye out.'

I shuffle closer to show Ember the scar under my eye.

'Ouch,' she says tenderly, hooking an arm around my shoulder.

'Yeah, ouch. It pissed with blood for half an hour, before it finally stopped.' Memories come flooding back. Memories of Rusty. 'The next day, my dog dropped dead.'

'And you blame the bird?' she asks, holding onto a frown longer than necessary.

My answer comes out in the form of a very unenthusiastic shrug. 'I didn't correlate the bad luck that followed the bird until …'

'Until …'

'Until, my best friend, Todd, died right in front of me.'

I shatter into a million fragments as I recall the horror. My throat in all kinds of pain … vomit threatening, legs brittle and on the brink of breaking beneath me. 'A car lost control and collided with his bike. It killed him instantly.'

I hear the sadness in her silence. And in her thoughts. 'And …' Ember says gently.

'AND …The bird was sitting across the road from me, watching.'

Glass shatters in my throat. I swallow but it doesn't help. 'We moved house after that. I couldn't stand to live there anymore.'

The softness of her hand against the back of my neck, her fingers gliding through my hair, barely registers. 'I'm so sorry, that you lost your friend, Skye, but it all sounds like a huge coincidence to me.'

I start to snigger but pull up before it takes hold. 'I thought that too. But now, it's all so clear to me. I didn't put it together for ages, not even after our other pets died.'

A mess of heavy lines on Ember's forehead stops me in my tracks. 'You're serious?' she asks.

'Deadly,' I reply, my face stoic. 'I've lived with this much longer than you and River, and certainly long enough to realise when something is or isn't of the *supernatural* kind.'

'Go on,' prompts Ember.

'Then, my parents went bankrupt, due to no fault of their own. My brother, who I was once close to, turned into a bully overnight.' I pause. 'All because the raven hung around me for one whole day.'

I swallow hard.

Words fighting me, drawing swords … drawing blood. The truth, so desperate to come out – wanting to be heard by someone … anyone.

'Then my … my … They were killed.'

Ember winces, but I carry on. 'The raven showed up every day before they died. It made an appearance from the struts of the airport hangar after their bodies lay on the grass outside, draped in white sheets … peering down at me ... at them. It followed me home and even perched on a neighbouring headstone at their funeral.'

Ember is quiet. 'You didn't kill them,' she says defensively.

'I played with their thoughts. I packed their *chutes*. They *jumped*. They *trusted* me, Em. They trusted that I would take care of them. And I didn't.'

Life stops living.

My heart is a block of stone, refusing to beat.

Ember opens her mouth to say something, but nothing comes out. She squeezes my hand tighter.

'They died because of me.'

My eyes feel full.

Tears spill out.

I choke as the pain finally makes its way to the surface.

46

'If I hadn't been born, then the raven wouldn't be here, haunting me the way it does, the bringer of death, and my mum and dad would still be alive. Either way, I'm responsible for their death.' This is the first time I've ever said the words aloud to anyone.

'I don't believe that.' Ember's voice is a lullaby in motion.

And yet, here I am.

Alone.

In this shitty little world I've created for myself.

'My brother has every right to blame me for it.' I try to hold it together. Push back the guilt trying to overthrow me.

But it's useless.

I can't.

Everything inside me has found its limit.

Sobs desperate to break free.

All the colours of the world become grey and lifeless. Happiness becomes hopelessness.

I retreat into my hands so she can't see me cry.

Long minutes pass and yet it still isn't enough time.

Ember sits with me until it's over.

'Everything will be okay. You know that, right?'

She says more words but my brain is in meltdown mode. I can't hear her. I only know she is there from the warmth of her leg next to mine.

I'm not sure how long she holds me. All I know is when the glass disappears from my throat. When my eyes become sawdust and barren, I finally say, 'During an English lesson, a few months later, we read "The Raven" by Edgar Allan Poe.' I pause, allowing the words to get used to being in my mouth. 'Then, all of a sudden, everything made sense. The voices I could hear in my head? Being able to read minds? I knew what was happening to me. I knew I was going mad. I was like the man in the poem who had lost his marbles.'

'Skye,' says Ember pitifully. 'The poem is about sadness and grief and how he struggled to get over the death of his lady. Not madness. You're no more insane than River and I.' She follows up with a nervous laugh. 'It's still not your fault. Like it isn't my fault that I made it out of the car my parents died in or how River's parents drowned. It's not us that has caused this to happen. Don't you understand that now?'

I kind of do. But there's still all this residual guilt and echoes of insanity lingering inside me from way back.

'Maybe,' I answer, 'but can you see why I'm scared whenever IT is around. I don't want anything to happen to you, or River. You're like my family now. The only family I've got.'

'Skye? Look at me,' says Ember. Her voice is crushed velvet and warm apple pudding. I swivel around to face her. 'I don't think this is about some vengeful bird sent from hell to punish you. It's way too coincidental for that. Plus, didn't River say something about the first clue being about a raven?'

'Yeah, he did. But, what if it's a red herring sent from Isis or Ra-Mon to trap me.'

'Who's getting trapped?' asks River, sticking his nose around the door. 'C'mon. Wally wants us downstairs. He says he's got something important to tell us.'

We find Wally peeling potatoes over the sink, a black apron protecting his perfectly pressed pants and collared shirt as always. Today, it has a Lacoste motif on it. The table in the kitchen is set with four places, ruling out us eating in the formal dining room, which I'm thankful for. That room makes me feel like I'm eating with the Royals, with its enormous chandelier, highly polished silverware and a thousand piece matching dinner set.

'Aahh, there you all are,' he says, turning briefly before continuing with the potatoes. 'Take a seat.'

River remains standing as Ember and I take a chair at the breakfast bar.

Wally turns. Looks once at River as though he expected him to do the opposite of what he asked, and then wipes his hands on the bottom of his apron.

'So, first things first…the only way to do this, is by working together. No more taking plates of sandwiches or bowls of cereal and skating off to your room for the evening.' He raises his eyebrows at River. 'I realise you've all got *issues*.' His lips tighten. Chews the inside of his cheek. 'But trying to figure them out on your own isn't getting you anywhere, *and* as the only *real* adult in the house, it's my wish that you all start acting like a team, and that includes dining together and exchanging ideas.'

He's right.

Since River's 'master of the living room' speech, we have barely spent more than ten minutes in each others company. Admittedly, I haven't been sitting on my hands. I've been researching Mithraism principles and traditions.

I was surprised to learn that a lot of Mithraic monuments are found here in England. A place called Hadrian's wall in Carrawburgh, close to the border of Scotland would be a great place to start. And then back in 2010, two Roman Altar Stones were discovered during the excavation of a cricket pavilion not far from Edinburgh. The front face of one stone had a griffin and lyre on it and an inscription dedicating the altar to the god Mithras. The other had four female heads on it, their hair adorned with spring flowers, summer foliage, autumn grapes and the last wore a shawl, representing the four seasons. There was also an inscription, partially obscured, still experts believe it is likely to bear the name of the Roman Centurion the stone was dedicated to.

If Wally hadn't gathered us together like this, I would've made a point to talk to everyone tonight. For a reason I can't explain, I have a strong urge to visit Hadrian's Wall, the same way I had to see Le Louvre. One thing I can count on, is my intuition. It has never let me down.

Without thinking it through, I blurt out my thoughts, 'I need to go to Hadrian's Wall tomorrow.' Wally places the lid on the potatoes, regarding me with a slight lift of his eyebrow. 'I mean, I need *all three of us* to go to Hadrian's Wall tomorrow.'

He looks at me with curiosity and then smiles, before taking the pot to the table. I take it as a sign he's ready to dish up. Ember picks up on the same cue, and we both stand, and slip into a dining chair, like a couple of synchronised swimmers. River joins us as Wally brings over the last dish. 'And I suppose you need me to drive you there?' says Wally. There's a playful tone in his voice.

I shrug. 'No need. I'm sure River will do it.'

River responds in a flash. 'Do you even know how far that is?'

Again, my shoulders find my ears as I load up my plate with Wally's best and most delicious potato bake.

'For your information, it's near Scotland, Dude! Do you know how long that'll take to drive?'

My only experience of long hauls is the vast distances my family and I used to drive whenever we visited Sydney. Sixteen hours was a blink, especially if you slept half the way. 'I dunno. Ten ... twelve hours, give or take,' I offer. I have no idea.

'It's five hours actually, depending on traffic,' says Ember, showing me her phone. 'That's what google maps say.' Her half-smile is cute.

'Five. Huh! That's easy peasy lemon squeezy. We could be up there before lunch.'

River seems to overlook my sarcasm. 'Why Hadrian's wall?' he asks.

'Trust me. It has something to do with Mithras. I don't know *what* exactly, but I've got a feeling we'll find out when we get there. Plus, there are these Roman Altar Stones I want to see in Edinburgh.' I share everything I learned about them. 'What can I say, it's calling to me,' I say around a grimace.

50

River looks at Ember and then back at Wally. 'Beats sitting around here twiddling our thumbs. We'll head off first thing,' he says.

'And if you could keep to the speed limit, bruv, I would sincerely appreciate it. My stomach took ages to settle after that last time.' I glance through the kitchen window noticing the raven, perched in the willow tree next to the driveway, listening to every word. Plus, I want us to get there in one piece.'

5am.

I wake tired and irritable, the nightmare still clinging to the last scraps of my sanity. I dreamt of a blinding light, like the one through the scope of River's rifle. I couldn't close my eyes. My arms pinned at my sides. Unable to move. Holes the size of apples scorched into my brain as the raven scratched deep channels into my chest.

I'd woken at 2am clutching my sheets, slick with sweat from head to toe, hardly breathing at all, my eyes, fixated on the window, positive I could hear that dreaded tap, tap tapping at my chamber door. It was almost four by the time I drifted off again.

My eyes, dry and grainy, itch from tiredness as I rub them. I stretch my legs down the bed, hearing movement in the house. Sounds like River is up. The second the thought is out of my head, my door opens.

'C'mon. I wanna leave in half an hour.'

I shower quickly and head downstairs to find Ember shovelling down breakfast. Wally is up, *as usual*, and immaculate, *as usual*. He lifts his head from yesterday's newspaper and bids me a good morning.

'You might wanna pack a bag,' Ember says, glancing up from her bowl. 'River mentioned we could be gone for a few days.'

In the time it takes me to throw some things into a bag and chow down on a couple of pieces of toast, River and Ember are already waiting for me in the car.

'Hold the fort while we're gone, Wal,' I call out, catching the blueberry muffin he throws to me as I close the door.

I sit up front with River whilst Ember sprawls out on the back seat, throwing a thick woollen blanket over herself. We haven't gone more than a few kilometres before she is snoring softly. Sometimes, I worry that she hasn't fully recovered from her ordeal. Her thoughts drift back to that pervert so often, I've lost count. She never says anything, and I'm certain if she wants to talk about it, she will. Or at least to River. There is still the topic of how we're going to get Iris's diary too. I'm positive there's evidence in there of how Ember's folks were killed. If I can help solve that little riddle of how she came to be fostered, I think she will sleep easier. I know I will.

The scenery passing my window is nothing like the wide-open spaces back home, where you might go fifty kilometres without seeing a blade of grass, another car, let alone a town.

And it's green.

Everywhere!

Not the dustbowl I'm used to.

River disturbs my thoughts. 'I researched Mithras last night and found out more on the Seven Degrees of Initiation.'

I turn in my seat to face him.

During my brief research on Mithras, I came across the Seven Degrees of Initiation. But ever since Ember mentioned it starts with raven, I chickened out of finding out more. Very coolly, very casually, keeping my voice as steady as I can, I ask, 'what are they?'

I suck in a breath…. waiting for *that* word.

'The first is Corax or Raven.'

I swallow.

Tongue paralysed in my mouth.

Legs tensing against the leather seat.

Breath, in no hurry to leave my body.

River peeks over at me. His frown comes and goes in under a second. He says nothing, but the scraps he allows me to chew on inside his head, tell me he's more confused than shocked.

'Ember told me a ra-ven was involved,' I manage to choke out.

I expect a sarcastic comment. I expect something smart to exit his mouth resulting in me feeling inferior to him. And yet, his words are simple ... surprising. 'The raven that's been following you, I believe, has something to do with this First Initiation.' I open my mouth to say something when he chips in. 'Ember told me,' he says with a sheepish grin.

Figures. It doesn't bother me he knows. 'What do you reckon?'

'It's possible,' I reply, mulling the idea over in my head.

'You know what I first thought of,' says River, taking his eyes off the road for a few seconds. I shake my head. 'How that black bird saved us in the crypt when it scratched out the Minotaur's eyes. That could've been your ... a raven.'

Again, I hadn't joined the dots there either. I was a little pre-occupied about being turned into a human tree.

'Raven, first and foremost, symbolises air,' River says.

'HA!' is all that comes out of my mouth. It takes a moment for more words to come. 'Are you serious?'

River raises his eyebrows. 'Makes sense, doesn't it?'

I still can't believe it. All this time, I've seen it as a curse, when in fact, it was a clue.

'Raven also represents the death of the neophyte and in ancient Persia, they used to place the bodies of the dead on funeral towers so they would be eaten by ravens.'

I shudder. 'That's sick, and what the hell is a neophyte?'

'I wondered that too. I googled it, and basically, it means a beginner or novice at something.'

'Oh. What were the other Initiations?' I ask.

'The second is nymphus or bride. The third is soldier. The fourth is Leo. The fifth is Perses or Persian. The sixth is Heliodromus or sun-runner, and the last one is Pater or father. And all have symbols attached to them.'

'So, how are we supposed to figure all of these out?'

'I've no idea. And to confuse the hell out of everyone, there are those who believe that Mithraism is connected to the Illuminati.'

'*What*?' I can see from the look on River's face he is deadly serious.

'Apparently, it was a secret cult for men only and was formed around secret meetings, symbols and codes.'

I'm stunned. 'Wow. This is so much bigger than I thought.'

'And,' continues River, 'a lot of the religion falls into line with Christianity, too. Right down to the Seven Initiations becoming the seven sacraments of the church, the marking of the forehead with a cross during baptism and the tattooing of a cross on the forehead during the Third Initiation, mithraic communions becoming Sunday mass, and even Mithras was supposed to be born on December 25th, the same day as Jesus.'

'That's unbelievable.'

River hums his acknowledgement.

'So, where does that leave us?' I ask. The task bears down on me, dragging my shoulders with it. It all seemed so straightforward yesterday.

'Suppose we'll find that out when we get there.'

FIVE

TWO thousand years ago, a Roman Emperor decided to build a wall, a wall that stretched a hundred and twelve kilometres in length, and three metres in width, right across the middle of the United Kingdom. And then named it after himself.

Hadrian's Wall is nothing like I expected.

I'd visualised some impenetrable fortress, so high you can't see the top, so grand it had become an eyesore in the middle of the scenic British countryside. Not this crumbling relic covered in white moss and blotched with lichen, low enough in some parts you could jump clean over it. Like something a farmer of old had thrown together to keep his sheep in, blending it into the environment perfectly as though it had every right in the world to be there. And yet there's this impressiveness about it that commands respect. A majestic presence of strength and valour, of legend and statement.

It remains as a warning.

The last line of defence.

Wisps of energy left behind, even after all these years, still linger in the air around us, painting a picture of what once was - a historical footprint, if you will, of blood, sweat and sawdust. Of horses and the rich aroma of tanning oils rubbed into leathers. Of blacksmiths and cheap wine. And most of all, of death.

The concept that people lived back then, let alone built a wall using primitive tools, dissecting England from Scotland is astounding to me. It's unlike anything Australia has, or has *ever* had, as far as man-made structures are concerned. Our modern history dates back less than three hundred years. Of course, the indigenous people of my homeland have centuries of knowledge and stories.

I stare at it, unsure if I'm qualified to come up with a worthy compliment, so I shut my mouth. All my body will allow me to do is take shallow breath after shallow breath.

River seems to take this awesomeness in his stride as I brace myself against the strong northerly wind.

I turn my back into it.

'It's just a wall,' he yells in order to be heard above the ninety kilometre winds.

It's not *just* a wall. It's iconic. 'How can you even say that?' I shout back.

He shrugs.

I don't care what he thinks. I'm amazed, to be standing in its presence. Our journey this morning began by zigzagging across the country. We then joined the motorway to Birmingham, through Chesterfield to Sheffield – a familiar ground for both River and I. In my peripheral vision, I'd noticed River's shoulders suddenly bunch, his fists had wrapped around the steering wheel so fiercely I wondered if he had the strength to rip the thing clean off. Once we took the final turn-off of where our old lives had once played out, he relaxed … a little.

There are still ghosts there for both of us.

We then headed north, right up the guts of England to Leeds, and then east towards Newcastle-upon-Tyne.

The scenery was mind blowing!

Old-fashioned villages, the kind you might see on coasters and placemats hurried past us as we drove. Cobbled roads. More thatched roofs than you can count. The whole sh-bang. Not a blade of dried, brown grass, no road kill or kangaroos anywhere.

We then took a bunch of A roads, whatever the hell *they* are, into the Northumberland National Park. From my uneducated guess, River had stopped us smack-bang in the middle of the wall – halfway between Carlisle and the North Sea.

Why?

Because I told him to.

I'm still not a hundred per cent sure why I asked him to stop right here.

Intuition?

Perhaps … But now that I'm out of the car, staring at this phenomenal grey, whitish stone wall that disappears into the distance on the back of this lush landscape of rolling green hills, the perfect backdrop to the Game of Thrones, I don't think so.

Nothing is coming to me.

No amazing flash of insight. No subtle clues lurking in the cold, damp crevices of the wall where clumps of weeds and boggy green sponges have made their home.

Nothing.

Nothing down the length of the wall. Nothing in my immediate environment. Not the tiniest of inklings.

This had been my worst fear during the entire trip up here, and the more I breathed life into it, the more it has become a reality.

The doubt in their minds, as Ember and River consistently glance at me when they think I'm not looking, isn't helping. Their eyes are like warm ants crawling all over me and their questioning thoughts ready to be unleashed. I inhale.

Nothing is coming.

Zero!

Zip!

I feel kind of stupid.

I wasn't expecting an overwhelming, guiding feeling to come over me, like I did when I first visited Le Louvre. But something at least.

This time, I'm a let-down.

No hot spots. No flashes of intuition. Not even a vision. I take a stab at summoning Amun, not that I know what the hell I'm doing. I mean, closing your eyes and wishing isn't the same as having a step-by-step instruction guide on effectively communicating with an immortal. But regardless, I give it a go.

Minutes pass.

And again nothing.

Now Ember is making no secret of staring at me, waiting for some out-of-this-world revelation.

I glance back at the wall. Then to the ruins of where a fort once stood. I pull my borrowed parka firmly around my body and zip it right up to my neck. The wind won't let up here, fierce in its efforts, and the temperature hasn't hit double digits yet.

'Do you think we'll have to walk the entire length to find something?' I shout out to River, so he can hear me above the howl. 'Because we don't have a spare week up our sleeves.' Back at the information centre in Haltwhistle, they had stacks of brochures advertising a range of walking treks.

'God, I hope not, and of course, you're right. Time is of the essence,' says River. He copies me, zips his coat right up to the neck, and tugs down on the cords on his hood to fasten it.

Ember has taken shelter close to the wall like she's part of the fixtures, her face as white and as cold as the stone behind her. 'Maybe we should go up to the fort,' she says encouragingly. Her lips quiver as she speaks. She fakes a smile. Looks frozen right through to the marrow. 'Perhaps you might *feel* something there.'

'I'm not sure, Em. It's like my whole antenna system is being thrown off by this wind or something.'

'Switch it off, then,' she says offhandedly.

I can do that!

Why is it that I forget that sometimes?

I'm not a hundred per cent sure it is the wind, but silencing it will at least give me half a chance to focus. I shut out the group of trekkers in brightly coloured rain jackets marching past me, and tap into my power. It's right there, waiting for my command … like turning on a tap.

Less than a blink later, the wind has dropped to a light breeze, whilst everyone around us is still battling through it. A young girl angles her head at me, her thoughts going a million miles an hour as to why my hair is hardly moving, whilst hers has become a frenzy of wild blonde straw.

'Better,' Ember says, dropping her hood and raking her fingers through her knotty auburn curls. 'Thank you.'

River and I remove our hoods at the same time. 'Handy that power of yours,' he says gratefully.

'Glad I'm good for something,' I mutter.

River nudges my elbow. 'I don't think that's the case, but check that out.' I glance over to where he's pointing. 'I believe that did the trick.'

Perched on the top of a jagged stone edge, feathers as black as the ace of spades and a little more ruffled than usual, is the raven. For the first time in my life, I don't feel that screaming urge to reach for my crossbow.

'We must be on the right track.'

'What do you think it wants?' asks Ember.

I throw my hands in the air. 'I've lost count the number of times I've asked myself that,' I reply.

River uncrosses his arms and blows out an aggravated breath. 'I've had enough of this shit. I'll be back in a sec,' he says, walking towards it.

'What do you think that'll achieve?' I reply, but he doesn't hear me, the light wind stealing my words, blowing them behind me.

River doesn't get ten metres away, before the bird flies off. I knew that would happen and chuckle silently.

River returns with a sheepish smile on his face. 'I guess he only likes Aussies for dinner and not Poms.'

'Haha,' I retort. 'Maybe being a complete tosser tends to stick in one's throat.'

River scowls at me, but I can see he finds humour in my words. Something tells me, we will always be like this with each other, after all, isn't that what brothers do?

'Maybe next time, you need to grow a pair and go check it out for yourself,' he replies.

I leave it at that, knowing he always likes to get the last word in, but he is right about one thing ... I *do* need to 'grow a pair'. I also know River is gutless when it comes to telling Ember the truth, let alone face a potentially psychotic bird with a chip on its shoulder – and I literally mean *chip*. Five years ago, I'd clipped it on the wing with a stone, using a hand-made slingshot. It fell to the ground and by the time I went over to check, it had disappeared.

I thought all my troubles were over.

That it had flown off to die somewhere.

I was wrong ... it was only the beginning.

'There are milecastles too, Skye,' offers Ember, showing me the flyer she'd picked up. 'They're placed every third of a mile, so we could walk to a few and investigate, if you like?'

I look down, past my hands and stare at my sneakers. My shoulders feel unusually heavy. Not the usual backpack of guilt I'm used to, but something extra, like two towels and a drawer full of jumpers have been stuffed in there too.

I'm exhausted.

Exhausted from trying too hard.

'Fuck! I don't know. I feel like I've dragged us all here for nothing.' The words come out before I realise I've said them. I wish Tomas was here to throw a little light on everything. I'm sure he'd know what to do.

'Then let's try the milecastles,' suggests Ember excitedly. 'It says in here, that milecastles were where Roman Centurions would stand and patrol. Isn't that what Tomas would've done? Act as a sentry, I mean?'

Sometimes, I wonder if Em can read my mind as she seems so intune with me at times. It's a long shot, I know, but I can't shoot her down, not with that desperate look of hope on her face.

'Sure. Okay,' I say. She skips up to me and links her arm in mine.

An hour passes. And then another.

Low grey clouds, heavy with rain, descend on us as we hang around the old milecastles ruins. We walk amongst the remains of what, I imagine, were once magnificent forts, full of soldiers and armour, spears, swords and pouches of wine. Primitive square footings, no more than fifteen inches high in some places is all that's left. I follow the mud trodden path around the perimeter, until I finally admit that nothing is working.

'There's always the Roman Army Museum,' suggests River.

'I'm not sure.' Indecisiveness is a disease growing stronger inside me every minute, and yet I feel like a fish being lured in, except I'm still a hundred metres away from the boat.

River looks down at his watch.

Looks at me.

'Maybe we should leave.'

'And go where?' asks Ember.

'Edinburgh,' I say around a smile. 'The Altar Stones are there. How about we find a place to bunk down for the night, get something to eat and pick the brains of the locals to find out more about the stones?' I'm grasping at straws. 'And then we can go and view them tomorrow?'

River sighs and checks his watch again. Even though it's only three o'clock, night is already on its way. His lips twitch to one side. 'Okay.'

Getting into Edinburgh takes a little longer than anticipated due to a truckload of pigs slipping down an embankment, blocking traffic both ways. Three hours in a car, barely saying a word, being privy to the thoughts of Ember and River hasn't been fun, especially with them both apologising to me every five minutes. By the time we arrive, I'm tired and cranky, and in desperate need of a shower.

The Highland Inn, a very cool fourteenth century pub, came highly recommended from a lady outside the Post Office, although it wasn't an easy find, regardless of the bold gold lettering splashed across the front of the building. We took two dead ends, and then got turned around on a one-way street, before eventually finding it tucked away down some back road, wedged amongst a row of red-faced terrace houses. The whole place is a walk back in time to when streets were cobbled and stained with the footprints of miners, thatchers and iron-mongers. The pub walls are rough-textured and painted such a brilliant white that if it wasn't dark, I'd be needing sunglasses. Stretching across the front of the ground level, eight glossy black pillars, used solely for decorative purposes, divide the whiteness into uneven rectangles, giving the appearance that the old place is leaning to one side. Hell, it's old enough, it probably is. Two white colonial windows hug a black wooden doorway that doesn't seem to cater to anyone over six foot, whilst three smaller white windows, bordered in black frames, sit above us on the first and second storey.

I pull my coat around me and blow into my hands as Ember and I wait out front for River to park the car. My intuition feels bang on that we've come to the right place. The very energy bouncing off the walls is evident enough.

I can't help grinning. 'I feel good about this,' I say, staring through one of the pubs big bay windows. My breath fogs up the glass and I wipe it away as a burly man with bushy black sideburns steps out from behind the bar, staring at me as he polishes a glass.

It doesn't take long to check in, and after twisting around two winding staircases, a tiny room with sloping ceilings greets me at the top. It's not the five star luxury I'm used to at River's place, my eyes immediately drawn to the lumpy, wrought iron bed draped in a faded orange bedspread. In addition, there's too much frill for my liking. Two saggy pillows assure me I'm in for a rough night. Regardless, I throw my bag onto the bed and flake out next to it, ignoring its squeaky protest.

I overlook the old, dark-stained wardrobe and chest of drawers that could easily date back to when the pub was first built, and ignore the brown spot on the carpet near the radiator that looks like it might leak from time to time. The sign outside my window, creaking as it swings back and forth, is easy enough to tune out.

I hear River's thoughts in the room next to me, wishing this was all over so that he and Ember can start their perfect life together, and Ember's incessant ramblings as she thumbs through the guest information, looking for clues and answers.

I close my eyes to think.

Clear my head.

And, try to tune into Amun.

It's not too difficult to block out the smell of stale beer and musty blankets, or the cool breeze seeping through the cracks of the loose window frame. In response, the wind picks up, rattling it a little more. I steady my breath. Focus on nothing but that slow inhalation and even slower exhalation. I'd often sneak onto our back veranda and watch Mum's yoga group sitting cross-legged on coloured mats, eyes closed, practising their kum-ba-ya's or whatever the fuck they called it. Although, I won't criticise it - the ritual has served me well when my mind becomes a warzone, and I need an escape.

I zero in, extending my Superhero skills to search out those impossibly unique and distinctive frequencies that Doc introduced me to all those years ago.

I need to go deeper.

To the next level.

Tap into what *no* human can hear …

Sound-waves.

Frequencies known to science, and unknown to the ears of man - energies that come directly from the earth, the air, plants, even rocks.

I don't hold out much hope of hearing much. The last time I went that extra mile, reached out farther than I ever have before, I got booted out at such speed I had a headache for a week. I guess it's no different to the way my body tires when I stay invisible or fly for too long.

But I'm ready this time.

I'm more prepared for it.

I drop in on a conversation from the bar downstairs, one bloke talking about his wife being pregnant, *again*. One lady complaining about the price of milk she bought from the corner shop this morning and how Daphne, the shop owner, is having problems with her gallbladder. Both conversations float over my senses easily enough.

I stretch out again … this time to the end of the street, listening to two children squabbling over whose turn it is on the Xbox, and the sound of an ambulance three more streets away from that.

And then the world slips into a state of tranquility. Not the kind of silence most know.

But something natural … almost *primal*.

The hum of electricity is lost, giving way to the stillness of life. My heart skips over a beat as the glorious silence speaks out, cheering from the mountains surrounding us, all whilst remaining trapped inside my head.

64

It's the wind softly blowing across the fields.

It's the sound of grasses swaying.

It's the buzz of a thousand locusts excited for the summer rain.

Magnificent roaring silence.

Until …

Pain crashes into my mind, reminding me of my limit.

I push past it.

Extend my range.

The agony bites down harder, shattering my concentration for a split second as the hum of a speeding train and the laughter of a child travelling on it for the first time, slip through.

I force myself to link back in. Back to a moment where time doesn't exist. Doesn't tick.

And then I hear them …

    Whispers,

        soft

           and many.

Random words and lost sentences, becoming tales of old. Of hisses and purrs of promises. Of secrets.

The voices of the dead.

Goosebumps prickle my skin as if the dead have invaded my room, brushed past me as they go about their business. The buzz of a hornet's nest beneath my feet travels to my knees and up my legs. I remember this feeling all to well and so does my stomach.

I dry reach.

It continues its journey up my chest to my fingers and along both arms to my neck. I'm suddenly struck with the strangest feeling of déjà vu.

I haven't been any further than this. Normally, once I hit spooky town, it's an automatic opt out. The ghostly whispers persist, but I have to push through the fear, see what's on the other side of this.

A voice with clarity and conviction stands out above the rest – *it is not time*.

Amun …

It has to be - the voice is internal ... part of me, so easily distinguished from the ghostly mutterings.

Finally! One small step for man ... my brain screams out!

I have a hundred questions to ask him.

It is not time, he repeats.

A sharp, zap to my brain and the connection is lost. My head fills with static - like someone is pulling apart my brain with claw hammers and pick axes. It jars me into consciousness and I pull out immediately.

I bolt upright.

Panting.

Sweating.

Blood streaming from my nose.

I wipe it away with the back of my sleeve, struggling with dizziness as it tries to take me. Consume me. Nausea swirls up my throat and into my mouth.

I swallow. Gently massage the pain from my temples as the pounding inside my skull intensifies. I swing my legs over the bed, fatigue smothering my bones. Knotting inside my muscles.

I hear a loud knock on the door.

'It's open,' I call out lethargically. I wait ten seconds, twenty seconds, not trusting myself to get up.

No one enters.

I gingerly push to my feet and hobble to the door through slightly blurred vision. I'm expecting to see River standing there with a stupid look on his face, demanding to know what time we are heading downstairs to eat.

But the hallway is empty. I lean into the doorway. Wait for a few breaths. Steady myself.

When no one shows, I knock on River's door.

'Good! You're ready?' he says to me, eyeing me suspiciously. He reaches out a hand to my shoulder. 'Is everything okay?' He studies my face, my forehead, my nose. He looks to my sleeve ... sees the blood and frowns.

'Just a bit run down,' I tell him, which isn't a lie. He pats my shoulder as Ember slides around the door. She too casts a curious glance at me, but says nothing out loud. *You've got this*, her mind says to me, *we're there for you*. She picks up her bag off the four-poster bed they'll be sharing tonight and closes the door behind them. When neither of them reveal they are the mystery knocker, I shrug it off, compile the anomaly alongside all the other weird shit that goes on in my life, and follow them into the bar.

A skinny woman with vibrant red streaks in her hair ushers us to a cluster of dark mahogany tables, handing us each a menu as we sit. The overhead light, fixed to the ceiling by a chain, and made from black-iron and wood, dangles above our table. I'm about to tell River to watch his head on it, but he sends the thing swinging before I open my mouth.

'I'll be back to take your order,' she says, before retreating behind the bar to talk to a middle-aged woman with enormous melons.

Ember pokes me in the ribs. 'Stop staring,' she mutters under her breath.

I shake my head, *and* shake the woman from my thoughts. 'One of the oldest pubs in Edinburgh, eh?' I say, very blase, struggling to ignore my ever-increasing headache. The walls share the same coarseness as outside, except they're a muddy colour rather than that brilliant white, and from my limited knowledge of interior design, the colour scheme, *dark brown on brown*, looks as though it's the work of a farmer with leftover fence paint rather than someone who has put a lot of thought into decorating as a career. Burnt mahogany beams criss-cross above us, closing the room in that little bit more. 'Is everyone in Scotland a midget?' I blurt out. Some might describe the place as intimate with the small glass wall lights, but to me, it's dark and dingy. 'Why do they have to make the ceilings so low?'

River looks up from his menu. His thoughts tell me he doesn't see anything wrong with the height and yet he says, 'Building materials were in short supply, plus it was designed like this so it would heat up quickly, and stay warm. No gas central heating back then.' He goes back to studying the menu. 'Let's order,' he says, beckoning the woman over again. 'I'm hungry.'

I pick something random off the menu, the slow suffocation of claustrophobia growing inside me. What can I say, small spaces aren't my jam. My lungs feel useless as heat rises up my body, finds my cheeks. I've got thirty seconds tops before total, nuclear meltdown.

I unpack my exit strategy.

Fill my mind with everything I can name in the room. It has a ninety-five per cent success rate - confusing my brain the more items I can list, the bigger the room must be to fill everything. The technique was suggested by the therapist I was seeing after Todd died. Ludicrous I know, but it works.

I start my list.

Dusty shelves full of jugs in the shape of fat-faced men, twenty-two in total. A hundred different types of knick knacks from snowglobes and little statues of wire fishermen. Proud African men, cast in bronze, bearing shields and spears. Dolls made from straw and a family of jade elephants. Framed awards thoughtlessly placed around the room, many crooked. Twelve different oil paintings of naval scenes and another five of herbs in a cottage garden. In fact, there's so much to record my head swims from the overwhelm.

I take a deep breath. Deeper than usual. And then wrinkle my nose. It smells old in here too. Not *quite* like my room upstairs, but similar to an antique shop in Sheffield I once found myself in. Years of built-up cigarette smoke, dirty boots soaked into the carpets and a barrel load of furniture polish fill in the rest of the blanks.

I feel myself begin to settle, the fear slowly subsiding. Headache waning. My eyes fall to a decorative shield with a family crest on it, on the wall behind River's head. It doesn't take a genius to see it's old.

'What does the date say underneath?' I ask.

68

River swivels in his seat to look at it as the man with the sideburns approaches.

'It says 950AD, and for your information, that'll be me family crest,' the man states proudly. 'Me family has been here since the Romans invaded.'

'Romans?' I hear myself say. We all spin around and stare at him. Of all the people, of all the towns and of all the things to say, what are the odds of someone bringing up the subject of Romans.

'Aye, Romans. Are ya hard of hearin', laddy?' I lock eyes with him before I loose a short laugh. 'Is ya friend all right in the head?' asks the Scot, jabbing himself in the temples with his finger.

River smirks. 'Don't take offence. He's Australian.'

Ember giggles.

'The names McTavish. Lachlan McTavish.' Ember jumps in quickly to introduce us when he doesn't offer us his hand to shake.

A shy smile lifts the corner of her mouth. 'Mr McTavish, would you know anything about the Altar Stones that were found here a few years ago?' she asks. 'I think *they* were Roman.' Her gaze lingers on the open fireplace as two logs of hardwood are devoured.

'Och aye, they were. Folk were plenty excited about it.'

I manage to locate my tongue. 'I read they're on display in a museum, *somewhere*.'

The Scot, dressed in a crisp white shirt and black pants, a tartan bowtie around his neck, scruffs his black sideburns. 'Aye, that's right. They were.'

'*Were*?' we all say together. My heart takes a nose-dive into my feet. Hunger suddenly vanishes.

'Aye. Up and disappeared, if you like. Been hanging around here for ten years and then …'

He doesn't finish his sentence, only stares at the crest on the wall. River and I exchange glances.

The woman with the red hair brings over our meals. 'And then …' says River. It isn't hard to miss the frustration in his voice and from the look on his face, I'm not the only one who has lost their appetite.

'We get a lot of young'uns up here, straight out of university, researching our heritage. Only last week a man came in here asking about the stones.'

Ten more seconds pass. River leans forward and begins to say, 'do you have any idea where they might be?'

'Aye, I do, lad. But eat your supper before it gets cold.'

We watch him return to his spot behind the bar. He picks up another glass and begins to polish it.

I regard my 'supper' and then push the plate away.

'You need to eat,' says Ember, 'you haven't eaten a scrap of food all day.' I smile at her and love that she cares, but the slow upsurge of guilt for dragging them on a wild goose chase supersedes her concern. All I want right now, is to find out what that giant Scot knows.

River and Ember finish their meals whilst I watch the gravy congeal over my roast beef. The Scot can't seem to keep his eyes off us, but all that changes when a tall customer walks in and sits at the bar. He attends to him.

'Can't you zone in and read his thoughts?' asks River.

'Already tried that,' I say between gritted teeth. 'It's like he has rocks in his head or something. Nothing coming in, nothing going out.'

'Then go and ask him,' urges River.

I deliberate, but only for a second. I'd rather set fire to my hands than sit here any longer not knowing.

I head to the corner of the bar to where he is standing. His eyebrows meet, his lips curl to one side.

'What can I be getting ya for?' he asks in a thicker than normal Scottish accent. 'Is it a whiskey you're after?'

'What? No! I don't want a drink. I want you to tell me where the Altar Stones have been taken to?'

'And who might you be?' he ask, like he's never met me before.

I peek over my shoulder at the other two. 'I was at the table over there with my friends,' I say, pointing back to

River and Ember. 'You told us about the Altar Stones that used to be in a museum but have now been moved. You said you knew where they'd gone.'

At first, the Scot seems confused. He then puffs out his chest, two buttons of his shirt pulling unnaturally against each other. 'Ah dinnae ken the game you're playing at lad, but you'll wanna finish it now.'

WHAT? my brain screams out inside my head. It takes a second for my mouth to catch up. '*Game*?'

'Aye,' he says, squinting at me.

Time slows.

The low hum of music playing in the background gets softer, even slurs. The air feels tight … like I'm inside a balloon that's been blown up to the point of popping. The only other time I felt like this was when River and I were at Chartres Cathedral before we entered the maze.

The woman with the red hair places a tray of glasses right next to me as though she's moving in slow motion.

I turn to look at her.

She casually gives me a wink and for one extended heartbeat, behind too much black eye makeup, I think I see Isis. I blink once and the image is gone.

The world returns to normal, the music back to its correct pace and the air as breathable as ever.

I turn back to Mr McTavish, who is now stacking cider bottles at the other end of the bar. I don't know what just happened. I try and tune into his thoughts, but all I hear are the repeated song lyrics of 'It's a long way to the top if you wanna rock n roll.' The red-haired woman is nowhere to be seen and even the man at the bar who left an empty glass with ice still stacked up in it, has gone.

On my way back to our table, I scan the entire room for the only creepy immortal I know … Ra-Mon.

Nothing.

'Well?' says Ember, 'what did he say?'

'Weird. Very weird.' I don't know what else to add.

'Well, where are they?'

Blankness comes over me.

71

'The stones?' she repeats.

'*Stones*?' I mimic, 'he didn't even know he had spoken to me, let alone what he spoke about.'

Ember looks at me and then at River. 'What's going on, River?' I hear the quiver in her voice as she says his name.

He offers her a smile, not full and glorious and sickeningly sweet like I've seen him do a thousand times before, but enough to take the edge off. I hear her saying over in her mind, *it's nothing, it's just nothing. Don't read more into it*.

But something is going on.

My spidey senses, as River once referred to them as, are now pinging. Adrenaline swamps my blood and every hair follicle would cut a salute if they were soldiers.

'Be on your guard,' I say in a low whisper. 'I think we have a visitor.'

Ember swings her head one way and then the other.

'Don't make it look so obvious,' River cautions her.

The fear on her face says otherwise. 'I see him. He's in the corner of the room talking to the barman.

'Are you sure it's him?' asks River.

Her lips pull tightly together. 'Are you for real?' she spits quietly through her teeth at him. 'I'll never forget his face as long as I live.'

River mutters an apology and draws her into his chest placing his arm around her shoulders. He kisses the side of her head. 'I'm sorry,' he whispers into her hair.

Ember bolts upright. 'Oh my god,' she says, 'he's coming over.

Hood covering his face, head hanging low, he advances. I see River suck in a breath and hold it.

And I do the same.

Suddenly the air changes.

Becomes lighter somehow.

And out of the shadows appears Tomas.

SIX

EYES wide. Skin dusted white. One hand on her chest, the other gripping River's arm. Panic exploding out of every pore. Ember is up and out of her seat, peering around Tomas. Examining every face in the pub. 'Where did he go? I saw him. I swear, I saw him.'

It's true, Ra-Mon was here.

I saw him, myself.

But, I also saw Isis for no more than a blink too. It doesn't take a genius to figure out we're being watched. But that isn't why my heart is hammering this hard.

Tomas!

I can't believe it.

Tomas, in the flesh. Well, *I think*. I mean, I'm sure he's human even though he's immortal.

'Dude, you're back. We thought you were toast that day, back in the labyrinth.' Relief breaks free from my body as I take hold of his hand and shake it hard.

73

Confusion flickers across his brow before realisation sets in. Very stoically, he says, 'I told you before, I cannot die.'

'But …the Minotaur …?' says River. 'You weren't breathing …'

Tomas heaves his thick, muscular shoulders. 'I cannot die,' he says, removing the hood of his cloak, his scarred face more tired and sombre than I remember. His eyes, as always, void of any emotion.

'The Altar Stones you spoke of were not moved to another location by the museum,' says Tomas. 'They were taken.'

'By who?' gasps Ember.

River raises one eyebrow. 'One guess.'

We all know.

Well, we thought we knew until Tomas clears his throat, his face evidently troubled. 'It was *I* who took them.' His jaw as rigid as rock.

Judging from River and Ember's faces, I'm not the only one who's shocked by this revelation. '*You*?'

'Yes,' says Tomas flatly.

'*Why*?'

'Because they are very important to me.' Tomas then does something I've never seen him do before … he smiles. It's not a full-blown smile. Doesn't quite touch his eyes, but he wears it well, with his blonde, shaggy hair and rugged *man-li-ness* that wouldn't look out of place as one of my surfie mates from Oz, minus the long jagged scar. 'And you were right to come here to view the stones,' he says to me directly.

Pride swells in my chest and I feel my back straighten, my neck elongate. Finally, I've done something right. I'd love to steal a peek at River's face right now, but I take the higher road.

'There is an inscription on one of them I need you to interpret.'

'Why *me*? And how do you know I'll be able to …'

74

Tomas checks over his shoulder before pulling out a chair and joining us. 'You found the book, did you not?'

'*Book*?' I say confused.

'Peri Phuseôs tôn Ontôn?'

I look to River before I respond with a single nod. 'What's that got to do with it …and…'

Tomas interrupts. 'Many years ago, I also acquired that book.' We are all leaning forward, open-mouthed before I finally find the words to say.

'You *acquired* the book? From *who*?'

'Is it important that you know this?' Tomas pauses and waits for an answer. I'm about to speak when he continues. 'Have you asked yourself if I hadn't, would you have the knowledge you need to defend your world?'

I shrug. 'I suppose not.'

'And does it not say in the book that *you* are the one to release the EarthHealer from her bindings?'

'Yes,' I murmur.

'*What*!' River swaps stares with Ember, his usual frown making an appearance. 'And you didn't think to tell us?' he questions. 'You were keen as mustard to know what was on my page, and not *once* did you mention this… to either of us. Why?'

'You didn't ask,' I reply, guilt leaking out of my skin. And it's true.

If I had answered one tiny question about my page, it would've triggered another and then another, and then I would have to tell them everything. Back then, I didn't know that the two people sitting across from me would become the most important people in my life. I suppose, it was the only way I knew how to keep who I was, intact.

River pushes to his feet, his palms pressing into the table. His head hits the low-hanging lamp again to which he throws a reproachful look at before his eyes come back to me. '*Didn't* ask?'

'Enough!' says Tomas, and River quickly takes his seat, rubbing the side of his head. 'You can battle this out between yourselves later.'

Tomas turns back to me. I get the distinct feeling everything is about to unfold. I'm unravelling at a pace that scares me more than jumping out of a perfectly good plane.

I hold my breath, cringing inwardly and wait …

'And does it also say in order to initiate the beginning of the end, you will have seven chances to prove your worth?'

I nod again, but this time, keep my gaze on my finger drawing continuous circles on the table. It's embarrassing enough to feel like shit around River, but to have it in writing … in a book dating back thousands of years, more than screams it from the rooftops. Why not skywrite to the world that I'm that hopeless, I get seven chances to redeem myself, in case I fuck up the other six.

I deliberately block out the sympathy inside Ember's head. She's debating whether to get me alone afterwards and assure me everything will be okay, or throw and arm across my shoulder and hope that does the trick. River is quiet, although his train of thought is skipping so fast, I can hardly keep up with which line he's going to approach me with. There is nothing, as usual, from Tomas … not that I expect it.

I return to my own thoughts. An answer is warranted. 'Yes,' I finally reply.

'Then why can't you see that these seven chances represent the Seven Rites of Mithraism?'

I sit up straighter, brain engaging as the thick, foggy haze dampening my self-esteem, lifts. *Why hadn't I put this together before?*

My confidence surges.

I fall back into my chair, relief spilling into every corner of my body.

I sense the change, as do my friends, the air around us suddenly shifting to a more ambient tranquility – a talent not manipulated from Amun, but something I think I inherited from Mum. She had a way about her that could calm the hottest of rages with a simple smile, or obliterate tension with just one hug.

'What does this have to do with an inscription?' River's face is lighter, less stressed, his hands clasped loosely across his torso.

Tomas's brow creases ever so slightly. 'Everything. And, am I right in saying, it's not only the living you hear?'

'Wha …' gasps Ember. 'You can communicate with the dead?'

I can only nod.

'That's so cool,' she says, first looking at me and then at River, 'Right, Riv?'

'Very cool, bro, although, I'm not sure why you didn't mention it before.' There is a little saltiness to his tone.

'Mmmm,' is my pathetic response.

It's not what I'm expecting … from either of them. But I'm certain of one thing … they won't think I'm *very cool* once they hear what the rest of the book has to say about me, especially the line about, *and I'm paraphrasing here*, that it'll be my fault for killing a close friend.

I know, mike drop, right!

Having this shit in my head all these years hasn't been easy, and there isn't a single day that passes I don't think of it. I hold my breath. Chance a glimpse at Tomas, praying he keeps this little nuclear bombshell to himself.

I suppose the one consolation is… my list of friends is thin. Five at best … problem is, three of them are staring right at me; River trying to pick up on my emotions with his watered-down WaterLover power. Ember wishing for the hundredth time that she can read my thoughts. And now Tomas has joined that list. All, *unknowingly* contributing to the torturous nightmares that accompany my raven dreams. It's an insidious torment of the worst kind … trying to save someone from death, never seeing their face, never knowing which poor soul is dangling at the end of my rope.

River and Ember say nothing, their eyes however, tunnel through my skin like a couple of wood-boring worms, and for now, I am the tinest bit thankful that I'm the one with the mind reading abilities otherwise it'd be *adios muchachos*.

A faint smile touches my lips as I regard my companions. I stand strong in my power, take a deep breath, aware of the peacefulness that transcends over us, and let their true thoughts assault me in which ever way they want to.

And yet, in that minuscule moment, their thoughts are not on me … not on the mammoth task ahead, but on each other. Ember is now tucked under River's arm, all cosy and feeling loved, the most laid-back I've seen him in a while, and cautiously planning their new life together.

Which brings me back to our resident Gladiator. My incessant curiosity, a disease I've yet to find a cure for, and will *ultimately* be my undoing, is getting the better of me. I want to know more about the book - how he found it, where it originates from, who wrote it, who else knows about it, altogether aware he might *accidentally* let something important slip that I'm not ready to discuss just yet with River and Em.

My teeth graze my lip.

Fuck it … it's not in my nature to hold back.

'How do you know so much about what is written on those pages?'

Tomas shifts in his seat. 'It is a very long tale. One that I do not have the time to tell at this moment.'

'You've gotta give us something,' I say frustrated.

He concedes. 'Simply understand that I could read it a very long time ago and now I cannot. Just like the Altar Stones.'

'I …' I begin to say.

'I have been searching for you, AirWhisperer, for eighteen hundred years.'

'*Me*?'

'Bringing the book to the land at the bottom of the world was the first time I'd travelled across the big water. The book drew me to you, the same way I knew, it would seek you out.'

'You *knew*? *How*?'

He ignores my questions.

Again …

'I buried it close to you so that when the time came, it would call to you and activate your power.'

'How did you know I wouldn't move house?'

'But you didn't, did you?'

'I *could* have.' I'm not meaning to be argumentative, I just want him to spill the beans. And fast!

'Enough!' Tomas has a real shitty look on his face that says I'll rip your head off if you continue with this line of questioning.

Serenity gone.

Tension seeps in.

I button it and he starts again.

'I knew you wouldn't move anywhere else, so let's leave it at that. The book was the start of the journey for you – to prompt you to search for the others. Which it did, yes?' His face softens, as much as a battletorn, scarred face can soften.

'Yes.'

Ember laughs. 'I can't believe you went all the way to Australia.' She reins in her smile.

We have sidetracked again, and it shows in Tomas's face. His cheeks crease as the light drains from his eyes. 'The Altar Stones are safe. You can trust me. They are hidden in a cave a short distance from here.' He glances out of the small-panelled window into the night. 'It is too late now, but when the sun rises, we must go there.'

'Sure,' I answer. 'No problemo, but, first you've gotta do two things for me.'

Tomas stands up. Stands tall. His taut body resembling the stones we seek.

'If you're gonna hang with us, might I suggest a pair of jeans and a hoodie rather than trying to hide your armour beneath that cloak?' Tomas looks down at his clothes, fanning out his cloak, confusion finding a place amongst his eyes. 'Dude, you need to blend in a bit.'

Ember and River agree.

'And second …'

'There's no way you're going to get me out of bed at dawn. We'll leave after breakfast.'

SEVEN

THE next morning, we bundle into River's car for the five-minute journey to a place called Arthur's Seat, a two hundred and fifty metre grassy mound keeping watch over the city of Edinburgh. Tomas had pointed out where he'd roughly hidden the Altar Stones on Ember's google maps.

'Did you know that Arthur's Seat is an extinct volcano?' says Ember, reading from her phone. She looks down at her shoes. 'I wish I'd bought my trainers ...'

'Sneakers,' I correct her.

'Trainers,' Ember says louder. 'You're in my country now ... *remember* ...and, we say trainers.' She nudges me in jest. 'It could be a bit of a hike.'

'We won't be going to the top,' says Tomas craning his neck around the front seat. He glances down at her feet. 'You will be fine.'

Ember smiles. 'This cave we're going to … is it the same cave where five boys found seventeen miniature coffins back in the early 1800s?'

'It is the same,' replies Tomas.

'Ha!' laughs Ember. 'This article says that the townsfolk suspected witchcraft was involved too.'

Whether from cold, although I doubt the weather would affect him, or from some unknown fear, which I would bet my best surfboard on, the second Ember mentioned witchcraft, I swear I saw a shudder pass over Tomas's back and shoulders.

'And there's more …' she continues. 'According to local legends, this is where Camelot was located.'

I draw my head back and stare at her. 'You mean, *King Arthur's Camelot*?'

'Is there *another*?' She fires back at me with a knowing grin. 'I'm happy to hear they teach some form of correct English at your school, even if it is literature and not language.' Her gaze drifts downwards again to her *trainers*. She twists her ankles one way and then the other, and laughs. She goes on to say, 'Apparently, that's how this massive hill got its name.'

'Knights are weak,' states Tomas forcefully. 'They are no match for a true Roman Centurion, like my father before me.'

Having no experience with either, I keep my opinions to myself. However, I need no convincing from the colossal size of Tomas's chest and shoulders, and brute strength to boot, that he would be victorious if it came down to hand-to-hand combat with any knight or swordsman.

No one else is keen to argue the point with him either, it seems, so safely tucked away on the back seat, I sneak a peek at him from under my lashes, unable to hide my humour. At this very moment, he has never looked less like a Roman warrior, dressed in a pair of faded jeans and heavy, navy blue overcoat.

As though on cue, we hear his sword and armour chink together from the boot of the car as we hit a pothole.

Ember leans forward in her seat. 'By the way, how old are you?'

Tomas grins. 'I was born in the year 20BC.'

'*Are you for real*?'

Tomas's answer is a straight yes.

'You know if someone told me a year ago, I'd be hanging out with a two thousand year old Roman Centurion, I'd have pegged grapes at them for lying,' I throw in.

'But, how *old* are you? repeats Ember.

'I am five and twenty years of age.'

Ember's little hive of questions doesn't look like it's about to stop any time soon. 'And what was the barman's deal?' she asks.

'The *barman*? *Deal*?' asks Tomas.

'Sorry. The *innkeeper*.' She turns to me, leans in closer to my ear, and says, 'I keep forgetting he doesn't know our lingo.'

'What are you talking about? ' I whisper back to her. '*I* don't know your lingo.' She smothers her clipped laughter with her hand before directing her voice to the front of the car. 'Why was the *innkeeper* acting so strange?'

Tomas twists in his seat to look at us, sighing loudly when his seatbelt locks up, restraining him. He tugs at it several times before River offers a more relaxed approach. 'He was possessed by the one you call Ra-Mon,' he eventually says.

Ember's mouth drops open. 'I knew it.' She claps her hands once. 'Didn't I tell you I saw him?' Her brain goes off on a little rant about why this isn't a good thing to be right about.

Until …

Her eyes turn cold and distant, and the colour from her cheeks become chalk. She draws a breath in through her teeth; the realisation of how close to danger we were, hits her with full force. 'And Isis … she was there too, wasn't she?' she says so quietly I almost miss it.

She teases a loose curl away from her eyes right before I freefall into her mind, seeing for myself the collection of dreamy images of Isis. Seems like I'm not the only one having sleepless nights. I don't imagine any of us will come out of this unscathed, *if* we survive at all.

'Yes,' answers Tomas bluntly.

Ember's breath comes quicker until I pick up her hand and squeeze it gently.

'But why?'

Tomas drops his head. His hands fall into his lap. 'She is luring us into a trap. To let us know we are being watched. To taunt us. Take your pick?'

'And you know this because …?' I add.

River and Tomas exchange glances. 'It's all a game to them. Manipulating. Changing world events …just to see how humankind reacts. Even as far as upsetting weather patterns to see how the earth will fare and what the minions will do to battle through it.' Something in the way Tomas says that makes me think we're not the only ones who have learnt from personal experience.

'It's like we're caught up in one gigantic movie,' adds Ember, 'And we are the characters …to move around at their will.'

Ember's words send a shockwave through my body, bringing our conversation to an abrupt end. The soft purr of the BMW is our only companion for the remainder of the trip. I barely get a chance to go over what we're in for today when River pulls into the car park. He decides to park a short distance away, mumbling something about not wanting his car to be an easy target for bored teenagers. I think he loves that car more than he lets on. Hell, I would if it was mine.

'*Teenagers*? Are you serious? You realise you're talking about us, *right*? I mean, w*e are* the only teens here in a five kilometre radius.' I gaze out of the window and then at my watch. 'And what kind of idiot chooses to hike up a thing like this before eight o'clock in the morning?' I say to him as I bail out of the warm car and back into subzero temperatures.

'The *Superhero* kind,' says Ember, super fast.

River smirks at me from across the roof of his car as I don my beanie and gloves. 'She's got a point.'

'She's got a point,' I echo back to him in a whiny voice. He sniggers, adding more fuel to my edgy mood.

I'd woken this morning uptight and more than a little confused from the dream I had. It wasn't the usual Alfred Hitchcock movie. There was no sinister screeching or daggerlike claws. No tweezering beak. No shadows of wings beating at my window. And that dreaded tap, tap, tapping sound was no more than the light breath of wind scurrying amid the slate tiled roof. This time, the raven sat on a large grey stone, a stone raised higher than all the others around it, staring fiercely at me from atop of Hadrian's Wall. The wind battering it from all angles.

And the weird thing is, it looked kind of sad, its head low, ebony feathers all ruffled, trying to keep itself warm. Every bone in my body wanted to go over there and pick it up. Comfort it, even.

Like I said … strange.

'You ready?' asks Ember, jostling the image free from my thoughts.

I throw my head back and stare up at the shaley rockface, thankful this isn't our route. Dark, heavy clouds gather above us, no sun either, and the air cold enough to shrivel your balls to the size of acorns. I stamp my feet and shove my hands into my armpits, wishing I was back in my lumpy old bed at the pub. I shrug my shoulders slovenly, trying to find the motivation for our next adventure.

She smiles. 'At least it isn't snowing.' She tucks a thick red curl under her hat before slipping her hands into a pair of matching cream gloves. 'Be thankful. We could be up to our knees in the stuff right now.'

Snow … I shiver that thought away too, stretching my neck one way and then the other. 'Let's do this.'

Arthurs Seat towers majestically above the city of Edinburgh. On a clear, sunny day, I imagine the view across the hundreds of rooftops to Edinburgh Castle would be pretty spectacular, although I doubt the group of tourists across the road from us, huddled at the base of this looming grassy slope, would be taking many photos. Not much to see here this morning except a thick blanket of swirling grey mist.

I'm quietly surprised at the volume of people who have braved the cold though. There's a cluster of avid walkers decked out in vibrant scarves and rain jackets to my left, some with hiking sticks. Joggers are stretching, or setting their watches, whilst the fighting fifty-year-olds, donned in expensive sportswear, and just as much money spent on the end of their dog leashes, are already powering up the dusty, worn tracks like they have something to prove. The same dusty track Ember mentioned only minutes before rises above Dunsapie Loch. And finally, bringing up the rear, is the occasional oldie wandering along like they've forgotten their way home.

'This way,' instructs Tomas, striding out in the direction of the tourists. We tag on behind him, Ember half running to keep up.

I'm expecting an hours hard slog to the top, but when we hit a grassy plateau not even a third of the way up, I realise Tomas has other ideas. He veers off the beaten track towards a rocky outcrop smothered in swampy green moss and dried algae. We traipse after him, trying to negotiate a path around large dense clumps of heather hidden amongst the knee-deep grass. The whole place has *rustic Scottish landscape* plastered all over it. I have to admit, the rush of blood to my cheeks and the crisp, cool air in my lungs has taken the edge off my shitty mood. In fact, I get so caught up in the joy of it all, that for a second,

I lose sight of Tomas altogether. It's lucky River and Ember are right behind him because I never would have seen him slip through a narrow crevice in the rockface. He's certainly mastered the art of blending into the environment.

I take a quick peek around before sliding sideways through the gap behind River, the entrance nothing more than a sliver of black and shadow.

I shuffle in a few more steps.

Three seconds of darkness meets light in the weirdest of ways, especially when I can't determine where the natural light is coming from.

'Bring back any memories?' asks River, nudging me in the ribs. 'Just like old times, hey?'

'Except it's light and airy, and we're not frantically hunting for Ember,' I say, 'other than that, sure Riv, whatever you say.' He clicks his tongue at me.

The walls are a smooth, shaley rock that looks as if someone has spent all week polishing them. I can't help but run my fingers over them. Flickers of peacock blue and green, lime and burnt orange as though the rock has rusted over time, remind me of a chunk of labradorite I've had for years, and which now sits on my bedside table back at River's house. The carved-out ceiling reaches upwards into a rocky peak and the ground is spread with a fine layer of hay that I'm sure isn't there by accident. The air tastes like freshly toiled dirt.

Tomas retrieves something from his pocket. 'Don't tell me you've got your own key to this place?' I say, laughing. He doesn't respond, simply shows us the same Roman coin that he dropped on the bathroom floor at Le Louvre when River got roughed up.

He slips it into a spot on the wall, and we hear the dull clunk of a lever engage. A door opens with a crunch.

'You're full of surprises,' says Ember. The smile she shares with us touches her eyes. Brightens my outlook instantly.

We all step inside.

This room is much smaller and colder – cold enough that our breath turns to fog. Tomas's belongings are neatly stacked in the corner of the room, including another broad sword and shield. A dirty brown blanket is folded over the top of what appears to be a backpack of some kind. Several pieces of fruit and half a loaf of bread are laid out on a small wooden box.

'Have you been sleeping here?' asks Ember, stealing the words from my mouth.

Tomas offers a grim smile. 'From time to time.'

He steps aside, presenting the Altar Stones.

They're much larger than I thought they'd be, six foot in fact, and way too heavy for the common man to carry.

But Tomas isn't a common man.

He is a Roman Centurion. And an immortal. And it'd be a walk in the park for him to sling one across his back to transport it here.

For their age, the Altar Stones are in much better nick than I expect. Then I remember - they'd been restored and on display in a museum for decades. I examine them more closely - two rough, hewn slabs of concrete, grey in colour, the corners crumbling away. The inscriptions, although legible, have faded with centuries of someone looking at them. And just like the internet article described, the first stone has an etching of a lyre and griffon, a jug and a bowl. The second has four ladies wearing seasonal headdresses.

'Is that Sol, the sun god?' I ask Tomas, pointing at the primitive god-like impression beneath the four ladies.

His teeth grind. 'Yes.'

I draw closer to view the inscription as Tomas inhales a sharp breath. 'Please tell me you can read it.' There is a shaky edge to his voice.

I take a moment, the air so slick with tension I can taste the immediate change at the back of my throat. Prayers come through thick and fast from inside Ember's head.

'There is a date and a man's name on it,' I start to say, tracing my finger across the worn stonework.

'But what does it say?' presses Tomas.

I'm curious – this is basic Latin … his native tongue. Don't ask me how I know this, I just do, and stranger still, I can read it perfectly. 'I'm surprised you can't read it,' I say casually.

'It's been encrypted.' I want to ask more, but his face says he is not in the mood for question time.

I go back to the inscription. 'It says …' I pause, trying to decipher the last letter. 'Tiberius. It says, Tiberius - 2AD.'

'2AD!' gasps Ember. 'That's like, two thousand years old.' She continues to stare at Tomas as he takes several sizeable steps backwards.

He turns away from us but not before I see a flicker of sadness replacing his worried brow. He presses both palms into the shiny rockface, his arms outstretched, his head drooping through the middle like it's too heavy to carry anymore.

And he stays like that for one minute, two minutes … five. I'm not sure if I should speak, his body language telling us everything we need to know.

'Who's Tiberius, Tomas? I know you know,' asks River before I can conjure the words from my lips.

Time finds a new beat.

'He was my father,' he finally says.

His voice echoes in this small, icy room. His posture slackens as the weight of his words hang pathetically from his shoulders.

Em is uncomfortable with the silence and abruptly blurts out, 'and what does this part say?' She points to the words beneath Tiberius's name.

I trace my finger under the first word. 'It says … bestiam,' I say slowly, trying the word on for size. 'And the last bit says, mansuescere.'

'Bestiam mansuescere means tame the beast,' Tomas informs us, the breath of life flowing back into his statue-like pose. Although I've never heard the words spoken aloud before, I do recall this line from the AirWhisperer page.

The expression on River's face doesn't need any explanation as the demons of his past race circles inside his head. I'm dead certain, however, this *new* beast doesn't have anything to do with the one that he was once familiar with.

'*Beast*?' repeats Ember. There is a definite tremble to her voice. The softness of her face has gone, and I'm given a brief insight into the fear she felt when she was shackled by the Minotaur beneath Chartres Cathedral.

The memory alone prompts her to shuffle closer to River, gently nudging her shoulder under his armpit. He obliges and pulls her closer, giving her arm a brisk rub before kissing the top of her head. 'Please tell me it's a metaphor for something else, Tomas?'

'*Metaphor*?'

'Sorry. I mean, does it stand for something other than a … a beast?' Ember's brow lifts in some kind of hope. 'Like a challenge or *something*?'

Tomas angles his head, his gaze drawn to a pile of straw heaped against the side of the rockface on the other side of the room. He strides over and reefs out a hessian sack partially hidden from beneath. 'Yes, it is a challenge that the AirWhisperer will need to complete. And yes, there is a beast.' He retrieves an item from the sack. 'This was left in my thigh the last time the beast and I met,' he says, producing an enormous tooth, not that dissimilar from a lion's canine except twice the size. He twists the tooth around his fingers before clenching his fist around it. 'The creature is undefeatable.'

The bottom drops out of my day - our gloomy surroundings close in on me, becoming my own personal coffin. 'I can't seem to catch a break, can I?' I say more to myself than the others.

I feel eyes on me, and so I scream the lyrics to a song in my head to shut out their thoughts. I don't want their pity. And I've had enough pep talks to last me until I'm fifty.

'No one said this was going to be easy,' says Tomas.

I swallow.

Feel the ground beneath my feet.

Paint on a smile.

'Shouldn't be a problem, right, Riv? We've already battled a Minotaur. How bad can it be?'

Tomas raises his eyebrows. 'A lot. It is a demon of sorts, controlled by the son of Sol and his witch.'

I sniff and scruff my hair, just because it seems like the right thing to do. 'Yeah, like I said, piece of cake.'

There is a pause. Not quite friction. Not quite confidence. But somewhere in between.

It's then, River bends down to inspect the stones. 'Why is your father's name on this stone, and why is it so important to you?'

'My father was a Praetorian Guard.'

We all regard each other like we're supposed to know what that means.

'He was chosen as an Elite member to protect the Emperor,' continues Tomas, 'and was in charge of five hundred men.'

'You mean like a general?' Ember injects.

'I think it's more like a cross between the CIA and the SAS,' says River. 'They were hired hitmen, masking as bodyguards.'

Tomas reaches for his sword so fast I almost miss it. Lightning-fast in my opinion. And directs the tip of the blade at River's throat.

Ember squeals.

'Hold up there, Conan,' I say. 'Think about this before you do anything stupid.'

Shoulders tighten. Muscles bunch. Tomas doesn't take his eyes off River. There is a steeliness to his gaze that makes him seem almost *inhuman*.

'No,' whinnies Ember, her hands flying to her mouth.

Tomas lowers his sword, his jaw remaining wired shut. 'They were nothing of the sort,' he explodes. 'My father was a true warrior, whose heart was pure.' Tomas takes a second to breathe. 'It was the reason he was murdered.'

I glance over at River, who shifts uncomfortably. 'No offence, Tomas,' he says, 'it's what we were taught in school.'

Tomas nods, the anger leaving him. 'The last thing my father said to me, if he was ever found dead from foul play, to locate his final resting place, and the legacy of his life would be revealed.' His face pales, running his fingers through his shaggy blonde hair. 'After years of searching, and hundreds of dead ends, I came across a man I thought seemed familiar to me. We shared a meal and he told me to go to Falicon.'

'*Falicon*?'

'It is a small town in France.'

'Oh,' I hear myself say.

'I found a pyramid there.'

'A *pyramid*? In France? I've never heard of such a thing,' says Ember.

'Believe me, it is there. And beneath it, I discovered underground caves where the son of Sol and his witch practiced rituals and worshipped their god.'

'Creepy,' mutters Ember, scrolling through her phone like a woman possessed.

Tomas continues. 'Three decades ago, I found a tomb there.' He takes a breath before he says, 'my father's remains were not there.'

Pain, in its rawest form, finds its way to Tomas's eyes. His jaw trembles - the first real emotion I've seen from him. 'I cannot bear the thought of my father's spirit lingering in The Underworld. Alone. Trapped for all eternity.' He turns away from us, breath after breath inflating his back ribs.

I am lost for words.

'If I cannot locate him …'

92

There is silence again.

He pivots on his heel, slowly, as though any sudden movement might unleash a tsunami of emotion. His eyes find a spot far above my head, his chin lifting towards the heavens. 'Then how will we be reunited after I've taken my final breath on this earth?' I can't imagine how many times that thought has crossed his mind. I'd hate to think.

'Isn't it customary for your father to have a royal burial and be cremated?' asks River.

Tomas's eyes drop to the floor. 'Yes. Except his loyal bodyguard confessed to me on his deathbed that my father's body was placed in a casket and removed from his burial chamber.'

'That's awful,' Ember says empathetically.

'But I did find something in the tomb in Falicon - the book - Peri Phuseôs tôn Ontôn. There was also a handwritten note, preserved between two palm leaves, saying that the book needed to be taken across the big water to a land of fiery red. There, it would need to be buried in a sacred place to await the one who would free us from evil.'

I swallow hard, and Ember looks over to me and scrapes together a weak smile.

'At the bottom was the scraps of a rudimentary map,' adds Tomas.

'So, is that *when* you buried the book for Skye to find?' asks Ember.

'No. That came later,' replies Tomas. 'It took me years to find the AirWhisperer and when I finally did, you were so young,' he says, turning to me. 'You had no powers, so I shadowed you until I was sure. The book was right in saying you would call out to me. You did. It took a further six years before I truly believed you were the one.'

'You followed me?'

With a solemn bow of his head, he answers with a simple yes. All those times … those crazy moments when I felt eyes on me, waking up from a fitful sleep positive somebody was standing at the end of my bed, or when I would hide beneath the monstrous magnolia tree at the bottom of our garden, crying because Dean and his mates had shot me with their potato guns. Not quite the guardian angel I'd prayed for, but hey …it feels like the next best thing.

Tomas reigns in a smile. 'Once I knew it was you, I buried the book on the other side of your town and sat and waited for you to come.'

I smirk. 'How many years did you have to wait?' I remember the day well.

'Four,' replies Tomas, finally unleashing that smile.

'What is so important about these Altar Stones?' asks River.

'I had to know for sure that these were the headstones of my father. The old man who told me about Falicon said the answer to my questions would come when I found my father's headstone. When the Altar Stones were unearthed, I dug deep into the ground, hoping once more that I would find my father's final resting place. Again, there was nothing.' He cuts off. Rubs his hands over his face. Steadies himself. 'You are my last hope, Airwhisperer.'

'Skye,' I inject.

'If you can truly hear the thoughts of the dead, you should be able to contact him.'

I wished Tomas hadn't mentioned about me hearing the dead. Not even *I* like to think of that. I feel my lips peel away from my teeth. Feel a stone drop into my chest.

'Where to from here?'

'Easy,' says Ember. 'We need to go to Falicon.'

She takes the time to stare at us individually before saying. 'Who's with me?'

She knows we all are.

And I agree.

Falicon is probably the best place to start.

EIGHT

WE arrive home from Scotland in the early hours of the following morning, tired but alive, which is saying something considering River's reckless driving. I totally get it, wanting to be home and all that, but bombing down the motorway at a hundred and forty plus kilometres an hour is a tad dangerous, even in my books.

Tomas isn't with us either, much to my frustration and disappointment. I wanted him to return with us, so I could learn more about the book, and the part his father played in it. Even after River had strongly insisted he come with us, he declined, adamant he had something more important that needed his attention, and that he would catch up with us later. Somehow, I feel better when he's around.

I fall into bed, shoes and all.

Now, alone in the dark, I wait for sleep to take me.

Except it doesn't … which is stupid, considering how many times I'd nodded off in the car on the way home. Sleep feels as far from me now, as my homeland does.

I go over to the window and open it a crack.

The cold hits me first … then the silence.

A stony, deathly silence …like someone pulled the ripcord on life, ordering the air to hold its breath. Trees seem to freeze in mid-sway. A spooky-grey mist clings to neighbouring fences and shrubs, slinking across the grass in curls of smoke, robbing my eyes of colour. The words *calm before the storm* slip in and out of my consciousness as a prelude that all is not right.

Y*ou're overthinking things again,* I mutter to myself before falling back onto my bed. I think once about kicking off my shoes and then nothing.

Nothing.

Nothing.

Nothing.

I wake sharply. *What was that?*

I look to the window. Nothing.

I look towards the door. Nothing.

But not *nothing … something …*

Something woke me.

And then I hear it. Tap, tap, tapping.

I bolt upright. My heart has become a fast car with no brakes, sweat beading on my upper lip. I rub my eyes so hard they seem to pound at the back of my eye sockets. Was I dreaming? Was it a nightmare? It feels real though. The icy breeze blowing across my face tells me it is.

I wait … listening … the darkness not willing to give up her secrets, the sound of my thumping heart all around me. Pulsing in my hands. My throat. The bottoms of my feet.

Slowly, and when I'm sure all is well, I lay my head back on the pillow, my eyes wide, staring up at the ceiling.

And then I see it.

Peripheral vision is a strange thing, even in the dark. Some kind of ESP kicks in, prompting me to look where it wants me to, wants me to move … to do something, although time isn't my friend.

Before I can stretch out an arm, the raven jumps off the headboard and makes a beeline straight for my face. Its sharp beak misses my eye by less than a millimetre. Any sympathy I once had for that black demon dries up in an instant. I reach up and grab it by the legs, ignoring the blood trickling down my cheek and into the corner of my mouth.

It shrieks out.

Like I knew it would.

Like it just read my mind.

Its high pitched cry, squawking, wings flapping furiously, trying to get away … flapping so hard the tips of its feathers beat against my hair. It sounds desperate, not to escape, but to wake the entire household.

'This is the last time you and I meet,' I growl through my teeth.

With that, the bird is suddenly still. Not squawking. No shrill cries. Not even a ruffle of a feather.

It looks me over, checking me out, unperturbed by my tight grip, which is getting tighter by the second. It looks down at my hands and then back at me. I glance over at the open window and then to the top drawer of my bedside cabinet. I have a penknife in there.

Cautiously, I throw my legs over the bed and sit up. The bird continues to watch me intently … in total silence. It disturbs me somewhat, as I'd visualised killing the creature in my fight for survival rather than through an unprovoked attack. I loosen my grip a little to see if it leads me into a false sense of security.

It remains calm, tilting its head slightly to one side, regarding me. The constant staring, the non-blinking, is beginning to freak me out more than the stalking ever did.

This is my one and only chance to rid myself of this nightmare. Forever. Blindly, I lean over and slide the drawer open with as much stealth as I can, never taking my eyes off the black demon. My fingers comb through receipts and chocolate wrappers, phone cords and porno mags until I find the smooth surface of the penknife. The bird senses the danger and immediately begins to fidget, tugging one leg, trying to get free.

Now comes the tricky part.

I haven't thought this through properly and will need both hands to release the penknife. The bird now yanks more fiercely at its leg, desperate now. I apply more pressure and pin down the knife with my forearm so I can pick at the blade easier.

As though the bird knows its chance has come, only detained with two fingers and a thumb, it jolts upwards and flaps its wings hard. Its leg slips through my grasp, and before I can extend the knife fully, it works its way free and out of the window before I can scramble off the bed after it.

'Fuck!' I repeatedly grumble under my breath, thumping my fist into the mattress half a dozen times until my fury subsides. I should've wrung the damn thing's neck when I had the chance.

I sit at the window and stare into the night for a while, hoping, wondering, dreading if it will return.

It doesn't.

I'm so cross with myself. *Fuck* … if I can't even take down a stupid bird, what hope do I have? *Way to go, Skye. Coming right up – gutless slayer, a hero to none.*

I close the bedroom window and switch on the bedside light.

A glimmer of something shiny on my pillow catches my attention. I pick it up, confused. It's like a small earring or something.

Then, like a shower of ice, it hits me.

The other day when I was looking through the scope of the rifle, a shiny object reflected in the lens. I glance at the ring and then back to the window. *Could this have been on the raven's leg?* At first, I wonder if it's an

98

ownership tag. I inspect it, convinced I'll find a telephone number or code on it.

But it has neither.

Instead, it has a seal-like clasp. I prise it apart, and a small slip of paper falls out. My heart is pounding again, but for a whole different reason. The words on the note say;

NEVERMORE PSYCHIATRIC HOSPITAL
HELP!

Now I definitely can't sleep.

I fight with the idea of waking River and Ember, but end up sliding in and out of sleep until I can stand it no longer.

I check my watch.

It's nearly six.

I get up and shower quickly, and then find myself tiptoeing down the hallway to River's bedroom, only to realise my desire isn't to be quiet at all but to actually wake the entire household.

I knock on River's door.

A muffled acknowledgement is all I need to hear to enter. His bedroom is almost the same size as the apartment I shared with my brother, Dean. I drag the heavy curtains open a little, not surprised in the least to see him curled around Ember.

'Sorry, dude. I didn't mean to wake you. But this can't wait.'

Ember stirs. 'What's wrong?' she mutters, half in sleep.

'Get up. Get dressed. Our plans have changed.'

River pushes himself onto his elbow but not before dropping a kiss on Ember's bare shoulder. Worry lines appear on his forehead. 'Is it life or death?' he asks. I shake my head. 'Good. Give me a sec,' he says, yawning.

I close the door behind me and head downstairs.

Wally is already up, gazing out of the kitchen window, coffee in hand. He turns when I enter.

'Not like you to be up this early?' he says, glancing up at the wall clock. 'Did we have a little night-time accident?'

'Very funny, Wal. Make yourself useful, *Geeves*, and get us a coffee. I get the feeling today is going to be an exceptionally long day.'

River is the first to show himself, nearly an hour later. I don't have to ask what's kept him; it's written all over his face. 'Em is in the shower,' he says, pouring a coffee from the percolated jug that Wally had just set on the table. He glances over at me. 'What happened to your eye? Cut yourself shaving?' Since I arrived in this house, everyone seems to be pulling pages from the "Skye Buchannan's book of humour".

'Haha,' I reply sarcastically.

Wally peers over the top of his glasses to inspect the wound. 'It's only a scratch, son.'

I don't respond to either of them even though my new-found knowledge is bursting to be set free.

Ember appears at the doorway another twenty minutes later, yawning and stretching. She loops her arms through River's, and he, in turn, wraps his arms around her and hugs her tightly. They do look cute together, I have to admit, until they start to kiss. Then I want to throw up.

Wally seems to hear my thoughts. 'For God's sake, lad. Put her down.'

'Sorry, Wally,' mumbles Ember, embarrassed. She slips around the table and pulls out a chair next to me. She lays her head on my shoulder. 'Is everything okay?'

'You tell me,' I say, setting the shiny ring and its contents onto the table. I lean back in my chair, arms across my chest.

River steps forward to take a closer look. He frowns, like he always does; like he's trying to solve a puzzle he's supposed to know the answer to. 'Where did this come from?'

'Oh, the raven,' I reply casually.

'THE RAVEN? It was here?' gasps Ember.

'Yup.'

'Is that how you got that cut under your eye?' she asks, turning my head. 'Didn't I tell you I thought I heard a bird in the house,' she says, now speaking to River.

River looks up from his coffee. Raises one eyebrow, the ghost of smile trying to find his lips. 'I've had worse shaving cuts than that.' I bite back my next words. Now is not the time for petty comebacks.

Ember picks up the piece of paper off the table. Looks to me. The questions swimming circles in her eyes, rattling her thoughts match those screaming inside my head. '*Nevermore*?' she says in a whisper we can all hear. 'What does it mean?'

'It means Falicon will have to wait. We have bigger fish to fry.'

Wally positions a giant plate of toast on the table, and I grab a couple of pieces and begin to butter them. 'This is far more important than going to Falicon. I think Tomas would agree if he were here. So would Doc.'

'Although, we need to figure out, w*hat's* more important?' says River, sliding two pieces of toast onto Em's place before loading up his own. 'Is there jam, Wal?' Wally points to the cupboard, but not before moving the pot of Bovril closer to his own plate.

I need a show stopper here … something that will make them sit up and listen. So I just come out and say it. 'The EarthHealer, for one.'

It works.

River stops in mid-spread. 'You're saying you think the EarthHealer is at this psych hospital?'

I shrug lethargically. 'Maybe. I don't know. But going to Falicon with four of us …'

'Five, including Tomas,' says Ember in a hopeful tone.

I nod. 'That's right, five. I think five of us have a better chance of success.' My ribs inflate from the mighty breath I suck in. 'I really think Nevermore holds answers

for us, and this piece of paper is the start of that journey.'
The truth of it fills me way past the point of contentment
as I pluck our clue from Ember's fingers and turn it to
face River. 'Plus, I don't think a raven knows how to
write. So, whoever it is delivering messages for … needs
our help.'

I pause.

Realisation breaks over me like a wave that has been
waiting too long. I crumble inwardly at how long this bird
has been stalking me … how long my help was needed
and ignored. A long, overdue sigh finds its liberation. I
take another reassuring breath, and stumble upon some
courage. This time I go for the forceful approach rather
than a *I've got this feeling we should* line. 'We need to go.
It could turn out to be a rescue.'

The sheer weight of this task causes the sudden change
to River's posture. 'Breaking someone out of a psych
hospital isn't going to be easy …' he says, his frown
joining ranks with his slumped shoulders. 'And, I can't
believe I'm saying this …' A smirk tugs at the corner of
his lips, 'but for once in my life, I have to agree with Skye.
We need to be at full-strength to face whatever is coming.
And, we need the EarthHealer for that.'

Straight after breakfast, we bundle into River's dad's
awesome Audi and head an hour and a half down the
A417 and onto the M4 to Berkshire. I have no idea how
the Poms remember all these numbers; it's simple
highways in Australia.

I'd set Ember the task of finding any information
about Nevermore before we left, and luckily enough for
us, it is the only psychiatric hospital listed with that name
in the entire United Kingdom. It's about time we got a
break.

I stuff my ear pods in and stretch out on the back seat,
the luxurious creamy leather pre-warmed by the touch of
a button. Ember takes the front, and I watch them
dreamily for a while at the way River cradles her hand in

his, reassuring her with long repetitive strokes and pensive gazes, that everything will be alright, making me half-wish I had someone who meant that much to me. I hope to have that kind of relationship one day, instead of the occasional one-night stands that come with little to no baggage.

Baggage I can't deal with.

Because I haul around a truckload of my own, loaded with enough guilt and secrets to rival the sappiest Netflix series. I mean, letting a girl in, letting her love me, know me, untangle me, fix me, whatever she wants me for … to be honest, scares the shit out of me. Since my parents died, I've found it difficult to get close to anyone. It's true, I haven't dealt with their death, and every time I try - guilt slides in and becomes my immediate portcullis. I suppose I've never found the right time between emigrating, and dodging blows from Dean, and then discovering I have an entire planet to save.

So, I stick to what I know.

What works for me.

And until the world is safe, Amun and the other Elementars are in their rightful places, and Ra-Mon is defeated, then it's the single life for me. And the safest for any willing contestant wanting to throw their hand in.

I must have drifted off at some point because I jolt awake. The car has stopped, and I'm alone. Through the front windscreen, Ember and River are looking up at a humongous mansion style building with immaculate gardens and an intense looking guard house and boom gate. It could be mistaken for a Lords Manor or country estate, and I'm about to yell out of the window and ask why we have stopped, when I see the sign which indicates it's Nevermore Psychiatric Hospital.

Not exactly how I pictured a looney bin and yet exactly how I pictured it, if that makes sense. The grounds are surrounded by a high stone wall, the same colour sandstone as the grand building at the end of the long sandy coloured driveway. Rows of white windows, four storeys high, race across the front of the building, boasting its magnificence.

I scramble out of the car and work the cramp out of my legs as I speed walk towards River and Em. The front of the hospital looks pleasant enough, but the high fence with razor wire over the top, visible only from the sides, says enter at your own risk.

I steady my breathing – evaluating a way in, looking from every angle, and at how much power I'll need just to enter the building. A plan is forming.

'The security guard says we need a pass to get in, and that we should've scheduled a visiting time on their website or by phone,' says River.

My initial reaction is *fuck*! Then I grin. Go back to my primitive plan. 'And when have we ever followed the rules?'

There is a sparkle in Ember's eyes. 'There's no doubt you have the coolest powers. But it could get dangerous in there. You might need us,' she says, touching my arm. 'Can't you turn us all invisible or something?'

I shake my head. 'I wish! Unfortunately, it doesn't work that way.' Of course, testing my power out on my friends was one of the first things I tried after discovering I had superpowers. My mate, Todd, was thrilled to find out I could be the next Superhero, although not too thrilled when I grabbed him by the hand to fly him around the block, and our feet didn't lift an inch off the ground. Invisibility was even worse, my air-hand disappearing straight through his solid palm. None of it worked. 'I figured out, any inorganic object on my person, or in my hands before I turn invisible, will become invisible with me, like a backpack for example. The same goes for flying.' I tell them. 'People, animals … are a no-go. Like your gifts, mine cannot be shared with others,' I add. 'Think about it. Your fire still burns me, Em, and River's flood almost drowned me.' My lungs feel heavy just thinking about how we almost lost our lives in the crypt in Chartres Cathedral.

'I don't think it's wise for you to go in alone. We could come back tonight,' says River. 'Or I could burst the water mains so they'd have to evacuate or something.' His gaze strays from me, across the lawn to an impressive fountain in the middle of the most perfectly cut grass I've ever seen. His frown then makes a return. It doesn't take a genius to work out, *even* if I couldn't read his thoughts, he is trying to formulate his own strategy.

'Dude, do you know anything about breaking into a place at night, especially a nut-house?' River shrugs his shoulders. 'Security will be doubled if not tripled. They'll be patrols, spotlights. This place will be lit up like a Christmas tree at Hyde Park. And, as for your little evacuation idea, aren't we supposed to be working a little more *covertly*.' I take a quick glance around. 'I assume the …' I mouth the word *EarthHealer*, 'is still off *their* radar.' Of course, I'm referring to Isis, Ra-Mon and anyone else tagging along that we don't know about yet. The last thing we need is to bust the EarthHealer's cover.

'Well, what then?' asks Ember, looking to River for ideas. 'We could apply for a pass and come back tomorrow?' she offers.

'No, that won't work,' I add.

'*Why not*?' asks River.

Oh my god, I'm dealing with a bunch of amateurs. 'Hear me out.' I pretend to walk up to the guard. 'Yes, good morning, Sir, I'm here to see … oh wait, I have no fucking idea who I'm here to see.' I can't help the cynicism in my voice. 'Because we don't know his or her name.' River rolls his eyes. 'I think that's an important thing to know, right?'

'Alright, sleuth. No need to get pissy about it.'

'It's now or never,' I say. 'And this time, you two will have to wait here until I get back. I also suggest you move your car. That guard up there keeps looking this way.

Let's try not to make it too easy to be caught redhanded. Hell, we're already looking a tad suspicious.'

River glances over at Ember, who shrugs her shoulders. 'I can't see another way around it, can you?' I can tell by the look on his face, he doesn't.

'Okay, we'll drive back up the road to the antique shop we passed a few miles back, and Ember and I will wait for you there. I'm sure you can hightail it over the fence without too much trouble.'

'Finally!' I say around a sigh. I've already made my plan. I'm going to stroll right through the front door. Sometimes, simplicity is the best way.

Less than five minutes later, I mosey up the driveway, like I'm walking through the bush back home, not a care in the world, taking in the well-kept gardens until I find myself standing at the entrance to Nevermore. All under the watchful eyes of NO ONE.

And yet, I feel eyes on me.

Not the guard on duty drawing deeply on his cigarette, scuffing his boots on the stoney driveway, or the groundsman, bent over, pruning last years roses.

My first thought is Tomas.

Good old comforting Tomas.

It takes another few blinks to realise it isn't him either. I casually look up to see the raven peering down at me from a neighbouring tree. It stares at me for five long seconds, squawks once and flies off.

'Alright, I'm coming,' I grumble under my breath at it, wondering how the hell it can see me whilst I'm completely invisible. The old gardener turns around at the sound of my voice, looks in my direction, his weathered face creasing in confusion, before returning to his roses.

Now back to the door.

What are the odds of someone opening it for me, so I don't have to draw on extra juice and walk through it?

I stand there, contemplating it for a while, questioning why the small-panelled windows aren't your standard size and style. A much closer inspection reveals steel bars have been criss-crossed over the glass to keep its residents secure, and the local townsfolk safe. If that isn't bad enough, the stone plaque next to the two front doors says 1836 on it. A place this old, I can pretty much guarantee there are going to be more than a handful of spooky psychos still residing within.

Great!

Superpowers and evil immortals I can handle, ghosts on the other hand, are a whole different ball of wax.

I reach out to turn the old-fashioned brass knob, when suddenly the door is wrenched open by a tall, thinnish woman in a straw hat. She drags a chubby boy through the doorway behind her. I can't believe my luck! The gods are shining down on me …well, the good ones, anyhow. I slip between the crack before the heavy door has a chance to close.

The second I breach the threshold, I screw my nose up at the smell. It stinks of disinfectant. And not the homemade kind Mum used to make, but that dreadful eye-stinging poison that peels paint off walls and leaves a metallic taste in your mouth for days. I swallow hard, wishing I had a mint.

Inside has all the familiar characteristics of a hospital. To my right is a standard nurses station, surrounded by glass, apart from a narrow slit used to address arrivals. Three women are inside, drinking coffee.

Behind them, a whiteboard stretches the entire width of the wall. Next to each number, which I assume are room numbers, are abbreviated names and a light that must flash if attention is required. I have no idea what the random numbers and letters stand for. It must be some internal code. As for the rest of the room, it could be mistaken for an old fashioned school or courthouse with its fifteen-foot ceilings, dusty black chandelier hanging in the waiting room, strands of cobwebs fluttering from the warm currents of a nearby vent, and walls washed with a dirty beige paint. Ornamental brass light switches break up the misery of the walls.

To my left, attached to the wall, is a row of equally depressing brown plastic chairs with several wheelchairs lined up next to it. Beyond that, is a corridor and what appears to be a pretty intense security door.

For me, it shouldn't pose too much of a problem. Slipping through doors or walls is easy, and my invisibility isn't just a cloaking device that masks my body shape either. Whenever I turn invisible, I no longer sustain a solid mass or matter.

I become air. Plain and simple - which is handy.

I can't bump into things, or have someone throw a blanket over me to see where I am. However, walking through solid objects does juice up the old batteries; juice I can't afford to waste right now. And although I've never fallen from the sky, or been busted for loitering in the girl's shower block at school, my energy does get excessively low the longer I am in that state, faster if I'm combining two powers together like invisibility and flying.

Right now, I'd say I have about half an hour before the fatigue starts to set in and my bones turn to jelly. And besides, getting into this place was never going to be the problem. Breaking out of here with the EarthHealer in tow will undoubtedly be my biggest challenge to date.

I might have failed to mention that to River, hoping that somehow, some way, I'd be able to jinx or fluke my way out and come out looking like the hero, like it was on purpose. The sad part is … I know who I am, and who I am not. I'm never the hero. I am the fuck-up, the disaster waiting to happen, or the someone who is in the way.

Two lights flash on the whiteboard and all heads look up. I can't begin to guess where to start looking for our *potential* brother-in-arms. I hope to high hell *he* isn't in the high-security wing, (I call him *he*, because I see the EarthHealer as one of the boys, you know, Adam being the first man and all that), because, from that massive red lightglobe over the top, it looks to have its own, more intense security system. I could systematically work my way from one end of the hospital to the other, although I will need to learn the hospital's systems, door locks and codes on how to get the EarthHealer out. One thing I do know. He has a helper.

He has the raven.

NINE

THE larger of the women slams down her cup, startling me, before sullenly pushing a plate of assorted cakes to one side. It seems the flashing light on the switchboard is the sole reason for her agitation as she looks up at it for a second time.

She heaves herself out of her seat with an exaggerated huff, cocks her head, eyes narrowed, and says to the young girl now standing beside her, 'Come on, Hayley, let's go and find Dane. We'll show you how to handle your first patient.' Here is my opportunity to tag along and see what the procedure is for getting *in* and ultimately *out*, of this place. 'And make sure you keep an eye on that board, Angela. I don't feel like cleaning up Mr Tyrell's mess again today.'

'Yes, Mrs Vera,' says the curly-haired woman, stuffing the last of a chocolate éclair into her mouth. I don't need to see Mrs Vera's name tag to know she's the head honcho because she has that shitty, bored, washed-out look of someone who's been in the industry way past her sell-by date. She's more arse than waist from behind, and her hair has seen more bleach than a public toilet. And I might not be qualified to critique her overly applied makeup except to say I've seen better heads on a ventriloquist dummy.

Hayley is the polar opposite.

Small, petite frame, no hint of makeup, pale skin that you can almost see your reflection in, and there's no mistaking the kind of shell-shocked look plastered across her face as she shyly tucks a caramel lock behind her ear. She looks too nice for this place, and I feel sorry for her already.

Hayley ventures towards the security door with Mrs Vera in tow. I silently side-step them to see the number she punches into the keypad - 37899461. I repeat the number in my head several times, praying there aren't too many doors with eight digit combinations, otherwise, I'm screwed. Numbers were never my strong suit at school. I'm more a "remember the face, not the name" kind of guy.

Three corridors later, we come to a large communal lounge and another code - 44390881. I now repeat the second code three times and then chant the first code in my head, alternating between the two. What I would do to be able to jot them down in my phone right now. Memorising them in blocks of four is easier.

I enter the room, squeezing in behind Hayley before the door shuts. I am half expecting to see everyone dressed in bleached white tunics, scuffing about in worn dirty tartan slippers and catching imaginary bubbles in the air, but to my surprise, they all appear normal, dressed in everyday clothes.

Mrs Vera frowns at two patients playing chess, and pats another on the arm who is fixing the last piece of a jigsaw puzzle of the Swiss Alps.

No one speaks. No one says hello.

The soft, eerie screech of violins filter through the speakers. It's the kind of music your brain conjures up during a nightmare to add that freaky, scarier aspect to it. The kind of music you hear for months afterwards whenever you're alone … or in the dark.

And yet everything else looks normal.

Two ladies are sitting by the window, looking out onto a small enclosed garden, clacking away with knitting needles. I take a few steps closer to inspect the garden as a possible way out, if I happen to make it back to this room. It looks like a no go, with a high wooden fence around it, and razor wire across the top. Fine for me, but not for the EarthHealer.

Shit!

The rest of the garden offers no other benefit.

I glance over a looney on the lawn, sitting crossed legged, head down, rocking back and forth, ripping up handfuls of grass with every forward motion. Straggly dark curls trail untidily down her back to her waist. Her repetitive silent mantra of *I need to get out, I need to get out, I need to get out* is easy enough to ignore, but perhaps not easy enough to forget.

I shiver.

I want to get out of this place. It gives me the creeps.

A middle-aged woman wearing a flowered shirt and high-waisted orange pants stands up so abruptly, her chair flies backward and smacks hard against the wall.

My body goes on full alert.

Her hands go to her hips as I take a few more cautious steps away. 'Feathers, feathers everywhere,' she says, flinging her hands into the air, knocking her glasses off her nose.

Mrs Vera has a voice like a foghorn. 'Now then, Mrs Winston. You need to sit down. There aren't any birds in here. We've been through this, haven't we? The birds are all outside.'

'Feathers in the hallways. Feathers in the cafeteria. Feathers in the Home-Room. Black feathers. Black

112

feathers. Silky, black feathers. Feathers, feathers, feathers everywhere.' Her hands seem to be swatting at imaginary feathers floating in front of her.

Immediately, my thoughts go to the raven.

This woman sounds like she might know something.

Mrs Vera wrestles Mrs Winston back into her chair, amid screams and protests, before injecting something into her arm.

And then nothing.

The feather looney flips a switch.

Calmly retrieves her glasses off the floor and says in a very polite and *normal* voice, 'Dane has taken Georgina back to her room. I can show you where it is because I know every room here, off by heart. I don't even need a map.'

This gets my attention, too, and I step closer to her. She might be my salvation if my weak-to-no-plan goes tits-up. Instinctively, she turns to look at me as though she knows I'm there.

As though she can see me.

This is a first … *she senses me?*

Maybe nuts isn't as insane as it used to be. I take a chance and dive into her thoughts.

'GET OUT, GET OUT! You didn't ask permission. GET OUT!' she shrieks as though she is an inch from death. 'These are my thoughts, and YOU CAN'T HAVE THEM.' She jumps up, waving her arms around like she's being attacked by an army of angry bees.

I reel backwards, arms pinwheeling as I'm thrown out of her head faster than I can blink. I gulp down breath after breath, my head in a spin. And then quickly refocus on maintaining my cover, willing myself not to become visible … the power surge like nothing I've ever experienced.

'There's no need for that, Mrs Winston. Sit down, NOW,' she growls softly between her teeth, 'and wait. Francis will be along shortly with your meds.' Mrs Winston is roughly handled back into her seat.

Mrs Vera and Hayley cross the room to the door.

I'm torn - join Mrs Vera for the rest of the tour, or stay put and learn what I can from wack-job Winston.

Fuck! I'm not sure, although I still manage to find time to berate myself for hesitating. I wrap my knuckles over my head … *Think, Skye, think.* The second option allows me to recharge my batteries for a bit, but it comes at a hefty price. I need to turn off my invisibility – something I really don't want to do, and yet, I'm fairly confident I wouldn't be noticed if I sit huddled in a corner somewhere and don't draw attention to myself. Besides, it could be a while before Francis comes around with those meds. It might be all the time I need.

In my moment of uncertainty …

As I pause to breathe and take another quick look around the room, with its cool minty walls and personality of a squash court, the decision is made for me. Cameras – two of them, spying down on us. Those ever-watchful eyes warn against such an idiotic move rendering the "staying put" choice as definitely out of the question.

Mrs Vera, it is.

I'm not quick enough to slip through the door after them, and the extra effort required to power through a toughened-glass security door sends a weary hum through my body to my shaking legs.

Focus Skye, for Christ's sake, I mumble.

Hayley swings around sharply and frowns at me. I feel her eyes burning through my clothes and into my skin. The chatter in her brain says she's hearing things again, or worse, she's convinced the place is haunted.

After turning around twice to check, she dubiously follows Mrs Vera up a wide flight of stairs, maintaining a three step difference between her, and the middle-aged overweight bully (Hayley's words, not mine). Without the aid of the wooden handrail, I doubt Mrs Vera would make it up the stairs by herself. Her excessive puffing and groaning as she clears each step also convinces me it's the

114

stench of her breath and not a dirty bedpan lingering somewhere close by. Like I said, becoming air, *any* aroma is intensified.

The staircase opens out onto yet another corridor, this time pale blue in colour, and it takes until we reach the tenth door on the right that Mrs Vera finally catches her breath. The door is open and the voices coming from inside are loud and angry.

'Dane, what on earth is going on in here?' asks Mrs Vera.

I stop in my tracks - the scene before me is a movie in the making. A chill skitters down my spine. Lands in my stomach. Filling my airy legs with lead. I deduce straight away that Dane isn't the kind of person I would be friends with.

EVER!

The air around him reeks of rotten corpses, his soul already on its way to Hell. The energy he sends out hits me before I enter the room - the airwaves revealing how sick and twisted his mind is. He is an open book, his naturally callous nature pinned to his chest like a badge of honour, unlike Mrs Vera, who is more calculated, her serial killer profile skulking just beneath the surface, ready to strike. I reckon she's the kind of sicko to keep a tally. Dane can't be more than thirty, and his acne-pocked skin doesn't disguise the way his beady grey eyes, too close together in my opinion, stab accusingly at Hayley as we enter the room. My thoughts ... sometimes the medical system gets it wrong about who belongs in here and who doesn't. Dane's shoulder-length hair is half hanging out of his ponytail, suggesting this woman might have had something to do with it. I look to her hand, frantically trying to scratch his face, to see several long dark strands caught between her fingers.

'The stupid bitch won't take her meds,' he answers, pinning her arm down with his knee. He's pretty much sitting on top of a squirming female who is screaming abuse at him. 'And Francis is off, who knows *where*, probably screwing Mrs Taylor in room sixty-two.'

Mrs Vera's eyes widen and her lips press out into such a thin line they no longer hold any colour. Women generally don't scare me, but this woman could be a serious contender for psycho of the year. In a tone that doesn't reflect her anger, she says very calmly, 'Hayley, come around this side and watch me carefully.' She waves her arm behind her back, guiding Hayley into a better position so she can see. I mirror her movements.

Mrs Vera throws her entire body weight, all one hundred kilos of it, on top of the poor woman, who is now bucking more fiercely than a rodeo bull.

'This will be over quicker if you do what you're told, Georgina.' Mrs Vera presses her elbow into the apple of Georgina's cheek, prising her mouth open. She then fires three red capsules into her mouth and clamps the woman's nose with her other hand whilst Dane forces her mouth shut.

Hayley has the same look of shock on her face as any *normal* person would. The natural dusting of rose on her cheeks is swallowed up by whiteness. 'Are … are you sure that's necessary?' she asks, chewing fiercely on her lips.

Mrs Vera gets up and straightens her light blue tunic. She looks like a five foot three dolphin jammed into a milk bottle. 'You have a lot to learn about looking after the mentally challenged. They cannot think for themselves, which is why they're here. They don't know what's good for them *or* what *potentially* could be life-threatening. It is our job to remedy that, and to keep ourselves safe at the same time. Most of the patients in here would harm you, given half a chance.' Worry has found a new home on Hayley's face. Her fingers twist into undoable knots in front of her. 'It is for the patients own good,' carries on Mrs Vera, 'and making up stories about what goes on here won't be looked on favourably by the Hospital Administrator, or by the Board of Trustees.'

Hayley looks to Dane, who still has his hand clamped over Georgina's mouth, even though she is no longer struggling, and actually looks as if she's ready to pass out. 'Do I make myself clear?'

'Yes, Mrs Vera,' replies Hayley meekly.

Mrs Vera looks to Dane, whose sadistic grin would drive fear into the hearts of any new father. 'Dane, do you remember the last girl who worked here?'

A low humourless chuckle gurgles in the back of his throat. 'Oh, it was Maria something or other. Didn't she end up being a patient in here for a while before transferring over to Hollow Pines?'

'*Hollow Pines?*' asks Hayley.

Mrs Vera says nothing at first, and simply raises her eyebrows. 'It's a rehabilitation centre much like this, except, the staff there are *deranged*. We hear some horrible stories come out of that place, don't we Dane?' An eerie silence punctuates the air. 'Sure do.' He winks and flicks his tongue at Hayley, and then laughs.

'So, what happens in here, young Miss *Hayley*, stays here. Are we understood?' says Mrs Vera. 'The outside world would struggle to comprehend the level of safety and security we have to maintain here.'

Hayley nods once and only once. I'm surprised she managed that much.

Part of me now understands the message written by the EarthHealer. *Help* is what all the residents of Nevermore need, including the staff, but for the latter, help of a different kind – a good old-fashioned lobotomy might do the trick or, in Dane's case, a castration too.

Georgina is now out cold.

Dane drags his arm from under her head, letting it flop heavily back onto the pillow. He then pulls a length of rope from his pocket and proceeds to tie her hands to the railings on the bed head.

This is wrong. So wrong. And definitely illegal.

117

Hayley turns her head as though she knows I'm there and bites down hard on her lip again. Tears bubble up in her eyes and instantly, I know she is an ally, even before I hear her thoughts. She is moral, right down to the core, and if I play my cards right, I can win her over and get her to help me. My whole game plan has changed. I need to stick to Hayley like glue.

We leave the room, Dane heading in the opposite direction. Hayley's head hangs low as she walks, her shoulders hunched, her caramel hair sliding out from behind one ear. Inside her head, I discover she no longer wants to work here and is trying to come up with a way to quit. She is in turmoil. It's the first job she's had in ages and her stepmother's hospital bills are piling up. My heart goes out to her.

We pass door after door, each with a glass viewing window threaded with wire mesh for strength, making it easy enough to look in. There is nothing else in the room other than a bed, a built in wardrobe, a table and bench bolted to the wall, a small TV dangling from a rod attached to the ceiling, and a second door, which I assume is a bathroom. And of course, not forgetting the cameras spying down on them.

Hayley lets out a squeal as a tiny mouse scurries in front of her feet, sending my heart-rate soaring again. Adrenaline floods my body.

I have to pause.

Grind my teeth.

Bare down with all my effort, tightening the muscles in my stomach, my legs, my shoulders, squeezing tighter, like I'm trying to hold back a piss, anything to stop the change. Adrenaline can shut down my entire power grid if I'm not focussing on the job at hand.

Being invisible for this long is starting to take its toll. My body has gone from a light hum to full on shakes. I must be close to hitting my all time record of an hour and fifteen minutes. I suck in a breath and struggle on, my body screaming at me to change back.

'Remind me to get the exterminators in when we get back to the hive,' says Mrs Vera. I take it that *the hive* is their ground zero or switchboard room where Angela has probably polished off the last of the chocolate eclairs.

I peek into the room on each side of the corridor, room numbers from sixteen to thirty-eight. Many of them are empty, which worries me after seeing so many rooms occupied on the whiteboard in the nurse's station.

Where is everyone?

I don't have to wait long to find the answer. Through the third doorway with yet another different eight digit combination, which has now taxed my mental ability to the max, the door opens onto a sunny room twice the size of the last communal lounge.

Here I find the rest of the horde.

And there's a lot.

At a quick count, over fifty at least.

And there are some fine specimens of society in here. NOT!

Old men with vague expressions, dribbling, staring blankly at walls. Women wearing clothes way too big for them, matted hair and the same vacant look on their faces as they shuffle about the room. For the most part, it looks as though I've walked onto the set of the Walking Dead. Young and old, all trapped in their own horrific reality.

Across the room, I spy a familiar figure - the rocking looney from the garden.

Instead of sitting, she is now standing.

Hands over both ears.

Hair dripping like thick black tar over her face.

Still rocking back and forth.

She truly epitomises what *nuts* is.

As I walk amongst them, there is a strange zombie-like hum from the horde, no doubt one of Mrs Vera's concoctions to keep them in these drug-induced wakeful comas. I weave my way through the forest of empty vessels, some swaying, mumbling. Mrs Vera is jotting down something in her notebook as I make one last sweep.

I stop.

Through the buzz of mindless chatter, one singular, familiar voice stands out…

The looney.

I zero in on her thoughts.

Must get out, need to get out, must get out, she mutters to herself. She is the only one I would call semi-cognitive regardless of her repetitive babble, and obviously immune to Mrs Vera's lethal cocktails.

Hayley makes no attempt to hide her horror. 'What's wrong with them?' she asks, her head jerking around to look at them individually as though at any moment they will chow down on her flesh.

'This sorry looking bunch are the dregs of society. We call them the LB's – the Left Behinds. They are the ones who don't get visitors and who have no contact with the outside world, mostly because they're unpredictable and beyond saving.'

'They don't look unpredictable to me,' says Hayley. She takes the words right out of my mouth.

'That's because you're naïve and lack experience in this type of work. We wouldn't be able to step one foot in this room if it wasn't for our top researcher and medicine extraordinaire, Dr Lionel Trott. He formulated what he calls the "Nurses Dream".

'Is that who you're blaming it on,' I grumble under my breath.

Hayley looks my way again, darkness flitting in and out of her eyes.

'Give them a couple of hours for their meds to wear off, and you wouldn't dare come in here without a loaded weapon and a couple of grenades in your belt.'

Hayley looks around, as do I. I can't tell if Mrs Vera is telling the truth or not, because in her mind, she is 100% convinced they all belong in here, which explains her volatile behaviour and short fuse.

'What about *her*?' Hayley points to the looney, who has stopped rocking and is staring in our direction. I say staring, but I can't be sure. Her face is still covered by her long, messy dreds.

As though she hears me, her slender fingers part her hair very delicately, almost in slow motion as though she is looking out for the very first time. Her face is ghostly grey from lack of sunlight and good nutrition, and her lips are burnt red as though she has bitten them for years.

'She is a lost cause,' says Mrs Vera, waving her off. 'It doesn't matter what we do to her or what meds she's on; nothing works. Normally, she is in the locker for trying to escape, but recently we've seen more cooperation from her, so the Hospital Administrator has granted her community time.'

Suddenly curious, I take a measured step towards her. Her eyes, cloudy and tired, have a hint of green to them.

'YOU!' she shouts out, pointing in my direction.

I freeze for a second, taking in her dark grey sweat pants and matching jumper.

Then I come to my senses.

She can't be talking to me because she can't see me. There's no way she can see me. I spin around to see Mrs Vera backing up slowly with a quivering Hayley behind her. I step back too as the looney springs forward.

'You have a nerve coming in here,' she hisses, still looking right through me, spit foaming around her mouth.

The skin on my back grows cold.

Mouth turns to sand.

It takes all of my willpower not to dive through the nearest wall to get out of here.

'Keep calm,' I hear Mrs Vera mutter to Hayley.

Calm is the last thing I am feeling.

'You think it's been fun for me all these years being locked away while you cruise around in your cosy little life,' says the looney with wild eyes that turn from pale lime to vibrant emerald in a blink.

Something jolts inside me.

NO!

It can't be … *can it?*

The looney lunges for me and swipes a hand right through the middle of my dust motes to where my stomach should be. Instantly, I double up and drop to my knees. I have the sudden urge to vomit.

She *is* talking to me.

She *can* see me.

I try to drag my invisible body over to the wall, energy draining out of me as though someone has let out the bath plug.

She then lashes out with her hand across where my face should be, giving me an immediate headache. I feel my invisibility slipping.

'All these years, I've been here,' she repeats, 'beaten, tortured, *ignored.*'

This can't be the EarthHealer.

It can't be.

It should be a guy … it should be Adam.

She's just some whacked out nutjob high on speed.

Her eyes flash at me again, but this time her voice is much softer, scared. 'Why didn't you come for me …' She pauses and looks directly into my eyes. 'Why?'

My head is caving in as the neurons in my brain finally unravel their jumbled mess, revealing the truth.

With lightning speed, she reaches for my leg as I try to crab-crawl backwards, away from her. If she touches me again, I know I won't be able to hold onto my power. As it is, I'm juiced out that I could sleep for a week.

Again, as though she's read my thoughts, the tips of her fingers graze where my ankle would be, turning me visible for one full second – long enough for her to see me, and me see her.

And … for Hayley to see me.

She then removes her hand and I use all the energy I have left to throw myself through the wall behind me.

I pant, lying on the floor of the corridor, totally visible, listening to the most horrendous, blood curdling scream I've ever heard in my life.

The life drops out of my body.

Becomes stone.

Dead.

And when I hear her cry out my name, a part of my soul goes into shock.

What the hell have I done?

TEN

LIKE turning over the engine of a rusted-out Ford Falcon, it takes a good ten seconds to switch my invisibility back on - and just in the nick of time too. The fat ankles of Mrs Vera coming backwards through the doorway, followed by the dark blue pants belonging to Hayley, sends my blood roaring through my veins. Hayley is upright for less than a blink before she is bent over, her head between her knees looking like she's going to hurl chunks. Mrs Vera says nothing, simply straightens her tunic and checks her pockets. Many minutes pass before Hayley finally lifts her head.

'I don't think I'm cut out for this,' she says, teeth chattering through every word, her face red and slick with moisture.

'Nonsense,' snaps Mrs Vera, 'it's only your first day. What did you expect? Balloons and party poppers?'

Hayley starts to cry. 'No, but not this,' she whimpers.

I prop myself up against the security door as Hayley slides down the wall next to me.

I have no idea where I'm finding the strength to hold on because my body feels like it's coming apart with every breath. I'm hanging on by a very thin thread - one wrong move, one lapse of concentration, and I'll find myself in here with the rest of the whacko's, rocking back and forth on my own patch of grass.

I let out a shaky breath as Vera lumbers over and drags Hayley to her feet. 'I'm going to give you fifteen minutes to get yourself together, and then I want you to meet me back at the hive. Okay?'

Hayley nods, but I can tell her heart isn't in it, not that it ever was.

'You have your codes?' asks Mrs Vera. Hayley slips her hand into the front pocket of her aqua coloured tunic and pulls out a small laminated card the size of a drivers licence. A dissatisfied groan emanates from Mrs Vera's throat before she punches in her own codes and leaves.

Hayley drops to the floor again, and cries.

Something inside me wants to comfort her, although I can't remember a time where I've willingly gone up to a stranger and asked them to lean on me. I'm about as stable as a drunk after a week-long binge. Ember was a little different in the beginning because she kind of felt like family; however I still feel awkward putting an arm around her and assuring her that everything will be okay.

I resist the urge to reach out to Hayley, instead; I gingerly push myself to my feet as she mutters a few positive affirmations.

On our slow journey back to the hive, Hayley moving at a glacial pace, using the walls for support, I come to the dark realisation that getting the EarthHealer out of here today is not going to happen.

Not in a million years.

I'm even second-guessing getting myself out of here under the cover of total invisibility. Sure, diving into a closet for a quick recharge, might sound like the ideal solution, but I also know, I'm likely to be out of it for hours, possibly even a whole day … who knows … The risk of getting caught is too high.

So, I grin and bear it.

As I always do.

And tell myself *I'll find strength in pain*.

Tomorrow is another day, and yet, I'd be lying if I said I was looking forward to meeting up with Riv and Em, and seeing that unsurprised look on River's face again when I tell him for the hundredth time, I've failed.

I drag my legs as quietly as I can behind Hayley. Her internal monologue keeps me company as she raves on about needing this job, how she hasn't managed to hold down a job longer than a month, how unfair her life has been and the shit deal she's been handed, and how she never accomplishes anything regardless of how hard she tries. But to top it all, she thinks she's going mad …seeing things as well as feeling paranoid someone is walking behind her.

It all resonates with me, and I immediately feel a connection to her. She has become my salvation and my ticket out of here.

Some four hours later, ironically, I can be found on the floor of the hive, under a desk, crouched into a tight ball, rocking back and forth to prevent any chance of materialising. Poor Hayley has been counting down the hours so she can leave. She can't wait to be out of here, and neither can I.

She's barely spoken a word all afternoon.

And yet her thoughts have betrayed her.

Because I've been listening in, privy to every minute detail inside her head.

I've sat through hours of agonising recollections, analysing and dissecting the meaning out of everything that's happened in the last eight hours, particularly when she thought she heard voices and seeing me for that blink of a second when I lost control. She even deliberated that

Mrs Vera might have slipped something into her coffee to cause the hallucination.

It's my fault she's going through this trauma. Like it's my fault for the suffering I've caused the EarthHealer too. I close my eyes and breathe into my knees, having no idea how I'm going to make it up to *either* of them.

Six o'clock on the dot, Hayley lifts her bag from the coat stand and fast paces it to the door without saying goodbye to anyone. I struggle to my feet and manage to squeeze through the front door before it shuts.

I gaze across the lawn, now swallowed up by darkness, no moon and no sprinkling of starlight. The fountain is no longer shooting up rockets of water, and the air is still, waiting for a frost. Ember and River are nowhere in sight.

Hayley turns right towards the car park. There are only three cars left there, and I can only hope one is hers because I'm down to vapours of energy. I can hardly see where I'm going, my eyes cloudy, distance-sight stolen from me. My legs shake with sheer exhaustion every time I lift one foot and place it in front of the other. I have never felt so utterly tired and ready to give up.

Hayley stops short at a Mini Cooper and rests her back against the door. The spotlight high up on the hospital wall beams down at the edge of the car park, providing just enough light for her to rummage through her bag for her keys.

I'm done.

I can't hold on any longer.

I drop to my knees and fall forwards.

The impact of hitting the car punches me back to visibility.

Hayley jumps and squeals.

I pass out.

My eyes eventually open. Slowly, painfully slowly like mini dumbbells are resting against my eyelids. A faint shard of light streaks across my face from up high, forcing my eyes closed again. The stinging, burning, too much to handle.

I try again.

Eyes dry and grainy, I open even slower this time. The weighted blanket over me is silky at the edges, reminding me of the woollen blankets Mum used to throw over us when we were sick. There's a low rumbling hum in the background like that of an old Aussie refrigerator.

I seem to be lying on someone's sofa. It smells like popcorn in here too, but food is the last thing I want. From my limited powers of deduction, my head seems filled with metal and glass, and wire and lead, and definitely not functioning as it should be. I rule out, that I'm *not* back at Nevermore.

I try to sit up, and can't. I pat down my pocket for my phone. Shit! It's not there.

I turn my head sideways and spot a glass of water on a coffee table just out of my reach. Even if I wanted it, my arm doesn't respond when I lift it.

'Wait. I'll get it for you,' says a timid voice. It's Hayley.

'Where am I?' I ask. My throat is dry and tastes like copper pennies.

'Rest. You're at my place,' she replies, picking up the glass. She scoops her hand under my head and gently places the glass to my lips. 'Not too much now. I don't want you vomiting again.'

'*Vomiting*? I didn't know …' I say, embarrassed.

'It's fine. You're all cleaned up now.' My senses return little by little, well … enough for me to notice I am missing my shirt.

'It's in the wash,' she says, putting the glass down. 'You were in a bit of a state.'

'How long have I been out?' I ask.

Hayley sweeps her hand across my forehead, removing my hair that was stuck there. She offers me a sympathetic smile. 'Seven hours. The fever broke about an hour ago. Are you a diabetic or something?'

'No.' I've never had to explain myself to anyone, and now that she's asked, I should've said yes, because now the questions will start.

'That's good,' she replies, relief breaking across her face. 'That's what I was worried about the most. My brother is a diabetic, and he's had some bad turns.' I am so surprised when no further questions come.

'How come you never took me to the hospital?' I say, frowning.

Hayley laughs a little and drops her head. 'And say *what* exactly? It's not every day ...' she pauses again.

'And, my phone?' I ask.

Hayley gets up, crosses a small dining room to a kitchenette. The place is a shoebox, not that dissimilar from hovels I've found myself in. 'It kept going off, so I put it on silent. I hope you don't mind. I didn't want it to wake you, and I thought it would need charging by the time you woke.' I am blown away by her selflessness.

'I don't know how to thank you,' I say, exploding stars dancing across my vision.

She kneels down beside me. Her lonely eyes, and mind, tell me what she wants before she even opens her mouth. 'I think you should stay a few days.' Her request takes me by surprise; that she actually followed through and spoke the words. 'Only if you want to, of course, and until you get your strength back.'

I start to say something, but she hushes me. 'Rest now. Tell me in the morning. I won't be offended if you say no. It'll be nice to have some company for a change, that's all.' She sweeps the hair off my forehead again, and for a split second I think she is going to lean in and plant a kiss there, like Mum used to do. But she doesn't. She gets up, and I hear the sound of a door closing.

She is right about one thing. I do need rest. And in the space between one second starting and one finishing, I lose consciousness again.

'How do you like your eggs?' asks Hayley.

129

I stir, slowly coming around.

My head feels too heavy for my shoulders as I try to get up. A muffled groan escapes my lips, and I hear the clatter of utensils in a frying pan as Hayley drops what she's holding into the sink and rushes to my aid.

'I told you last night not to go pushing yourself. Here, let me help you.' She has quite a grip and good upper body strength for a slender, fine-boned girl. Effortlessly, she hooks her arms around the back of my shoulders and lifts me into a sitting position.

The room shifts slightly until my equilibrium kicks in. 'Easy now,' she coo's, 'you've had a rough few hours.' She heads back into the kitchenette and cracks two eggs into the pan.

'I need to phone my friends,' I say, knowing River and Ember will be out of their minds with worry. It's been twenty-four hours since I last saw or spoke to them.

Hayley unplugs the phone and hands it to me. The words blur a little as I bring the phone to my face. I have ten missed calls from River and eight from Ember, not including the countless texts and Facebook messages. I don't stop to read them and enter River's number. It doesn't even ring once.

'Skye!'

'Yep. It's me.' Ask him if he's okay, I hear Ember say. 'I'm fine,' I answer before he has a chance to ask. 'I'm at a ...' I pause, '... a friend's place.'

I see the corners of Hayley's mouth turn upwards as she gets something from the fridge.

'What happened? Do you have the EarthHealer with you?' I was waiting for this question.

'There ... were ... *complications*.' I think about each word carefully before speaking, so it doesn't draw undue attention to Hayley. River asks me if I am going back in there today to get the EarthHealer out, and again I have to use tact. 'I overdid it yesterday and had an uncomfortable night. I'm not sure what special tasks I'll be able to perform today. I think it's best if I gather my strength.'

River clicks his tongue, and I hear Ember in the background asking what I've said, and to put me on loud speaker so she can hear. I agree with him that we don't have time for this, but this isn't something I can rush. I need to be at full capacity to be able to go in there again. And I need Hayley to help me.

Hayley is hovering. I need to wrap this up. 'I'll get it done,' I say, before hanging up, 'Trust me.'

'Get *what* done?' asks Hayley. The smile on her face says she doesn't care what it is, as long as I have a full stomach before doing it.

'Oh, nothing,' I say, attempting to brush it off.

'I think someone has some secrets,' she sings the last few words.

'I don't know what you mean, Hayley.' The second her name is out of my mouth, I realise we haven't been formally introduced and I hear the short intake of breath that happens in her mind.

And she pounces on it.

'So, you guessed my name was Hayley, then?' Her eyes flit around the room searching for something with her name on it. Reading thoughts is so easy for me. It's like doing a crossword and having all the answers. I copy her actions immediately, hoping, praying, there is a certificate or birthday card hanging on the wall or propped up on an old bookcase somewhere, lilting to one side. There must be something … anything to bail me out.

As usual, I'm shit out of luck.

I could bullshit my way out of this, or, I could really spin her out as my eyes pass over a familiar selection of multi-coloured crystals and some incense sticks. From this small clue, I deduce she could be open to the possibilities of powers that don't require an explanation, and that won't get me into too much trouble.

'No,' I say confidently. 'I didn't guess. I *knew* your name was Hayley.'

Hayley removes the eggs from the heat and comes to stand at the end of the sofa. My feet are sticking out and she casually drapes the blanket over them. 'Really? How?'

'I can read minds,' I say with a smile. 'Go on. Test me. You have a brother, right?'

She nods.

'Think about his name, but don't say it out loud.'

Hayley purses her lips, but before she even has time to ask anything else, I blurt out, 'Bartholomew. But you all call him Barty for short.'

Hayley lets out a sharp laugh and claps her hands. 'That is so cool. What about the name of my high school?'

Again, less than a fraction of a second later, I say, 'St Catherine's Trinity College.'

Hayley bursts into fits of laughter. 'Oh my God, you *are* good. You could make a fortune with that trick.'

'Nah,' I say, playing it down. 'It's more trouble than it's worth most of the time.' Her eyes question me but she says nothing.

'Okay, last question.' Her eyes lift towards the ceiling as her lips twist to the right. 'How many boyfriends have I had?' She crosses to the coffee table opposite me and sits down. Her hands fold into her lap and she stares at me, long and hard, like she's trying to work me out.

A tremor passes over my body as I struggle to find the words. I sigh. And then lift her own words straight out of her mind. I offer a commiserating smile. 'You've had two boyfriends – Paul, who treated you okay, and Matt, who was the love of your life, but dumped you after a month to date your best friend, who he is now engaged to.'

Her eyes well up, but she ruffles her hair and smiles away the pain. 'He didn't even give me the chance to love him,' she says and returns to the eggs.

'That's his loss, Hayley,' I call out to her. I keep staring at her until she turns around. She swallows and then shrugs her shoulders. She doesn't say anything, and miraculously, she keeps her thoughts at bay, but something in her eyes tells me she wants to say more. I commend her for keeping it to herself. Most girls I know, are all too keen to dump their life stories in your lap and claim the poor-me victim.

She shares the scrambled eggs onto two pieces of toast and tops it with some chopped chives. I can't remember the last time someone made me breakfast. Come to think of it; I don't think anyone has *ever* made me breakfast.

She takes a quick look at a solitary chair and pathetic excuse for a dining table positioned under her kitchen window and brings the two plates towards me. 'Let's eat here today,' she says brightly.

'Alright,' I say. I swing my legs around so she can sit down. The room spins a little and I grip the arm of the sofa to steady myself.

'Easy now. You'll have to slow down a bit today and find your feet.' Her cheeks then flush at my semi-nakedness as the blanket falls to my waist.

Her eyes drop to the floor as I try to hold back my smile. For some strange reason, it doesn't seem weird to be sitting on a strange girl's sofa, shirtless and eating eggs.

'How long have you been able to read minds?' she asks. She pops a piece of toast into her mouth and waits for me to answer.

Before she's even finished, I've shovelled down a third mouthful. I can't help myself. 'Fuck! These are the best eggs I've ever tasted.' And they are. I don't know what she's done to them, but holy shit. They are amazing. Again, a small, tight smile pulls at her lips as her gaze wanders the length of a scrappy old mat under the coffee table. She doesn't answer because she is still waiting for my response.

'I've always been able to do it. Even since I was a kid. Naturally gifted, I suppose.'

Hayley hums and nods her head. 'Is that when you learnt to become invisible too?'

133

ELEVEN

I cough.

Hard.

Spraying eggs everywhere.

Stay cool, Skye. This is still salvageable.

'Last night,' begins Hayley, 'you were talking in your sleep, and kept mumbling something about failing again.'

'Really …?' I begin to say.

The colour rushes out of her cheeks. 'Then, all of a sudden, you disappeared. Right in front of my eyes.' She frowns as though the words don't belong in her mouth. Are bitter to taste.

'I … I …' I don't know how to explain that.

'I didn't know what to do,' begins Hayley again. 'I immediately knew you weren't having a seizure, or were a diabetic because how often does someone …' I drop into her head, listening to the way her brain is struggling to say the word *invisible*. 'And then you were back and then gone and then back and…' She breaks off and stares at my food until finally, she says, 'I sat with you for five hours, watching you appear and disappear, wondering who you were, why you were here, should I be afraid, were you an alien?' Hayley rests her fork on her plate. Her hand is shaking as she cups her mouth. 'I didn't know what to do,' she repeats.

'I'm sorry you had to go through that. You must have been scared to death.' I balance my plate on my knees and reach for her hand. Guilt slides under my skin. 'It's okay, Hayley. You weren't meant to see *any* of this, and I'm sorry that you got caught up in it, especially when I kinda dumped my problems at your feet.' I stall, trying to find the right thing to say. 'Your kindness has been … more than I deserve.' Words are being murdered, strangled in my throat. 'I didn't think I would keel over like that.' I stroke her hand, tracing the delicate lines across her wrists.

She scrapes together something resembling a smile. 'I'm alright now, but I have to admit … I was a bit scared when I went to bed because I wasn't sure if you'd be here when I woke.' She looks me over from head to toe. 'All that praying paid off because, well, here you are.'

'Here I am,' I say. I check her face for clues because her thoughts have faded to nothing again. 'Are you *sure* you're okay with this because I can leave if you want me to?'

Hayley wraps her fingers around my hand, her grip tightening. 'No, I don't want …' she stops short and closes her eyes. 'I mean, I don't *think* you should leave, not until you are well enough.'

'I *think* you're right,' I say, after hearing her pleading thoughts of not wanting to spend another day alone in this place. I know we are on the clock to get the EarthHealer out, but one day can't hurt.

Hayley perks up right away. 'Well, it's certainly a first. I can't remember the last time I played nursemaid to an invisible psychic.'

We both laugh.

And then there is a moment of silence.

'Perhaps now is a good time for introductions,' I say more softly. 'My name is Skye. I was at Nevermore yesterday.'

A light frown casts shadows over her blue eyes. 'I don't recall seeing you ….' No sooner are the words out, an internal light seems to shine from beneath her skin, and her face immediately softens - the proverbial penny dropping. 'Ahhh …you were invisible?'

'Yes,' I say.

That proverbial penny drops a little faster. 'It *was* you then! That I thought I saw –for that split second.' If there was a first prize for the best sheepish face, I would win it by a mile. I nod once.

'And here's me thinking I was going nuts.'

I stifle a laugh. 'I know. I heard,' I say, tapping my temple.

Hayley's cheeks take on that rosy glow again. 'Oh my god, yes, you did. Then you must have heard everything else ...' That rosy glow blooms into a deep crimson red.

This time I can't hold back my laughter. 'All jokes aside, though, you have the purest mind I've had the privilege of listening in on,' I say in my best and most serious tone.

This seems to comfort her a little.

'So, why were you there?'

This is the part I have to be careful with. I need to put my mouth on a leash and keep it simple. 'I have a friend in there that I needed to see.'

'Oh!'

'She actually doesn't belong in there at all, in fact she's totally sane … I think.' *God, I hope she's sane.* 'I have to get her out.'

'Is she your girlfriend?'

'*What*? No,' I say quickly, 'to be honest with you, I never met her until yesterday.' I pick up my fork and pile down the last of the eggs. Hayley slides her eggs onto my plate, seemingly no longer hungry, which I then devour in two mouthfuls. 'But, she is … important to my friends and I. Can we leave it at that?'

Hayley smiles. 'Secrets, right?'

'I don't want to worry you or add any extra stress in your life.'

Hayley takes a piece of hair and twists it around her finger, her caramel locks the colour of buttermilk toffee. She flicks it a few times before staring directly at me. 'You're going to ask me to help you get her out, aren't you?'

'Now who's the mind reader?' I say, grinning. 'Am I really that *transparent?*'

Hayley cocks her head at my pun.

Squints at me … a laugh dying to come out but doesn't.

'Look, yesterday, I thought I would be able to stroll right in there, locate my friend and get us out before anyone noticed. Zip in and zip out again. Nobody the wiser. Except I juiced up all my power and …'

'Now, you need my help,' finishes Hayley.

I sigh deeply. Play with the satin ribbon on the blanket before zeroing in on Hayley's waiting gaze. 'Yes, now, I need your help.'

The sunshine on her face turns to nightfall. Her eyes lose their vibrancy. Her lips become something to chew on, like how Ember does when she's upset. 'I should've known …'

I cut her off.

'It's not the only reason I'm staying, though.'

Her lip trembles, like she might burst into tears at any moment. The turmoil in her head that she's simply a means to an end, just like always, that she is never anyone's first choice, but a substitute until something better comes along, tumble about in desperate, sorrowful circles. I can't get into that right now with her, so I pick door number two. 'You're right. I'm not 100% myself right now, and staying here is a safe option.'

'You mean safe from the psychotic black crow that keeps trying the smash through my window.'

'It's a raven,' I say without thinking.

And then I realise... *Holy hell!*

'*Wait*! It was here?'

'Yup. Last night ...for about half an hour. I had to throw my shoe at it in the end, to get it to leave.' She gazes over at the bay window to where a pair of tatty pink striped curtains hang haphazardly. 'Pretty good shot, if I say so myself. Went down like a spitfire.'

'*What*?' Panic strikes me, and I upend the plate on the floor in my rush to get to the window. I stop short, two steps away, out of breath and feeling the eggs making a return. I put my hands on my knees and let my head drop forward.

'Now, don't be doing silly things like that.' She rushes to my aid and presses down on my shoulders, forcing my arse to the floor. The sudden bump rattles my brain inside my skull. The eggs make a swift exit.

'I'm sorry. I didn't mean to push you so hard. Sometimes I don't know my own strength.'

'S'okay,' I call after her, but she's already raced off to grab a cloth. I sit, hands out, not wanting to touch anything, partially digested eggs hanging off my fingers in slobbery strings. I still try to look outside though, and Hayley catches me on her return from the kitchen sink, trying to stretch my neck to see.

'Don't stress yourself. It's gone,' she says, somewhat disappointed.

She doesn't hand me the damp cloth to clean up after myself.

She does it for me.

Carefully wiping my mouth before attending to my hands. 'The stupid thing must have flown off because I can only see my shoe on the back lawn.'

Relief floods through me, and my heart returns to its normal rhythm. Something as simple as a shoe could have dire consequences for the fate of the entire world, but I don't say that out loud.

'What's the deal with it, then?' she asks. Psychic abilities and watching me turn invisible can be seen or explained. Being haunted by a bird, isn't, even though that's not *quite* what it is now.

'I'm not sure, but anyway, we've spoken so much about me, what about you?'

Hayley looks down at herself. 'What you see is what you get. There isn't any more to it than that.'

It's a vague answer, especially when her inner monologue has suddenly switched back to mute again. Thinking absolutely nothing is a fine art that I haven't come across much in the telepathic world. I mean, even the women in Mum's yoga classes still had random thoughts during their meditations, like taking the dog to the vet, remembering what to pick up from the shops or why the lady from across the street shoplifts when she can clearly afford it. If I didn't know any different, I would say Hayley's fuzzy blank moments seem almost practiced. Almost deliberate.

'I might take a shower then, if you don't mind.' I smell my hands that still stink of vomit.

'Second door on the right,' says Hayley, walking back into the kitchenette and sliding the dirty plates into the sink.

Gingerly, I push myself upright, much slower than earlier, and test my feet before raising my head. I really gassed myself yesterday, but at least I know now, I have more in the tank if I need it. This whole episode has made me aware of one thing - I've been playing it safe with my powers, and not pushing myself to my limits.

That is all about to change now.

'Is there any chance we can go tonight?' I ask Hayley later on that afternoon.

I feel much better now, and even managed to float a few feet off the ground and turn invisible a dozen times without feeling too drained. Of course, I made sure it was when Hayley had nipped out to peg some washing on the line, had a shower and whilst she was making her bed. She doesn't sit still for long, which I like about her.

'Not a good idea,' she says, 'all the patients are locked in their rooms for the night, which means we'll have to break into the hive and steal the keys from a box I don't have the code for.'

'Fuck,' I mumble.

'And besides, with yesterday being my first day, I haven't had a chance to learn who is in what room yet.' She grimaces. 'Sorry. Tomorrow morning is your best shot, plus Mrs Vera doesn't work on Sundays because she has church.'

I let out a sharp laugh, and Hayley's eyes widen.

'I know, right. Doesn't compute, does it?'

'No,' I say, shaking my head.

'At least by going in tomorrow, I can say to the facilitator in charge that I left something there on Friday.' She pauses. Bites on her thumbnail. 'I'm sure they won't think to question it.'

I get on the phone with River straight away and inform him of the plan. His new robotic attitude seems to have slipped a little since we last spoke and he sounds much like his old self again … thank god. I mean, he wasn't even that worried about delaying things an extra day, which isn't like him. And from the few thoughts I did pick up on, he's enjoying time alone with Ember … without *me* around. Sometimes, it totally sucks being able to hear people's thoughts.

'Will you have a glass of wine with me?' asks Hayley as she starts to prepare dinner.

'You don't have a beer instead, do you?' I ask, sitting on the edge of her bronzy coloured sofa. 'Never been much of a wine drinker.'

Her lips turn down. 'Sorry, it's either wine or milk.'

I deliberate for a few seconds. 'What the hell. Sure, why not.'

Hayley has already poured the glass and brings it over to me. I take a sip, surprised that I actually like it. First the eggs, and now the wine. Everything tastes good around this girl. I take a larger gulp and let the crisp, bite of grapes introduce themselves to my newly appreciative tastebuds.

'This has to be the best wine I've ever had. Better than beer.'

Hayley toasts her glass to me. 'To better things.'

'Better things.' I guzzle down the rest of the glass as she hovers, bottle in hand, ready to top me up again. She then places the bottle on a low table scattered with magazines as I lean back into the sofa and make myself comfy.

Hayley joins me, sitting closer than I expect for two would-be strangers. She tucks her legs beneath her and looks up at me from her glass. The icy blue shirt she's wearing really sets off the colour in her eyes. Earlier I'd swear they were more aqua blue, but with the afternoon sun peeping through a high window, they look closer to lapis. It's odd, remembering eye colour … it doesn't usually hit my radar with girls.

She lowers her gaze, surrendering a shy smile. She's pretty cute. Different to what I usually go for, and under any other circumstances, I'd probably make a move, but getting a glimpse into her head, she seems kind of fragile, and River would do his nut if I scared her off, especially now she's my ticket into Nevermore.

'I think I'm going to quit my job at the hospital,' she says, refilling my glass for a third time. The carefree buzz of alcohol is doing its thing. 'Don't think I'm cut out for that kind of carework.'

I recognise the look on her face.

It's the same image I see in the mirror every day. I stretch out and touch her hand.

'You were meant for so much more,' I say to her.

She shifts position.

Nervously.

Skols the rest of her wine and swivels to face me. 'I'm not sure. I seem to keep making the same mistakes over and over – the wrong job, the wrong house, the wrong friends, the wrong …' I hear the word boyfriend in her mind although she doesn't actually say it. Instead, a tear runs down her cheek. She suffers from the same affliction I'm plagued with – failure.

I cup her cheek with my palm. Her tear disappears into my hand, dissolves into my skin. It's unusually cold, where tears should be warm. That curious part of me wants to check, to see if it's a drop of ice - melting against me until the coldness is not longer a sensation. She leans her head into my hand, more tears prickling my skin with tiny frozen droplets.

In a flurry of movements, she's caught up in my arms. Our kisses are wild. Frantic. Desperate. Hands searching, exploring everywhere so fast my brain can't process the pleasure. My fingers tangle in her hair, spilling across my knuckles like wonderful toffee waterfall. I grab a handful and pull hard as she bites down on my neck, causing me to cry out. And yet the pain is sweeter than a new rose. Our breathing is heavy, gasping, my body aching in a way it's never known before. She doesn't taste like any girl I've ever been with. And I want to tell her that. I want to tell her I'm about to explode from the intensity but I can't drag my lips away from her for a single second.

She scrambles into my lap, her delicate, slender hands working feverishly to take off my hoodie and t-shirt. Her head drops back as she begins to remove her shirt, ripping buttons from thread, leaving nothing more than a lilac bra with a small rosebud in the middle. The shirt is soon airborne, over her head. Her eyes are closed, caught up in a moment all her own. Her mind, silent.

The wine is dulling my ability to think straight and I know I shouldn't be running my hands under her skirt and up the insides of her thighs but I can't help it. I can't stop myself. I don't want to stop.

I touch her where I know I shouldn't, where she wants me to, and she moans softly, arching her back.

But then, her hands stop twisting in my hair.

Her body stops gyrating.

Gingerly, she eases herself off my lap, turns towards her bedroom door and holds out her hand. I stand and slip my fingers into hers and follow her in her lair.

I wake to the sound of tap, tap, tapping. Instant fear doesn't inject into my veins like it usually does, instead I feel a sense of relief. I turn to look at Hayley, who is fast asleep.

I slip out of bed and venture over to the window to where a small black shape is waiting for me. Quietly, I open the window. The raven boldly hops onto the ledge and surveys me with its haunting green eyes. That part of me, who used to be afraid, is long gone, and in the light of the full moon, I notice its wing feathers are matted together. I tenderly brush my fingers over it, and its soft squawk tells me its hurt. I pat my wrist, and without hesitation, the raven hops onto my forearm. I check back on Hayley who has not moved in the slightest, and creep out of the room to the bathroom and close the door.

Under the fluorescent light, it's dead obvious the raven's wing is hanging much lower than the other, and at an odd angle. My guess, it's broken, and I don't know the first thing about administering first aid to a bird. Blood has congealed the feathers together. I hold back the urge to wake Hayley. She might know how to take care of it, but being her shoe that likely caused the damage in the first place, I'm not sure she'd be all that keen to help.

I throw Hayley's yellow face washer into the sink, allowing the warm water to run over it. Carefully I stretch the wing out, a pair of curious green eyes watching my every move. I squeeze the water from the washer over the wing several times so it's completely soaked. The water in the basin is stained red. There is a small incision that looks to be on the mend.

Without warning the raven tries to flap both wings, letting out a loud squawk for good measure. I freeze, blood thumping through my ears.

'Quiet or you'll get us both busted,' I whisper to it. It makes a soft throaty cackle as though it's laughing, fluttering the feathers around its neck. *Oh my god, I can't believe I'm talking to a bird.*

It settles instantly, and that's when I notice the ring fastened around its foot, just like before.

A message.

I cautiously remove it and release the strip of paper from inside. All it says is … *whatever you do, don't lift the curse.*

I glare at the bird, trying to conjure the meaning from its tiny brain, knowing full well my mind-reading capabilities are exclusively for humans.

It's now or never.

I have to go back to Nevermore.

NOW!

And this time, the raven is coming with me.

I locate Hayley's car keys, partially hidden behind a matching blue and white striped sugar bowl and jug, and head out into the night; the raven perched comfortably on my shoulder. Thankfully, Hayley's small weatherboard home resides on a slight hill, so I opt to push the car down the street a little, so as not to wake her. According to Google Maps, the psych hospital is straight through an intersection and down a couple of back streets. Less than ten minutes away.

I pull the car over much further down the road than River did, and tuck in as close to the bushes as possible without scratching the paintwork. Thinking about River, makes me question whether I should be calling him for help. I start to punch in his number but then hang up.

I can do this.

I don't need him looking over my shoulder.

Under the cover of darkness, only a sliver of moon to guide me, and still in my visible self, (I don't want to juice up my power until it's absolutely necessary), I stick to the shadows, dodging the multiple spotlights illuminating the grounds and car park at the front of Nevermore. I shoot a quick look towards the guardhouse. It's appears to be empty and the boom gate is down.

I make my way towards the back of the building, staying close to the boundary. The prison-like fence and accompanying razor-wire, looped over the top, looks downright menacing to anyone who cannot fly. A wide grin spreads across my face. This should be easy as …

Swallowed up by shadows, I look up at the colossal building, trying to locate my best entry point … steering clear of as many windows as I can. Windows in a psych hospital are a horror movie waiting to happen – I don't know what I'd do if I saw a figure dressed in white, long hair, greyish features, fists silently pounding against the glass. This place gave me the creeps enough during the day, it's dead-set petrifying at night. Hell, give me a Minotaur any day of the week.

The raven tilts its head back and looks up at the roof.

Sweet! I kinda guessed it would take refuge up high, and like a homing pigeon, it would return to its nest, home, master, or whatever is controlling it.

I take a deep breath.

This is when the old Superhero battery is about to get gassed. In less than a blink, and under the cover of darkness, I float towards the roofline. The slow leak of energy begins as though I've punctured a tyre. When my shoulders finally align with the gutter, the raven hops off and struts across the roofline. It seems to know where it's going.

The mossy, clay tiles are more challenging to navigate than I initially thought, especially when I can barely see one foot in front of the other, causing me trip several times. The raven, however, finds no difficulty keeping its balance.

I follow the bird the length of the building before it stops. And then, through a crack between two broken tiles, the raven disappears.

We have arrived … at last.

I switch to invisibility mode and follow after it. I zip through the roof tiles to find myself in some sort of attic, except, like no attic I've ever seen before. No cobwebs or furniture draped in musty old sheets. No boxes of photographs and books. No haunting mirrors or broken hatstands. *This* attic still has that clinical look, and smells faintly of bleach. Aged timber floorboards, dusty in the corners, replace the grotty beige tiles from the floors below.

A row of beds, with just the mattresses on, no linen, line up symmetrically against the far wall, whilst a bunch of white medical bedside cabinets are stacked up in one corner. There are linen baskets and mop buckets randomly placed, and a tray of plates and cutlery stacked up on the draining board of a small sink. There are no curtains, only thick white bars at every window. Finally, I check for cameras, and when I'm certain there aren't any, I flick back to visibility, shaking off the fatigue – no point in dumping fuel if I don't need to.

The raven is strutting towards a stainless steel bowl with shallow edges, filled with water. It drinks heartily from it, then looks to a pillow with all the stuffing pecked out. It then proceeds to pick at a few pieces of fluff before settling itself down. It offers me one soft squawk, turns its head and then nuzzles its beak into the glossy feathers on its back. The poor thing looks exhausted.

'Righto, Skye, that's your good deed for the day. Now what's your plan,' I say to myself. As usual, I don't have one, but if all else fails, at least I can make it back up here and hideout to gather my strength, if needed.

My thoughts drift back to Hayley, and wonder what she'll think when she wakes to find me not there. In my defence, there wasn't time to explain, and this can't wait.

I take a quick stock of the room, and spy the only way in or out of the attic. I go over to the door.

Ha! What luck. Even though it's locked, there's a key that's been left in the keyhole. That might come in handy later. I suck in a breath, and give myself three seconds to mentally prepare. Back to invisibility, I zip through quickly, feeling no worse for wear.

In front of me is a rickety old spiral staircase. I've no doubt it would creak from my weight if I was visible. I hurry down it to find myself on a small landing. There's no left or right option.

Only down.

This second staircase is much wider, large enough to fit ten people on one step side by side. I peer over the balcony determining it must go all the way to the ground level, and more than likely connects up to the one that I followed Mrs Vera and Hayley up.

I don't hesitate and race down the first flight. I'm not surprised to find the first security door locked. It's nighttime. It would be stupid not to lock the place down. I don't have the code for this, and I'm not game to enter any of the three codes that I'd memorised to see if they work. Again, I pass through steel and glass, this time aware of the slight spike in energy it devours.

From memory, I need to find the second floor where the patient's private rooms are - where Georgina was being forced to take her medication. So, I repeat the process, heading down the next flight of stairs and passing through another locked security door.

I stop to take a breath. Glance down at where my hands would be, feeling them start to shake. *Keep going, dude, you've got this.*

The main hallway lights are off, with only the emergency lighting left on, ample light for hourly rounds and bed checks. I work my way along one side of the corridor, looking in each window and then doubling back to inspect the other side. I'm hoping that the

EarthHealer's black dreds are going to be distinguishable enough to identify her.

After checking thirty rooms, a dozen bald heads, and blonde and brown hair of all styles, I'm convinced she is not in any of those. I pass through another security door and head back up to the third floor.

Fatigue is slowly setting in.

Again, I peer through every window on this floor, taking more than a minute with each one, to be absolutely certain she isn't in there. I pull up short when an orderly walks past with an iPad. I give him ample room, and he hums as he walks past. The only door I haven't checked is the one at the very end of the corridor. It doesn't have a window but does have a number, L-50.

I'm curious.

Rather than draining unnecessary energy, I perform my signature Casper trick – leaning my head through the door instead of committing my whole body.

It pays off, I think.

A person is lying on the floor, out cold. Her hair is tar black and just as thick, and conceals her face as it fans out in a perfect arc around her head.

It could be the looney – I mean, the EarthHealer.

It looks like her.

Whoever it is, has fallen out of bed and gone back to sleep. The bed looks recently slept in, so I take a chance and press the rest of my body through the door.

My eyes are immediately drawn to the wall closest to her bed. Dozens of pictures, sketched in pencil, are randomly scattered across the dirty grey paintwork.

All with the same image.

Each picture is dissected in half with one part in sunshine and the other in darkness. In the sunshine picture a girl with long black hair is sitting in a chair, and in the darkness picture, a black bird is perched on the back of the chair.

I'm now convinced it's her.

First, I scan the room because I know there has to be a camera in here somewhere. I find it snuggled in the corner, behind me. I have no idea how to switch it off, so I'll have to deal with it the good old fashioned way – by force.

The room is about twelve feet high, so even if there were a chair in the room, which there isn't, I wouldn't be able to reach it. So, it's time to try something I've only accomplished once before - partial invisibility.

I float up towards the ceiling, feeling the once steady trickle of power leaving my body in a much bigger hurry – like someone letting the air out of a balloon. I see a wire attached to the back of the camera. I know what I need to do. And this takes some concentrating. I focus on my hand … so hard in fact, I feel nauseous, even though, technically, I don't have a stomach.

I visualise my hand, four fingers and a thumb, rough callouses across the palms from years of riding dirtbikes without gloves, the silver ring my father gave me on my middle finger - every tiny detail including, my skin tone and texture.

Before my eyes, or rather, appearing out of thin air, is my hand – not transparent or ghostly, but fleshy, real and made from solid matter. I feel the strength return to my hand as I curl my fingers into a fist.

Without thought, I yank the wires out from the back of the camera and drop to the floor, completely visible and running on empty. I would say I have about five minutes tops before someone comes to investigate.

My next dilemma - do I wake her now or drag her out once I've dealt with the orderly? Bricks and mortar weigh heavily on my chest as I deliberate.

I crouch beside her.

Look sideways at her.

And frown.

She has a cast on her arm that wasn't there two days ago. Slowly, my hands now shaking more from fear than a flat battery, I cautiously sweep her hair back from her face. I am appalled to see one side of her face is several shades of purple and there's a deep gash below one eye. My first impression – she's had a visit from Mrs Vera and Dane.

I tap her uninjured arm gently. 'Wake up.'

Her body feels cold to the touch, she might as well be dead. But she isn't dead. Her chest rises and falls with slow, even breaths. I wipe the sweat off my brow with the arm of my hoodie, confused why her body doesn't feel warmer when the heaters are cranked up to the max in here.

'Wake up,' I whisper, shaking her arm a little more vigorously.

She doesn't move. She doesn't even stir.

And then, it slowly sinks in – she's been sedated.

Fuck!

I hadn't even considered the idea she might be knocked out for the night. Giving me no reason to prepare a backup plan.

Just like always.

Skye, the screw-up, is in fine form and setting himself up to fail ... yet again.

Decisions, decisions, decisions.

Where is Doc when you need him? I try calling him telepathically, but his line seems to be busy ... as always. I think about phoning River, too.

Fuck!

I do nothing. I slide under her bed. And wait.

Wait for the Orderly. Wait for the EarthHealer to wake. Wait until a new plan surfaces.

A gutless move, one that River wouldn't do, but at least this option allows me to recharge my batteries for a few hours. I watch her sleep for a while, wondering what the second note means – what curse shouldn't be lifted. My body is slowly drowning in exhaustion, my eyes growing heavier by the second. I fall into a deep slumber I might never wake from.

150

TWELVE

I have no idea how long she's been staring at me for. To be honest, I don't want to know. She kind of gives me the creeps.

I open my mouth to speak, but she places her finger against her lips. Then, very subtly, she points to the ceiling to warn me about the camera. 'I've already pulled the wires,' I mouth to her.

Her head shakes slightly, enough for me to see. Her lips become a snarl, and her eyes look like they're about to pop out of her head. Something tells me the camera isn't the only problem.

Slowly, she drags her body across the floor until we are nose to nose, her hair still covering most of her face. My first thought … she needs a shower, and I don't think her hair has tasted shampoo in six months. Or a brush come to that.

'Stop evaluating me and listen,' she growls softly. Again I open my mouth, but she continues, 'that camera hasn't worked for months. They get sick of me destroying it all the time so they just leave it now.' I roll my eyes at the effort I went to in dismantling the damn thing. 'But they *can* hear us.'

'Okay,' I mouth, 'how do you wanna do this?'

A low, albeit fierce growl rumbles at the back of her throat. 'I don't give a fuck. You figure it out. Just get me the fuck out of here. NOW!' She whispers the last few words through clenched teeth. And here's me wishing I had a mint to give her.

'I have a friend who's helping us,' I say, thinking of Hayley.

'Not her! She's one of them.' I've never heard anything so ridiculous in my life. Anger rises.

'I *assure* you Hayley is not *one of them*. She is a friend.' She warns me with another one of those intensive glares to lower my volume.

'Well,' she says even softer than before, 'I don't know what kind of friends you've been keeping of late, but I'm not going anywhere with *her*.'

The sound of the door unlocking has me turning myself invisible.

'Good morning, Terra.'

I can tell by the voice, it's Dane.

Terra grunts.

'And, what are *you* doing out of bed, Blossom?' he says in a condescending voice.

'You should know! You put me there, you gutless wanker. And, just so you know …you hit like a girl.'

Darkness drops into his face and alters his smug look. 'I see your attitude hasn't improved. You're still a smart-mouthed little bitch.'

Defiantly, Terra gets to her feet, protecting her newly broken arm and hisses at him. 'I see you're still an impotent twat with a small dick.'

Dane raises his hand at Terra and she lifts her chin, daring him to hit her. This is not okay in my book, no way am I going to let this happen. Not on my watch.

Recharged and ready to rock, I switch to Superhero mode and summon the heat flowing through the air duct above his head. I scoop up the air into a vacuum and fire it down on Dane's head - a nifty little trick I learnt after some thug tried to hold up our local service station when I was fourteen. He scarpered pretty quick.

Dane lets out a surprised yelp, clamps his hand to his head and looks up. 'What the fuck!' he shrieks. I holster my laugh. It's enough of a distraction to sidetrack him.

Terra smirks. 'Like I said … gutless.'

Dane's face goes from demon to demure in the blink of an eye. 'I forget,' he says in an unusually calm voice, 'violence doesn't work for you, does it, blossom? I know what you want.'

I hear Terra's throaty gulp from under the bed.

I slide myself out from under the steel frame as quietly as I can, in time to see him shake a small bag of white pills at her. 'Want a little Benzo to take the edge off?'

She seems to look at them longingly for a considerable amount of time before saying, 'you know where you can stick those.' I have to admire her spirit.

'Now, now, you really don't wanna go there. You know I'm much better at this game than you are.' Terra backs up a couple of steps. And as fearful as her actions suggest, her deep emerald eyes flash with hatred.

'And how's that arm today?'

'You'd know,' she says beneath her breath.

Dane crosses the room and rips Terra's hair back from her face, her messy dred-like clumps tangling in his fingers. 'I told you,' he growls, digging his finger beneath her chin to tilt her head, all so that he can check out his handywork - the plum coloured bruise sliding down her cheek. 'I had nothing to do with that.'

'Yeah, sure you didn't. I just woke up with it like that. Just like all the other times.' She spits in his face.

And, he leaves it there.

Grins.

Licks his lips.

'You're so predictable, blossom,' he says, releasing her hair and shoving her away with his forearm. Terra regains her balance and stands her ground as he dives into the bag of pills. 'I have some nice yellow ones today. Your favourite.'

Terra freezes as though an invisible force has turned her body to stone … the only movement is her eyes. They stare at me, scorching with intensity, demanding me to make a move.

But I am already one step ahead of her.

I'm standing behind Dane, ready to king hit him if he so much as lays one finger on her.

I swallow hard, witnessing the pulse pounding in her neck. She hasn't moved. Not even blinked. Her tone changes. 'Please, not those. I'll do whatever you say.'

Any idiot can see she's lying. There's a steeliness to her jaw, and a slow steadying breath of a predator about to pounce. And yet the idiot in the room seems to be buying it.

Dane smirks, drumming his fingers against the bag, deliberating. *I can't believe he's falling for it.*

Whilst Terra buys some time, I scan the room for something to use as a weapon. In truth, I want to strip the air out of this fucking pig's lungs and be done with it, except murder isn't my style, or on the agenda right now. I'm sure karma will eventually see to it. And besides, the dude is my height, not quite as muscular, but wiry enough to overpower the residents. I need no other evidence that I can take him.

I spot a towel draped over a silver rail.

Perfect!

'If only you meant that,' he says, a sinister grin snaking across his lips, revealing crooked yellowing teeth. 'And you know what special sauce comes with the yellow ones …?'

Her whole face becomes stone, apart from one muscle that flickers in her jaw. A fierce, untamed rage explodes in her eyes. 'Bring it on, cunt. That maggot in your trousers isn't worth being conscious for anyway.'

The lightning-fast backhand across Terra's face catches us both off-guard, and she drops to her knees.

She spits blood onto the washed-out grey linoleum, then wipes her mouth against her sleeve.

That's it - game over for me.

Before Dane knows what's happening, I switch to visibility, grab the towel and throw it around his neck. I tighten my grip, twisting the two ends together like a vice. He lashes out at me, but I am well out of his reach.

'Don't kill him,' warns Terra. I've no intention of killing him. I'm trying to render him unconscious.

Arms flailing, his body weakens after several volatile attempts to wrench himself free. The second his body goes limp, I release him and he drops heavily to the floor.

'C'mon. Let's go.'

Terra's lip is split, and the cut beneath her eye has reopened. Still, she wastes no time getting to her feet and follows me to the door. The corridor looks clear.

'What's your plan?' she asks.

Great question. 'I don't have one,' I say, shrugging my shoulders, 'but I do know the door codes to get out of here.'

'Wow, you're the classic Houdini, aren't you? I learnt the codes the first week I was here.'

'You know they *change* them every week?'

Obviously, that was the wrong thing to say. 'Remind me who's been living here again ...' She throws me a side-eye. 'Even when they blindfold me, I still find a way to hack it.'

'And yet you're still here,' I say sarcastically.

Terra sneers. 'It's the hive. I can't figure how to get around it. It's the one area that holds me back every time.'

'I take it you've tried this before then?'

'What do you reckon, Einstein. That I've been sitting in a puddle of my own piss for the last eleven years, twiddling my thumbs.'

She is ballsy. And I get a taste of what River must feel like with me constantly yapping at his heels. The difference is, I won't back down. And I can't help always wanting the last word – what can I say, it's a disease.

'Hold onto your dreds, Whoopi. If you can get us through the doors. I'll take care of the hive.'

She shoves me in the back with her cast, forcing me into the hallway. 'Move.'

The overhead cameras beam down on us, but now isn't the time for indecisiveness. It's all or nothing. We walk swiftly along the sterile beige hallway to the sounds of waking patients banging on the glass and hollering for release.

'Meds have worn off,' says Terra, jerking her head towards them.

'Never would've guessed,' I respond as we approach the first locked door. She punches in the numbers, and to my surprise, the door buzzes open.

'See,' she says triumphantly. A muscle beneath my eye twitches in irritation.

We make it down the stairs without a hitch, and I'm kind of amazed that no alarm bells have gone off. No sooner are the words out of my mouth, the stairwell is bathed in red light, and the distinct errrr errrr errrr errrr of a siren wails around us.

'What now?' she asks. My mind spins up a gear. I could turn invisible and get the hell out of dodge, and come back for her another time, but somehow, I don't think she'll agree to that, considering I've bailed on her twice already. Or I could blast everyone with a vengeful hurricane and we could stroll out the front door without so much as a whisper of opposition, but that will also mean I will be on the looney's most wanted list alongside Terra, and we don't want to draw unwanted attention to the weird and wonderful powers we have.

Voices grow louder.

'In here,' I say, opening the closest door and pushing Terra inside. As I hoped, it is a secondary fire escape; however the stairs only go up.

'Good thinking, Sherlock. Now you've got us trapped.'

I remember the attic. 'I think I have a way out.'

She heaves a sigh. I have to agree. I'm not that confident in my flimsy plan either.

Terra takes the stairs two, sometimes three at a time. I'm impressed at her fitness, especially for someone who has been incarcerated most of her life, and I match her stride for stride. Once on the landing, she races towards the rickety spiral staircase like she knows where she's going. I take a quick look around before closing the last security door behind me, and take off after her. Just like I thought it would, the stairs creak loud enough to wake the dead.

Thankfully, the door to the attic is still open.

I hang back in the doorway, half keeping watch, half intrigued as Terra makes a beeline for the far corner where the raven is still asleep in the pillow stuffing. She stands over the poor thing, head down, hands clenching and unclenching so many times, I lose count.

Something inside me says I should call out to see if she's okay, except it's pretty clear she isn't. The floorboards tell their own tale as her weight shifts from foot to foot. I expect the raven to wake any minute. It doesn't.

I shut the door behind me, drowning out most of the siren, and clear my throat. She casts a quick glance towards me as she sits down, cross-legged, back straight, before turning back to the raven. She runs two fingers over the bird's head and down its back, making the glossy feathers shine like freshly polished boots. In spite of all that, it still doesn't wake.

'Is it dead?' I ask.

She simply shakes her head.

'What's wrong with it then?'

Terra sits in silence, stroking it a few more times before saying. 'Isn't she beautiful?'

I come closer to inspect it and peer over her shoulder.

'Looks like a stinking raven to me,' I say.

Terra's hand stops in mid-stroke and her shoulders stiffen. I take a step back.

'You still haven't got it, have you?' Her voice is soft, but deadly.

I back up again and she swings around to face me.

'You read the message, right?'

'*Message*?'

She rolls her eyes and pulls at her hair as though she wants to rip it from the roots. 'Why did I have to get you? Why couldn't I have gotten River in the rotation? At least he has half a brain, regardless if it's in his trousers most of the time.'

I think hard. And then it comes to me. 'Oh, you mean from the ring on the bird's foot. Yeah, I read it. Something about not lifting a curse.'

'*And?*' she says looking between me and the raven several times.

Why the fuck do girls play these stupid mind games? It usually doesn't bother me because I take what I need from their minds, but Terra is different. I get a sense of what she is thinking, but not actually what it is: like I'm blocked or something.

'The *bird* is cursed?' I finally ask.

'*And …*'

The fact that she is biting down hard on her lip says she's about to rip me a new one.

The penny drops. '*You*? You mean …'

'Oh, finally. Congratulations, Skye. It only took you ten years to figure it out.' She rolls her eyes.

'You're the bird?' I say, trying to catch my breath.

'You're the bird?' Terra repeats, 'oh my God, you are the dumbest motherfucker I've ever met. Of course I'm the bird. Who else would it be?'

158

'A *messenger*?' I offer, hopefully. She drops her head into her hands.

'But if you're the bird, and you are *you*, then … how …?' Her head snaps up, her eyes daring me to open my mouth again. I can't help it. I'm really confused.

'I'm *me* now, in the flesh, talking to you … *right*?'

I nod.

She picks up the sleeping bird. I remember it was injured. 'Be careful, I think its wing is broken,' I say.

'No shit! You think I don't know that?' she says, shaking her plastered arm at me. 'And while we're on the subject, do you recognise this?' She lays the bird into her lap and roughly drags the sleeve of her shirt past her shoulder to show me a scar the size of a pea.

I feel my face creasing. I don't see the connection.

'Pellet gun. A few years ago … *remember*?'

Horror strikes at me hard. A blow to the gut would have been kinder. I do remember. 'I didn't know. How was I supposed to …?'

'Just so you know, it stung like a bitch.' She is not interested in hearing my excuses and I don't *blame* her, but now is not the time. We have bigger fish to fry.

'But you accused Dane of …'

'Wow! You are so dumb. How *ever* did you make it through puberty in one piece?'

'*Puberty's done?* Yay. Go me!' I reply and throw in a smirk for good measure.

Terra rolls her eyes, pressing the dusky pink colour out of her lips. 'If you quit being a total dick for a moment, I'll tell you.'

She pauses.

Waits for a smart comeback.

'The second I'm unconscious, I turn into the raven – if they drug me, like I have been, the last two days, I remain as the raven.' I frown. 'Dane did give me one parting gift before he drugged me.' She turns her head to show me her eye again. 'The arm, is courtesy of your little friend's shoe.'

159

I look at the cast on her arm. 'Then how …'

Terra shrugs. 'No idea. Woke up like it. Someone must've checked up on me whilst I was bombed out on Dane's yellow smarties.'

'So because you're awake now, the bird is asleep?'

The siren stops, and I make a dash for the door. I look to the keyhole to see the key is missing. 'What the fuck!' I look for something to wedge against the door. 'Help me drag these beds over.' Terra sets the bird down, grabs the closest bed and hauls it across the room, slashing a deep scar into the timber flooring.

As it happens, the bedhead fits neatly under the door handle. 'It was made for it,' says Terra, pleased with her effort. 'Now what?'

I hate to say it, but she is right.

We are trapped.

I could blast the iron bars off with my high powered wind device, but how am I going to get Terra off the roof? No point in rendering her unconscious because the raven still can't fly, plus it still leaves her body here. Nope, strike that option out.

She angles her head at me. Sees the surrender on my face. 'You should get out of here. I can deal with them,' she says wearily.

'Not on your life.' My jaw sets firm. There is no way I'm going to leave her. 'I have an idea. Pull the bed out a little further.'

'But they'll get in,' she gasps.

'Exactly,' I say, a smile spreading across my face.

Terra drags the bed out a few inches and I instruct her to lie on the floor, face down. Begrudgingly she complies.

As weak as it is, my plan is to get as many of the staff up here, overcome them, *somehow*, and then stroll right out the front door. It's pathetic, I know, but I'm out of options. And the clock is ticking.

Standing by the solid oak door, I hear voices and a rumble of footsteps striking the stair treads just outside. I turn myself invisible as Dane shoulders his way into the room, twisting the key around in his hand. I growl internally – it was him that took it. He is accompanied by Mrs Vera, who must have been called in at the last minute because she's wearing a dark brown tweed skirt and jacket, and not the standard pale blue nurses tunic. Three more fellas accompany them, two male orderlies, and a middle-aged man wearing a pinstripe suit. He looks to be someone of importance, so naturally, he's my first target.

'Silly, silly girl,' says Dane, walking over to her, swinging a set of restraints in one hand and a lethal-looking syringe in the other.

Terra remains still.

'Playing dead, are we?' chants Dane. 'What do you think, Mrs Vera – isolation or shock therapy?'

'Definitely shock therapy,' answers Mrs Vera. She laughs, and yet Terra refuses to budge. Standing between us and the door, I step around the orderlies each holding a syringe. Mr Pinstripe hovers close by.

Without totally thinking through my actions, I switch off my invisibility the second my arm locks around his scrawny neck. He gurgles half a scream, causing Dane and Mrs Vera to spin in our direction.

The shock and surprise on their faces is just what I was after. It takes a few moments for it to sink in that I'm holding a royal flush.

Mrs Vera takes a tentative step towards us. 'You should think this through, lad. Don't do anything reckless now.'

'HA!' I can't help the burst of laughter. 'You're messing with the wrong person, lady. Reckless is my middle name. NOW BACK OFF!' Mr Pinstripe chokes off another gurgle as I intensify my hold. Mrs Vera stops. 'If you don't want Professor Pinstripe here to hold his breath indefinitely, I suggest you back up.' I add a little more pressure to my forearm. Mrs Vera and Dane obey, both slinging daggers at me through every blink.

'Terra, get up,' I command. She's on her feet in a heartbeat, regardless of her broken arm.

161

'You two, over by the window. Move!' I yell to the orderlies, who comply without question. 'Tie them up,' I say to Terra.

She scours the room and comes back brandishing a reel of thick silver tape. 'This should do nicely.' She rolls them onto their stomach and binds their hands to their feet before dragging over Professor Pinstripe and doing the same to him.

'I saved the best till last,' she says, fronting Dane, who looks like he's about to piss his pants. She snatches the syringe out of his hand. 'You remember where I said I was going to stick this ...' she pauses for a few seconds, 'well, I lied.'

She boots him fair and square in the balls, without shame or remorse.

He coughs hard.

Doubles up.

Drops to the floor in a mess of his own making.

She then snatches up the restraints and spins Mrs Vera around, reefing her arms behind her until she cries out in pain. Terra clears her nose and throat and conjures something green and slimy in her mouth before gobbing it at Mrs Vera's face. 'That's been a long time coming, you sick bitch.'

Now this is where I come in. 'And if any of you so much as whisper one word about what went on here today, I *personally* guarantee, I will haunt you all from dawn to dusk.' I switch to power mode and levitate, hovering for a good twenty seconds. Once I'm convinced they've all got the message, I turn invisible, adding my best, scariest laugh.

Grey faces and wide scared eyes stare up at me. 'Do I make myself clear?' I add, as I switch back to visibility. They all shake their heads in unison.

Score one to the AirWhisperer – I hold back the urge to fist pump the air.

'*You* finished?' I ask Terra, who still hasn't taken her eyes off Dane.

'Almost.'

Almost will have to wait as I hear more footsteps hurrying up the stairs. A part of me isn't surprised to see Hayley standing there. She's holding two syringes – one in each hand. Fearlessly, she walks over to the orderlies and jabs them both in the neck at the same time, before picking up their unused syringes. Their eyes glaze over, before face planting to the ground.

'Hayley,' I say around a sigh. 'You shouldn't have come …'

'What is *she* doing here?'

I reassure her. 'Hayley's a friend.'

'She's one of them,' says Terra, squinting her eyes at Hayley.

'What did I do?' asks Hayley, blinking away her confusion.

'The bitch threw a shoe at me.'

Terra and Hayley stare each other down. We don't have time for a full on catfight.

'Get over it, Terra. She's come to help.'

Hayley winks at me as she approaches, and then casually jabs Mr Pinstripe in the leg. His body becomes a lead weight as he loses consciousness.

'That's three,' says Hayley. There's a satisfied smile on her face. 'Want me to take care of that one for you,' she says, pointing to Dane still writhing around on the ground.

'I've got this,' says Terra sulkily, placing her thumb over the end of the plunger. Dane has curled into a ball, and Terra rolls him onto his back with the blade of her foot.

'Stretch out,' she commands. Dane can't do anything other than rock from side to side with his hands cupped over his balls, groaning. 'I said, stretch your legs out.' He still refuses to obey. 'You wanna play hardball with me, then I'll give you the choice of where I'm going to stick this.' She looms over him, throwing his body into shadow. 'Eye or dick?'

Anyone knows that being stabbed in the eye can lead to blindness or possible death, depending on the force, and yet that doesn't seem to matter to Terra. Her bedside manner expired the day she was bought in here.

Dane starts to whimper, a soft high-pitched whimper, the kind a dog might make when it needs to take a leak. 'Your choice,' she continues, brandishing the syringe, aiming it closer and closer to his face.

Dane begs the same way any man would beg, when his life is on the line, in fast, short sentences that make no sense – 'please, no, don't, please, wait, no, don't, please.'

With less than an inch to go, Terra throws her arm back to plunge it into Dane's eye and at the last second, he straightens out. She changes her trajectory and stabs it straight in his dick.

He screams out as Terra casually gets up and walks to the door, leaving the needle embedded in his groin.

I wince.

But she doesn't look back even after Hayley follows her out.

I make my way to the door, satisfied the girls are safe and already halfway down the stairs, and stop short. I glance backwards to see Dane has inched his way over to the raven. He grabs hold of the bird.

'Screw you,' he says and twists the poor bird's head clean off before passing out.

Fuck! I have a bad feeling about this.

THIRTEEN

DUMBFOUNDED, we arrive back at Hayley's house. I can't believe how easy our escape was, in the end. We managed to coax Terra into a straitjacket, just for show, and with me invisible, Hayley calmly walked Terra through the building to that final security door, the door Terra could never breach. There were a couple of tense moments along the way when Hayley accidentally punched in the wrong door codes, only for Terra to impolitely shove her out of the way and take control, keying in the numbers herself.

Then Jackpot! We reached the hive!

Hayley confidently entered the last eight-digit code, and the second the door buzzed open, the tension immediately dropped, the air much easier to breathe, even though, technically I was air myself. The only staff member manning the front desk was Meryl, a middle-aged woman with painted-on eyebrows and hair scraped back so fiercely into a ponytail she looked almost bald. Meryl could have been our only hurdle, except she seemed more interested in reading her novel. Hayley casually waved a sheet of paper at her, that Mr "unconscious" Pinstripe had just authorised regarding the commotion upstairs. Meryl had reluctantly swung her legs off the desk to come and look, and, with a little manipulation of the airwaves inside Meryl's head, she saw a quote for Hayley's dental work she was due to get next week, as an Emergency Transfer Order. She buzzed the door open, and we breezed straight through the front door without so much as a word from anyone.

One massive win for Team Skye! High five!

My biggest concern now ... is how the hell am I going to tell Terra about the raven?

I need advice.

River and Ember should be my first choice, but somehow I figure Doc has the answers I'm looking for. I'll never forget the first time I bumped into him. It was four months after my parents were killed, and I literally bowled him over as I rushed out of a café in Kings Beach. Kings Beach is a small seaside town on the sunshine coast in Queensland, just north of Bribie Island, known for its awesome surf and long sandy beaches. We moved there after my mate Todd, had that tragic accident. It was a tough time for me, and his death hit me hard. I'd never known anyone who had died before, and Todd and I had been friends since kindergarten. Every park we hung out at back in Rocky, every waterhole we swam in, every classroom, every ... well, let's say, everything around me was a vivid reminder I was alive and he was dead - everything sucked. Now, when I look back, the move to the coast was more disastrous than it was favourable. If Todd hadn't died, we'd have never moved. Mum and Dad would still be here, and the tonne of guilt piling up on me daily, keeping me up most nights, wouldn't exist.

So Doc had been my saviour. Doc, who had been created by God himself, and brother to Ra-Mon. Doc, who had been stripped of his powers, save a few, and banished to earth to live as an immortal in a mortal body until the end of time. In all honesty, I don't even know if Empedocles is his real name because his true self had been hidden from him by the Creator. A man, if you can call him that, so humble, so good, so hell-bent on helping us stop his evil brother, has always been there for me. And I don't know what I would've done if he hadn't come along when he did.

Dean and I were a mess. Dean with his anger issues and me blaming everything that went wrong in the world on myself. Riddled with guilt, for knocking him to the ground, I bought Doc a cup of coffee, and we sat on the edge of the pavement for two hours, and talked. This man I've come to rely on, confide in and have complete trust in, listened to my life story, even though he already knew it, but let me prattle on anyway.

He didn't offer the advice he does now. Didn't interrupt me whilst I poured my heart out … just let me speak until my mouth ran out of words.

A week later, he showed up at my school … said he had some important stuff to tell me. We chatted for a bit, and that was when he asked me if I'd turned invisible that day, or whether I'd been out for a midnight flight like I often did. Of course, I was shocked he knew. Initially, I had him pinned as a stalker, I mean, I didn't know him from a bar of soap. However, it took no convincing that he was an immortal, especially after introducing me to his unique way of travelling – one minute we were sitting eating ice-cream in Australia, and the next I was being chased by a llama in Peru. What's not to believe after that? So, regardless of what his name is, Doc is the only person that can help me now.

I leave Hayley and Terra on the sofa to see who can outstare the other the longest, and step outside onto Hayley's front porch. I pass two tin buckets either side of the door overflowing with lavender. The rest of the space is taken up with potted ferns, and every hanging plant you can think of, making the entrance near impossible to see or manoeuvre out of. The air is damp and heavy, and definitely not a great day for flying or invisibility.

I start to think about how I might bring up this new development with Terra, well aware Doc can hear my every thought, although his telepathic hearing aid seems more turned *off* than on these days. I know we share these frequencies with other immortals, but this simply cannot wait.

I slip between two parked cars in front of Hayley's place and head across the lush green verge to the man-made lake overlooking the town. The row of trees ahead, branches naked and still feeling the brunt of a brutal winter, stand tall and strong, like a row of soldiers ready to charge. I'm confident this place would be teeming with people in the height of summer, but seven-thirty in the morning, heading towards the middle of March, it's quite another story. Apart from a young lady walking a fluffball on a leash, the wooden seats are bare, and the jogger's path is empty. It starts to rain, so I throw my hoodie up. Hands in pockets, looking across the lake, I wait for Doc.

'Had a rough day?' I hear from behind me.

'You could say that,' I answer, picking up the gruff familiarity of Doc's voice. 'Suppose you know what happened?'

Dressed in a long grey mac and tortoiseshell flat cap, he nods his head once and scratches his beard. 'Doesn't take a genius to work it out.' From that statement alone, I'm more confident that his Houdini act is deliberate.

'I could've done with your help.' A tired breath escapes.

'Why? You had everything in hand,' he says coolly, shrugging his shoulders. 'What you need to do, young Skye, is to learn to trust your own abilities. If I came running every time you were faced with a tiny hurdle, you wouldn't appreciate the win, and never truly learn that through grit and determination, victory will be found.

Have faith in yourself, son. Believe in the fact that you hold everything you need to succeed.'

Mental note: Remember never to *ask* that question again unless I need a *Go Skye, you can do this* kinda pick-me-up.

'Alright already. I get it. Now let's get back to the serious stuff.'

Doc sighs. 'Good thinking, so ...why haven't you told Terra yet?'

His words catch me off-guard. He's like that, Doc, just comes out and says things without ever giving a hint of what he's about to say.

No mulling it over in his thoughts to give me an idea.

Simply straight out of the air and to the point.

Damn! I could do with that skill.

I answer truthfully. 'Have you seen the way she stares you down?' I suck in a shallow breath.

'I don't know what you're talking about.' He frowns, his forehead becoming more rippled than a low tide.

'*What? Are you serious?* She looks like she could rip you limb from limb.'

Doc sniffs and shakes his head. A soft smile peeks out from under his bushy beard. 'You should try and cut her some slack. She's had a tough life – worse than all of you.' He narrows his eyes at me. 'At least you've all had a family. You know she's been in there for almost twelve years?'

I find I'm blinking, hearing the words, but my brain is scrambled, trying to find a way to comprehend that.

'*Twelve years*?' I eventually say, but it's more like a huff of breath. 'How? WHY?'

'Her parents threw her in there when she was seven years old. Confused. Unsure what to do with her.' There is a hum of silence between us. No traffic sounds, no dogs barking, even the wind is scared to breathe. This is getting worse and worse.

'*Her parents? WHY?*'

'It's a strange thing, that all three of you believed you were destined for an institution for hearing voices.' He sighs. 'You all questioned your sanity. You all thought you were …'

'Nuts?' I throw in.

'So, imagine being able to converse with animals … and I mean, really understand them, talk to them, hear them, not being *nuts* at all, and still being locked up for it.'

The words I want to say won't come out. It's difficult enough to get my lungs to work, the air so thin it doesn't feel like it's sustaining me as I breathe in. I shake my head. I can't imagine what would make a parent give up their child like that.

'The poor kid was tormented by the voices of animals since she could crawl.' He pauses and looks up at the sky.

'Go on,' I prompt.

'It was normal for her. She thought everyone could hear them. I watched over her, knowing exactly who inhabited her body, reassuring her that she wasn't mad, but that she was a very special girl with special powers from heaven and when she was old enough, she would have to use those powers. And she believed it for a while.' His face grows dark. 'Then when she told her parents about possessing heavenly powers, she was thrown into that *prison* and all that positive reinforcement was for nothing.'

The air around us has stilled.

Almost becoming non-existent, and, for once, I have nothing to do with it.

I'm counting time again – time for Doc to stop reminiscing … to stop taking those long, pensive stares to where the far edge of the lake greets those rolling green hills that we don't have back home. Finally, he takes a breath, smooths his beard and looks at me. 'It was a bad time for Terra. She spiralled downwards and got caught up in a world of drugs to shut out the voices … to shut out Gaia. Slowly, she fell apart until she hardly recognised

170

herself. A lightness finds its way back into his eyes. 'She's better now.' I raise my eyebrows in disbelief. 'Over the last few years, she's fought her way back with such courage ... such courage.'

'*Gaia?*'

'The EarthHealer,' Doc clarifies.

'Wow,' I say, a little impressed. From the brief time I'd spent in that horrible place, I'm shocked that anyone could find the strength to fight back.

'Skye, you realise Terra can communicate with all forms of life?'

'You mean like fish and birds?'

'Fish, birds, insects, plants, flowers, trees ...'

'She can talk to *trees*?' Once I've said it, I realise that talking to trees is the least of our worries, but OMG, I can't get my head around that. I can't believe what I'm hearing, but most of all, that she isn't an orphan like the rest of us.

'And ... Terra's folks are *alive*?' It shines a little hope into my soul. 'I still don't understand how they could do that to their own daughter?'

'They were alive the last time I checked. I guess Terra will fill you in on the other details. Oh, and the *I hate the world thing*, isn't real, you know,' he says, nudging his shoulder against mine. 'It's all superficial. Once you get to know her ... you'll see.'

'I hope so.' A mother duck and her ducklings swim by, momentarily distracting me. I bring on my serious face. 'The raven was bound to her, wasn't it?' The drawings on her wall explain so much now.

'Yes. Two years after Terra arrived at Nevermore, Gaia cast a spell using earth magic to bind Corax to her.'

'Corax?'

'Corvus Corax is the Latin name for the common raven, and the preferred term for the First Initiation.'

'Oh right. Well, what's going to happen ... now that it's dead? Terra said something about not breaking the curse.'

'What else did she say?'

'Nothing. Just *don't break it.*'

The pinched look on Doc's face, his eyes tired and full of concern, says I'm not going to like what he's about to say. 'You knew that *her* raven was the First of the Initiations, didn't you?'

'I had an idea it was, but I wasn't certain.'

'Gaia knew Ra-Mon would try to milk Mithras's strength to get to Amun, thereby giving him an easier path to herself. So, she bound the Raven to Terra to suppress her powers, to protect her and to hide her from Ra-Mon. But she had a second motive - to keep the first of the Seven Initiations of Mithras hidden.' I need to be writing all this down, so I don't forget. I'm sure River will drill me the second I get home. 'And was the ritual performed correctly when the bird was sacrificed?'

'*Sacrificed? Ritual?* What are you talking about? Dane ripped the birds head clean off.'

'*Dane?* Who in God's name is Dane?'

'The fuckwit, sorry, I mean, the orderly who had it in for Terra.'

Right before my eyes, I witness the colour drain out of Doc's cheeks. 'You mean it wasn't you who released Terra from the raven?'

'No.'

The sound of my voice is hollow, like a stone dropping from an incredible height into a hole forged deep into the earth.

Doc twitches his lips to one side and makes a strange clicking sound with his tongue. 'This complicates things slightly.'

I still don't see his problem. 'How so? The way I see it, Dane did us a favour. There's only six to go now.

'Unfortunately, pup, it doesn't quite work that way. Incorrectly breaking the curse will undoubtedly have consequences for you … with Isis. To start with, these Initiations are *your* tasks … *your* duty. And although the

172

First Initiation is complete, *technically* ...' Doc winces slightly, 'you failed the task as it was set out.'

BOMB drop!

No surprises there.

I wish I could bury my head into my hoodie, run away from this place, to a desert, to the sea, forget about this stupid end of the world shit that keeps pointing out how much of a complete loser I am. FUCK! The first damn task and I can't even get *that* right, just like it said on my page of Peri Phuseôs tôn Ontôn.

I feel myself sinking into the murkiest bog imaginable. Into that deep, dark hole I dropped that stone into. 'Wow! I'm awesome,' I mutter to myself.

'Come now, lad. Don't be so hard on yourself,' says Doc so casually it makes me look up. 'You weren't to know. You didn't know about the ritual, anymore than you knew Dane would slay the bird.' I roll my eyes at him. 'It was an easy mistake.' For a moment, I thought he was going to say it was a rookie mistake, but it's easily ten times *worse*! There was nothing easy about it ... because I wasn't even involved in it ... and I should've been.

I should've known.

'And here is the lesson in it for you, young Skye. Don't dwell on what you can't change. You need to look to the next Initiation and focus solely on that.' *Easier said than done!* 'There may be consequences for that mistake.' He pauses to scratch his beard again.

I try his words on, ten different ways, until I realise the shocking truth. 'So, are you saying I'm in her debt now?'

'Maybe. Isis has her own agenda, and *will* find any loophole to get what she wants. Believe me. Even if it means reneging on her side of the bargain. It's what she does. It's what she's always done. Just know, she can't be trusted.'

I find myself answering him with a huge exhale, my hands running through my hair ... massaging my neck ... needing my temples.

173

'Son, we are dealing with dark magic here. Not the pure kind that comes from the earth - the kind that comes from Gaia. But dark magic that Isis stole. Magic from The Underworld. Dark magic and powers that Ra-Mon is syphoning. It is why he is more powerful than me.'

'Great,' I reply. 'If I'd known how *anal* this immortal witch was, I would've kept a much closer eye on that bird.' I don't realise I've said the words out loud until I see Doc nodding.

'And I hate to say it, but it does come down to you now.'

I'm aware as every single muscle in my body relaxes.

Becomes water.

Becomes unusable.

Fuck!

I've said it once and I'll say it a thousand more times before this is over … I'm not the right man for the job.

'Isis will use Mr Fulton any way she can … even as leverage if she has to. However, she will not want to give up her new Bloodslave. If these Seven Initiations aren't achieved, according to her rules, River will remain in her service forever. You already have one strike against your name, you can't afford any more mistakes.'

Short. Sharp. And aimed straight at the heart. I feel its sting. Feel the pressure mounting that I need to concentrate, slow down, take stock of every decision I make, consult with the other three when I need to, and above all, stick to a plan.

'What's next then?' The wind blows around me, driving the rain straight into my face, dampening my clothes. My hands instinctively dive into the front pocket of my hoodie as I brace myself against the cold.

I wish I'd bought a coat. But who needs a jacket when you can control the weather?

I zone in, under the watchful eyes of Doc, who looks on like any proud father might, focus for all of one second before sending the wind to play in the treetops behind me.

174

'At least you have one thing in your corner. You've had the most time to learn about your power, and show an incredible amount of control. That'll help.' He pats my shoulder.

'Thanks,' is all I can think of to say.

This time, we both gaze into the distance.

'For now, spend every waking moment trying to decipher the whereabouts of the Second Initiation.'

'Nymphus, right?'

'Exactly. What do you know of this?'

I call on the research I'd done before we headed to Scotland. 'It means bridegroom. Apparently, as part of the Mithraism religion, dudes had to marry dudes.'

'That's right,' says Doc.

'It had something to do with women not being allowed to be part of the Mithraism cult. The male bride, notably a Roman soldier, was joined to Mithras through a marriage ceremony, although not like ceremonies we have today.'

'The difference being,' begins Doc, 'was that these soldiers didn't have a choice. If they wanted to be part of the army, they were forced to go through with the proceedings.'

'Doesn't sound fair?' I add.

'They didn't know any different. Nymphus can also represent a veil, a mirror, lamp or a diadem.'

'So it could be any one of those things,' I say, blowing out an irritating breath.

'Yes.'

'Perfect! Where the hell do I start looking for one of those … in a *haystack*? And how will I know which one it is?'

'You will know.'

'How?'

'You will know,' repeats Doc.

'You sound very sure of that.'

'I am,' says Doc smugly. 'First, you have to tell Terra that the curse is broken, which I'm pretty sure she's already figured out.'

'Okay.'

'There is some positive outcome here.'

'Being?'

'At least there won't be any more air rifles to dodge.'

My eyes widen. 'You knew! And you did nothing. I could've killed her.'

Doc chuckles softly and then breaks into a guffaw of laughter. 'You really think I'd let that happen. There was a reason your shots always went wide, why a dog barked or another bird flew into your field of vision.'

'But I did shoot her. She showed me the mark.'

'And she knew the risks. She was determined to open your eyes. Make you see who she truly was.'

'*Why*?'

'Because I told her to.'

'*You*?'

'Who else would it have been?' It's a fair point. 'I've been watching over all of you, way before you were born.'

A huge WOW explodes in my thoughts. 'But I thought you said …'

'A magician never gives away his tricks,' says Doc, grinning. 'Besides, I used the one power, the one gift that Ra-Mon doesn't possess …'

'Which is?'

'Intuition.' I find myself frowning. 'Intuition is a human gift, something immortals only read about.'

'Aahhh. That explains why Ra-Mon couldn't find the Elementars.'

'Precisely. Humans don't realise how much power they possess. They might not be able to fly or turn invisible but that doesn't mean they aren't powerful beings. Some powers only work if you tap into them, if you flex them like a well-exercised muscle. You need to believe in them. Trust them. I used my intuition, my

176

human gut instincts to locate your family lineages. I tuned into the elemental powers of earth, fire, air and water, like I wrote about back in 478BC. From then, it was easy enough for me to trace the Elementars.' Doc pauses. Teeth grazing against his lips. 'I'm sure the Creator knew this when he assigned me this body.' Revelation after revelation has me coming apart as though each stitch of my learnt experience is being plucked out and replaced with something new. This is the first time he has spoken about his own existence. My thoughts still come back to Terra. 'She *knew* about us?'

'Of course, she knew about you all. Ember was not the first piece of the puzzle. She was the last.' It all began with Doc making himself known to Terra, to get her to make contact with me, which then stimulated me to look for River, spurring River to seek out Ember. I can see now that this has all been orchestrated by more than mere coincidences. And here I was thinking Doc had simply been sitting on the sidelines, watching the end of the world unfold. He was the trigger, the one responsible for waking us from our slumbers. 'Enough now. You need to contact Mr Fulton and Miss Riley and formulate a plan to meet up with Tomas to determine your next course of action.'

He's right.

It all starts now.

FOURTEEN

'**WHERE's** Hayley?' I ask, dragging my wet hoodie over my head. I find Terra gazing out of the lounge room window, still in the same grey tracksuit pants and top, hair backcombed and needing way more attention than a local hairdresser can offer.

She shrugs. 'I don't know what you see in her. She's one of *them*.'

That's the second time she's said that, and I won't have her gnawing at the hand that has just helped free her. 'You need to let up on her. She's okay.'

Terra grumbles something under her breath, and I take a cautious step back, ready to go another round with her. She's explosive and impulsive, and I never know what she'll do next. The corner of her lip turns up, sending a cold shiver over my body. To me, she will always be that looney I saw rocking back and forth.

I turn towards the door, hearing a key in the lock. Hayley enters with three bags, offers me a warm smile and drops them at Terra's feet. 'I thought you might need some clothes,' she says meekly. 'You can't very well wear that *gorgeous* outfit for the rest of your life.'

Terra squints evil thoughts at her, looks down at the bags and then goes back to staring out of the window.

'You're welcome,' says Hayley sarcastically and disappears out of the room.

'That was rude. The poor girl is only trying to help.'

Without looking at me, Terra says, 'I didn't ask for her help. And, I don't like her. End of story.'

I grit my teeth, wondering how the hell I'm going to bring up the raven when she is likely to take me apart regarding something less important. The only way is … death by bandaid.

'The raven is dead.'

She spins in her seat to face me, her eyes narrowed, her lips thinner than a pencil line. 'You think I don't know that, Einstein? You think I wouldn't know if it has been killed? I was tied to that damn thing for ten years. You have no idea what chain reaction this has set off. I have opened the Gates of Hell.'

'Don't be so melodramatic, for Christ's sake.'

'I know everything, Skye. EV-ery-thing! I know about all of you. Who you are, what you've done, and not done, *and* I'm not spilling another drop until we're all together. You don't get it; you never have. And you don't get me.' She folds her arms tightly across her chest and swings her body away from me.

An hour later, River and Ember arrive, much to my relief. Hayley welcomes them in and then quietly withdraws to the small kitchenette. Silence rocks the room; tension shifts uneasily in the air that only I can taste and feel.

'Sit,' I say, gesturing to the sofa. Ember takes one of the chairs, laying her hands calmly in her lap. Her eyes flick between River and Terra, but not once looking at me. River leans against the lounge room wall, rubbing his chin with his hand. Somebody needs to start this conversation otherwise, we could be here all day. I take it upon myself to be who everybody knows me to be, cocky and irresponsible, and unleash my opinion on the situation whether they want to hear it or not.

'Good to see you guys,' I say to Ember and River. 'I don't think introductions are needed because Terra knows everyone and everything.' She turns and scowls at me whilst gnawing on her thumbnail. Those vivid, cat-like green eyes devour me, scorching me like they might burn a hole right through me.

River looks disapprovingly at me and goes to stand beside the chair Terra is in. 'I'm happy to meet you, Terra. So is Em.' Ember smiles.

Terra glances up from under her straggly dark hair at them. 'Don't worry about him,' says River, 'he takes a while to warm up to.' They all turn to look at me.

I sneer at him, sensing a need to walk. I contemplate it for all of four seconds and decide not to, only because I'm curious what Terra has to say, and I'm bound by the promise I made to myself and Doc.

'The First Degree of Initiation is complete,' says Terra quite openly.

A loud crash from the kitchenette has us all looking in Hayley's direction as she picks up a large black pot from the floor. 'Sorry,' she mutters.

'What does that mean for you?' asks Ember. I love her question because the First Initiation means I have six left to go.

Terra tries to smile, but it doesn't quite reach its mark. Actually, it's kind of scary.

'Whilst the raven was linked to me, it meant that Mithras could never rise. You know of Mithras, right?' I watch River and Ember nod. 'For some reason, that even Empedocles can't comprehend, my mind has been imprinted with the Akashic records. It's all to do with Gaia, and the whole EarthHealer Elementar *thing*.'

180

'The *what*?' I hear myself say, and not in the nicest of tones either. I am rewarded with another scary glance, this time from both Terra and Ember. At this rate, I am becoming public enemy number one. If Doc were here, he'd tell me to simmer down a bit and take a breath. I push aside the wise guy cracks, the *ego*, and focus with everything that I have.

'The Akashic records are fundamentally the universe's personal diary.'

I look up to see Ember drop her head.

Her thoughts betray her as she flicks through the extensive list of things on her mind that she hasn't yet put to bed, the major one being *Iris's diary*. She needs closure around why her parents were murdered, and why that information was in Iris Perkins diary.

Terra begins again. 'It is a record of every event … past, present and future that has ever happened since the world began. Every thought. Every action. And not just on earth, but with every life form.'

'That would explain why you know everything,' I mumble under my breath. Time to eat humble pie, Skye boy!

I take stock of the room.

It's not the rosy coloured walls or the cheap framed pictures which portray two almost identical paintings of three long-stemmed tulips hanging a little lopsided. It's not the crocheted rugs over the back of two dodgy second-hand leather chairs, or the old record player in the corner with a stack of old records piled on top, that draws my eye. It's the utter disbelief on everyone's faces.

Including mine.

Terra certainly knows how to muzzle a room.

I've never seen River so speechless, and Ember can't stop shaking her head.

Me … it drops into my body, making me slightly disorientated and yet somehow euphoric because I know what this means.

This is a gift.

A welcome gift to help us know our enemies better, their past, present and future movements. A second is all it takes for Terra to bring everyone else into the picture.

'And with that, comes all of the Mithraic heritage. I know about Mithras's former plan to take over the world. I know how he was banished into exile. I know everything about him, as though I've walked in his shadow.'

'Cool,' I say, 'then you'll know where to find the next Initiation - the Nymphus.'

'Not cool. Do you have the slightest inkling of what this knowledge has done to me? How it has robbed me of a life?'

Yes … of course we fucking do.

We all do, but I don't say that aloud.

This girl seems to know exactly how to push my buttons.

And when.

And I was playing so nicely then.

Fuck this!

I let rip.

'Pick a number and get in line, sister,' I reply without thinking about it too much. 'Get over the poor me, *I've-had-such-a-shit-upbringing* speech. We've all been there. Ember has had to live with a …'

River cuts me off with a loud cough.

'I'm not looking for sympathy, you moron,' says Terra, staring me down. 'And I don't want yours … ever.' Fury burns in her eyes. 'You have always been the second pebble in my shoe.'

Ouch! I swear I see her eyes well up before she blinks it away.

River sniggers. 'This is getting us nowhere. 'Do you know where we can find the next Initiation?' His tone is much softer than mine.

'I know where we can find them all.' Terra looks straight ahead, her jaw set firmly.

'Great, now we're getting somewhere,' replies River around a tight smile. 'I suggest we head back to my place, regroup, and make our plans from there.

Ember shifts in her seat.

Twirls a strand of auburn hair around her finger. 'Hold up for a second, Terra. You said when the raven was …' Ember stalls before saying the word *killed*, 'that this would start a chain reaction.' There's a slight tremor to her voice. 'What kind of chain reaction, and how will it affect us?'

'It means that we are now being watched. Our every move is not only been closely monitored by Isis but by Ra-Mon too. So, breaking the curse, even though it wasn't done correctly, has exposed us.'

'Wait,' says River, butting in. That *gorgeous* furrow on his brow is back again. 'What do you mean wasn't done *correctly*?' He looks at me, and I shrug my shoulders.

'I've known about the ritual for years.' The light in her eyes fade away. 'It was downloaded to me from Gaia.' She takes another breath. 'The ritual, releasing me from Corax, was supposed to be performed using the branch of an Ash tree.' River crosses the room and sits on the corner of Ember's chair, listening intently. 'The Ash tree is critical to the First Initiation.'

The sadness in her voice isn't hard to miss.

She gathers herself, straightening her back and lifting her chin.

She is re-setting.

Going through the motions.

Going through learned behaviours of picking yourself back up when life threatens to drag you into those dark chasms we all try to avoid. Her lips press together and her hands are released from the tight balls that once sat in her lap.

'How?' questions River. 'There's something else, isn't there?'

Terra nods. The colour grey has found her cheeks. Has wrapped her up and drained her of every last shade. 'The ritual not only shielded us from watchful eyes but it has awoken every mystical creature in the universe.'

'*What*?' I cry out.

'Are you serious?' cries River, rising to his feet.

'Oh dear,' mutters Ember to herself.

'Fuck! When are we ever going to catch a break with this?' I say to no one in particular.

'It's going to make our job that much harder,' adds River.

'No shit!' I blast out.

'They'll be gunning for us now. Super! So, not only are we dealing with Ra-Mon, the most powerful immortal ever, so he can rule the earth the way he sees fit, *AND* defeat a couple of ancient gods and goddesses along the way, but now we've got a boatload of mystical beasts to contend with. PERFECT. This is just *perfect*!'

'Well, not quite us, more me.'

We all turn to look at Terra.

Her hands have begun to shake and if her body was made from ash, she would crumble into a million tiny pieces with one breath.

'They're after Gaia's powers. They want the power to know everything, past, present and future. Gaia is the bringer of life and death, and with these powers, any creature can create life, build an army and destroy anything that gets in their way.'

Ember lets out an exaggerated breath. River turns to her and rubs warm circles into her back. He squats beside her, takes her hands into his and kisses them gently. 'It's just one more bad guy, Em. We've been through worse. We'll get through this,' he says, his tone so warm and soft even I believe him.

'I'm sorry, everyone. I've failed you.'

My brain switches tracks … actually more like derails itself, the second Terra closes her mouth.

Hang on one freaking minute here… Those are *my* words. I failed that First Initiation, not Terra.

'It's not your fault.' I hear the words come out of my mouth, taste the tone which is uniquely sweet, my body language doing all the right things. I'm not surprised to see everyone gawk at me.

Although, I'm only looking at one person … wearing guilt so thick it could pass as makeup.

Ever so slightly, so slight you might not even notice, Terra's head angles a little to one side, her eyes penetrating every layer of my skin, diving into my muscles, anchoring in my bones. I don't think I've ever been looked at quite like that, like my whole body has been supercharged with plutonium.

'What would you know?' she spits. There's no doubt in my mind that she's fully aware of all of my inadequacies.

I swallow loudly.

So loudly I wonder if anyone heard it. Of course, she knows my past, present and future.

I deflect the question with a question. 'Why didn't you tell me about the curse. I would've taken better care of the bird.'

Terra grinds her teeth, sending a grating shiver up my spine. 'I did. I told you not to break the curse,' she snaps.

'But if I'd have known how serious it was …'

She slaps her hands against her thighs. 'Forgive me if I didn't trust you. You know you've only tried to kill me like a hundred times.'

Silence descends.

Natural silence, the kind I long for above everything else.

No thoughts …from anyone.

No inner monologue.

Eight long seconds of pure and unadulterated bliss.

Until …

'Is there any way to undo the damage?' asks Ember, shrugging her shoulder, a hint of hope in her voice. Terra turns her body away from me to face River and Ember.

'From my understanding, Ash trees are often described as the Tree of Life, you know like from the garden of Eden. They represent the foundation of humanity past, present and future, which is why Gaia said it needs to be used for the ritual. They live an incredibly long time, centuries even, and are robust, sturdy trees. They're also known for their healing abilities, and in mythology, can cross between Heaven and Hell. So, who knows … maybe there's a loophole, but I haven't discovered it yet.'

Ember slumps back into the chair.

'And I'm sorry to be the bearer of bad news, but that's the least of our problems. We have another, far more pressing matter to contend with …' We are all waiting … wondering … guessing. 'I'm not sure if you all know, but we're on the clock with these Initiations.'

'Since when?' I ask. I notice Hayley hanging in the doorway.

'Since always.' Terra's confused look morphs into disbelief as she takes in our surprised faces. 'I take it Isis never mentioned it.' Her eyes flick to River but she doesn't wait for his answer. 'It doesn't shock me though, she's always been a slippery piece of work.' The problem with someone who knows *everything*, is knowing they have all the answers, and yet you don't know if you're asking all the right questions.

River pipes up. 'She never said anything to me about a timeframe.'

'Figures,' says Terra, warding off a laugh. 'Isis was also known as the Moon Goddess. And one thing we know about the moon is, it's surrounded by illusion and deception. Everything that comes out of that whore's mouth is a lie.' Now there's no mistaking the fact that this isn't the first time Terra has encountered Isis.

'How long?' asks Ember. 'How long have we got?'

'A month,' answers Terra flatly before following it up with a tight smile.

'A *month*? Why?'

'Remember, Ra-Mon hasn't set this timeframe; Isis has. And from what I know of her, she'll have her own agenda, ensuring she's at the height of her power for a reason.'

'Why?' *Why, why, why*, is all I can think to say. She glares at me but doesn't say anything.

'Why is that, Terra?' River asks softly.

'I'm sorry, I can't tell you that. It's hard for me to say that to you, but trust me, I can't. Being the font of all knowledge comes with a heavy price, and because I know everything, it doesn't mean I can tell you anything you want to know. There are other players in this game. Others want to level our planet. Others that want to wage war on us or at the very least, listen in on every conversation to gain knowledge for their own benefit. Indulge me if you will, but a Grand Master wouldn't give away his next chess move before he makes it, would he now?'

River slowly nods his head. 'I understand. We all do.'

'We have until the next full moon; otherwise we'll not only feel Ra-Mon's wrath but Isis's too. And trust me, you do not want to be in her pocket.'

My recent conversation with Doc comes back to me – *River is already there, and now I might have accidentally dropped myself in there, too.*

However, there is something settling about not knowing the outcome, and for now, I feel that we have all said what we needed to say.

'If we leave now … we should make it home by dark,' I say, picking the words directly out of River's head. He nods his acknowledgement at me.

Terra and Ember rise simultaneously and that's when I turn to see the empty look on Hayley's face.

Her eyes ask me if last night meant so little to me? It didn't, I don't think. I do feel an obligation to her for helping me, and to be honest, I don't know what made me have sex with her. I certainly wouldn't put it down to a momentary lapse of concentration, like I usually would, because that's not what it was ... I don't think. The whole event is kind of foggy in my mind, but the residual high from it still lingers in my body. All I know is, this feeling inside is more powerful than anything I've felt before, where if I couldn't touch her, I'd go out of my mind. I wonder if this is what love is. And if it is, I don't want to leave her here. Plus, this underlying ache in my brain says she's meant to join us.

'I think Hayley should come with us too,' I blurt out. I watch as she takes in an exaggerated breath.

'Well, I don't,' snaps Terra promptly. 'I think it should be us four, like it is meant to be.'

River and Ember exchange glances, and Ember shrugs and pulls a face of *I don't know*.

I come up with the perfect answer. 'I think it's up to River. It is his house, after all.'

Terra and Ember both flick eyes to River, and he voices a very loud *thanks, dickhead* in his mind to me, which echoes in my head tenfold. And as an afterthought, he adds, *my gut instinct says she should join us.*

He sighs. 'It makes no difference to me,' says River, crossing the room to stand nearer to the kitchenette, closer to Hayley. 'You're welcome to join us, if you want, Hayley.'

Hayley squeals out her excitement.

Jumps at me, kissing me passionately.

Then blots the corners of her mouth.

I feel all eyes on me, as though they've peeked inside the back of my mind and seen us going for it last night. Now, left with messy hair and a guilty expression, River simply shakes his head as he downloads a bunch of silent expletives to me.

Hayley offers Ember a timid smile and glances over at Terra, whose eyes could rip flesh from bones in under ten seconds. Not meaning to, but I dive into River's mind to double-check that he's thought his decision through, and all I see is an image of him having sex with Iris. I bail out, quick as all hell, flick him a look of *what the* … which he looks extremely embarrassed about. *Don't mention anything to Ember*, he says to me in his thoughts.

'I'd love to come,' says Hayley, beaming at Terra which, in my opinion, goes on a little longer than it should.

Still in her zombie clothes, Terra snatches up the bag and heads off to the bathroom, slamming the door behind her.

'What's up with her?' asks Ember.

'Me,' says Hayley, her voice so soft, I hardly hear her. 'She hates me.'

'And me,' I chip in quickly.

FIFTEEN

THE end of our mini road trip is over as quick as that, leaving our journey back to River's house, quiet.

And tense.

River mucked about with the radio, repeatedly turning it on and off until Ember told him to leave it. And what little conversation there was, stemmed around what Wally might be cooking for dinner, or whether Doc would show up and give us some more insight. I didn't mention our little catch-up. Not sure why. I suppose I didn't want Terra to think I was snooping.

I ended up in the back of the car with Hayley and Ember. Terra had refused to get in the car until we were both as far away from her as possible, even though that was less than a metre. God! I hope this hate-hate relationship can move forward in some kind of positive direction soon or the next few months are going to be *fun*.

And, did I mention it was tense?

190

In fact, the air reeked of it.

Like someone had emptied a garbage bin at my feet and mixed it in with fish guts. The only way I could stop myself from throwing up all over River's posh upholstery was to take shallow sips, or wait for him to slow down so I could open the window a crack and let some fresh air in.

Totally disgusting!

We pull into River's driveway.

Time to face the music, River says in his mind, although I'm not sure what he's worried about; Wally will be chill as. In fact, he isn't the least bit surprised when he sees us dragging home another two girls. He politely bows and greets them, and then casually asks them if they have any food allergies or preferences.

Wally shakes Terra's hand. It's the first time I've seen her happy to see someone. 'I've been hanging out to meet you, Wal. I know so much about you; I feel like we're friends already.'

'We are indeed friends, young lady. Now, would you like to get showered and changed before dinner, or are you all ravenous?' He looks around at us all.

'I'd like to change first, Wal,' says Ember, 'if there's time.' She looks to River, who nods.

'Very good,' answers Wally, drying his hands on a tea towel tucked into the pocket of his trousers. 'Although, no longer than half an hour please, girls. This stirfry won't last any longer than that.'

'C'mon, Terra, I'll show you to your room,' says Ember as River and Terra take off upstairs.

It's good to be home … well …River's home.

'I'm going to give Hayley the tour,' I say to Wally as he makes his way into the kitchen. He waves his response at me, and I pick up Hayley's hand and lead her into the lounge room.

'Wow. I don't think I've ever been in a house this big or this fine before.' She trails her fingers across the back of a plump, cream sofa, looking around at everything. Her eyes are alight with wonder, her mouth forming a cute O at every little thing that catches her attention.

I stretch out on the sofa as she glides past the open fireplace. She stops and turns to me. 'You know, if you need me to go at any time, all you have to do is ask.'

I question where this has come from. 'Did someone say something to you? Was it Terra?'

She shakes her head delicately, innocently, her caramel curls swaying from side to side. 'No. I know how it feels to be in the way.'

'Let me reassure you,' I say, extending my hand out to her, encouraging her to join me. She meanders over, slowly, unsure of her own footsteps. 'You are not in the way.'

'Are you sure?' she says around a wobbly smile.

'C'mon, let me show you the rest of the house.'

We barely make it out to the lounge room when the doorbell rings.

I know it's Doc. He flicked me a casual heads up three seconds beforehand.

Wally gets the door.

'I'm glad you're all back in one piece,' says Doc. removing his cap and coat. Wally takes it from him and makes himself scarce. 'I guessed all the fireworks would be over by now,' he says with a smirk.

'*Guessed*? That's a laugh … Mr see-all-and-know-it-all,' I say over my shoulder as I retrace my steps back into the lounge room.

Doc takes the armchair closest to the fire as Hayley and I occupy one end of the sofa.

'It's much easier to keep tabs on you when you're altogether like this.' His brow creases, and he tries to rub out his frown with the palm of his hand. And we have an extra … how,' he pauses, leans forward, examining Hayley's face. A soft chuckle bubbles out his throat. 'Well, well, now this is interesting.'

Hayley smiles politely, and I'm about to ask him what *exactly* is so interesting when I hear the others coming down the stairs. They casually stroll in and plonk themselves down in the remaining seats.

They are all showered, although Terra is still wearing her old grey sweatpants and jumper. What kind of person refuses fresh, new clothes when they're offered to them? Hayley doesn't look bothered by it, so I shrug it off. Let her sit in filthy clothes if she wants.

Terra catches me looking at her and sneers, not just through her mouth … it comes from her eyes. I'd love to know where this deep hatred for me comes from. At least she looks semi-normal now, although she hasn't done a great job combing out the dreds. They're still clumpy, regardless that her hair is long enough to tickle the small of her back. And, because it's still wet, it seems much flatter like she got caught in the rain and hasn't had chance to brush it. I fear our happy little threesome has now turned into a horrid little foursome.

Terra glares at Hayley. 'I don't think *she* needs to be here.'

Hayley rises swiftly. 'It's all good,' she says to me, waving me back into my seat. She offers me a smile. 'You guys need to work this out by yourselves. I'll go help Wally in the kitchen.'

As she leaves, head held high, I spearhead a stare straight at Terra, who responds with a middle finger salute. My teeth grind. Jaw tenses.

'Now then, who is ready for round two?' says River, keen to defuse the situation. Tiredness settles in his eyes, … into his cheeks. No hint of happiness. No frown either, which is a first. I sit up, angle myself forward, trying to give the impression I'm interested in what he has to say. 'Terra says the Second Initiation, the Nymphus, isn't a person like we originally thought.'

'That narrows it down a bit,' I offer.

River carries on. 'So, we're not looking for a bridegroom.'

'Excellent.' The visions I'd had of turning up at a church and abducting some poor newlywed and torturing him until he cracked, bleed into thin air. I release a breath. 'What is it then?'

'Mithras called it a diadem, which is a sort of tiara or crown,' Terra informs us.

'A *crown*?' says Ember, 'please don't say we have to break into the Tower of London and pinch Lizzie's jewellery?'

I let out a laugh. 'Could you imagine …?' I'm still laughing long after the smiles have left everyone's faces.

'No, we don't have to do that,' Terra says to Ember with a friendly wink. 'I know exactly where it is.'

'That's a relief. And what about Falicon? And Tomas?' asks Ember. 'I thought they were high on our list of priorities. Isn't Tomas waiting for us?'

River offers her a sweet smile. 'Tomas will have to wait for the time being, I'm afraid. This is far more important.'

I agree.

'Just so you know, I'd rather go and pinch a crown from the world's most fortified location, risking life imprisonment, than face a creature from the Black Lagoon because that's all we've got to look forward to, meeting up with Tomas again.' I run my hands through my hair for no reason other than I want to. 'Finding a crown sounds a much safer option. Tomas doesn't exactly have a great track record of steering clear of mystical beasts, you know? And right now,' I glance quickly at Terra, 'the least of those we come across, the better.'

'Amen to that,' says Terra. 'However, finding our crown won't be a walk in the park either.'

I sift through everyone's thoughts, trying to pick up on a theme. Terra is deadpan again – no big news there. Ember mulls over the same question as I am, although River might be onto something. I casually shoplift his thoughts.

'What's this crown made of … *thorns*?'

River narrows his gaze at me.

I shrug my shoulders. '*What*? If you weren't going to say it, then I thought I would.'

'Yes, that's exactly what the crown is made of,' answers Terra, surprised.

River sniffs, holds back that smug, arrogant smile of his and says, 'what a guess.' He stares at me as though it should mean something.

'*And*?' I say to Terra. 'Let's go get it.'

River's eyes widen. 'Are you talking about *The* Crown of Thorns?'

I still have no idea what he's talking about, and it obviously shows on my face.

Terra pounces. 'Oh my god, you are so frigging dumb, Skye,' she snarls. 'There was only one person in the history of the world to wear a crown of thorns.'

Okay, it's penny dropping time again. 'You can't possibly mean the Crown of Thorns that Jesus wore during his crucifixion?'

'Well done. Everyone give Skye a round of applause.'

River sniggers.

This ganging-up shit, blows. 'I guess I'm the only one who didn't go to fricking Sunday School. Shit! We can't all be religious buffs and choirboys.' I stand to leave.

'Sit,' says Doc.

Since he's been here, he hasn't muttered a single word and yet one word is all it takes to level the room. It has the same effect as lightning striking a tree. 'Running from life's ups and downs when life doesn't go your way is no longer going to work for you, pup. Listen up. You might learn something.' Doc pushes his way to his feet with a groan, clears his throat, and takes up River's favourite position in front of the fire. 'First and foremost, lad, *you're* the only one who can retrieve the crown and destroy it.'

'He's right,' confirms Terra, a weary mask shadowing her face. 'The crown disappeared soon after the crucifixion. And according to the Akashic records, Mithras, the deity of the time, was contacted by Amun.

195

They struck up a bargain … no human or celestial being, be it a god or powerful entity, other than themselves, would be able to touch it *and* destroy it, else they would suffer the same fate as its previous owner.'

'I suppose because Skye is human and has Amun hidden away inside him, that he is exempt, right?' says Ember.

'Exactly. Humans can touch it but don't have the power to destroy it, and celestial beings have the power to destroy it but cannot *physically* touch it. Only Mithras and Amun can. Let me give you some backstory of how it all unfolded.'

'Go ahead,' says River.

'Sometime during the fourth crusade, when the Crown of Thorns was still in the possession of Mithras, it disappeared from Jerusalem. However, when Mithras …' she pauses and turns to Doc, 'maybe you might be the better *person* to explain it, considering you were there, and have firsthand knowledge.'

'Alright,' he says, taking a handful of beard and performing several downward stokes on it. 'It was around the time Christianity kicked in. Mithras became less of a deity because fewer people prayed to him.' He turns directly to Ember and River. 'Do you remember when we spoke of this last year?' They both nod. 'Mithraism ceased to exist from lack of prayer, whilst Christianity flourished. When this happened, Mithras and his power diminished, causing the Crown of Thorns to lose its protective shroud, making it vulnerable to all manner of creatures.'

'What happened after that?' asks Ember.

'It sat in a cave for a thousand years before it was discovered,' continues Terra. 'It was taken from Jerusalem to Constantinople in 1063, and finally ended up in King Louis IX's possession, in 1239. He even built a chapel to house it. Can you believe that? During its brief stay there, some of the thorns were broken off and given as gifts to those who married into his family. And yet, the crown renewed itself, restoring itself to its original glory.

'It has magical powers then?' interrupts River.

'Yes, in a sense, but not in the way that will help us. The thorns themselves date back even further than the crucifixion. In fact, they date right back to Adam and Eve sinning in the Garden of Eden.'

'It's true,' adds Doc.

'Thorns were thought to bring evil and a curse upon the world, and part of that curse upon humanity was, if I can quote "…cursed is the ground because of you; in pain, you shall eat of it all the days of your life; thorns and thistles it shall bring forth for you…" So the Crown of Thorns was not only to inflict pain on Jesus, it was also to mock him.'

'That's fascinating, Elvira. I'll sleep much better knowing that.'

'Skye,' whispers Ember, her eyes disapproving of me.

Unleash instant guilt.

'Don't you see? Roman soldiers took a cursed object and twisted it into a crown. I think if any of us knows about a curse, it's me.'

She has a point.

I take the bait. 'I assume this crown is in a chapel somewhere then?' I ask, trying to keep my tone in check and failing miserably.

'Actually, it's at Notre Dame,' answers Terra.

Paris …urgh!

The last place I want to go back to. 'Wasn't Notre Dame burnt to the ground last year?' I say, 'we could be totally out of luck.'

'Not totally,' says Terra. 'Two-thirds of the roof was destroyed. The rest, including a magnificent spire, fell onto the stone vault beneath. Somehow, miraculously, the Crown of Thorns survived.'

'Of course, it did,' I add sarcastically. 'I take it from that, the cathedral isn't open to the public?'

'Nope,' says Terra matter of factly. 'When has that ever stopped you before?'

I can't stop my lips from breaking into a smile. 'Was that a compliment?'

'No,' she snaps back.

'I think that was a compliment,' I say again.

Terra turns her lip up at me, although there is no *real* rage behind it.

'Enough you two,' says River. 'You two need to put away your toy swords and focus on what's important here.'

'Hear, hear,' chimes in Doc, leaning back into his chair, looking more like he's here for a social catch up than any divine inspiration. He coughs and raises his eyebrows at me, letting me know he heard me.

'Fine with me,' I say. 'When are we leaving?'

'Every flight is fully booked,' informs Wally, carrying a tray of drinks in and placing them on the coffee table.

'Even first-class?' I ask, sending River a sly wink.

'*Everything*,' replies Wally. 'I read in the paper there was talk of a strike or perhaps it's another one of *those* music festivals. Unfortunately, I could only get tickets for next Wednesday. It's all paid for, but you'll have to hang out here for a few extra days.'

'Can't you zip us there with your magic?' Ember says to Doc. 'You know, like you did when you took me to the desert.'

Doc chuckles. 'Sorry. No can do. I don't have the power for all of you.'

'Fine,' says River, 'I *suppose* a few days can't hurt.'

Hayley follows in behind Wally, phone in hand. 'In case you were interested, the crown is on display on Fridays.' Terra mumbles something under her breath that I don't quite catch. I don't miss the overly exaggerated eye roll either. 'And then when its not in use, it's stored at the back of the Cathedral in a container for holy relics.' Hayley flashes her phone at us to show a miniature picture of the inside of the cathedral. 'However, I suppose that doesn't really apply to you guys now,' she says, turning to face me. 'I guess you'll find your own special way in.'

'Thanks, Hayley,' I say, patting the seat next to me. She gingerly makes her way between the sofa and coffee table as though she is walking over glass, and sits beside me. She lets out a breath, and I put my hand in hers to show her my thanks. She beams at me, and I sense a slight shudder go through her body.

'I only want to help,' she says. 'I used to read the Famous Five books when I was younger and it kind of reminds me of what real friends can mean to you, and how they have your back.' Ember smiles graciously, and so does River. Terra grunts and takes off, drawing the panelled sliding doors behind her. 'Awesome Foursome, at least then,' she says and laughs.

'Sounds like Terra has some issues to work through,' says Ember. 'I might go and see if I can offer her some advice.'

'Good luck,' I add, but I don't think she hears me.

'And I'll finish washing those veggies,' says Hayley, following Wally back into the kitchen.

As usual, Doc evaporates before our eyes, leaving River and I to stare at the walls. His thoughts take him back to the crypt filling with water, and Ember's panicked cries for help.

'It's not even worth asking her to stay,' I say before he says anything. 'You can't protect her forever, you know, and asking Ember to remain here while you run headlong into danger isn't going to make her feel any more at ease. Anyone can see she'd cut off her hand than spend time away from you.'

'I know,' he says, sighing deeply. 'I have a horrible feeling about it this time.'

I'd be lying if I said I didn't feel the same. 'The stakes are higher, dude. That's all. We both know Ra-Mon is serious, and it's time *we* started to take it seriously.' The sound of those words on my tongue send a ripple of fear over my body.

It's not *just* serious for us.

It's serious for the whole world.

Everything rests on us, and at this very point in time, rests with me.

'I need some air,' I say, feeling the enormity of it bearing down on me. I take the stairs two at a time, to get my jacket.

It's raining again.

I can smell it coming through the vents.

I groan as I pass Ember's door and overhear my name mentioned.

I stop.

'Why do you hate him so much?' asks Ember. 'He means well. You just have to get to know him a bit more.'

'That's the problem,' replies Terra, 'I *do* know him, more than he thinks. I've spent the last ten years of my life around him, even hitching a ride on a cargo ship to be near him.'

I hear her crying.

'You have to talk to him. Explain to him how you feel. I'm sure he will be okay with it.'

Okay with *what*? I don't need her to explain anything.
> She hates me.
>> It's as simple as that.
>>> And, I don't particularly like her either.
>>> What's to explain?

'Hayley is no good for him. She's evil. Whenever she's around, I get this really bad feeling.'

I press further into the door and it squeaks. The second it takes Ember to yank open the door, I turn invisible. A nifty trick to have in your back pocket at times like this.

'Skye?'

I hold my breath.

She looks up and down the hallway before closing the door, although she leaves it open a crack this time. 'Please help yourself to my clothes too. I don't have many, but you can't go to Paris in sweatpants. And let's have another go at your hair.'

I'd love to be able to see the look on Terra's face, but the narrow slit in the door only shows me her shoulder and I don't want to risk Ember throwing a fireball at me if she suspects me listening.

'Thanks, Ember. It means a lot to me that we are friends. I've never had a friend before. And, I just wanted to say, I'm so sorry for what happened to you. I know everything *he* did to you.' There is silence. 'I've had to fight off my own share of creeps too, and it's no easy feat. So, I commend you on your bravery and for remaining true to you. Unfortunately, it changed me, and there is no going back.' There is no inner monologue from either girl.

I back away from Ember's door, retrieve my jacket and head out into the rain, wishing I'd never heard any of that conversation.

The night before we're due to fly to Paris, I lay in bed, wide awake. A tremor has found its way into my body that doesn't belong there, and doesn't want to leave; some kind of nervous energy that begs to be unleashed. If I had to guess, I'd say it has everything to do with Ember and Terra's conversation, and not the buzz of tonight's secret and very solo mission to Sheffield to get those damn diary pages from Iris.

The idea struck me as I said goodnight to everyone, and in true me style, there's nothing like leaving it to the last minute. And, no, I haven't thought it through properly.

But what's new, right?

Leaving for Paris tomorrow means it's now or never. I need to redeem myself in some way… especially in Ember's eyes. The disappointment in her thoughts these past couple of days has been the worst, and each time she catches me redhanded, she smiles apologetically, knowing I've heard every word. I hope that tomorrow will be a day of healing for her, and finally lay those demons to rest.

I check my watch.

I figure it'll take me an hour and a half to fly to Iris's place – stop for an hour to re-group, break-in, steal more pages from the diary, if not the whole damn book, power down for an hour and recharge – fly home and I should be back in time to leave for the airport.

Yes it's risky, and things could go drastically wrong, but I have to try.

I throw on a pair of black jeans and then layer a couple of t-shirts under my dark hoodie. Initially, the bubble of warmth from switching to flight mode is glorious, shutting out the cold. Unfortunately, it won't last long. The height I'm aiming for, minimising my flight time, means it will get frigging cold up there. I chuck on my beanie and gloves. A coat would be good, but I don't want to risk sneaking into River's room and borrowing one of his. Mine seems to have gone walkabout.

My room is warm and comfortable, and the thought of freezing my arse off doesn't send rockets of pleasure through me. Hayley stirs but doesn't wake as I tiptoe over to the window to open it.

Cold air rushes in and I brace up before throwing my legs over the edge of the window sill. I sit there for a second, and take a quick look back at Hayley sleeping. I'm pretty sure I can be there and back before she wakes.

I power up, slip out of the window and take off like some kind of Peter Pan leaving behind his Wendy.

Wind rushes up to meet me.

Any other time, this is the highlight of flying – ascension. That rush I can't explain because no one apart from me has ever flown before, as far as I know. The thrill of going from zero to a hundred, to a thousand kilometres an hour, if I want to, body buzzing with a unique flavour of electricity is almost better than an orgasm. That warm, cradling embrace that I feel amongst the clouds, regardless of how cold it is, basically feels like home, a place I feel accepted. Welcomed. Loved. To be honest, I'm not sure I want to ever give this up. To be honest, I'm not sure I'm ready to be … just me.

When I said it was cold, that is the biggest understatement of the year. I could tap in and warm the air around me, or more to the point, take the chill out of the air around me, but that takes up juice I can't afford, so I buckle in for a shitty flight across chilly old England.

Dark puffy clouds offer adequate cover for the trip so I don't have to use my invisibility. Whenever I needed to go to River's house, I'd fly on a night like this and like River's built-in sonar, my flying is guided by my own internal magnetic compass. I'm still a little old school and prefer visual landmarks to guide me, but I'm in a rush and sometimes the cloud is too thick to do that with. So, I use my own GPS.

Some eighty minutes later, fingers and toes so cold I could snap them off like broken twigs, I decide to drop down just below the cloud cover and take a look around. I can tell I'm getting closer because the air becomes smoggy, and I can taste the remnants of the Industrial Revolution in the air.

The most vulnerable time for me is ascending and descending – anyone could see me, so I switch on my invisibility as I drop down into an alleyway, several streets away from Iris's apartment. I always like to ground and walk for a while when I've been airborne for more than an hour. It helps with the general fatigue, but more so to get the blood flowing back into my legs and feet.

It's rained recently.

Puddles dot the alleyway, some large enough I have to jump over them. I haven't missed this place one bit, with its dreary old brick houses butted up so close you can smell what the neighbours are having for dinner, and the gloomy, overcast weather that seems to put everyone in a constantly shitty mood.

I head out of the alley and onto Taunton Street. The fish and chip shop is closed, which of course it should be at 1230am, although some of the local pubs are still kicking out that last of their punters for the night. It feels good to stretch my legs, and doesn't take long for the tingle of blood to trickle back into my toes.

I turn the corner to see the entrance to Iris's apartment.

I check in with myself – energy-wise.

I'm not as tired after the flight, which surprises and worries me too. However, I think I will take a ten-minute break just to be sure.

I haul up under the roofline of a vacant shop and go over in my head what I know of Ember's parents and what happened to them. I flick on my phone and go to my notes, checking out the screenshot I took from Iris's diary the last time I broke into her place. I know River told me not to keep a copy, but hey, daring is my middle name, and where would I be now if I couldn't check it. From what we understand, Iris was already watching Ember's foster father, I think she called him Mr Creepy for short, which makes me wonder … *why. Why* was she watching him? Ember's parents were killed in August 2018, and this particular diary entry I'm reading right now is dated April 2017. So, I need to find an entry before this date to determine Iris's motives if any, or if anyone contracted her to watch him. And yet, if I had to trust my intuition, it doesn't feel like a contract. From her diary entry, it sounded personal … to her.

The time to think has cleared my head, removed the sludge out of my joints. I feel good. I check my watch – it's 1245am. At this rate, I can be back in bed and catch a few zzzz's before the onslaught of the next few days.

Keeping to the shadows, I head towards Iris's apartment block, turn back a few times to make sure no one is around and flick on my invisibility button before I reach the door. I'm sure it would be a sight to see if anyone was watching – there one second, gone the next.

I activate my flight power and float upwards.

Being here twice before, I know exactly where to head, and less than thirty seconds later, I am standing in her apartment.

It's quiet … unusually quiet. What I mean is, there are no humping noises and that's very odd for Iris. For a second, I wonder if I'm in the correct apartment, but then I see her décor - her colour design of red, white and black, her modern furnishings and not an item out of place. Yeah, this is Iris's place alright.

Maintaining my invisibility, I search every room until I find her tucked up in bed … alone.

Immediately I shut down my invisibility. The added strain leaves my body in a big hurry and I feel immense relief … until.

'Who are you?' I hear Iris say.

I freeze.

To the carpet.

Not even daring to blink.

Silence.

That delicious silence I crave for, is all around me, except my blood is racing so fast I can hear my pulse pounding in my ears. Hear it inside my veins, threatening to burst.

I think about turning invisible again, but then stop.

Her eyes are closed.

I venture closer to her bed, taking each step with measured accuracy … so I don't trip … so I don't fuck up … to show how focussed I am.

She is fast asleep, albeit a bit irritable.

'Who *am* I?' she says.

She must be having some wild dream.

I need to do what I came here to do and get out. It's then I see my muddy footprints on her luxurious white carpet. That's certainly going to freak her out when she wakes, but I can't think about that right now.

I backtrack out of the room and make for her study, knowing that was where I located her diary before.

Jackpot!

I'm astounded at how bloody precise she is. I find her desk has been left the exact same way as before - two white pots positioned next to each other, one with pens, all the same colour, one with pencils, all sharpened to the exact same length, and a lined notepad sitting neatly alongside. An elegant looking desk lamp, not the suspect ones you get from Home Bargain Basement, but a real classy one from Harrods, is positioned in the middle of the desk, and a new glass... waiting for a refill.

And, of course, her diary.

I want to be thorough this time.

I have as long as I need.

No need for hurried screenshots.

No mistakes.

No distractions.

I thumb through the pages, locating the entry I took back in April 2017, and start to work backwards. It's still written in French, but again, I am looking for keywords. She always refers to Mr Creepy as a disgusting slug, so that, and obviously Ember's name, is what I'm looking for.

And then I find something.

February 15th 2017, it mentions *La limace dégoûtante,* the very word I'm looking for. It's on three consecutive pages, and I line up my phone, and snap each page. I then scroll through each page checking they are legible and clear enough to translate.

A high-pitched, panicked scream from the bedroom startles me so much I drop the book.

I can't breathe.

I can't move.

Blood feels like it's stopped pumping in my body. Congealed into thick lumps. Strangling my heart.

'Who am I?' she screams out. I hear panting and the sound of ruffling bedsheets.

She's not having a good night.

Not taking any chances, I hold my position. The last thing I want to do is bang into her as she stumbles out of bed to get a drink of water. Better still, she'd probably go for a scotch.

Quiet again.

I pick up the diary and lay it back in the exact same spot, making a minor adjustment to set it square to the edge of the desk,

I release my breath; confident she has gone back to sleep and continue with my investigation. I thumb through to the last entry. I'm surprised to see it isn't in French. It's not in English either, but some weird kind of code. Man, this is one fucked-up woman. Talk about paranoia at its finest – she *definitely* wouldn't want anyone reading this.

I take a couple of snaps of them.

The remaining three entries in the book have been scribbled down, the last one dating more than a month ago. Again, very weird! And totally out of character for someone so meticulous and habitual –all her other entries are either weekly, or at least every four to five days.

And that's it.

I'm done.

With that, I hightail it out of there.

I end up back in my bed by 4am, knackered, cold, and thankful for the body of a warm-hearted girl to cuddle up to. I only stopped once on the other side of Birmingham for a quick breather and recharge before continuing.

But I did it.

Nobody is any the wiser. And for the first time in my life, I completed a task successfully and feel pretty proud of myself.

SIXTEEN

PARIS.

Spring is here, although you wouldn't know it. March, generally one of the warmest months of the year back in Oz, is barely reaching double digits on the continent. The sky has all the hues of a washed-out blue paintbrush with clouds if you can even call them that, flat to the sky and very unobtrusive. The sun is shining, *just*, which is a big plus, and clearly a secret to England, although people do seem to be coming out of hibernation to sit outside in cafes and parks and soak up the atmosphere of one of the most romantic and extravagant cities of the world.

It's great to be back … NOT!

Familiar grey buildings of immense proportions crowd around us as we hurtle through the noisy traffic to our hotel. It's a sombre reminder of the last time we were here and how we'd almost lost Ember.

Police sirens and car horns double in effort the closer we get to Notre Dame, and brave cyclists and even gutsier pedestrians chance their luck at getting across the road in one piece. River's suggestion that we choose a smaller, less known hotel, and something in plain view of the cathedral as a low profile option, to me, is freaking ridiculous. He insists on trying to keep the entire operation more covert, but like I keep telling him, we aren't dealing with assassins or the CIA, but immortals that can see what room we are hauled up in. As usual, my words float over his head as though my opinion isn't needed.

Yesterday, I did manage to corner Terra for a blink of her time to show her the book - Peri Phuseôs tôn Ontôn, and, like the rest of us, the book flipped over to her specific page the instance she touched it. A page that only she could read. I asked her several times what it said, but she just huffed and sighed like it was no big deal. She promptly closed it and handed it back to me, not murmuring a single word. Since then, I've tried as many as fifty times to break through the barrier into her thoughts, but she's a vault and well-trained in the art of feeling and thinking nothing. It has become a new crusade for me to know what she read and more to the point …what she thinks of me. And in the last eight hours alone, she's barely met my gaze, and when our eyes do eventually meet, they are loaded with hatred and disgust. I must've done a real number on her, yet when I search my memory, nothing other than the shooting mishap sticks out. It could be that, I suppose, I just get the feeling down low in my gut it's something more. I certainly can't imagine the horrors she's had to endure, which does get my tick of sympathy, but we all have scars. It does, however, make my life seem insignificant and rather boring compared to what she's had to endure … her *and* Ember … and I try to keep that thought at the back of my mind every time she throws me one of those looks that could wipe out an entire civilisation.

While we're on the topic of getting shit done, I know Doc told me to do this a few weeks back, but with the agenda we've had, this has been the first chance I've had to catch up on my homework. Acquiring the rest of Iris's diary, even though I haven't translated it yet, was number one on my list, and I'm relieved it's over with. I also made a concerted effort today to try and communicate with Amun. I've tried pressing every button and tweaking every channel … and nothing. He is refusing to budge an inch, and I have no idea why. Shit … I must be the worst Superhero in the world!

River nudges me in the ribs.

We're here.

We finally check into the hotel, the lobby the size of River's bathroom back home.

'*Nice*,' I tell him. '*Ree-al* classy.' He discreetly steps backwards onto my foot until I dig him in the ribs with my thumb. 'Dick.' Ember and Terra shake their heads at us.

I leave him to check us in, and haul the luggage over to the lift and press the button.

There is a scraping, metallic sound that no elevator should ever make. The bottom drops out of my stomach when the doors open. 'I'm not getting in there,' I say, failing miserably to stem the panic from my voice. 'I'll take the stairs.'

River walks over. 'Good luck. There aren't any, and we're on the third floor. So, unless you're gonna fly, I suggest you get in.'

'I-I can't …' The back of my neck is slick with sweat. The lift is barely big enough for one person if you turn sideways, and a piece of luggage.

'Pussy!' says Terra, picking up her's and Ember's bag and then gesturing for Ember to get in. She follows in behind her. The two girls are nose to nose, yet it doesn't seem to worry either of them. The cramped elevator doesn't look like it's going to carry this much, and Terra

210

ends up shoving her bag out with her foot before the doors close.

'I didn't know you were claustrophobic,' says River, turning to me, surprised.

'I'm not. I just don't like small spaces.'

'Yeah, claustrophobic,' repeats River, one eyebrow raised. The doors reopen a minute or two later, and like the magic trick it is … it's empty inside. 'It's either eaten them or the girls have made it to their floor. Get in,' he says to me, but I wave for Hayley to take it. She too doesn't seem put out by it.

She steps in … the doors close, and we wait.

And then it's back again.

This time, it rattles the instance I step in. There are no mirrors inside, only wooden panelling with posters of the Eiffel Tower. 'You're really struggling with this, aren't you?' he says, a longed-for smile ready to burst at any moment. He's enjoying this way too much and I go to step out as he steps in.

I say nothing.

Only hold my breath.

A trickle of sweat streaks down the side of my face, and I reach up to wipe it away.

The doors close, and it jolts upwards.

Instinctively, my hands fly out to steady myself. One hand finds a poster, which suffers a major tear, the other smacks River straight across the chest.

'Watch it,' he groans.

'Do you hear that? That's not normal. That noise? Lifts aren't meant to sound like that. It's like Wolverine trying to peel back the doors to get in.' Terra's duffel bag falls against me after an exceptionally jarring bump, and I'm just about to turn invisible and bail out of this hellhole when the third-floor button turns red.

The suspension feels way too bouncy to be certified as safe as the lift stops, and the fact that it hasn't plummeted to the ground in a smash of blood and stray limbs is still not very comforting.

I wedge my foot into the door and slide out the luggage.

'See,' says River sarcastically. 'Safe as houses.' I want to educate him on the hurricanes we get back home, the devastation left behind and the fact that houses are far from safe, but I can't be bothered. 'There's no such thing,' I mumble back instead.

The room that River and I share is no bigger than the reception area downstairs. There are two single beds, a white painted dressing table that wouldn't look out of place in a beach house, and a tiny ensuite that you can barely step inside without having the door brushing against your back. The wall behind the beds is a collage of black and white photographs of Parisian living. There is a balcony overlooking Notre Dame, though. But again, there's only room enough for one person. In my opinion, the French are either a very small race or very lonely.

River throws his bag onto the floor. 'I'll go drop this off to the girls,' he says, picking up Terra's bag.

'I still don't see why I couldn't share with Hayley and you with Ember.' Ember had suggested bunking in with Hayley because Terra wanted a room to herself.

'You heard what Em said. Terra will feel like a fifth wheel.'

I shake my head. 'Whatever.'

For as small as our room is, the ceilings are extraordinarily high, evident by how long the curtains are at the balcony window. I draw them back, inviting more warmth and light into the room. The gold-coloured paint has almost completely peeled off the door handles and it takes a considerable force to prise open the narrow glass panelled doors. I lean my shoulder into it as River strolls back in. He huffs and falls backwards onto his bed.

I step out onto the balcony.

The cool breeze embraces me, plays in my hair, caresses my face. I close my eyes for a beat, just to enjoy it, to savour its warmth, its touch, that place I call home, before I come crashing back to reality, bringing with it all its problems.

I glance down at the park below, alive with school children in uniforms of olive green and light blue. Their shrieks of laughter as they skitter around several street performers doesn't ease the fear that, inch by inch, has been growing inside me.

I lift my gaze to the reason we came here – that majestic stone lady who's seen better days. That ominous feeling of dread taps on my shoulder and steps onto the back of my shoes as I look across at Notre Dame, the front of her face unharmed and yet the scaffolding clearly visible from the sides and roof.

That nervous energy is back too.

I feel it nipping at my knees and thighs, begging to be used. I could finish this all so easily, so quickly. And with the newly found confidence, from my last snatch and grab, this should be a piece of cake.

And, to top it off - I have a plan. Locate the crown, perform a small pyre to dispose of it, and hey presto - Second Initiation done and dusted.

Mind made up.

I'm going.

I step back into the room to see River still laying on the bed, his hands behind his head, eyes closed. He's kicked off his shoes.

'I'm ducking out for a bit,' I tell him.

'Can't it wait?' he asks. 'I thought we could all meet up for a spot of lunch and work out a plan. Ember just messaged me with some news.'

Shit! I'm all psyched up … *and* I have a plan, I want to say, but don't. I suppose there isn't any hurry. Notre Dame isn't going anywhere. 'Sure, I guess.'

We find a little café a few doors down from the hotel, and contrary to popular opinion, I've come to my own conclusion that the French really are a cultured lot. I could definitely get used to the freshly ironed white tablecloths and shiny knives and forks. The neatly pressed napkins are fastened with a single piece of ribbon. The smell of freshly baked bread at everyone's table. The bottles of wine encased in little wicker baskets. It's a real contrast from eating out of takeaway tubs, using plastic cutlery, or chowing down on whatever you've thrown in the esky like we do back home. This is the good life, and I feel as though I've found my people at last. What can I say, I'm a snob on a dollar a day budget.

We tuck ourselves away into a corner.

'Listen,' says Ember, keeping her voice low. 'The crown isn't at Notre Dame anymore.' She takes a sip of her coke. 'The lady at reception mentioned all Notre Dame's antiquities have been moved to Le Louvre.'

'Into the safe,' chips in Terra.

'Shit!' I blurt out.

They all turn to me, and each have their own responses – Em tilts her head. Terra rolls her eyes. River blows out a breath. Hayley is the only one on my team and gives me a cute smile and a wink.

'However,' continues Ember, 'she did say that the Crown of Thorns will be on show at a *Veneration* Ceremony at some church, not far from here. Maybe we could intercept it on the way, or during the ceremony?'

'When?' I ask.

'Good Friday,' Ember replies.

I shake my head. 'That won't work.'

'Why's that, Einstein?' asks Terra rudely. There's a know-all smirk on her face I would love to rub out.

'Because Good Friday is two weeks away and in case you've forgotten, *we* or more to the point, *I*, have one lunar month to complete these Initiations …remember?' I tap my temple. 'Otherwise, River is toast.'

If smoke could come out of anyone's nostrils right now, it would be Terra's. A ghost of a smile finds my lips, and I sit back in my chair, arms crossed behind my head and revel in this small victory.

Terra's eyes become shiny white daggers.

'Bit risky anyway,' adds River, still glancing over the menu. 'Even if we could hang this out till Good Friday, it means we'll have to go like a cut-cat to finish the rest of the Initiations, and I'm not sure that will leave us enough time.' He scratches his slightly stubbled jaw. 'Breaking into Le Louvre isn't exactly a walk in, walk out robbery.'

'I agree with River,' says Terra. 'And the last thing we need, is for every copper in the world to be looking for us. Because that's what it will be. We're not exactly nicking a bag of sweets here, are we?'

'True,' says Ember. 'Then how are we going to get it?'

I'm sitting here, listening to them chat. Le Louvre could be the ultimate heist - the bank job of all bank jobs. 'I could get it.' Their faces show a vote of no confidence. 'It would be easy. Turn invisible. Walk through walls. Nick the crown. Easy.'

'Not so easy,' says Terra, her once vibrant green eyes suddenly transformed into slimy green swamp water. 'Did you know there are dozens and dozens of crates of fake crowns in that safe?'

A frown pinches my forehead. 'And you know this because …?'

'I've seen it.' In a flash, her emerald eyes light up …pierce right through me. My heart skips a beat.

'*You've* seen it? *When*?'

'Believe me, I know. The room has eight cameras and the room is heat sensitive. The floor is also pressurised so you can't stand on it, so you'd have to be either floating or invisible. Trust me, your power would max out before you even got through the first five crates.'

'I could brainwash them into letting me take it. Like I did with River's ex-stalker chick.' The words are out before I've had a chance to realise their impact. I should have said, miserable Meryl but my brain malfunctioned. River calls me a string of profanities in my head as Ember glares first at him and then at me. 'I'm sorry,' I mouth to him, my face wincing under the apology.

'Again, that won't work. You might be able to get five or six people to believe you, but you will still be gassed to get out of the safe in one piece.'

'And you know this because …'

Terra chokes back a laugh. 'I know you, Skye. I know what you're capable of and what you aren't. I know the strength of your powers …' she trails off.

My shoulders become heavy, dropping in submission. 'What do you suggest then?'

She shrugs. 'Frankly, I dunno. I was hoping, *together*, we might come up with something.'

'Great.'

So much for planning.

I still think my way is better.

Sure, I might fly by the seat of my pants, but sitting here with our thumbs up our arses, totally blows. Nothing is being done. *Doc*, I yell out in my head. *We could really do with a hand here*. No reply comes back.

Typical!

We finish up lunch in near silence. Hayley said less than ten words the entire hour, and strolling back to the hotel, she whispers to me, 'I know you said you wanted to go for a walk, but I'm feeling a bit tired. Do you mind if I go back to the hotel and have an afternoon siesta?'

Her face is pale, her posture wilting slightly. 'Are you sure?'

'Positive. You should still go. Go get some fresh air into your lungs. Go stretch your wings.' She giggles.

I walk her back to her room, and she lightly kisses my lips. I could quite easily spend the afternoon in bed with her, but before I get the chance to ask, she politely closes the door on me.

I head to our room.

River is already there.

'I'm going to do some sightseeing,' I say to him, switching out my light hoodie for something a little warmer.

216

'Cool. I need a shower anyway,' River mumbles, diving through his bag. 'Although, don't be too long. I don't want to have to come looking for you.' There's a look on his face I know all too well and the words in his head are an exact match – *I don't want a repeat of what happened to Ember*.

'Chill,' I tell him.

His face creases. 'Can I ask you a personal question before I go?' I'm not sure if I should, not when I've sifted through his thoughts already, but the words are out before I can take them back.

River arches one eyebrow. 'Depends on *how* personal.'

I plunge right in. 'Is it … *easier* for you, now that Nereus is gone?' There's a legitimate reason for my question. Lately, his internal monologue seems more focused on the dreaded *urge* returning than what is currently at stake – hence why the shower is calling to him.

River makes for the door. Then stops. It takes a whole ten seconds before he finally turns and walks back to the dressing table. He drags his hand across his chin and up his face. I know it's a tough question for him to answer.

He props one of his arse cheeks on the edge of the dressing table. 'It's complicated,' he begins. He buries his head into his hands and slowly peels them away, combing his fingers back through his hair. There's another pause. He looks me straight in the eye. 'Initially, it felt awful. I felt empty, like I had to get to know myself all over again. That sounds weird, doesn't it?'

I shake my head. 'Not at all. And I'm sorry to eavesdrop on your thoughts, truly I am. You know I can't stop it. But the urges are …?'

'*Were* under control for a while,' he interrupts. 'It's easier now with Ember and I being *together* … and Nereus is no longer driving it. But, the last few days … '

Darkness descends, the light from his eyes is snuffed out, revealing that haunted expression from back at Iris's place. 'I think the blood is changing me.' I thought as much. 'In fact, I'm sure it is. I don't feel the same as I did. I put on a brave face for Ember's sake because I know she worries like mad. The problem is, I can feel it inside me, trying to corrupt those parts of me that want to do the right thing. It's like poison every time I swallow.' The aqua blue of his eyes disappears, leaving behind still, glassy millponds. 'Can I be honest?'

I nod. Here it comes.

'The first thing I wanted to do when I saw Hayley was …' River pauses, his teeth clenching, 'well, you know. I haven't had it that strong in weeks.' He gazes out of the window. 'It's better today. Nothing a shower won't fix.' His mind goes off on a rant about how he's choosing not to be with Em during these times because the impulses are marred with blood magic.

I offer a commiserating smile. 'Wish I could say I was that strong. There's something about her, isn't there … something so different from other girls …?'

River's head spins sharply to face me, his eyes glance over my chest, shoulders, arms and legs as though he's looking for a clue. 'Don't do anything stupid. She seems like a nice girl.'

'Yeah, she is nice, and no offence, stud, but you're the last person to talk about how to treat girls.' I know I'm out of line, his tight jaw tells me I am, and that he wants to fire something back. To his credit, and our friendship, he doesn't. Instead, he walks to the bathroom and shuts the door. I suppose some labels are not worth arguing about.

I return my gaze to the open window.

I need to blow off some steam, and have nothing to lose by acquainting myself with Milady. And, I would rather fuck up on my own than have an audience around to watch me repeat the failures of my past.

I'm about to leave when the bathroom door opens. 'Don't do anything stupid, okay?' He then promptly closes the door. When the shower has been cranked right up, I slip around the door, hold my breath in the elevator and make my way across the road to the huge cathedral.

Situated on a small island in the middle of the Seine, sits a humongous stone structure. Two rectangular towers climb towards the heavens … way more impressive, in her own right than Chartres Cathedral, but what would I know. I've only been to two cathedrals in my life. Today, the brickwork is more yellowy than grey, courtesy of the overcast day, altering her true colour. Apart from twenty-eight stone figures looking down upon three magnificent carved archways, her most obvious feature is the immense circular stained-glass window positioned directly above.

It's impressive if I do say so.

I cross the Pont au Double, a wide footbridge over the Seine. Flocks of tiny birds twitter in the trees above me, mingling with the accents of many passers-by. An old woman, sitting on a park bench, dressed in a dark green coat and matching hat, eyes me curiously as though she knows the ins and outs of my flimsy plan. I pay her no mind and head for the forecourt in front of Milady. Thankfully, the forecourt is still open to the public, however, a menacing fence has been erected around the whole cathedral.

First minor setback …for the average human.

White makeshift tents have been set up in front of the cathedral's three stone archways on the other side of the fence.

Again, simple enough to navigate.

I know what I have to do.

Under the cover of a wide, leafy tree, I shift to invisibility and walk through the wire fence to stand at the foot of the most famous cathedral in the world. I'm expecting to see teams of scientists and historians, architects and archaeologists – people in suits, and men in overalls swinging off the sides of the scaffolding, but then realise it's Sunday and they're probably all at home watching the tennis. Several well kitted-up security guards, or they could be federal police from the artillery they're packing, converse in low voices on the east side of the building.

Without waiting for permission, I mount the ten or so steps and head inside.

As far as my limited knowledge of cathedrals go, I'm expecting a cold, smelly, dark, musty church, with the strange scent of dust and candles, plus the comfort of a soft and ambient energy - I got that last bit from the brochure I swiped at reception.

I am wrong on all accounts.

According to the brochure, before the fire, there were rows of wooden benches, trying to take shelter beneath fifteen-metre arched pillars. There were tombs with stone dudes lying on top, clutching swords or hands clasped together in prayer, and dark, chilly corridors for parents to lose their kids in. Now, it's a near-empty shell of rubble and carnage and heavy-duty canvas drop sheets. The carcass of one of the oldest gothic cathedrals now stands before me, gutted and without glory.

I walk beneath the arches, dodging rock chunks, occasionally gazing up at the massive hole in the roof. For a second, I think I see someone standing up there, but it must have been a trick of the light. I keep watching, waiting, but it seems only pigeons are out to enjoy what little sun there is.

I head towards the back of the cathedral …where shadows become pitch black and devils dwell, to the place Hayley mentioned where the Crown of Thorns was once kept. And because the large front doors are closed and possibly locked, who knows, I feel confident enough to turn off my invisibility. The moment I become solid, the immediate fatigue from Amun's power vanishes.

I continue on with my search.

The stain-glass windows throw a little light my way as I complete my first lap. I realise the crown isn't here, but

I keep getting this feeling that I've been drawn here for a reason.

'Come to pray, my dear.'

I swing around, heart in my throat, eyes searching every rock, every shady corner.

I don't see anyone.

My first thought … is ghosts. *Please don't let it be ghosts,* I murmur under my breath. This place is old enough to house more than its fair share.

'Not ghosts,' says the voice.

'Who are you?'

I've become a confused compass that won't stop spinning. Spinning in every direction trying to find the owner of the voice … the voice of an English woman.

'Where are you?'

'I'm here,' answers the voice.

'Show yourself,' I shout.

Something rustles behind me.

I spin around so fast, dizziness slaps me in the face, almost taking my legs from under me. I try to shake it off, but nausea takes over, dropping me to my knees. I seem to be at the mercy of someone's childish game - like something Terra would do. 'I said, show yourself, you coward.' I clutch my stomach as a deep ache grinds inside me.

'Games, games, games. We love to play.'

It can read my mind. I don't have to be a genius to work out it is supernatural. I slowly get to my feet.

That's when I see it.

Lurking in the shadows …a figure.

Wearing a dark green coat and matching hat, carrying something the size of a dinner tray. 'Hey, I know you,' I yell out, remembering the old woman from the bench. 'How did you get in here?' She doesn't turn around. 'Wait,' I shout out, but she keeps on walking. My instincts tell me to follow her as she ambles along in slow, shuffling steps towards the north tower.

I race, the best I can, from the east side to the west side of the cathedral, confident I can catch up with the old duck before she disappears from sight.

I've never been more wrong.

She must be wearing rollerblades or something because, by the time I reach a set of stone stairs in the far corner, she's vamoosed.

I peer up the spiral stone steps before doing one final sweep of the area. When I'm satisfied she's definitely not down here, I grab hold of the black handrail and pull myself up the uneven white steps two, sometimes three at a time, convinced I'm going to run into the back of her at any moment.

The first tier of steps, approximately three hundred at my last count, brings me to a dark terracotta-coloured security door that has been propped open. Whether by fate or accident, I'm grateful.

I chance a quick look inside.

It looks safe enough.

There's a grey counter where you can purchase tickets directly to my right, with brochures, postcards and souvenirs still left on display covered in a thick layer of dust. And at the back of the room are two long reception like counters covered in drop sheets.

I glance up.

This room must be close to a hundred feet high, the ceiling, carved into an elaborate octagonal shape. I have to give it to the French – they might know a thing or two about style. The lean-to, that Dad and I threw up a few years ago, barely stayed upright. Yet the sophistication of this makes me remember my dream of becoming a carpenter. Carved archways and ornate pillars break up the flat whiteness of the walls, and as my eyes travel upwards, more arched, stain-glass windows, outlined in coloured glass, hover regally above me, letting in ample amount of light.

I get lost in the awe of the place and, for a moment, forget that I'm still in pursuit of the spook and not here to sightsee.

One thing I am sure of … I'm in here alone - the shifty old cow has definitely given me the slip.

My patience is ragged.

And so is my breath.

I wrench open the door to my left, the only other way in or out, and the sweetness of the fresh air hits me. Soothes me.

No dust.

Too high for car fumes or pollution.

Just sweet, fresh, clean air.

I take in a breath and then another. It revitalises me. Clears my head.

I re-group.

Before me, is a stone walkway. Actually, now that I'm looking at it, I recognise it as the bridge that connects the north tower to the south. A steel cage has been constructed overhead to prevent anyone from falling or jumping.

It's the best ride in the park.

Tiny hairs on the back of my neck stand up as a cool shiver pays my spine a visit. Other than being purposely lured into this modified chook-run, my initial thought is …I'm being watched …evaluated. There's only one *person* I can think of.

'Amun,' I whisper.

SEVENTEEN

SILENCE.

That's all I hear.

It's weird!

Maybe my intuition is off.

Stepping out onto the stone footbridge, I half expect it to crumble beneath my feet, it looks that old. I peer over the side, examining the forecourt below. Miniature figures are going about their business, and I quickly realise they'll be able to see me. I flick on my invisibility and half run, half walk between the two colossal towers. I don't bother to check if the door to the south tower is locked or open, I simply zip straight through. I'm faced with a similar room to that in the north tower, except for one very distinct difference - the subtle aroma permeating the air. I've smelt this once before, back in the labyrinth in Chartres, and mistook it for dust and acid and the balms used in the cathedral, but I know better now. And even though today, my heightened sense of smell detects chocolate and burnt honey, cinnamon, roses and ash, they both leave the same unmistakably unique taste of pink marshmallows, aka the sweet stench of magic.

Once I have the initial ingredients, it's easy enough to track, and seems to be coming from yet another spiral stone staircase in front of me.

I launch into the next flight of stairs, going as fast as my wobbly legs will carry me. It would seem obvious to power up and fly, but that dread I felt back at the hotel … that unease still lingering in my muscles, forewarns that my power is meant for something more than a joyride and easy access. An internal voice, of sorts, warning me to be fully loaded and ready to pack a punch.

I'm puffing by the time I clear the top step. And, as anticipated, old Granny Green has done a Harry Houdini on me.

The uppermost balcony of Notre Dame is pretty similar to the last walkway I was just on, except to say the steel cages have been removed, and the panoramic splendour of Paris is spread out before me.

I tilt my head back, inviting the wind to play in my hair, to cool my red face, drenched in sweat. I forget for a second what I'm doing up here until I sense I'm not the only one admiring the view. The entire rooftop is littered with hunched stone gargoyles, some ready to take flight. A collection of them are perched on the balcony ledge, peering down at the city, horns protruding from their foreheads and long goaty beards, seemingly frozen in time. A number of them look like eagles. A few, are part men, part beast. Some have grotesque, agonised faces and long talons for toenails, whilst others crouch in crevices and in archways.

That sugary tang of magic suddenly saturates the air around me. 'We're not in Kansas anymore, Toto,' I whisper into the wind.

'Finally,' says a voice.

This time, there is no shiver up the spine.

No ghostly presence of old English ladies. And definitely no need to spin around to catch the owner of this very distinctive voice off-guard either.

This voice is internal.

'Amun?'

There is no answer.

'For fuck sake, I know it's you, dude. You wanna throw me a lifeline here? I am the one shielding your sorry arse, you know?'

Still nothing.

A pigeon lands on one of the gargoyles heads. It coos down to me. I lift my chin and glare at it. 'This is serious. We're in *real* trouble this time.'

I wait … hoping.

'Fuck! As usual, Skye, it's all left to you,' I huff under my breath.

The pigeon takes off and flies onto the wing of the next gargoyle – an ugly looking brute with fangs and bulging eyes. 'You use your power too recklessly,' says Amun. There is a harsh tone to his voice.

I thump my chest hard. 'Reckless or not, at least I've got the balls to stand and fight. You're hiding in the shadows when you should be, I don't know … training me?'

'You want *training*?' The voice vibrates out of my pores.

At last. 'Yes!' I stand, poised, looking to the skies, to the ground, speculating where my first lesson might come from.

I don't have to wait long.

The sound of stone grinding against stone sets my nerves on edge.

Then stops.

I grit my teeth together.

The sound begins again, a little louder this time, and my initial thought is that the building is about to give way, and I'm going to be taught some cool flying trick I didn't know existed.

226

I glance down at my feet.

The ledge looks stable enough. No dangerous, see-through cracks or holes forming.

I'm confused. The grating gets louder still, closer somehow that I can actually feel the sound screeching and scraping across my teeth. Then darkness descends over me - too sudden to be weather-related.

I glance up.

'What the hell,' I scream out as a scaly grey beast hovers over me. The neck of the closest gargoyle is slowly rotating, twisting until it's looking right at me. It rolls its bulbous, gritty eyes in my direction, the corners of its hanging maw lifting into a sinister smile.

'You call this training?' I yell out to Amun. 'A tad unfair, don't you think?'

'How better to prepare you, than coming face-to-face with a real-life gargoyle.'

Real and *life* aren't words that come to mind when I think of gargoyles. 'Fine,' I growl between my teeth.

The thing is *hideous*.

It looks more like a hound from Hell than a gargoyle. Its hunched-over body is grotesquely demon-like with its bony vertebrae poking through skin, if it had skin. It slowly straightens its back as though it has woken from the longest sleep. The sound of makeshift bones crunch and echo around us as the reptilian creature pushes itself upright from its powerful, muscular arms until it's fully erect.

No word of a lie, it must stand close to seven feet tall, and even though this beast has no legs, it somehow doesn't detract from how lethal it appears, and what kind of damage it can do. The strange thing is … I don't recall them being this big before they were given Amun's magic fairy dust.

And then I get it.

'Have you super-sized this chunk of masonry on purpose?' A gigantic claw flexes, inches from my face, each digit tightening and contracting, turning my limbs to jelly. I half expect it to howl as it throws its head back in an almighty stretch, an arched horn protruding from between a pair of erect ears.

The water in my mouth evaporates even before I swallow, and my body becomes one giant, trembling, internal earthquake.

'I may have exaggerated certain features.'

'*Certain features*? You've created a monster, Dr Frankenstein.'

Of course, there's no answer.

I am about to live my worst nightmare, except it's daylight. And my eyes are open. And this is real.

This isn't going to be an easy victory. Still, with no game plan in place, I tell myself, I've got this.

In order to gain a better vantage point, I power up to hover above it, except my legs won't move. They've become two solid blocks of concrete embedded into the stone. I grit my teeth and push off hard, only managing a few feet off the ground before being suctioned back to the stone ledge.

'What the …'

I try my invisibility power this time, which flickers on and off like a faulty light bulb before exposing me back to my human form.

Frustrated and impatient, the gargoyle flares its nostrils. My blood freezes as a foreboding smirk creeps across his shaley grey face.

'You wanted training?' says Amun. 'You are, how do they say in your world, about to learn defensive arts 101.'

'Ha-ha. You're hilarious, spook,' I call out to him. Even though I can't see him, I know he can hear me just fine. 'How can I learn if you take my powers away?'

'It's temporary,' echoes Amun. 'To get you to think. Get you to plan. Don't go for the obvious attack. Change your tactics. Have a strategy in place before you act.'

Except, I'm not given the chance to think. In one swift movement, the huge gargoyle leaps from its position, shuddering the stone ledge beneath my feet as it lands. My arms fling out to brace myself against the impact.

The fear suddenly settles.

And a sense of confidence floods in.

I realise, a heartbeat later, there is nothing to worry about. This chunk of sandstone moves slow and clumsy like a drunken chess piece. A hum of courage filters into my body.

'One lumbering mutt of a gargoyle? Is that all you think I'm capable of handling, oh Mighty Ruler? At least challenge me.'

'You want more,' answers a voice in a crisp English accent. The woman in green appears from behind the gargoyle.

'You!' I knew I wasn't going nuts. 'Who *are* you?'

'I said, do you want more?' she repeats. A smile, the kind that *doesn't* make you feel the warm and fuzzys inside, breaks through her lips. 'I'm impressed.'

The crunching of larger, grainier stones grows in volume. Stones that have been roughly hewn and much coarser in texture cause me to look to my left, look to my right.

Behind me, bigger and more fierce than the first, stands another monstrous gargoyle. His skin, if you can call it that, has a green tinge to it, from the build up of moss and lichen over the years. It has a strange monkey face and yet the torso and arms are clearly human. A pair of neatly folded wings are almost impossible to see until it breaches the adjacent wall. It arches its back and flaps its enormous wings, the sound mimicking a pair of rusted iron doors caught in the wind.

Now I need eyes in the back of my head.

I spy another pair of stoney hands grappling over the ledge as though it has scaled the entire cathedral. This one resembles a dragon. There are no wings this time but it has a cool crest on its head and down its back. This one might be tricky as it has all four limbs – complete with sharp, stone talons.

Three? I gulp. *You've got this*, I say to myself, clenching my fists and muscling up to them. 'Who's first?'

'I'll leave you to it then,' says the old woman.

'Isis,' I hear Amun whisper into my blood. 'She is Isis.' If I had my own set of claws, they would've surely sprung from my fingertips. That conniving witch – I now see where Tomas is coming from – friend one minute, foe the next.

'What if they kill me? Who will finish the Initiations and raise the big fella?' I yell into the wind. I'm obviously talking about Mithras.

'Trust me. This will help you.'

Major alarm bells go off in my head. Trust her – *yeah right, when hell freezes over*. And Isis offering her help? And then it dawns on me. Something that Doc said - s*he will have her own agenda.* For now, and for as long as it suits her, I might have an ally. That has to count for something.

I turn to see the three rock monsters focused on me … waiting.

'It will help you to be battle-ready for Zurvan.'

'Aha!' I knew this was about something bigger, although I have no idea, who or what the hell Zurvan is. 'And when might that be?'

Like all supernatural beings, she only answers when she wants to. Transfixed, I stare at her, until her body slowly becomes more and more translucent until she disappears completely.

'What's your plan?' I say to Amun, keeping a keen eye on the nearest gargoyle, who seems to be inching closer.

I give him ten seconds to reply.

No response.

Typical. 'On my own. As usual,' I add.

With Isis gone and Amun as elusive as ever, I test out my powers to see if they're back, curious if Amun's *temporary* block has been removed.

I focus inward, tapping into that place I call on, to create a tornado. Each power requires a slightly unique trigger – flying, for example, I have to concentrate on feeling as light as a feather. Turning invisible, I focus on seeing through objects. A tornado, however, comes from the pit of my stomach.

My body tenses, like so many times before, as a whirlwind of extreme velocity swirls up from my gut and into my chest. Gratefully, Amun has removed the barrier, and I straighten up, full of self-assurance, and raise my hands.

An enormous gust of wind channels through my arms and into my hands. I have to say, it blew my mind the first time I saw a hand-made tornado spinning through my fingers, just like when Ember created her first fireball, I imagine.

I know exactly what to do with it.

The first one, with the bulging eyes, doesn't know what's hit him as I aim the twister straight for him. He stumbles backwards, feeling the full brunt of my power. The noise of his clomping stump on the stone walkway is so loud it could pass as thunder.

I need to finish him off before the whole of Paris hears it.

Quickly … and quietly.

Before the beast can regain its balance, I summon a mattress of air and sweep it under his feet. Caught up in a bubble of air, tumbling head over stump, again and again, I manoeuvre my mini-tornado until he's suspended over the edge of the cathedral. The people in the forecourt below have no idea how close to death they are. I make a slight adjustment, ensuring my swirling mass is well within the *keep out* fenceline, and let the brute go.

Silence lasts for three seconds before an almighty crash and a plume of dust billows up from below.

I wince as it makes its mark and give myself an internal pat on the back for being so clever. One down, two to go. In my stupidity to watch the win, I spin around to see the other two gargoyles are now on top of me.

The dull thud my body makes being whacked against the tower wall rattles my bones, leaving me with a ringing inside my skull. I take a second to check in with myself to make sure nothing is broken.

Two blinks later, a giant hammering fist comes my way. I dodge it easily enough. Gargoyles aren't the sharpest tools in the shed, and I grin and lift my chin at the one that missed me by a mile.

'Is that all you've got?' I smirk. 'You're like a couple of granny's in sumo suits.'

The larger one lets out a gravelly roar.

Left wide open, it gives me time to rush at it. I drive Monkey Face into one of the towers, my head wedged under its stony armpit, arms around its waist. A thin spire above us, stretching to the heavens, wobbles too much for my liking as the gargoyle slams into the wall. Thankfully, the spire stays its course.

Blood trickles down my cheek as my skin scrapes alongside its abrasive ribcage. I shake it off, ignoring the sting, and find my footing. Coldness clamps around my wrist as Dragon gargoyle latches onto me. My hand, sandwiched in its stone mitt, might be my downfall. It might be my last day on earth if I was simply a human.

But that isn't the case.

I smirk as I turn invisible and slip from the giant's grasp. It looks about, trying to find me.

A moment later, after evading another haymaker from Monkey-face gargoyle, I appear at his side. I step left, deftly dodging the strike, its claws as sharp as freshly cut flint. The cathedral wall doesn't fair as well as the squeal of its talons leaves behind proof of its short-lived existence. Three perfectly parallel scratch marks are etched into Notre Dame's history books forever.

Without a moment to lose, I charge along the walkway, certain they'll follow me.

They do.

A corner approaches and I fly around it, ready to dish out the same fate as their buddy, who got dropped on his head a moment ago. The minute they are close to the edge, I whip up a hurricane into an angry frenzy and hurl it behind them to continue their momentum over the edge. They land as a pile of stones on top of their already dismembered counterpart.

I dust my hands down my pants, pleased I have completed yet another task successfully and without the help of *anyone*, especially River.

I straighten up, throw my shoulders back, feel the gentle breeze on my face, and smile.

'Your prize,' says a ghostly, English voice.

I turn, unable to believe what I'm seeing.

Looking like a game of ring toss, the Crown of Thorns dangles from the horn of a nearby gargoyle – a non-living gargoyle, I might add.

'How?' I ask.

No response as always.

I retrieve the crown, ignorant of how sharp the thorns are. A blob of red breaks through my skin as it punctures my thumb. I immediately stick it in my mouth.

'So this is what you do in your spare time,' says a voice. I yank my thumb out of my mouth and turn in the direction of the voice, not that I need to.

It's Terra. 'You're in so much shit. You wait till the others hear this.'

'Terra … I …' before I can get another word out, she transforms into an eagle and flies off.

The air seems to have been sucked from my body, my legs unstable, my hands prickling with an inner tremble. 'And when were you going to tell us about that?' I yell after her, brain-scrambling, trying to make sense of her newest bird transformation. Seems I'm not the only one with secrets.

I scowl at the crown, and having nowhere else to put it, gingerly go to place it on my head, then think better of it. I flick my visibility off, step on the ledge and follow Terra. She will beat me hands down, but I have the crown. Again, that must surely count for something.

The four of them are gathered around the TV as I step onto the balcony an hour later. Like tank turrets lining up their next shot, they all turn to look at me in sync, their minds churning with an assortment of questions. I can only imagine what bullshit lies Terra has made up.

On cue, she lifts her chin at me and smirks, her eyes glistening like polished emeralds.

'Where have you been?' asks Ember, a thousand emotions on her face at once. 'We were expecting you back ages ago.'

'I took a detour,' I say, looking directly at Terra. 'Needed to clear my head.'

Hayley, tucked in the corner, looks the happiest to see me. She gives me a little wave but holds her position.

Ember and River are glued to the TV again.

'And, I suppose you had nothing to do with this?' asks River, not bothering to look at me. Ember lifts her head, waiting for my response. Taking a guess, it must be centred around Notre Dame.

'Nup. Got no idea what you're talking about.' Through my jeans, the sharp barbs of the crown prickle into the back of my legs.

He glares at me. '*Really*?'

'Okay. I *might* have had something to do with it.' River looks disapprovingly at me and shakes his head.

'*What*?' I feel my anger rising.

'It's your sledgehammer approach, Skye. We were supposed to do this together and with the least amount of fuss. Now look at the shitstorm you've caused.'

I pause to look at the TV, a ribbon of text along the bottom of the screen:

BREAKING HEADLINES - Vandals responsible for the wilful destruction of three of Notre Dame's most famous and valuable gargoyles.

'A little collateral damage,' I say offhandedly.

'*Collateral damage*?' River comes back with. 'Is that all you have to say is ... *collateral damage*? Just when I think we are finally ...' he cuts off, but I hear the words *becoming brothers* in his mind, which seems to dull his anger.

'You doubt me?' I say after a few seconds of silence. 'You all do.' The lightness leaves Terra's face, and darkness finds a way in. 'Hopefully, this might make up for it.' I gingerly bring my hand out from behind my back, producing the crown.

'Skye,' Ember gasps.

She stands.

Shakes her head in disbelief.

I'm just about to relax, about to receive my commendation when thunder strikes and lightning flashes.

'Great!' cries River. 'This is perfect! Pack your bags, everyone, we'd better clear out before Interpol get here.' A siren outside causes us all to freeze. I edge over to the window. A police car comes into view in pursuit of a speeding car.

We all release that breath.

'I can't believe you stole it,' says River, his hands in his hair and all over his face. I frisbee it over to him although he makes no attempt to catch it. Instead, it glides over the bed and ensnares itself on the pillow.

I don't believe this. 'You're mad at me for ... You think I stole ...' I bite back the words.

'Your stupidity and recklessness is going to put the whole country on alert, Skye. Do you realise what you've done? We'll be lucky to make it home.'

Anger isn't an emotion I'm all that familiar with, but today I'm getting a double dose of it. 'I didn't *steal* it.'

My hands are trembling and I hide them behind my back, squeezing them until they pulsate.

They all stare at me. Sure, I might be a hotdog, but they know I'm not a liar. 'It was *given* to me.'

'Yeah, by who?' I am stunned it's Terra who asks this.

Realisation hits me between the eyes and I struggle to hold back a smile. 'You obviously can't see everything now, can you?'

Her lips press so firmly together I'm amazed she can get the words out. 'I wouldn't be asking if I knew, would I, *genius*?'

I can't help it and let out a laugh. 'Wow! You aren't the all-seeing-eye, after all.' She bares her teeth at me and some part of me registers if we were ever to fight, I would come off second best. I don't mean anything by it; in fact, it has opened my eyes. And it's just a theory at the moment, but perhaps if Isis and Amun are around, then maybe Terra is blocked from getting the full download on what's happening.

'Isis gave it to me.'

I let my words hang there for a moment, enjoying the silence, enjoying the glory, but still really pissed at their judgement of me. 'I went to Notre Dame because I felt drawn to it. I wasn't drawn to inform or invite any of you, so I went myself … to satisfy my curiosity. It was actually more of an experiment.'

'How so …?' asks Hayley, timidly stepping forward.

'Not everyone gets a rule book on how to interpret intuition, you know, or even how to communicate effectively with a God living inside you.'

Hayley sucks in a breath.

'Amun?' says River. 'You spoke to him?'

'Yes,' I say, shrugging in my usual *whatever* way.

'I used my *special techniques* to get into Notre Dame, *unseen*, and this old lady wearing a green hat and coat showed up. I followed her to the top of Notre Dame.' I pause for a breath.

'And?'

'And Amun reckoned I needed some training. So, he bought a gargoyle to life. Then Isis bought two more to life because she said I had to be ready to face Zurvan ...'

'Hold on a minute. Amun bought a gargoyle to life?' says Ember, blinking repetitively.

'*Isis*?' asks Terra.

'Who the hell is *Zurvan*?' adds River.

'Yes ... and yes, and I don't know,' I say, addressing each individual question. 'That is why the so-called *vandalism* took place. It was them or me, and I couldn't very well leave those *things* up there to ravage the city now, could I?'

'It's still incredibly foolish ...'

I cut River off, fury fuelling me. 'There were people below. So, I weighed it up and took out the threat with the minimal amount of destruction.' Another rumble of anger boils away inside me as I brush sweat back into my hairline. 'I neutralised a dire situation without loss of civilian life. I was careful not to be seen, and then ... I get back here, and you fuckers bite my frigging head off for it, without even giving me the chance to explain. Well, fuck you. Deal with it yourself.' I grab the crown off the bed, turn invisible and take a left turn straight out of the window.

It's after 3am before I finally pluck up the courage to return to the hotel. The room is dark and the heating is up too high for my liking. I see the bulk shape of River in one bed and turn to look at my own. A dense shape is also curled up against the pillows. It has to be Hayley.

I slip my jeans and shirt off and slide into bed next to her. The single bed idea from River is now not a smart move. She stirs a little and I roll in closer, longing to be in someone's company that truly gets me.

'Where have you been? I was worried,' she whispers as she rolls over to face me. Where indeed ... and there's no doubt in my mind she would've worried. After all, I've barely said more than ten words to her since we got here,

237

and then abandoned her to four virtual strangers to deal with my own shit.

But I had to see if I could destroy it.

Had to see if I could earn back their trust.

Had to see if I could chase away the doubt in their eyes.

She runs her fingers over my cheekbone, stopping at the abrasion. She opens her eyes, and with the low street light peeking through the gap in the curtains, she inspects my injury and winces. She squirms in closer and very delicately kisses it. 'For the record, I believe what you said earlier,' she says and then kisses me softly on the lips. 'Sleep, we'll talk in the morning.'

EIGHTEEN

I'VE been awake for hours, trying to work out what the hell went wrong …

You see, I needed to find a place to conduct some experiments. Needed a place where I wouldn't be disturbed, where no one could see what bizarre antics I was getting up to. It took much longer than I thought to find the right place, and the secluded farm south of Paris, ended up being a last resort.

Two hours it took me to discover the crown is impervious to fire. That it can't be destroyed when dropped from a great height. That it remains intact even after being smashed by the biggest boulder I could lift. That no matter how hard I chopped it with an axe or the countless times I ran over it with a tractor … it would not succumb.

Now I'm at a loss.

What the fuck am I going to tell them? Terra said I'm the only one who can destroy it, and I can't even do that. Like I said, World's Worst Superhero.

The alarm on River's phone goes off, and he rises lethargically and heads into the bathroom. A few minutes later, I hear the shower. *Just like old times*, he grumbles to himself. The poor fella is struggling.

Hayley rolls towards me and whispers my name. I'm not ready to talk to anyone yet and pretend to be asleep. She slips out of bed, resting a hand upon my shoulder for a couple of breaths before leaving, the sound of the hotel door quietly clicking shut behind her.

Once River finishes up in the bathroom, he quickly dresses and leaves without uttering a single word. I wait a while before I throw off the covers and rub the sleep from my eyes.

The hotel notepad that I spot on the bottom of my bed when I sit up has a message scribbled on it from Hayley, saying they've gone to breakfast and to join them when I'm ready. She's drawn a loveheart next to her name.

I need a shower before I can face any of them.

I find them crammed into a retro-style dining room on the first floor, the walls washed in soft tangerine paint. Dozens of tables of varying sizes and designs, partner up with a collection of non-matching chairs … certainly not the white tablecloth set-up I've become accustomed to in Paris. If it wasn't for the high ceilings, this room with its six waiters squeezing between adoring couples, families with noisy children, several grey-haired ladies with miniature dogs on their laps, and the old gentleman in the corner wearing one of those dodgy neck scarves, it would double as the damned screeching elevator that I can hear from across the hallway.

I spot River and the girls in the far corner. They've pushed two mismatched tables together as best they can, leaving one vacant seat for me.

'We thought we'd let you sleep,' explains Hayley as I pull out a wooden chair. It wobbles slightly as I sit on it. River, Ember and Terra don't even look up.

Balancing on the uneven ridges of the two tables sits a fancy two-tier cake server filled with buttered croissants and jam-filled pastries. A rack of toast, two jugs of orange juice and a large bowl of fruit salad has pretty much taken up the rest of the table and I push aside the paper napkin and re-arrange the cutlery to suit. At this rate, I might be eating out of my lap.

Suppose I should jump right in. 'Sorry about yesterday.'

Ember is the first to acknowledge me. Her bronzy eyes hold me like a deer in headlights. 'No, we're sorry. Aren't we, River?'

River and I exchange a look. Not quite sympathy or forgiveness. Simply plain old acceptance. 'Yeah. No hard feelings, hey?' he answers as though he's rehearsed those lines all night. His face creases slightly, and I hear for myself how drained he feels living day to day with Isis's blood inside him, and how putting on a brave face is beginning to take its toll. He also asks me to keep this news to myself, which I will, as long as it serves us all. The second he starts going downhill in a big way, I'm spilling it.

'None,' I reply solemnly. He cuts me a quick grin that has no feeling behind it, re-enforcing to me that we need to get these Initiations completed as quickly as possible, for his sake, save none.

Terra, of course, says nothing. She sips on a cup of black coffee, peering over River's head as though she is the only one at the table. I try to catch her eye several times although her thoughts remain blank, her body language closed down. At some point in the near future, words will need to be spoken between us. I only hope the outcome won't be to the detriment of the group.

Hayley welcomes me with a warm, sympathetic smile and brushes my newly forming graze with the back of her fingers. Ember notices and winces. 'Do you wanna tell us what happened?'

'What's to tell. There was a fight. The end.'

Ember's mind turns over with guilt. 'Sorry we weren't there for you,' she says.

I shrug it off, like it's no big deal. 'Nah. Although I am interested to know who this *Zurvan* is.' I stare directly at Terra for five whole seconds until she looks up.

The burning curiosity in River's eyes doesn't miss the swift change on Terra's face either. Her thin mask of indifference moves into stone and then shadow. I'm tempted to ask her again, but I don't have to. River's ability to pick up emotions is all over it, and I'd bet my entire bank account of £183 she's having way more internal experiences than her mouth is letting on. I just wish I could get inside her head for five minutes to see for myself.

In plain and simple terms, River comes right out and asks her. 'Who is Zurvan?'

Terra buries her face in her hands.

Time freezes all things except the violent shudder that ripples across her shoulders and down her back. Even the room loses its voice for those few microseconds.

Her head lifts slightly.

She massages her forehead in deliberate circles as though the very action might rub out some terrible image.

We all swap glances, River shrugging. Terra sits back, drops her hands to the table, slowly raises her head. Her eyes go from luminous emeralds to mushy pea soup in one solitary blink.

'Zurvan, originally was half-man, half-lion. And although he can be killed, nobody has ever come close to defeating him, giving him an unusual claim to immortality.' Her jaw clenches, creating a domino effect down her neck and into her shoulders. Her fingers nervously drumming on the yellow, metal table.

I find myself perched on the edge of my seat, salivating for her next words. 'And …'

Terra takes her time.

A dark moment finds her.

Binds her.

Slips a noose around her neck and unleashes its inky blackness into her.

I catch my breath, feeling every living second of it as it radiates out of her skin towards me in scratchy, thorn-like airwaves.

My gut seizes.

My appetite falls away.

My ability to think becomes boggy and unclear. She pauses before saying, 'it has mutated over time.'

My teeth grind together, trying to purge the unsteadiness of an empty stomach, my bowels turning to water. I pour a glass of orange juice and take a sip, just to clear the bitterness from my palate. 'Mutated into what?'

'A beast of immense size.'

'Ember places her hand over Terra's, and in a soft, kind voice asks, 'how do you know all this?'

For the first time ever, I see a change in Terra's expression. A blaze of fire in her eyes, so different from Ember's lava eyes – but strong, powerful, purposeful, as though she's held onto this secret for so long, and can finally set it free.

'He sees me.' Her eyes zero in on the contents of her cup. She stares longingly into her coffee before taking another sip. Her lip trembles a little. 'He knows who I am. He visits me in my dreams,' she says, her voice getting slower and softer with every word. 'Along with every other supernatural beast of this world.' Her fingers stop drumming. Every blink, trapped behind her lashes. The heavy, throbbing pulse in her neck, the only sign she's alive.

'Oh my god,' murmurs Ember under her breath. 'We had no idea.' Perspective always hits at the most inopportune time. Here's me worrying about a little guilt for killing my parents and potentially having to fight some giant mutated alleycat, and then there's Terra, who hasn't had any love in her life, been abandoned, drugged, beaten, abused, and now being hunted by every evil mythical beast this world has viciously spat out. Nobody deserves that much shit, so I decide to cut her some slack.

Terra swallows. 'I didn't want any of this.' A tiny fracture in her voice lets me know her a little more.

I offer her a tight smile.

'None of us did, Terra,' says River, his voice the gentlest I've ever heard it. 'But we don't have a choice. The more we know, the better we can handle this, and the more prepared we are … for *whatever* life has in store for us, we'll do it … *together.* We have each other now.' He stretches out and places his hand on top of Ember's. I feel as though I should throw my hand on too, but the moment comes and goes before I make up my mind. 'I know it's upsetting, but you need to tell us everything you know about Zurvan.'

Terra inhales a long breath, teeth nibbling her lips a few times and straightens up. 'I don't know how to tell you this …'

'It's okay,' assures Ember.

Terra nods, taking another breath. 'Okay.' She pauses again. 'Gaia says Zurvan will challenge one of us.' Her words drop a heavy weight into my chest, and all is silent for a moment. 'To the death. She says he has been created for this sole purpose.'

'Well, obviously, that's me then, isn't it?' I say, deflecting the seriousness with humour as usual. 'I'm the biggest fuck-up there is, so it goes without saying. It was nice knowing you all.' I throw in a laugh for good measure.

'I don't think so,' she says directly to me, her voice all but a whisper. Her eyes are a little warmer, her cheeks a little softer. A thaw has begun, be it in its smallest degree.

'And, technically, as I will be the only one qualified to fight him …' Terra cuts off and draws in a shaky breath.

There is no way I will let her take a hit for me, or any of us. No way! Even if we aren't best buddies. And from the resounding echo in everyone's mind, it seems we're all on the same page. 'Riv and I have fought a Minotaur before, so a lion-mutt should be no probs.'

'Zurvan is not just a lion-mutt. He has the strength of ten men, maybe more.' She looks directly at me and finally permits me into her mind. The image sends a shockwave through my body, double punching my heart and dampening my armpits – *now do you see*, she says to me telepathically. 'And he doesn't play by the rules, so I can't get a fix on him.'

I'm glad River speaks because I've run out of words. I skol the remainder of my juice, even if its only purpose is to return some wetness to my mouth.

'Okay, we'll tackle that problem when we come to it.' He has that *stuck up* air of authority to his voice again that we've grown accustomed to. River rises a little and hands his plate to the waiter before sitting back in his chair. 'But right now, we need to figure out what to do with the crown.'

I jump right in. 'About that …' I say, 'It might not be as easy as we first thought.' I look to Terra. 'Is there any weird voodoo ritual I need to perform this time, like with *your* bird, I mean …*the* bird, whatever, I mean … the raven? Corax?' I should stop talking.

Terra stops chewing on a piece of melon. '*Why*? Has something happened?' I shrug, and Terra rolls her eyes at me, but there is no malice behind them. 'The Crown of Thorns doesn't exactly come with a set of instructions, Skye.'

That is the first time she's said my name without twisting up her mouth or adding a sour tone to it. Things *are* looking up. She goes on to say, 'however, don't be surprised if you try to blow it up and it doesn't work.'

'Really? Because it *didn't* work.'

'You *tried* already?'

'Yup. Last night … for two hours. And nothing. Not even a dent. Didn't you say only Amun and Mithras are the only ones who can touch it and destroy it? I thought I was the *chosen* one.'

Terra's lips twitch to one side, her nostrils flare. 'As you've plainly pointed out, I don't *always* know everything, and sometimes the downloads I get are subjective and not altogether, a little cryptic. You being able to destroy it, was an educated guess, based on what I know. There are other forces at play here.'

'Like what?' We are having our own little mini conversation.

'The Crown of Thorns was plaited by a Roman soldier, right? Therefore, we must assume it can only be *unplaited* by a Roman soldier.'

Genius, my thoughts blurt out before I can stop them.

'I'll take that as a compliment,' Terra says, playfully popping another piece of melon into her mouth, a smile curling at her lips.

I pay no mind to her because that blinding epiphany has fired up the lazy neurons in my head. '*Tomas*! We could get Tomas to pull it apart, then I should be able to destroy that sucker anyway I see fit.'

I actually smile at her.

We need Tomas right away. 'Riv, can you whistle for him or something. He seems to like you the most.'

'Sorry, dude. Not my jam. You're the one with the freaky antenna system. Radio him and tell him to get his arse over here. And you might want to mention we're facing a new monster, too. I could really use that sword of his.'

'Roger that,' I say, cutting him a salute.

Ember stacks up the empty plates and puts them to one side. 'We do need to start thinking about the Third Initiation, too. Terra, what are we up for?'

I refill my glass with the last of the juice and pop two pastries and a croissant into my pocket. 'Can we not do this right now? I'm not saying it isn't important … it totally is, but my brain is fried, and I can't handle anymore chat right now. You know, input overload from everyone.' I discreetly include those around the room before tapping my temple. 'Plus, I have somewhere I need to be.' I check my watch.

'Where?' asks River, his tone not altogether polite.

'Don't stress, princess. I promise I won't demolish any more historical buildings. It's more like an errand I have to run. Trust me.'

River scoffs and shakes his head. His next words aren't heard by anyone else except me – *you make it hard sometimes, brother. Please don't do anything stupid.*

I flip him a subtle wink and lean over to him as I rise from the table. 'You worry too much, you know that?' I whisper. And I wasn't lying about my brain being fried either. A dull headache has slowly been getting worse since I woke.

The small dining room has cleared considerably since I first came in, leaving a couple chatting beside a colonial window, and the neck-scarf dude scrolling through his phone. The waiter floats in and out, glancing our way, ready to clear our table.

River nods. 'Okay. Let's meet back here in an hour or so.'

We scatter like seeds to the wind.

Ember and River head to the lift. I eavesdrop on his thoughts about them taking a romantic walk along the Seine because it might be the last time they get to be alone. Terra practically disappears from view before I can ask her what she is up to. And Hayley wants to buy some souvenirs to take home for her sister that I don't remember her saying she had. Which leaves just me.

So, back to my so-called errand.

And, although I told River it doesn't involve any mischief, it does, however, require a little covert action.

NINETEEN

AFTER the weight of gravity finally sloughs off and I become one with the air, I travel east of Paris, under the cover of invisibility, to the sleepy village of Chatillon-sur-Marne - to the ramshackle cottage of Henri du Garcia, historian extraordinaire and ex-curator of Le Louvre.

Henri was there for us when Riv and I had no one else to turn to. Em had been kidnapped by Salvatore, or Horus as we now know him, leaving us with nothing but a Roman coin as a clue to find her. Henri had bought us up to speed in the Mithraic cult before sending us to his protégé. Without either of their help, I don't think Em would still be with us.

The last time Riv and I were here, we'd come by road and with a guide. This time, it's quite different. The view is spectacular from up here, the air crisp and so damn clean I can taste the earthy tang of freshly ploughed fields. A vision of Mum planting rows of zucchini's and red capsicum in the back yard, brings a lump to my throat, catching me unaware.

I miss her.

Miss all the little things she used to do to make me laugh. Silly things. Things only her and I shared. I don't let myself go there because I know I'm not over her. Or Dad. I haven't dealt with the pain or loss. I haven't dealt with any of it, and I'm not sure where to start. So, I swallow, push them from my thoughts and get back to the job at hand.

I re-check my position.

Meadows criss-cross below me in every shade of green you can think of, laying resolutely at the base of gently sloping hills of tangled vineyards. Tall, yellow cornfields sway to the tunes of a thousand crickets as farmers busy about, herding their sheep.

I zip over red roofs and churches, people on bicycles and a lady walking with flowers in her basket, all whilst keeping a keen eye out for that winding country road that leads out of town to Henri's place. The journey has taken around twenty minutes, and I feel like I've hardly juiced up any power.

I spy a lone haystack and drop down behind it.

By my rough calculations, Henri's place should be just on the other side of this field. I hop over the gate and take a leisurely stroll down the road, the light breeze on my face, the morning sun at my back, the smell of freshly baked bread in the air and the sound of ducks quacking a short distance away. If the world wasn't about to be swallowed up by evil, this would be close to the most perfect day.

I round the next bend, a little shocked by my accuracy, to see a familiar cottage with its ancient stone-pitched walls and roof in disrepair. I'm even more surprised to see Henri outside, clipping the heads off a bunch of dead daisies.

'Henri,' I call out as I approach. The old man turns in my direction, his weathered face creasing with confusion.

He pushes his shoulder-length grey hair aside, before shielding his eyes from the sun.

He raises his hand, beaming a smile at me you just can't fake. 'Salut, jeune homme. You 'ave another coin for me to look at?' he asks as I draw closer.

'Hello, Henri. You look well.' I'm thrilled he recognises me, and more thrilled he's outside and that I don't have to sit amongst the women's clothes on his sofa that were laid out during our last visit. I've no idea what he called me, and I don't much care. Knowing Henri, it would be something honourable. 'No. Not this time. But how is your French to English translation?'

I've thought long and hard about who to give the pages of Iris's diary to. God knows what they'll reveal – nothing good I imagine. And even though I've only met Henri Du Garcia once before, somehow, he doesn't seem the kind of person to dob me in if the pages are incriminating.

'Not too bad. Maybe a little crusty,' he says, raising a single black eyebrow at me. I holster my laughter, knowing he means *rusty*. A few seconds of doubt pass over me, debating if he's up to the task. Too late now, I'm here.

'I have a few pages on my phone for you to translate, if you have the time?'

'Of course. Of course. But I'm sorry, I cannot do it now. My son, Gervais, who you met before at z 'otel is coming very soon to take me to z market square.' He points to a box of pumpkins and squash. 'I 'ave to take zem to z church on top of z 'ill.' He looks off into the distance and I can just make out a roofline and a church bell. 'But, if you leave z pages with me, I can translate zem and send zem back to you.'

I suppose I don't have a choice, and Henri isn't someone you can rush.

'Sure. Do you have a phone?'

Henri pulls a phone from his jacket pocket. In the sunlight, I notice the pinky nail on his left hand is painted vivid purple. I like him … he makes me smile.

He hands me his phone, and I don't bother to ask whether his Bluetooth is on. I simply airdrop the pages to his phone, wait for them to appear and then accept them.

'There you go. All done,' I say to him. 'They'll be saved in your photos. I also popped my contact details in there so you can send me the translation when you're done.'

'Okay,' says Henri, his lined face wrinkling even more from his smile. 'I will get my daughter, Gabriella, to 'elp me, if I get, 'ow you say …sticked.'

'*Sticked*? Oh, you mean stuck.'

That's good enough for me. 'Great,' I say, handing back his phone, and shaking the old man's hand.

There's nothing supernatural about Henri, or even Chatillon-sur-Marne come to that. No mystical presence or even the aroma of magic in the air, and yet the second our hands collide, I'm barrelled into his head so fast, I can barely stand upright.

Images of Mithras.

Of a spear sailing in mid-air.

A staff.

A cup.

A passage through Hell.

Isis.

Hayley.

Everything blended together in a jigsaw, except I sense all the pieces are in the wrong places.

Henri releases my hand.

And I'm left reeling, gasping, head foggy, words desperate to spill out and yet remain imprisoned within my mouth.

Henri frowns. 'Are you well?' the old man asks. 'Sit,' he says, taking my arm, and leading me over to an old tree stump.

I sit.

'I don't know what happened,' I say, shaking the visions free from my mind. 'I saw …' Except I can't explain what I saw. Not to him anyhow.

I feel my body come back online, the dizziness subsiding. 'Thanks, Henri. I'm sweet. Sorry to trouble you.'

His eyes flit over my face and down my body. 'You are sure?' he says. 'Maybe you should come inside and 'ave some tea.'

I am okay, I think, blinking through the last of the spots. 'I've got this,' I say, 'call me when you send through the translation.'

He nods, and I make a slow, wobbly beeline for the haystack.

Back to the honking of horns and pollution of Paris, I've come to the realisation I can't tell the others about my visit with Henri, or what happened when I shook his hand.

Not just yet.

It's shit, I know, keeping another secret from them, but without the translation, what good would it do Em. Her thoughts drift often enough to how her parents were murdered, so bringing it up again without any closure isn't going to achieve anything except more worry and sleepless nights for her. My big announcement will have to wait.

The flight back was just what the doctor ordered, and I'm thankful to be feeling more like my old self again as I arrive back at the hotel. Noticing the balcony doors open, I fly straight in.

Much to my surprise, the room is empty.

I'm concerned, but relieved.

Where is everyone?

I check my watch before flaking out on the bed. I kick my shoes off and shut my eyes to recharge my energy and for a few minutes of peace.

It is not to be.

A low pitch whistle – less than a kettle, more than the wind, is gradually getting louder. The pitch changes into the sound of a mongrel cat chasing its buddy through an alleyway of tin cans.

Damn antenna!

I pull the pillow over my head, but it doesn't lessen the noise. It then grows in volume until I think my skull is going to split open.

Then silence.

And a small squeak.

Skye, I hear inside my head.

Doc? Is that you? I reply. The buzzing and crackling starts again. *Doc!*

Tomas heard your call for help. He's on his way.

Great news.

I don't get a chance to ask anything else as a high pitched squeak signifies Doc has hung up. His attempts at communicating with me are getting harder and harder to intercept, which prompts me to try and link up with Amun again. Yesterday was a fairly successful outcome as far as our personal interaction went, so I try my luck at dialling his frequency. After several, persuasive yet failed attempts, all I hear are crickets. I will try again later.

I flick on my phone to check if there are any messages. There's one from Dean asking where the fuck I am, and a free family pizza with my next order. Other than that, my inbox is clean. I reply to Dean's text with the middle finger emoji and slide my phone onto the bedside table just as Ember and River return. Amid everything going on, these two lovebirds look the happiest I've ever seen them. Ember hasn't stopped smiling since they got back in the room, and River hasn't taken his eyes off her. How nice would it be, to feel half of what flows out of these two? I try to keep out of their thoughts but love is addictive and hard not to want more of.

A knock at the door reveals Terra, and then Hayley turns up a few seconds later. She waits for me to wave her over, and makes herself comfortable, using my legs to rest her head against.

Terra gets straight into it. 'The Third Initiation stands for Miles, or Soldier.'

'Do you think that could be Tomas?' I throw in.

Terra eyes Hayley stroking my calf, her face dead-pan. 'Not this time, sleuth,' she answers. She pauses, still watching the intimate sweeps of Hayley's hand on my skin, before going on to say, 'the soldier *does* indicate a Roman soldier, however, I believe this man doesn't want to be found.'

Hayley glances up when all is silent. Something in the way Terra is glaring at her, ceases her stroking and prompts her to sit up, using my pillow as a wedge behind her. She flicks on her phone. 'I was doing some research earlier. Does this have anything to do with Longinus?' she asks.

We all stare at her in wonder. All except Terra, who squints her eyes and presses her lips together like she might be tempted to rip her throat out at any second if she doesn't hold in the urge. 'How could you possibly know that?' she retorts.

Hayley half shrugs one shoulder as a smile emerges around her semi-serious face. 'Logic, really. I've been reading up on these Initiations, and the Third one also represents a spear, right? So, I typed in spear and up comes the Spear of Destiny, which was thrust into Jesus's side, as he hung on the cross, by … none other than …a Roman soldier by the name of Longinus.' She turns to each of us in succession, beaming from ear to ear. 'It's amazing what you can find on Google.'

The darkness on Terra's face hasn't lifted one bit. 'She's right,' she says, practically spitting the words through her teeth. 'The Spear of Destiny, also called the Holy Lance, is a bit of a mystery though. There are three historical artefacts that all claim to be the Holy Lance, but only two have real credibility.'

'Please, tell me you know which one the true spear is?' I say.

'What do *you* reckon?' Terra fires back without looking at me.

Hayley jumps in when the silence goes on for too long. 'One is said to be located beneath the dome in Saint

Peter's Basilica, a church in the Vatican City, which also happens to be the burial place of Jesus's first apostle, Peter. However, the tip of this particular spear has been lost. And, the other one is in the Imperial Museum in Vienna.'

'It's a little more than a museum,' retorts Terra.

But Hayley doesn't seem to hear her, and continues on. 'This spear was known as the Vienna Lance. Records show that it was stolen by Hitler before the Second World War. He believed the spear had mystical powers. You know he was interested in the occult, right?' she asks. We all shake our heads. 'Well, he'd done his homework. Apparently, Charles the Great, or commonly known as Charlemagne, acquired it in 744AD and carried the spear through forty-seven battles. Legends say, the moment he dropped the spear, he died. Every man and his dog has been after this spear. Armenian monks say they have it. Even Napoleon went after it, but never found it …'

Terra looks ready to boil over and jumps in the second Hayley stops to take a breath. 'Basically, the owner doesn't live long once the spear leaves their possession. The most up to date records say that US soldiers, under General Patton, found it in an underground bunker in Nuremberg. Soon after that, Hitler committed suicide in his bunker.'

'Bloody hell,' says Ember. 'And we have to find this thing? Touch it, even? Can we back up a minute, though? Tell me more about this other Roman soldier. What did you mean he might not want to be found?'

Terra shrugs. 'A feeling is all. Tomas will know how to locate him.'

'You know *Tomas*?' asks Ember.

'We've never *formally* met, but I know *of* him,' replies Terra, her green eyes ablaze. 'All Gaia said was that the old man, I assume is the Roman soldier, has done his time and needs to be put out of his misery. I mean, how many Roman soldiers do you hang out with these days …?' I'm about to jump in and say something smart, when she adds, '*other* than Tomas?'

'So, I assume we're off to Vienna then. I've always wanted to see the Imperial Treasury,' says Hayley.

Someone lets out a low whistle and from the incredulous look on River's face, my guess is, it was him. '*Imperial Treasury?* I don't like the sound of that.' *Probably going to be ten times harder to break into than Le Louvre*. I nod, letting him know I heard his thoughts loud and clear.

'How are we going to get in there?' asks Ember.

'They hold daily tours to the Treasury, which is part of the museum,' butts in Hayley again, displaying her screen at us. 'The cost is twenty pounds per person.'

'Are we going to Vienna, Riv?'

We all look to River. 'I guess. Seems like the best lead we've got right now,' he answers, 'I'll get Wally to book us some flights for tomorrow.'

River steps onto the balcony to phone Wally as Terra turns on her heel in the opposite direction. I glance over at Hayley, still tapping away on her phone. The jury is still out on what I think of her. There is a kind and selfless chick in there, which also has a ballsy, excitable and highly sexually-experienced nature, which is kind of strange considering her limited relationships. And for all the reasons I normally ignore, I'm treading cautiously. She seems to recognise secrets in me, which I hate, but which also reflects she has them too, and yet I feel as though we've known each other forever and could possibly be soul mates. It's like there are two very different sides to her, and I never know which one I'm chatting to. Everyone likes her, except Terra, and although we don't get on well, I don't believe Terra is the kind of girl to hold a grudge without a motive. She's too streetwise for that, regardless of being cooped up in that hellhole for twelve years. I need to talk to her, and find out what she knows. Plus, there's still the topic of how she morphed into that eagle. Talking to animals is one thing – changing into them, is something quite different, especially when the curse has been broken. I haven't told a soul about this, and perhaps that's the reason she's never dobbed on me about what happened at Notre Dame.

'We leave tomorrow at noon,' says River, walking back over to his bed. He stretches out next to Ember and she quickly snuggles into his shoulder.

How about a little alone time, he says to me silently. He lifts his chin to see if I understand and I give him a sly wink.

'I think I'll go find Terra. I need to know more about this Zurvan character,' I tell them.

Hayley rises. 'And I can tell from the look on your face that this is one of those times when you need to be alone.'

I'm about to say, no, it's okay, you can come too, except she's already heading out the door.

Ember throws me the card to their room, and it lands on the end of the bed. 'I think she said she was going to lie down for a bit.' She leans back into River's arms as I make a grab for the card. By the time I look up, a small flame is dancing in the palm of her hand. She sees me staring at it, and smiles. 'Got to keep practising.'

I leave them to their *alone time* and let myself into the girl's room with a loud knock as I open the door. I find Terra on the balcony, feet up on the same white, iron table we have on our balcony.

'You busy?' I concentrate on keeping my tone light. She lifts her head and raises both eyebrows. The blank stare cowering under her expression isn't hard to miss.

'What does it look like?'

I take that as a no.

'Can we talk about Hayley?'

Terra rolls her eyes. 'I thought you were here to talk about the *eagle*.' A ghost of a smile touches her lips, ignoring all other features on her face. 'What's to talk about? I don't like her. End of story.'

'*Why*? There must be a reason.'

Terra sniffs. 'There is. It's a gut instinct thing. You wouldn't understand.' She picks at her nails. 'She's not right for you.'

'And you know what is right for me because …' I'm trying not to be argumentative but she isn't making any sense. I step out onto the balcony and lean against the railings. I wait for her to look up.

'Because I know you better than you know yourself.'

I feel myself frowning. I get the impression I've been spied on way more than I realise, plus she'd said the same words to Ember when I listened at their door.

'Explain?'

'What for? You're not in the right place to hear anything I've got to say.'

I work on my smile. 'Try me.'

She tilts her head back to look at me. And I mean, really looks at me. It's the first time our eyes have met for more than a couple of seconds. It's strange to say it's almost comforting, like being probed with a gentle feather-like wand that every fibre in my body somehow remembers from way back.

My cheeks suddenly feel hot, and Terra quickly averts her eyes.

'All I'm going to say, is there is a darkness in her soul that you haven't seen yet.'

The door opens and Hayley strolls in.

Terra lets out an aggravated breath and abruptly turns her head to take in the view, ending our conversation.

'Did you get what you needed?' I ask Hayley.

'Yep,' she replies and hands me a white box. Inside is the best looking strawberry tart I've ever seen.

TWENTY

ARRIVING at Vienna International Airport after a turbulent hour and forty-five minute flight, to a day of cloud and rain, does little to dampen my spirits – not when the bumps heightened an experience of a lifetime with Hayley in the toilet cubicle.

YES! I am now a proud member of the Mile High Club!

A little juvenile, I know, and I don't mean anything by it, like it isn't my ego talking, it's more like… wow that was the most mind-blowing, hottest sex I've ever had.

In.

  My.

    Life.

In truth, it all started yesterday afternoon.

Hayley and I left Terra's room and spent the entire afternoon in bed. I have no idea where the sudden sexual tension came from, and I don't much care if I never find out – one minute I was finishing the strawberry tart and the next I couldn't keep my hands to myself. Neither could she. I might as well have been drugged or under a spell or something. And then the evening came, and I'd sat with the boner from hell during dinner, totally sympathetic to what River has to deal with on a daily basis. After we paid for the meal, I had screamed into his head to *fuck off for an hour* so we could go back to our room. He got the message loud and clear, and casually suggested to Ember they should stretch their legs before retiring for the night.

And, even now, I keep visualising her naked, imagining all the erotic fantasies we could play out.

I can't shake it.

Hayley flashes me a smile as we wait for our luggage. River rolls his eyes at me, informing me of *how reckless and irresponsible I'm being, and that this won't end well*, all the while never once lifting his gaze from Ember and Terra, who are cueing up at the ladies toilets.

Things on the Terra front have gone from bad to worse in less than twenty-four hours. The only time we exchanged eye contact was after Hayley and I burst out of the bedroom door, half-naked, laughing and red-faced, to accept food and drinks from an embarrassed waiter. Other than that, she has started referring to me in the third person as though I don't exist. I don't get it – just when I think we are making progress, she goes psycho on me again. To be honest, it's giving me whiplash.

After collecting our luggage, we eventually head outside to wait for our driver. The smell of rain still hangs in the air and the sky warns there is more to come. A long, sleek limo pulls up a few minutes later and a short, plump man with a curly moustache steps out and greets River like they're old friends. River informs us, as Gavin packs our bags into the boot, that he used to be one of his father's regular chauffeurs but had given up the corporate life to start his own Chauffeur service. Gavin casually chatted about all the things he missed about not living in

England, until he offered his condolences about River's parents passing away. After that, the mood changed a little, although he was good enough to drop our luggage off at our hotel first. He then drove us straight to the Hofburg Palace, the home of the Imperial Treasury and Museum. Apparently, checking into our hotel first to freshen up, according to River, wasn't an option. *We've wasted too much time already, and need to get a jump on this*, he'd strongly suggested via telepathy.

Initially, Hofburg Palace reminds me of Buckingham Palace, except it's crescent-shaped instead of rectangle and doesn't have the looming black gates out front. Horse and carts seem fitting enough for the backdrop until you see tourists racing around on electric scooters and hoverboards.

Gavin drops us off outside the palace and we make our way through a reddish-brown archway, that Hayley informs us is called the Swiss Gate. From there, we make our way into a courtyard.

There's no cue lining up to get in, and Hayley leans in closer, breathing into my neck. 'It could take us a while to find the S.O.D.' I love her code talk. 'Maybe we should split into two groups.' No way am I deviating from River's plan – my life, jokingly, on the line. I casually inform Hayley that we need to stay together as one group. She goes on to tell me there are twenty-one rooms of rare treasures, including the Imperial Crown of the Holy Roman Empire, which dates back to the eleventh century. 'There's even an agate bowl claimed to be the Holy Grail.' I turn to face her and immediately think that it could come in handy. River also hears and raises his eyebrows at me in a way that says, *don't even think about it.*

'The question is, do we have a plan?' asks Hayley.

'*We* have a plan,' retorts Terra, 'it just doesn't include you.'

'Hey!' I pipe up.

'Well, it doesn't … *technically*,' chimes in Ember. Her face softens. 'No offence, Hayley. This is dangerous stuff. We are all risking our lives here, and none of us wants to add another casualty to that list.'

Hayley smiles. 'No problem. I thought you might wanna use this though.' She dives into her bag and pulls out an exact replica of the spearhead.

I open my mouth, but only air comes out - the shock doing an excellent job of keeping my words tethered.

Not so much for River. 'Where the hell did you get that?' he says abruptly, shoving the spearhead back into her bag and taking a three hundred and sixty degree turn to see if anyone saw it.

Hayley shrugs matter of factly. 'At the souvenir shop.' Her tone light and playful. 'They had heaps of them in there.'

'She's a liar,' growls Terra, taking a step towards her. I glare at Terra. Had she been a dog, her hackles would be standing up. Mine go up for an entirely different reason. For the first time, I question Hayley. I mean, we came straight from the airport to the hotel, then directly to the Treasury. When on earth did she stop to visit a souvenir shop? Now is not the time to ask, but I *will* need an answer to that question.

'Prove it,' snarls Hayley.

My eyebrows raise. So do Embers.

'Walk away, Terra,' suggests River. Forever, the peacemaker.

Hayley's tone stuns me. I've never seen her snap like that. An analytical process begins in my brain. Is Terra's assessment of Hayley correct or has Terra simply worn Hayley down until she breaks? Something picks at the back of my mind, like an itch that wants to be scratched. I revisit it, time and time again, searching for an answer and then dredging through everyone else's head to see what they've come up with.

Terra walks ahead in the direction of the Treasury, the rest of us trailing behind her in silence. What turned out to be such a promising day, with adventures galore, now muddies around our ankles as we drag our feet. And yet, I am unable to shake the way that Terra stood rigid, her shoulders hunched, her teeth exposed, like a lion waiting to tear down a deer.

The scratch that was once an itch, turns to doubt.

The Imperial Treasury, for the most part, is nothing short of amazing. I've yet to see the Crown Jewels, so Hofburg Palace is everything I imagined it would be - marble walls, marble floors, marble ceilings, pillars, statues ...you name it, everything is made of marble. Everywhere you look there are Michelangelo styled paintings, high ornate ceilings and more extravagance than you can poke a stick at, not to mention swamped in history, which wasn't my best subject at school.

We have nothing like this in Australia.

Beaches I know heaps about, rips, tides, where to catch the best rides, shark pits (the water kind not the pick-up kind), where to buy the best boards, and not forgetting where to get a good feed. Royalty on the other hand, I'm a fish out of water.

And if our mini-expedition was to wander around these lavish surroundings, I'd be thrilled. Instead, we find ourselves in the cellar of the building. All of the rooms inside the Imperial Treasury are dimly lit, obviously to preserve the precious relics down here, but the whole place gives me the creeps. The walls actually feel like they're closing in on us, getting smaller and smaller with each room we enter. And to top it off, I'm hearing more voices through the airwaves than usual. The voices are lower and take a little longer to decipher but considering my environment, I'm pretty sure I know where they're coming from.

I'm hearing the dead.

A heavy shiver, the kind that touches your toes and even makes your eyelashes tingle, creeps up my spine from the hundreds, if not thousands, of nearby spooks.

Somehow, they have sensed my energy or something, and swarmed in, the volume suddenly going from a dull hum to a riotous pub on Finals Day.

I cup one hand over my ear, immediately attracting Ember's attention. 'What's wrong?' she asks as we walk through an entire room dedicated to old clothes. Velvet and fur ceremonial robes, encrusted with precious gems and jewels belonging to kings and queens of the past, hang off a bunch of headless mannequins. And like most of the antiquities here, all safely tucked away inside glass cases, bound in rich mahogany wood.

'Speak up, I can hardly hear you.'

Ember studies my face, confusion finding a home in her eyes. 'There are like eight people in here, Skye … including us.' She places a hand on my arm, slowing me up. 'If you're starting to get the jitters …' She pats my arm twice. 'Don't stress … we've got this.'

Part of me wants to laugh out loud.

She thinks I'm worried I'm going to screw up.

How ironic?

I decide it's not the right time to bring up *ghostly* hurdles, when we already have a full plate. 'Thanks,' I say around a tight smile.

Each room is similar to the one before, drab walls, colourings of maroon or mouldy green, polished floors and more and more frigging mahogany cases. We pass countless paintings of grumpy old men in stupid outfits, women posing, faces bored and weary, and children painted to resemble dolls.

I am so bored.

If I see another frigging crown, orb, sceptre, display of keys, coronation tunics or tray of jewels, I'm going to barf up a lung. I blow out a breath of irritation.

'Oooo, there's the biggest emerald,' I hear Ember say to Hayley. The girls hang by the display whilst River and I walk ahead.

'Where is this bloody thing? I wanna see some action and get this over with,' I whisper to him.

'Patience. We need to be sure it's here before we send Ember off to start her part of the plan. Because after that, all hell will break loose in here.'

I siphon the rest of the plan from his thoughts, to double check my role. I, of course, am the burglar part of this operation. I mean, why wouldn't I be? I'm the perfect burglar. You can't catch what you can't see. I'm performing a partial snatch and grab – invisible hand through the case, turn off the invisibility in my hand for a split second, grab the spear, turn invisibility back on, and float out of there. Em's little fire in the ladies toilet, will create enough smoke to blur the overhead cameras, and River, naturally, will take care of the sprinkler systems that he casually keeps glancing up at. Easy as pie.

'You really think this idea of yours is going to work?' I add, noticing Terra standing at the same display for more than five minutes. 'It's so cliché.'

'And you've been the mastermind behind so many robberies before.' He stretches his neck in irritation. 'It's the best we could come up with in the time we had. If you don't like it, sit it out.' The good old River temper is back again, and snippets of doubt I manage to pluck from his mind, that his plan has serious holes in it, makes me snigger.

'Calm the farm. You should take up yoga or meditation or something to keep that anger thing of yours in check.'

He clicks his tongue at me.

I turn back to look at Terra again. Arms behind her back, she is still peering into the same large glass cabinet that towers over her head. I know my presence will irritate her if I go over, but I'm curious what's captivated her for so long.

River grabs hold of my arm, anticipating my move. 'Be nice.'

'*What*? I'm *Mr* Nice.'

I wave my arm in front to allow River to pass, sticking to his shadow as he crosses the room.

Standing a foot away from the case, he inhales sharply. It's enough to cause me to step out from behind him. I shouldn't be surprised at what they are staring at, and yet my head spins in delirious excitement.

An impressive golden cross, standing upright and embedded with jewels, takes up most of the available space. Beside it, is a smaller wooden cross. My eyes fall to the object on the left … my head, spinning a little faster, adrenaline surging beneath my skin …

It is the Holy Lance – the Spear of Destiny.

The molten grey spearhead, bound through the middle with a gold metal sheath, is nestled on a plush velvet background. I was half expecting the replica in Hayley's bag to be a dodgy knock-off, but it's a convincing imitation.

River ushers Hayley and Ember over, and Hayley reads out the inscription. 'It says, "In order to hasten crucifixion, the Roman soldiers used to shatter and crush the bones of the legs with an iron club to ensure that all the crosses were empty by the day of the Sabbath. However, when the Roman Centurion, Cassius Longinus, came upon Jesus, he noticed that he was already dead and refused to smash his bones. To prove to all, that he had died, Longinus pierced Jesus with a lance, causing blood and water to flow from the wound. Longinus, suffering from a severe eye disease, almost blind, was sprayed by the blood and was instantly healed. This was the first miracle.'

'It goes on to say, "the lance is made of iron and has a gold sheath wrapped around the middle of it, small hammer marks evident by the primitive nature of the workmanship. It is fifty centimetres long, and has been stored in the royal cross to keep it safe. The staff of the spear was wooden but has been lost over the years." It also says, "that this *might* not be …' Hayley looks to me and then River. I can't keep my eyes off Terra who has the worry of an entire world etched upon her face.

Hayley continues. ' …might not be the Spear of Destiny because an English metallurgist found the lance dated back to 7AD, but that the 'Nail of the Lord' held by silver wire, is iron. X-rays showed that some fragments of a genuine crucifixion nail might have been beaten into it and is consistent in length and shape with a first century Roman nail".'

'Shit,' I mumble under my breath. 'So, this could be a fake?'

'We've come here for nothing?' gasps Ember quietly.

'Wait a minute,' says Hayley, 'all may not be lost. Forensics did reveal a few sloughed skin cells, some microscopic mineral particles and spores, although no traces of human blood.'

'Is it worth stealing something that could be fake and risk going to jail for our entire lives for it?' River voices the worries in my head.

'I say we do it,' says Hayley. 'The evidence is there to suggest it's real. Perhaps they say it's fake to deter thieves. What do you reckon? Do you want to wait? Do we have time to wait?'

'*We*,' mumbles Terra, clearly irritated.

I drag River to one side. 'Hayley's right. We shouldn't be concerned about the consequences if we get caught. We should be more worried if we do nothing. Serving the world up on a platter for Ra-Mon's consumption isn't something I want on my conscience.'

River ponders for a moment, his customary frown pinched between his eyebrows. 'You're right. Let's do this before I come to my senses and change my mind.'

The girls are gathered, waiting. 'We're on,' whispers River. 'Em, you know what to do. Terra, clear the place out, and Skye, take yourself off somewhere and Houdini yourself invisible.'

'What are you going to do?' asks Hayley.

River pulls a bottle of water from his bag. 'Don't you worry about it. Now, go and find an exit, and be ready to leave.' And for the second time, I see an expression on

Hayley's face that doesn't look like it has permission to be there.

'What about this?' she says, patting her bag. 'You might need me.'

'It's not up for discussion, Hayley. River said go,' snaps Terra.

Hayley's eyes widen, straining against the lids as though she cannot possibly open them another millimetre.

Her nostrils flare.

Her cheeks suck in.

A vicious snarl changes her soft features in an instance. She has the hardened look of someone who always gets her own way. I don't know whether she thinks I can't see it because when she sees me watching her, it disappears right away and the doey, kind girl who nursed me back to health, returns.

I'm slightly petrified of her.

Ember leaves the room and right on schedule, even before the fire alarms start blazing around us, I smell and taste smoke, even in its minutest quantity.

Now for my part.

Tourists start streaming for the exits, scurrying from adjoining rooms, congregating in a large communal area like rats in a stormdrain as the smoke starts to thicken.

My *disappearing in the middle of the crowd trick*, is the one I go for, rather than singling myself out. Away from the watchful eyes of cameras and staff ushering everyone out, I duck down slightly amongst the mob and turn myself invisible. I then step out of the herd and backtrack to the room where the Holy Lance is.

The room is now filled with smoke, and I'm impressed at how Ember has managed to confine it to one area to block out the cameras.

I smile confidently.

This should be a breeze.

I head over towards the case, assuming the room is empty. What I'm not expecting is to see River slumped beside the cabinet, unconscious, Hayley standing over him. I have to make a snap decision, bring myself back to visibility and help him, or do what I'm supposed to do.

It's a no brainer.

I become a solid mass again, with the help of a nearby pillar, and rush back to River.

'Hayley! What's going on? Help me get him out of here,' I croke as the fumes fill my lungs. Visibility sucks in situations like this. No body, equals no fumes to breathe in.

'You take him. I'll be right behind you,' says Hayley, cupping her hand over her mouth.

'Hurry,' I warn.

She gasps for air again. 'But what about the spearhead?'

'Leave it,' I order, 'we'll come back another day. It's not worth dying over.'

I scoop River under the armpits and haul his body out into the main foyer, thankful for the strong arms of a nearby security officer, who helps to drag River to the front doors. The security officer rushes back inside to search for any more survivors as Ember comes running towards us.

'What happened? I thought it was all going to plan,' she says, catching her breath.

'I don't know what happened. He was like this when I found him,' I say, spitting and coughing.

'I'll try and suck the smoke out of his lungs,' says Ember, leaning in and giving him what looks like mouth to mouth.

'Get off me,' says River, pushing Ember off him, dazed and confused.

'It's okay,' I hear her say, and he relaxes into her arms. I look back to see where Hayley is and she is nowhere to be seen. What I do see … is the tail of a rather large snake going in the direction of where we've just come from.

Terra!

269

'I'm going back in for the girls,' I tell Ember, crouching in the shadow of her body and disappearing before her eyes.

'Be careful,' she calls out as I race back inside.

The room with the Spear of Destiny in it, is empty of people by the time I reach it. Nothing looks tampered with. Nothing out of place. I'm thinking about how to break the glass when I hear a whistle.

The sound is up high. I allow myself to become weightless and drift towards the ceiling so I can see through the smoke.

On the highest ledge, is a blackbird.

It promptly flies off as I reach eye level.

Back through the hallways and out into the fresh air again, I follow it until it finally goes to ground outside a café two streets away from the Treasury. The blackbird hops onto the back of a chair and I immediately notice a message clipped around its foot.

'Wait there,' I say, diving into a desolate alleyway for a second before returning to visibility. I remove the clip and receive a forceful peck for my trouble. A trickle of blood slides down my finger. 'Thanks for that, Terra,' I grumble loud enough for it to hear before she flies off.

The note reads: Meet me in Rome. Hayley knows where.

TWENTY-ONE

ROME.

My passport is getting a major workout with our constant jet-setting across Europe. It must be costing River a small fortune, and yet, he doesn't appear to be the least bit put out by it.

All he's worried about is why I didn't *follow the plan* … why I keep *re-writing the script*.

His first reaction, biggest eye-roll on record.

Second reaction …I did the wrong thing, AGAIN.

I see his point … to a certain degree, and yes, it keeps happening. However, he struggles to comprehend the variables in his seemingly failsafe plans because there is no such thing – there are always going to be those spur-of-the-moment decisions, those dying seconds when something goes wrong. In River's world, *obviously*, that kind of thing doesn't occur because if it did, then he'd have a little more compassion for those of us who screw up a lot.

Recovering outside Hofburg Palace, gasping for breath, enough smoke in my lungs to be considered a twenty pack a day man, he'd torn me a new one …

In front of everyone!

In fact, I'm positive the entire city of Vienna heard him, even when Ember told him to keep his voice down.

Irritated much … is the biggest understatement of the year, and I'd be lying if it didn't leave me feeling as though my life is one huge mistake all over again. I get the bigger picture and all that … that we won't have any friends if we fail, and yet, I would still drag his sorry-arse out of the Treasury again instead of stealing the spearhead.

And I think he would do the same for me.

He's just pissy because going-off-his-head is the only way he knows how to process his feelings. His knee-jerk reaction is to lash out first until realisation sinks in. And even after all this time … in his eyes, and *mind*, I can't do a thing right, and he sees my decision-making skills as a real threat to our success. In my eyes, what can I say … I thought I was doing the right thing.

Since Terra left, Ember has barely spoken to me either as though somehow, *that's* my fault too. I explained about the note, and that I didn't know anything else; however, the endless string of questions running through their heads that they forget I can hear, triggers suspicion that I'm holding something back. I don't know another way to say *I'm in the dark as much as you all are*. I'm meant to be part of this dysfunctional and exclusive quartet, and yet I feel more of an outsider than ever.

Hayley seems to be the only person who has any time for me, regardless of her bipolar moods. I still cannot pick up anything telepathically from her, which is strange considering, at one point, she was an open book.

And, let's not forget the bombshell she dropped as we all caught our breath outside the front of a very smoky Imperial Treasury …

She stole the real spearhead!

Apparently, during the commotion, she had somehow switched the spearheads without setting off the alarms. None of us could speak for a few seconds, and I'll never forget the look on River's face after she told us. Questions weren't raised at the time, as to how she did it, because we were all desperate for water, River especially, and his welfare was paramount to Ember. But it's stored away, to be bought up at another time. All River did was open her bag a crack, and we'd all peered in, staring at what we thought was the souvenir, but which Hayley swore blind was the real deal. I was half expecting to see the Agate bowl in there but the only other item was a wooden cup that she offered zero information on.

So it appears, we're not public enemy number one on Britain's Most Wanted list after all. This morning's news headline mentioned there was a fire at the Imperial Treasury, which had been contained. No mention of a robbery.

The spearhead, now wrapped in a flowered tea towel, is stowed in my backpack. This brings me to Customs …which was quite an exciting challenge for me. But hey, I'm the kind of guy you want around when there's a need to manipulate the airwaves and influence someones thought patterns. A few words here, a few suggestions there – and hey presto, I have a permit for a rare and quite sharp implement, even though in reality, it was a printed A4 copy of our hotel receipt. I flashed them my driver's licence, explaining I was a world reknown archaeologist and a collector of ancient artefacts, settling any concerns about bringing a lethal weapon out of Austria and into Italy. No problemo.

And, I think I saw a little respect and a dash of amusement, albeit in the smallest amount, return to

River's eyes as I unleashed my airpower on two unsuspecting customs officers.

So, after finally locating our luggage, checking in to another less than extravagant hotel, we are now heading to some nature reserve about six and a half kilometres southwest of Rome.

Hayley has been a tad cagey about where we were meeting Terra, other than informing us that we needed to find a cave. Ember wasn't satisfied with that answer, and produced a map, politely demanding Hayley pinpoint exactly where we were heading.

The Riserva Naturale della Valle dei Casali is not a real nature reserve, not like we get back home, anyhow.

'I thought there would be more trees,' he says, plucking the thoughts directly from my head, 'and perhaps the odd stream or boulder.' His lip turns up. He looks left and right. 'There isn't a hill or mountain in sight. Are you sure this is the place?' he says, turning to Hayley.

'Yeah,' adds Ember, 'what's with all the houses? It looks like a country village, not a nature reserve.'

'We're in the correct place,' replies Hayley. 'Don't fret. Terra knows what she's doing.'

Two things trigger my spidey senses – one, Hayley sounds like her and Terra are the new dynamic duo, which is more than a little odd, and two, the way she screws her mouth up suggesting she's eaten something bitter reflects the true nature of their relationship. And yet her eyes haven't stopped shining since we touched down earlier this morning. There are no mind-clues to help me out and I get the distinct impression she knows when I'm trying to shoplift her thoughts. A curtain of static seems to drop over her mind the second I venture in for a little look-see.

'Follow me,' says Hayley confidently.

Ember shrugs as River and I exchange worried glances. What choice do we have, he thinks, knowing I will pick up on it. My face creases with uncertainty before

I concede, and continue to trail behind the one person this has nothing to do with. Terra must have a solid reason to trust Hayley, because right now, the doubts we are all feeling is louder than the dry, coarse grass crunching beneath our feet.

Clouds pass across the sun as we walk, patchworking the ground in assorted shades of grey, until our view alters slightly. A line of thick, bushy trees, bordering the edge of a recently ploughed field, plunge the nearby houses into shadow, giving the illusion we are miles from civilisation.

Ember drops back from the group and I slow my pace to walk beside her. 'Everything okay?' She's been unusually quiet about her personal life the last few days, not letting too many thoughts venture my way.

'Yup,' she answers, studying River's back before returning her eyes to the ground. Her mind is jumbled and random thoughts thread through each other, making it hard to decipher a theme.

'I'm worried about him, Skye.' With a heavy brow, my mood slides into dismay. 'I don't think he's letting on how much this poisonous blood is affecting him.' I absolutely agree and choose my words carefully.

'He's strong, Em. He'll get through it.'

She nods unconvincingly. 'You will do everything in your power to save him, won't you?'

'Of course,' I say, resolutely.

'Promise?'

'Promise,' I answer, squeezing her hand in mine. To an outsider, her cheeks appear less pinched, and her mouth has softened, yet her mind prolongs the agony.

'We're almost there,' calls out Hayley, glancing behind, zeroing in on our clasped hands and then straight at me, her eyes, a new kind of wild. I release Ember's hand immediately.

Hayley says nothing, although it isn't hard to miss her fists ball up as she walks in front. I never took her as the jump-to-the-wrong-conclusion type before, and as though she hears me, she slows her pace so I can catch up.

She smiles sweetly at me. 'You trust me, don't you, Skye?' I peer into her mind. There is nothing there that says I shouldn't.

'Sure.' I wonder if she picks up the wobble in my voice.

She brushes a strand of hair from her eyes. 'We're not *actually* looking for a cave, per se.'

'What?' My response is almost rude in tone, prompting River and Em to turn around for a second before carrying on.

'We're looking for a windmill,' she informs me, her voice no more than a whisper.

'A windmill?' I hear myself repeating.

'Seems totally ludicrous, doesn't it?' I nod and she continues to speak. 'I wanted to tell you because I need you to know I am here to help you complete these tasks.'

'I know that,' I say in a softer tone. This is the Hayley I remember.

'I get the feeling the others don't like me very much,' she whispers across my chest, 'but don't let it concern you,' she says, examining my face, 'their opinions of me don't matter … only yours does.' She offers me a brown paper bag. 'Fudge?' I take a piece out and pop it into my mouth. 'Wally and I made some before we left. It's been in my bag all this time, and I keep forgetting to give it to you.' The chewy, sweetness is out of this world, sending me straight back into the bag to get another one.

'Not all at once now,' she coos, snatching the bag away, 'otherwise, you'll get a tummy ache and then what good will you be to me?'

They say the way to a man's heart is through his stomach …I wonder if it's the same for a man's desire, because my head is suddenly filled with wild, hot fantasies about her. I actually have to bite down and count to ten to ward off the overwhelming impulse.

276

She smiles at me ...innocently, clueless as to my intentions. I inhale a deep breath to help me through the throbbing urge in my pants.

The afternoon sun makes a welcome appearance as we hike over hedges and along shady laneways. I feel a little more confident we are going in the right direction from the older styled stone houses we pass ... something a stonemason would've been proud of two hundred years ago. A windmill certainly wouldn't look out of place here.

The second I think it, I see the flat, paddled fins of a windmill poking through the tree line. River sees it too and points.

'I see you've spotted our destination,' says Hayley.

River raises his eyebrows and addresses me. 'I thought we were looking for a cave? Did you know about this?'

I shrug, not wanting to get into another full-on row with him about who knows what. So, I lengthen my step and stride away from him.

Hayley half skips to catch up and hooks her arm through mine, squeezing out a short giggle. 'You two will never learn.' She says it in a way that sounds like she's known us both for years.

Partially hidden behind a run-down haybarn, we find the windmill. It was probably quite remarkable and glorious in its day, but now there are stones missing from the walls, the sails are weathered and in disrepair, and birds have nested under what is left of the roof. The only sturdy element is a thick wooden door with an equally heavy-duty bolt.

River grimaces as he inspects the lock. 'Looks like this place has been off-limits for a while,' he says, untangling a spider web from his fingers. He forces back the bolt, taking a chunk of his palm in the process. He swears under his breath before trying to open the door. He steals a glimpse over his shoulder to Hayley, sweat gathering around his hairline. 'Are you sure this is the place? The door won't budge.'

'Positive,' she answers without hesitation before turning to me. 'Fly up there and see what's inside.'

I was just about to, although not before becoming invisible. The last thing some poor farmer and his wife need to see is a teenager hovering twenty feet in the air.

A sense of peace washes over me the second my feet leave the ground. I float up higher, and when I become level with the top row of stonework, I lean forward and peer over the edge just as a few birds fly out, startling me.

'It's an empty shell inside,' I yell down, a little surprised. There are no inner workings of the mill. No giant rusted cogs to turn the sails. There's no sturdy wooden beams holding it in place, doubling to provide internal structure for floorboards. Nothing.

I flick back to my visible self, weave between the remaining roof struts and drop down into the belly of the windmill. Tufts of grass surround the edges of what looks to be a black manhole cover, several inches thick and several feet in diameter. I don't think I'll be able to prise it up myself.

I hear River putting his shoulder into the other side of the door, huffing with each thumping shove, and that's when I see it. The door appears to be locked from the inside. *How odd?*

Three thickset bolts are placed at the door's top middle and bottom. I can reach the top one, the ground level higher inside the windmill than out, and have no problem shifting it without injury.

'I think I'm making progress,' shouts River, wrestling with the lock.

I slide back the second bolt, less weathered by the elements than the outside one, and it obeys without hesitation. The bottom bolt is a tad harder, and I end up throwing my boot onto the end of it to get it to shift. The second I do, River comes hurtling through the door and lands flat on his face on top of the manhole cover.

'Fuck! You could've given me some warning,' he says, picking himself up and brushing the dirt off his

278

jeans. Ember and Hayley hang in the doorway, both trying not to giggle. Subtlety isn't my strong suit, and I loose a riotous laugh.

Hayley doesn't seem to see the funny side of it as she steps across the threshold. 'Who would have thought to disguise a Roman slave-keep as a fourteenth century windmill,' says Hayley, very matter of fact. 'It's pure genius.' We all turn to look at her. Her expression changes from wonder to indifference, 'I suppose it's obvious really …isn't it?'

To her maybe, but not to us. Her knowledge of European architecture stuns me.

She continues on. 'Back in Roman times, they built these structures to imprison their slaves, so they wouldn't run away, and now it has been remodelled over the years to represent a windmill. What better way to conceal a cave, or more to the point, a tunnel leading into a cave.'

All eyes fall to the manhole cover.

'I don't think I can go in there,' mumbles Ember, finding that same worrying spot on her lip.

River goes to her side immediately and puts his arm around her shoulders. 'I'll be right there with you, and Skye will be in front. You can do this.' Ember's lip trembles.

The same worry gurgles in my stomach. Another small space, but worse, a small, *dark* space. Much worse than an elevator. 'If I can do it, Em, then *you* can,' I say, focussing on the calmness of my voice.

Hayley looks on sympathetically. 'First, let's get this cover off and see what we're dealing with.'

'And we can always use our phones to light the way,' I chip in, switching on my phone torch. 'Or you can use your flame, Em. You've always got one of those handy.'

She forces out a smile. Seems a little braver.

Although her thoughts are frantic.

The manhole cover is much harder to pry up, with years of grass and weeds anchoring the lid in place. After multiple attempts to loosen it with the help of a piece of wood, it comes off clean.

I lean it against the wall of the windmill.

Ember peers in just as three bats decide to exit, sending her reeling backwards into the stoney wall. Her face resembles winter's first snow. 'I'm definitely not going in there now.'

'Toughen up, princess. You've been through much worse than this,' snipes Hayley.

Instinctively Ember takes a step back.

I find myself doing the same, my hands sliding through my hair, momentarily holding it back before releasing it.

River stares openly, lifting a single eyebrow at Hayley, his brain going double time deciding whether to say something or not.

Realising the effect of her words, Hayley's face scrambles to reverse what she said. 'I didn't mean it like *that*. I just meant …' She drops her gaze towards the hole, 'it's just, we're not going to get very far if we don't all go together.' Without warning, she descends into the opening as though she's jumping into a puddle. 'I'm all good,' she calls up, shining her phone up at us. 'There's heaps of room down here too, Ember.'

Ember squares her shoulders, stares first at River and then at me. There's something different in her posture, in the way that familiar bronzy-fire lights up her eyes again, that I haven't seen in a while. I dive into her mind, suddenly curious. I don't know how it happened, but the growing fears in Ember's mind, concerning everyone and everything, has vanished. Like it had never even been there. As though Hayley's tough-love speech has erased the frightened little girl syndrome that has been slowly creeping back in after Nuria was removed. She looks ready to slay dragons again.

'I'll go,' I say, teetering at the edge. It's not the drop or even the confined space that worries me. It's what might be down there waiting for us. Caves are rarely empty and even more so, when dealing with supernatural shit. Besides, something at the back of my mind keeps jabbing at me. Something from the book – Peri Phuseôs tôn Ontôn. 'Make sure you bolt this door behind you, Riv. We don't want any kids falling in.'

River nods and throws the top two locks into place.

I float down with ease and take in my surroundings. It is much wider than I anticipated, eighteen to twenty feet across, and the ceiling height at least ten foot, even though we only came down eight feet. It is definitely more of a cavern than a tunnel.

I flash my phone light across the walls. They're shiny with moisture and the small indentation in the rockface suggest it's been hand chiselled by the slaves Hayley referred to. The air smells sulphurous and less earthy, which surprises me. I'd wager there's an underground water supply around here somewhere.

'Riv, lower Ember down and I'll catch her.'

A few minutes later, I see the soles of Ember's shoes. 'Don't you dare drop me, Skye,' she grumbles. I feel for her shins and that's when River lets her go. Her body slips through my fingers. I manage to catch her around the ribs before she hits the ground. 'Thanks. You've earnt the right to live a little longer.' Lightheartedly, she punches my arm.

River is the last down, landing feet first with a heavy grunt. There's only one way to go. River points, 'lead the way.'

'I'm not saying we will, but has anyone thought what might happen if we get stuck down here? We have no food or water with us. What then?' Ember has picked those thoughts fresh out of River's mind.

'Don't stress. I can float right out of here and bring us back a KFC, no probs.'

Ember sighs. 'You know what? You have the best power out of all of us right now.'

TWENTY-TWO

THE further we venture into the tunnel, the better the terrain gets, which seems totally weird. You'd think it'd get worse. Now that there are less rocks to kick and fewer potholes to fall in, the cries and groans about twisting ankles or stubbing toes are long gone. River and I have also switched off our phone torches to save the battery. We are now being guided by the soft glow of Hayley's phone. It makes sense. God knows how long we'll be down here!

It's pretty hard to see anything except the loamy dirt scuffing up from beneath our feet. Except for the odd occasion when Hayley swings her phone around to check on us, I manage to get a fleeting glimpse of the walls. It's hardened natural ground, not rock like I first thought and carved out with almost perfect precision. Other than that, there is nothing else to see. Except how spacious it is down here, which totally blows my mind – enough for six men to march through, shoulder to shoulder, decked in full battle gear. I have to admit, I'm a little happier about that. I think Ember is, too.

The air, which should feel denser, has a crispness to it that says fresh, breathable air is being ventilated in from somewhere, but I have no idea where, and it gives me hope that we are not journeying to the centre of the earth … not being swallowed whole by a planet.

We push on in silence, the near darkness starting to dampen everyone's mood.

'How much further, do you think?' Ember groans. Her hand, slapping against my back, makes me jump. 'I feel like we've been walking for ten hours.'

My hoodie is damp under the armpits and around the neckline, although I suspect it's from a lack of fresh air and not fatigue. It hasn't been hours like Ember thinks, but I understand how it might feel that way. We've only been walking for two hours, and my guess is we must have covered around eight to ten kilometres, but who knows. We could be going in a straight line. Hell, we could be going around in circles for all we know.

'Keep going,' I reassure her. 'I'm certain we're almost at the end.' I listen to her constant mutterings of *it'll be over soon, and then we can go home* mantra.

Before we'd set off, I had suggested flying on ahead to see what's up there, although the definite "NO" from River as I'd whispered it to him screwed up that plan. He wants us to stay together.

Surely it can't be that much further.

We'd have to be right under the city of Rome by now, if we are heading in that direction. If we were above ground, I could use my GPS system, but as my typical lousy luck would have it, it isn't working. Hayley speaks, disturbing my train of thought.

'Can you smell that?'

I inhale deeply. I can't smell anything except more moisture in the air, meaning I'm definitely going to need a new t-shirt soon. The humidity in here is rising.

'It's water,' says River, confidently. 'And it's fresh too.'

'How can you tell that?' I ask. My mouth salivates at the thought.

'Oooh, I don't know. Why don't you read my mind and find out?'

Fair point.

The tunnel is widening, and I flick on my phone torch. To my left is an enormous cavernous room that could be a place to sleep or some kind of holding area for soldiers or slaves.

'There,' says Ember. 'Shine the light there,' she says, guiding my hand. It looks to be some kind of primitive well made from stone, the height and diameter of a small car tyre. 'Do you think it's safe to drink?' She plunges her hand into the water and lets it run through her fingers.

'Go for your life,' comments Hayley, 'but you won't get me drinking it.' I angle my phone so the light hits her directly in the face. She squints her eyes and places a hand up in front of my phone. 'My guess is, this is the off-shoot from the River Tiber.'

I frown.

How the hell would she know that?

'You know they used to dump dead bodies in there?' She pauses. 'A king drowned in the River Tiber once too. And the bodies of murderers and traitors, who were strangled first, then bound and thrown down the Gemonian stairs, where their corpses were left to rot, or scavenged by dogs, were then disposed of in the river. So … do I want to drink from it? I think not.'

'That was hundreds of years ago,' retaliates River, 'and besides … my nose says it's uncontaminated and I'd trust that more than a shitty history lesson.' He struts over and scoops up several handfuls to drink, wearing most of it down his shirt. 'Good old fashioned bore water.'

'Good enough for me,' says Ember, joining him. I find no problem in it either and take my turn when Ember is done. It's a little chalky at the back of my throat but other than that, it does the job.

As much as I don't want to be down here longer than I have to, a five minute break is warranted. Ember is sitting down, her shoe and sock off, inspecting a blister, whilst River stands over her, offering her the light from his phone.

It gives me a chance to take a breath and inspect our surroundings a little closer. I let my torch do the exploring for me, the light passing over Hayley, twitching, and eager to get going.

'What's that?' Ember calls when my light finds something orb-like a few feet away. I don't need to get any closer to see it's a human skull. 'Is that what I think it is?'

'Yep,' I say, nodding. 'I'd say it's been here a few hundred years.' I hadn't wanted to say anything out loud that there are more shadows and lower-toned voices down here than I care to count. Hearing the voices of the living is doable … voices of the dead can fuck right off. The one and only time I opened up a discussion with a spook was when I was twelve. My Pop's best friend had died, and the persistent old spook had bugged me for days to get me to listen to him. The message he wanted me to pass on to his wife was sweet, although the whole experience zapped my energy like I had the flu, left an ashen taste in my mouth for days afterwards, and I couldn't seem to warm up, no matter how many layers I put on.

And besides, it's just wrong.

Once you die, you don't get to come back … unless of course you're an immortal Roman Centurion, and actually have flesh on your bones.

'Skye.' I reign in my thoughts. 'We need to leave,' urges Hayley. 'Now.'

I am about to agree with her when the air pressure suddenly changes. Too much gravity exists, squeezing what air is left between the ceiling and the ground. My lungs have become a vanilla thickshake and I'm breathing through a straw.

'Skye …' mutters River, his fist massaging his chest. 'What's hap…happening.' His words are brittle.

I direct my light over to where we came in, expecting to see a rockfall had silently caved in around us, trapping us.

'I'll be back in a minute,' I manage to get out.

My first guess is Ra-Mon. Only he would do something so bold as to squeeze all the oxygen out of the air to get his jollies.

I venture back into the tunnel, my light jumping from wall to floor back to the wall again. A deep impulse presses against my mind, urging me to turn invisible. I feel a challenge coming, the same way Notre Dame suddenly came to life.

    I breathe
        and breathe,
            and breathe,

slow and controlled. A familiar smell taints the air. Something up ahead moves across my lightbeam.

I freeze.

'Who's there,' I call out. I hear the shuffle of feet and what sounds like the clink of metal on metal. 'Come out.' Random thoughts, from my mystery visitor, stream through my brain. I can't make any sense of it. I block out the blood whirring in my ears and try to zero in. A couple of words stand out, like my name.

There's a reason I can't understand what is being said. It isn't English.

'Don't be a coward. Show yourself,' I call out to the darkness again. My light touches every area of the floor and walls in quick successive bursts so I don't miss anything.

'I am least of all, a coward,' replies a familiar voice.

'Tomas?' I can't hold back the jubilation in my voice. 'I thought you were … never mind.' His broad outline appears around the edges of my light, and I accidentally fire the light directly into his eyes. 'You're the last person I thought I'd bump into down here.'

Tomas steps into the light, his square-set jaw and vacant stare as present as always. 'You are lucky I am the only one you have *bumped* into.'

I feel a lump in my throat. 'What's that supposed to mean?'

'You mean, you don't feel its presence. Do your lungs not feel heavy?'

'Yes, it is difficult to breathe,' I answer shakily. I don't want to ask the rest, but I know I must. 'And *what* presence are we talking about?'

'Othniel is here.'

'Oth …?'

'A beast of mammoth proportions.'

My legs lock into position. 'I was racing ahead to see if we were close to the end of the tunnel.'

'No. There is still a way to go. You are within the walls of Rome.'

That's good to know.

'Three tunnels will appear before you if you follow this path to its end. The middle tunnel will take you beneath the Colosseum. You must not take that one unless you wish to be a meal for a hungry beast.'

A rumble of thunder steals my next words. It takes a minute or so before I finally come up with, 'What was that?'

Tomas grasps the hilt of his sword. 'Like I said, we are not the only occupants of these dwellings.' *Dwellings …* *I thought it was a tunnel.*

A scream, the kind you pray you'll never hear in your lifetime, rips the deathly silence from my ears.

'Ember.'

'You cannot help them.'

'Are you *nuts*? My friends are back there.' I turn to go but Tomas grabs me by the shoulder.

'You must fulfil your part in this.'

'And that is why we have to go back. I can't do this without them.'

Tomas lets go. 'You can … and you must. Your destiny, for now, lays on a different path to theirs.'

I deliberate.

Fuck!

I don't know what to do.

I'm always in this predicament where I have to make a decision and to be honest, I'm frigging over it. Every time I choose, I seem to do the wrong thing. And so, for once in my life, I fight my gut instincts and choose the wrong thing, hoping to God, it's right.

'Okay. I'm right behind you.'

Five minutes into our fast-paced march, my phone dies – great! Even if I wanted to, I have no way to contact the others now. I have no trouble following behind Tomas, the chink of his sword consistently bumping against his studded leather tunic. I breathe a sigh of relief - at least someone is dressed for a fight.

'You have the spear?' asks Tomas, after we've walked a short distance.'

'It's in my backpack.' I'm trusting Hayley with more than my own life right now. God, I hope it's the right one.

For as far underground as we are, the area I now find myself in is somewhat lighter, and I can make out the three tunnels in front of us, just like he said.

Tomas raises his hand for me to stop. 'Now we wait.' He seems edgy, muttering softly to himself in what I guess is Italian. I feel the air on my face as he passes me with his troubled pacing, the language barrier keeping his thoughts a secret from me.

I jump to my feet as a light approaches from the left tunnel. Tomas notices it too, and instead of unsheathing his sword, he backs away as the person draws nearer.

An old man, hair as long and as grey as Ra-Mon's, has me reeling back in terror until I see his weathered face by the light of a fire torch. His eyes are kind, and he bows courteously to me around a wooden staff that supports his frail being. A thick woollen cloak is pulled tightly around him, hiding what lays beneath.

I look to Tomas for guidance. His face, ordinarily a blank canvas, conveys a hundred different emotions as his fingers clutch at his throat, his mouth agape.

'You should not have come,' says the old man. He neither looks at me nor Tomas.

Tomas offers no response. I want to say it was his idea to come and that I wanted to go back for my friends but I don't. I have an idea who this man is. 'You're Longinus, aren't you?' I say.

He turns slowly to face me as though his head is a tight cork on a prehistoric bottle. 'That I am,' he replies. He shuffles closer, leaning heavily into his stick. I take the torch from him, his arm shaking. 'If you know of me, then you know what I have done.'

'Only what I've read, but you can't believe half the stuff in print these days,' I add, scratching my head, and adjusting my backpack with one hand. The spearhead suddenly feels much heavier in my bag than before.

I slide the torch into a wire bracket above my head. 'I'd like to hear it from you, if you will tell me.'

Tomas still hasn't moved even as the old man passes him, looks him up and down, and comes to stand at my side.

'He healed me, you know. The Son of God. His blood splashed upon my eyes and gave me back my sight, even after I forced my spear into his body to make sure he was dead.'

'You weren't to know,' I offer sympathetically. Two thousand years of guilt is a lot to carry. I try to ease his burden with a few well chosen words. 'How were you to know? You were simply following orders.'

Longinus is quiet for a short while before saying, 'And now I endure an eternity of misery for defiling our Lord's body. I am condemned to these caves, to suffer the harshest of punishments every single night.'

'Punishments? What kind of punishment?'

The air loses its freshness, not that it was ever there in the first place, and is replaced with a sour, rancid aroma, not that dissimilar from the morning breath of our old dog, god rest her soul.

A low, intermittent thud tremors beneath my feet that at first, I wonder if it's water rushing beneath, or the way a house might groan throughout the different seasons of the year. The second time it happens, I realise it's an impact tremor.

From the look on Tomas's face, who thankfully has the breath of life back in him, he knows what it is.

Hunched, sword drawn and ready to strike – that's my man.

A deafening roar rushes through the tunnels towards us, shaking the walls, juddering the small rocks beneath my feet. My chest clenches between beats, trying to avoid the slightest noise through respiration.

'He's coming for me,' says the old man, without a hint of fear in his voice. 'You must leave, before he picks up your scent.'

'There's no time,' says Tomas. 'Get behind me. I will fight the beast as was the way.'

'You mean like … *gladiator-style*? This is nuts! There must be a way out, somewhere.' My thoughts scramble, and I blurt out the only thing that might make a difference. 'I have the Spear of Destiny.'

Within arms reach, the old man lashes out for me, gripping my forearm fiercely in his gnarly fingers. 'You have the spearhead?'

'Yes,' I say, nodding.

Longinus stumbles and falls to his knees, his hand still clamped onto me. 'Do I dare hope for a way out of this afterlife?' he asks. 'For I have repented every day for my sins. Surely he must know that.'

'He knows, Uncle. But your penance is not orchestrated by the Lord anymore and I'm not sure it ever was. It comes from a far darker place.'

I replay the last sentence. 'Uncle? He's your uncle?' I look between the both of them, waiting for one of them to answer as sizeable, pounding footsteps draw nearer.

'If you wish to save me, I beg you. Do not put your steel through the beast,' says Longinus. 'Did you not, but escape with your life the last time you were here? You know being slain by this beast will break the curse between you and the witch, and you will dwell in The Underworld forever? Never to be reunited with your family.'

'You knew about that?' replies Tomas, struggling to compose himself.

'Yes. The witch knew that one day, you would come looking for me. That you would consider ending your long existence, like I long for mine.'

Another shuddering footstep echoes in the tunnels around us.

At the most inappropriate time, I let out a laugh that borders along the lines of hysteria. 'In case you haven't noticed, you both share the same genetic disposition of immortality. And having at least two thousand years under both your belts, I'd consider this life a life well-lived, whereas me ... I'm very much of the mortal, humankind and in the early prime of my life, so whatever is coming, you better power up and quit the family catch-up because I don't much feel like being supper for a hungry cave-troll.'

I sense its presence before its monstrous frame comes into view.

'A *lion*?' I hear myself say. 'I was expecting a dinosaur or mammoth or some kind of monster from the black lagoon.' Admittedly, it's the biggest fucking lion I've ever seen, but *still* ...a lion. Its head is the size of a Range Rover bonnet, teeth longer than a ruler and paws that could break every bone in your foot if it stood on you.

'This lion cannot be slain,' says Longinus, stepping forward to meet the beast, not a shred of fear in the old man's eyes. The giant feline stands seven feet tall.

291

The rumble of a voice, not quite human but still very distinguishable, reaches my ears. 'It is time, old man. Face your penance, and let us be done with it.'

'What's going on?' My body quakes with some unknown dread. 'Is this a need to know thing?'

Nobody is laughing.

The lion and the old man regard each other. Moments pass between them, an exchange of ancient knowledge and familiarity fills the space around us as though I am part of someone else's dream. Before I can move, or speak, or even flinch, the lion lethargically swipes a hefty paw at the old man's frail body, sending him to the wall in a clatter of cloth and bones.

It doesn't take a genius to see the old man won't live. Each struggling breath in, is shallow, each breath out rattles through his spindly ribcage. He only has seconds. 'Do something,' I scream at Tomas, finally locating my voice.

'The end is inevitable,' he replies as the lion moves towards the old man and stands over him.

'Are you going to help him or not? He's your uncle for Christ's sake.'

Tomas inhales a hearty breath, his face creasing in all kinds of anguish. The lion suddenly changes its focus – man and beast exchange glances, with something passing between them, something I am not privy to.

In one ravenous movement, the lion rips out the old man's throat until his last breath is cut off with a gurgled groan.

I take a step towards the lion, having no idea what I can do. It bears its teeth at me, the fur around its muzzle stained red from the old man's blood. The only weapon I have is the spearhead which is pretty much useless without a large stick to fasten it to. And who am I, to go up against a lion when Tomas, decked in battle uniform and wielding a sword, is ready and able to kill this beast?

The lion slinks away into the darkness, retreating back into the tunnel.

'So, you pick and choose who you save? Is that how it works? That man was your family. Why …'

'Enough!' yells Tomas. 'You have no idea what we are dealing with here.'

'Then how about filling me in. I have …*skills*.' I feel kind of dumb adding that last bit, but I can do stuff.'

'I can't kill it. You heard what my uncle said, I will remain in The Underworld forever.' Tomas pauses for a breath. 'My uncle, Longinus, as you know, pierced the Lord's side with a spear after he perished on the cross.' I nod. 'His penance for that crime was that he was condemned to a cave for eternity, and every night a lion would maul him until dawn, after which his body is healed back to normal.'

I don't see the downside to Tomas's remorseful tale. Instead, a spark of hope flares in my chest. 'He's not dead? We just have to wait for him to zap back to life?'

'It's not as simple as that. I see the pain in his eyes, the memories that continually haunt him. He suffers horrendously … every time … as does the lion. It is the reason it did not attack us.'

'The lion suffers, too? Who cares about a stupid cat and since when have you been able to speak lion?'

'I can't. The EarthHealer told me. She spoke to me of his weariness and his will to leave this life.'

Something familiar about this sparks a conversation off in my head that Terra mentioned. She'd said, "Gaia spoke of an old man having done his time and needs to be put out of his misery". Technically, that could be Longinus, or Othniel, or *both*.

'I cannot. Only you can face Othniel. It has been set down that way for centuries - the one who returns the Holy Lance to its owner can undo what has been done. Did Terra not part with that knowledge?'

'No,' I snarl. 'It must have slipped her mind.' I wonder what else she's forgotten to tell me.

'You know that the Lion is the Fourth Initiation?'

'Yeah,' I say solemnly. 'I kinda figure that. But what about the third? The Soldier? I haven't completed that Initiation yet.' The second the words are out of my mouth, I make the connection. 'The two are combined, aren't they? The soldier and the lion – they are woven together in this tapestry of deceit?'

'Yes.' Tomas drops his gaze, releasing a shaky breath.

'So, how do we kill it?'

'It is immortal. It cannot be killed. Like my uncle.'

I feel my brow furrowing. 'But, I have the Spear of Destiny. Surely that must account for something.'

Tomas nods gravely. 'It does. I do not know how. Terra would know.'

I yell out her name, hoping she can hear me. There is no answer. 'When did you last see her?'

'Last night. She is within the city walls, but she will not speak with you.'

'Why not?'

'She did not say.'

'And you didn't think to ask? She could be in danger and we need her ... NOW.'

Tomas places a hand on my shoulder. 'She is more concerned about the dangers you are about to face.'

Going toe to toe with a lion is about as scary as it gets. I need answers and something tells me Amun is the one to cough it up.

TWENTY-THREE

WITH the initial threat of Othniel over, for the time being, I use this opportunity to double back and check on the others. My thoughts have been dark, worrying about them, to the point I can't focus on much else, especially with an oversized feline on the loose, who may or may not be harbouring a grudge.

I move faster by myself, switching to supersonic flight mode, arriving at the well in less than half the time it took marching behind Tomas. Of course, they're nowhere to be found, just like I thought, and yet I couldn't be more relieved. My heart immediately feels lighter and more optimistic, having not stumbled across any freshly chomped body parts. I am pissed that they didn't think to leave a clue where they might be going though, so my best guess would be, with the threat of suffocation bearing down on them, River did the smart thing and retraced their steps back to the manhole. I've no idea how, or if, they managed to climb out, but being a resilient group of individuals with a unique set of skills, I'm sure they figured something out. What I need to do now … is trust they're okay.

Upon my return, I find Tomas propping up the wall where his Uncle once lay. It's no surprise, that the old man's body has vanished. I figured as much. So, it shouldn't be long before he's back to his decrepit old self again.

Tomas tells me we have to leave, so we push on through the tunnel until we come to the junction he spoke of. He doesn't hesitate in electing the middle option, both of us aware we are walking into the lion's den, *literally.*

There is a significant drop in temperature too, as we approach a formidable metal door, the bars burnt with red rust, and yet still robust enough to give you the finger. Tomas informs me that this is the entrance to the slave quarters beneath the Colosseum. He also assured me, this area is not accessible to the public.

The slave-cell we set up camp in, is dark, dank and smells of mildew. There are no windows except for a small grate at eye level in the wooden door, which I demanded to be left wide open. The thought of being trapped in one of these, *for real,* gives me shivers.

Tomas suggests I get some rest because I need to be at the top of my game when Longinus returns. The fire torch he has strung up above our heads, entice ghostly shadows onto the wall in front of me, so I close my eyes to block them out. I pull Tomas's cloak tightly around me, drawing up my legs to keep a little heat in and lay my head against my backpack. I don't realise I've nodded off until I wake with a start.

I check my watch.

Shit! I've been out of it for three hours.

'Why didn't you wake me?' I rub my face awake, my cheeks cold, the tip of my nose even colder.

'It shouldn't be too much longer now.'

I get up and stretch, walk around the edges of the cell thinking how I can help. What can I do?

Amun.

I need to speak with him.

Like so many times before, I focus inwards and call out his name.

Tomas regards me.

'Dude, we need your expert knowledge on this. Just one tiny, incey wincey clue as to how to kill two birds with one stone would be greatly appreciated.'

Silence.

Amun isn't playing nice with others, and no amount of begging, bribing and pleading seems to summon this sluggish God to the party. My thoughts drift back to River and Ember, and then Hayley, hoping they have made it out safely. Terra, however, is a complete mystery. She is hiding in the shadows, clearly more informed about all this than we are, and yet isn't playing by team rules either. She still hasn't spoken about Zurvan, and I just wish she'd spill her guts and let us all in on it.

Tomas goes back to dragging his whetstone over his sword. 'I don't feel right about leaving your uncle back there. How will he …?'

'He knows where we are, and will seek us out when the time is right. When he does, I need to speak with him alone.'

I frown. 'What for?'

Tomas stretches out his legs and rests his head against the carved stone wall. The icy coldness of the stone doesn't seem to bother him. 'He knows where my father's final resting place is.'

'Where he was buried, you mean?' He nods. 'Why? Why is it so important to you?'

'I believe my father has something more to do with this. You remember how I told you I found the book, Peri Phuseôs tôn Ontôn, inside a pyramid in Falicon?'

'Yes.'

'The journey leading up to this moment has become my life's purpose. I have to free myself from the witch's curse, ease my uncle's pain, and place my father's soul at rest. And it all starts with you.'

'*Me*? What does it have to do with me? You stumbled across *my* destiny, I think.'

'You are wrong. We are part of the same twisted plot.' I ponder that thought for a moment. 'I know contacting Amun is of great consequence, but right now, I need you to speak with my father.'

'Your *father*? How? Hasn't he been dead for like, *two thousand years* ..' Ice needles prickle my skin. 'I don't think I can go back that far.'

'The dead is *the dead*,' replies Tomas forcefully. His jaw grinds together. 'We need to wait for the resurrection of my uncle. He will help bind the two worlds so you can communicate with him.'

'Great!' I mumble under my breath. The thought of channelling a two century year old spook doesn't excite me one bit. Tomas shifts his position several times before getting up and walking to the cell door.

He looks to me, his face saying he isn't thrilled about the idea either.

I place my backpack behind me and recheck my watch. This waiting around is almost as bad as what's coming. I just want this over with.

And, I can't get comfortable.

My pants are wet from this damp ground, my arse is numb, and my back …

Then I remember.

The crown.

I reach into my bag. 'Here, I have a puzzle for you while we wait.'

Tomas steps out four large paces towards me. In the dim light, I see the whites of his eyes glow as he gingerly plucks the crown out of my hands. 'You know what this is, yes?'

'Yup. I know all that. Terra says, only a Roman Centurion can unplait it, before it can be destroyed.'

Tomas's face is grim. 'This cannot be destroyed.' The scar on his cheek creases into a heavy line as worry sets in.

'What do you mean … I can't destroy it? It's part of the Seven Initiations of Mithras set out for me to complete.'

'Complete, yes. How do you know it has to be destroyed?'

I think for a minute. 'I-I don't. I assumed I had to.' Thinking back, Terra never mentioned anything about destroying the crown. That was all me. I'm more curious about *why* he thinks keeping the crown intact is so important.

'You need to hold onto this until we are finished here.'

'Fine.'

I rest my head back – the crown safely inside my backpack. I close my eyes for a moment and when I open them, Tomas and Longinus are standing over me. 'We have very little time. You will need to follow my instructions to seek a connection between this world and The Underworld.'

'Okay. Let's get this over with.'

I consider dead people being … well, *dead*. The Underworld, on the other hand, doesn't sound like a fun place to be.

Longinus hobbles closer to me, leaning heavily into his walking stick. 'Take off your footwear and tunic.' I removed my shoes and socks, and then drag my hoodie over my head. 'And the undergarment.'

I look at my t-shirt, pinching at the thin cotton material. 'Are you serious? It's freezing in here.' Plus, I'm already missing the warmth of Tomas's cloak.

'Remove the shirt,' adds Tomas.

'Your heart will lift you into The Underworld as your feet anchor you to this world. Only those pure of heart will come back.'

'Come back! You didn't say anything about being stuck there.'

'You've been there before. You simply didn't remember it.'

'Oh, I remember it okay. That's why I don't want the refresher course.'

It was the day Todd was killed.

Little did I know, I raced headlong after his spirit as it was yanked from his body. The corridor was dark and cold, where no light had ever lived, and no warmth had ever visited. I know now, it was my guilt that took me there as much as Amun's power inside me. Todd couldn't hear me calling him, and when I saw him disappear through a wall of light, too bright to look at, I knew he was gone to a better place. And, I knew then, I was never going to be the same again.

I remove the shirt and sit on my knees as Longinus commands. 'Now, clear your mind of any impure thoughts.' My first thought is to laugh - that's gonna be tough. 'Those who enter The Underworld with selfless thoughts, and not for personal gain, will have a stronger connection.'

'Why can't I do it my way? I know how to connect with spooks, I mean, spirits.'

'Yes, when they have come to you. But did you ever have to go searching for one?'

'No,' I say sulkily.

'There are many realms that exist. Not just this one.'

'Well, which one am I going to? A heads-up would be good.'

Longinus sighs. 'You have much to learn.' I have no idea what he means.

I look to Tomas. 'What was your father's name?' I ask.

'Tiberius,' he says solemnly. No sooner are the words out of Tomas's mouth, I remember his name from the Altar Stone.

I take a deep breath, my lungs filling with the freshest air I can imagine. By the time I inhale a second time, my body not only feels lighter, I also hear the birds tweeting on a telegraph wire ten kilometres away. Don't ask me how I know it's that far, all I know is, my perception of distance over sound has become so finely tuned that I can pinpoint a sound to the nearest inch - far better and more precise than my existing inbuilt compass. I wish I'd been able to tap into this when we were looking for Ember.

I close my eyes, shutting out the expectant faces in front of me and travel down a familiar cold and lonely path. This time, however, there is no dark corridor. I am walking through a wide canyon of rocks and steep cliff faces, Grand Canyon-like, minus the tumbleweeds, and … I am lucid enough to know I'm still kneeling in the cell. Shadowy figures glide past me by the thousands as though I have joined the procession of some kind of ghostly pilgrimage.

I call out the name, "Tiberius" in my mind. Certain spooks stop to look at me as others continue on their journey to nowhere. "Tiberius, father of Tomas," I call out silently. Some of those who had stopped, now continue on their way, leaving others in their wake to stare intently at me. "Tiberius, father of Tomas, brother of Cassius Longinus, who plunged the spear into the Lord's side," I say.

All but one man resumes their course.

He is broad in the shoulders, wearing a worn leather breastplate beneath a tunic that falls to his knees. He has decorative leather bands strapped to his forearms and plain open-toed sandals on his feet. He looks semi-ready for battle, a sword clasped tightly in his hand. But most importantly, bearing a striking resemblance to Tomas.

'Come forward,' I command. The man no longer glides but approaches with strong, deliberate steps. The furrowed brow and concentrated look on his face convince me I've found the right man.

'Your brother and son are with me on the earth plane,' I say slowly. 'Will you speak with me?'

The man stretches his arms above his head as though he has woken from a sleep his body didn't know it'd had. 'Who are you? And why should I trust you?'

'My name is Skye Buchannan. I need to talk to you about the *book*.' A slight twitch above Tiberius's eye alerts me that he knows what I'm talking about.

'Nothing good can come of it,' says the Roman. 'And you would fair better if you let it be.'

'I can't. I have to complete the Initiations so we can stop this evil once and for all.'

His eyes drill through me, jaw as strong as steel. 'You cannot stop it. It is beyond any power us humans can wield.'

'I don't believe that. Look at me. A human talking to a two thousand year old ghost. I'd say that is beyond most human powers.'

'It will not work.'

I don't have the time or energy for an argument. 'Look, Pal, you might've given up, but we haven't. So, you either help us, or go back to your flock of spooks and let me get on with the job.'

Tiberius glances back at the wandering herd, and between the slivers of silence, fatigue sets in. Talking wireless to the other side is draining me at a much faster rate. There is a weary look on the man's face and he heaves an exhausted breath before saying, 'I was given the book by a scholar who told me, one day, someone would come looking for it.'

'*And*, that would be me,' I interject.

'No. Someone evil, who will use the book to unravel the entire fabric of time and recreate it in his image.'

The word comes out with a sigh. 'Ra-Mon.'

Tiberius stiffens, if that's possible a ghost can. 'I stumbled upon his rituals and ceremonies after joining the Mithraic Cult.' The light fades from his eyes. 'I bear witness to the good strong men, like my son, turned into slaves to do their bidding.'

'And now you can make him pay,' I chip in.

'My brother also suffers at the hand of this monster, and when I tried to release him from this curse, she cast me out.'

'So it wasn't God that punished him?'

'No. The curse was spat up from Hell, from the witch herself. Our one true God is love and forgiveness. Ra-Mon insisted I be locked away to keep his secret hidden from the world.'

A pain bolts through my head, almost slicing our flimsy connection. I have to speed things along. Secret? What secret? 'Tomas is hell-bent on finding your final resting place. Tell me why?'

'The reason I am here, is because I took something of great value. So precious that not even death was punishment enough.'

Riddle time is over. I'm short with him and to the point now. A severing feeling takes over me ...as though my soul is being lifted from my body. 'What did you take? Tell me where your body lies so that we can retrieve it, before *she* does.'

'I wish to be reunited with my son.'

'Yes I know that.' I can't hold on any longer as the echoed, alarmed voice of Tomas seeps through the cracks of my meditation. '*Where*?'

'You will need to choose. Some have the right to die, others have the will to die.'

'What does that even *mean*?'

'He will find my body where he has already searched.' His ghostly appearance fades into the background of molten rocks, wisps of a once-mighty Roman warrior floating on the breeze until there is nothing.

I come back to my senses, feel the darkness of the cave around me, shake off the dreaminess before vomiting myself into an exhausted heap.

TWENTY-FOUR

DISCOVERING my head nestled in Tomas's humongous hands is strange enough without his confused expression drilling down on me. The rough rim of a cup at my lips and the taste of chalky water are what finally bring me around. 'You could've warned me,' I say, grabbing for the cup and downing the contents. I want another.

'I did,' says Tomas indignantly. 'And drink it slower.' He refills the cup. 'You have used much of your strength.'

A smile presses its way into my lips 'You're just like your father, you know that?' Tomas frowns, and opens his mouth to speak. 'You go about telling me in your roundabout way, just like he does. Not really saying anything, but somehow answering a question without actually giving an answer. You should've said, you're gonna puke your guts up after this, so don't stay too long in there. That's what I would've said.' Longinus stares at me as though I should've known this.

'Did he tell you?'

'Yes and no.' I find myself mimicking their irritating habits and then realise it isn't just them. I've been doing this my entire life aswell. 'He said you've already been to the place before, but he was hidden.' A shadow creeps across Tomas's eyes. 'I got the feeling he's been watching you.' Tomas shivers as though ghostly fingertips have found his spine and lightly danced their way from his neck to his pelvis. 'Please tell me you haven't searched in a thousand different places otherwise, we're screwed.'

His forehead creases, reflecting a deep level of concentration spreading across his face, pinching his lips into a thin, tight line. 'There are a few places we could try again.'

Off the top of my head, I think of two. 'Scotland?' I offer.

Tomas shakes his head. 'I don't think so.'

'What about Falicon? You did mention we need to go there?'

Tomas's face tightens. 'I was convinced my father's body was laid to rest there, but I checked thoroughly.' He sighs. 'I suppose we can look again. It does seem the most obvious place.'

I finish the second cup and push myself upright, immediately throwing my arm out to steady myself. The headspins are a killer.

A low, muffled roar crashes off the walls, echoing through the tunnels. Tomas and Longinus turn simultaneously in the direction of the noise, faces creasing with apprehension. 'Hurry,' says Longinus. With one either side of me, they support my weight like a couple of lop-sided bookends. I feel stupid, leaning against an old man that looks ten times older than my Pop. 'It is imperative that we leave now. Othniel will return, and *we* need to be ready for him.'

My body feels wretched and weak and there's a deathly cold making a cosy home amongst my bones. The fatigue is way worse than being invisible for eight hours. And, although my brain isn't fully back online yet, the *We* sentiment they keep using, I believe, is more *me* than *them*.

'We need to get to the practice arena and prepare,' I hear Tomas say. There's that word again, we.

'For what?' I respond.

'Battle. You will have to kill Othniel.'

'*Me*? Why *me*? I can't even stand up straight.'

'You need to kill the lion with the spear.'

Dizziness dives into my head and limbs. 'Are you nuts?'

'The Spear of Destiny holds a great many powers,' says Longinus, 'least of which, it will undo what has been done.'

'Undo …' Words crash into my brain that seem to have no meaning.

'Aim for the heart,' adds Tomas. 'That way you can complete both the Second and Third Initiations at once, and break the curse at the same time.'

'Great. Thanks for the heads up – I was going to aim for his arse.'

'He will be fine,' says Longinus, pouring a liquid into my mouth from the leather pouch around his neck. The two men half drag, half carry me out at speeds unfathomable to dudes of their age, ignoring my slurred objections that I can walk on my own.

Several tunnels later, dimly lit with standing fire torches slung every twenty feet, I find myself in a vast circular underground room with a high domed ceiling carved into the rock above. The small black spots are slowly disappearing from my vision, making the claw marks, mixed with blood, and the slashing chunks out of the wall more visible the closer I look. Whatever was in that tonic is starting to work. Tomas thrusts another cup of water under my nose.

'Stand up. I need to show you how to use this.' He draws his sword, and I stumble back a few steps after he pulls me to my feet.

'Swordplay isn't my thing,' I say, smirking.

Tomas isn't smiling. 'This is serious. Othniel will kill you.'

'Not if he can't see me. Have you seen Lord of the Rings?'

Tomas frowns, glancing at his uncle.

'We have no time for this,' says Longinus. 'Pass me the spearhead.' I reach into my backpack and remove the spear from the tea towel Hayley had wrapped it in. 'Here.'

The old man hesitantly takes the spearhead. Something dark passes across his eyes, a fear or memory, something so unbelievably hard to describe, it would take me an eternity to find the right words.

'Just as the Lord humbly gave me back my sight, the darkness dwelling within the spear saw fit to withdraw his gift.'

'You mean, you can't see?' He looks up at me, the colour in his eyes, opaque and lifeless. 'What the …?'

Tomas takes his staff and fixes the spearhead to it. 'Now, remember, the boy must be the one to kill the beast,' he says softly, although loud enough for me to hear.

Tomas then spends the next five minutes, showing me how to position my body whilst holding the spear. It's more complex than it looks, with Tomas, constantly kicking at my feet to ensure I maintain a solid stance.

'Where did your other companion come from? The girl?' he asks, his brow troubled. He swings his sword at me, and I think I've avoided it until I feel the flat of his blade against my backpack. I lose my footing and he pushes me back with force.

'You mean, Hayley?'

Tomas lunges towards me. 'Do not trust her. She has other intentions.'

I block his punch with my body. 'What evidence do you have?'

He drums his fist on his chest. 'You have to trust me.'

I heed to his warning as it is the same one I have also been feeling. And the same as Terra. 'You have to give me something to go on? You can't accuse her without cause. That's not how life works in our world.'

In the time it takes me to finish my sentence, Tomas has me around the throat, his sword caressing the base of my neck. 'She has lied to you.'

'About what?' I whisper onto the blade.

Tomas unwraps me from his grasp and chops at the air in front of me. 'Everything. But start with the small, sweet delicacy she feeds you.'

'The *fudge*? What's so wrong about that?' Hayley said she'd made that with Wally. 'Why would she lie about that?'

Tomas says nothing, but the grim expression on his face says it all. Why would Hayley lie about something so insignificant, unless it wasn't *insignificant* at all?

'Any last tips then, before I meet Aslan?' Tomas frowns, and I forget that many of my jokes go over his head.

'Don't die.'

'Great!' I take a minute and close my eyes, hoping to hell I make it through this.

The earth-shattering sound that needs no explanation blows through my body like a Queensland hurricane, uprooting my nerves and taking down my courage. Instinctively, my body freezes, my fist re-tightening around the spear. A slow, tired thud of paws grows infinitely louder. The air has become a wet sponge again, syphoning the oxygen from my lungs. A cool dribble of sweat slips between my shoulder blades and down my back.

My senses feel suddenly heightened.

I'm not sure if I'm delirious, seeing the tiny dust motes floating in the air or my vision has become that much clearer in the torchlight, but whatever it is, I'm thankful for it. Even my hearing is sharper, turning to see the shiny black beetle scurrying away before being trampled.

'I will be here if you need me, but remember, it must be you to strike the fatal blow.'

Tomas no sooner finishes his pep talk when a monstrous shadow grows larger and larger, creeping up the wall in a wave of black ink. In the doorway, the lion stands - much bigger than I remember it. Without adjusting its head, it looks me directly in the eye.

Tomas and Longinus have stepped back, giving me the whole arena. I chance a look at Tomas as the lion draws closer, but his face reveals nothing.

'You think you are the one to vanquish me, youngling?' The sound of the lion's voice inside my head is in perfect English and yet my ears hear nothing more than a soft growl. It takes me a moment to respond.

'I don't think … I know I can.'

His sly grin grows wider, revealing teeth that could kill a gorilla with one small lovebite. 'Such confidence. Others have tried before. And failed.'

Perfect! I'm in familiar territory. 'Then I have no expectations to live up to.'

Othniel stifles a laugh. 'You have courage, I'll give you that. But nothing more than a fool's courage. Lay down your spear and walk away. You are fighting a battle you cannot possibly win.' And yet, Othniel hasn't taken his eyes off the spear.

'We'll see about that.' He is close enough that I jab at him with the spear. He laughs again as it misses him by almost a foot.

'A lamb to the slaughter,' he mutters, shaking his sandy coloured mane. It's like wildfire caught on a hot summer breeze.

There's no denying it, his strength and superiority are intimidating. And, he knows I am the weaker of us, regardless of my extra abilities. We're a couple of chess pieces – he steps, I step, tracing a wide circle marking out our battleground. I accept that his first strike would easily kill me, and he knows it too. There's nothing like being toyed with, to give you that extra boost of confidence.

In one stride, he advances quicker than I thought a lion could move, as fast as a cobra striking. His massive head thumps me in the ribs, lifting me clear off the ground. I sail through the air, hitting the dirt just short of Tomas's feet, my back crunching into the solid earth. I cough, trying to knock the wind back into me.

'Get up,' shouts Tomas. 'You need to be quicker on your feet.'

'No shit, Sherlock. Anytime you wanna step in here, be my guest.'

I get to my feet, empty-handed. The spear, now on the other side of the arena.

'Your sword,' I demand, but Tomas is already two steps ahead of me and has unsheathed it. He launches it at me as Othniel returns for another go. The heat from his breath warms my face before I turn invisible.

'You are not playing by the rules, youngling.'

I appear on the other side of the arena and revel in the anguished howl as I flick on my visibility briefly and bring the sword down against the lion's flanks. 'I've learnt the hard way that rules are meant to be broken, especially when faced with Minotaurs who want to rip my head off or when gargoyles come to life. Call me a cheat, I don't care. I live by my own rules now.'

Agitated, the lion struts back and forth, cagelike, looking for a way in. I anticipate his move and jump clear over him as he pounces at me. If a lion could frown, I swear it was right now, fierce determination replacing the playfulness from before.

Othniel lunges at me again and again, each time, I find it easy enough to slip from his grasp, turn invisible or sail over his head, dispensing a slashing blow every time. This game of chess is beginning to look a lot like us both being in perpetual check, with him healing after every strike. Hell, this could go on for hours.

The lion senses this, and he looks to the old man and Tomas. 'If you will not play by the rules ... neither will I.'

I don't get chance to warn Longinus, for that is who Othniel targets first. He snatches the old man up in his teeth and shakes him like a dog with a toy. The sound of his spine snapping convinces me he's dead. The lion spits him to the ground and looks to Tomas, unarmed.

'Here,' I yell, lobbing the sword in his direction. His skill with a sword is poetic to watch, and it takes a few seconds to realise that I can use this distraction to cause some real damage to the beast. Every stab, every slice against the lion's skin seems to heal up within seconds.

'Nothing is working,' I call out to Tomas as he chops frantically, trying to gain the upper hand. I notice the tip of the spear in the shadow of the torchlight. I turn invisible and take it up.

But in the space between light and dark, in the moment between heartbeats and breaths, the sword is knocked out of Tomas's hand and he stumbles backwards. The lion stands over him, bearing its teeth.

'Put down your spear or I will tear his throat out.'

'Don't,' I shout in a shaky voice. 'Please don't.' I place the spear at my feet. Both of us are unarmed, both vulnerable.

'I have lived since time began. Did you think you would vanquish me with such ease?'

In truth, I didn't. 'I don't even want to be here. I shouldn't be here, except my life is woven into this mess that you have also been created for.' I feel my shoulders slide down my back. 'I want to go home. Except I can't. I have to finish this. And yet it seems impossible. It is my responsibility and it's the one thing I've been put on this earth to do. I cannot fail. I will not.'

From the corner of my eye, I see Longinus is coming around. He tries to prop himself up on an elbow, his eyes unfocused and in pain. I feel a sharp twist in the pit of my stomach when I see the old man hasn't healed as he should have. His pelvis and legs are lopsided as though he has been wrung out and left to dry in the wrong position.

'He's not going to heal, is he?' I say accusingly.

'No,' answers Othniel. 'Not whilst we are in the presence of the spear. You should destroy it.' This doesn't sound like the weary lion Terra had spoken about. Certainly not ready to meet his own death, that's for sure. There is an arrogance about him that reminds me all too well of Ra-Mon. And then it clicks.

'I should've known. Come out and face me, you coward. It's very easy to puppet a lion and have him do your dirty work.' I remember Doc saying that it drains Ra-Mon's power when he walks on our earthly level, so mind controlling a mythical beast seems to be an alternative solution.

Ra-Mon appears, clapping his hands in a sarcastic manner, a sinister grin spreading across his face. 'You really are the most intelligent of the four. Who would've guessed? You hide it well under that dumb exterior you seem to fool everyone else with ...'

'I don't know what you're talking about.'

'But my guess is, it is not you who senses me, but Amun.' He chuckles to himself, his arms stretching towards the heavens. 'Amun, my master, my teacher, my friend.'

'*Friend?*'

'Amun wishes to be summoned. He wishes to be released from your heavy mortal body and retake his rightful place at my side.'

'I don't believe you.'

'And you speak with him often, do you?'

The little conversation we've had, has had nothing to do with him wanting out of this situation. And yet, nothing to say he doesn't.'

Not only am I screwing this whole thing up, but my immortal is defecting to the other side.

I can't believe it.

I won't believe it.

My thoughts return to Longinus. I can't begin to imagine the kind of pain he must be in, and all this small talk is delaying the old man's death.

'Finish him,' commands Ra-Mon.

The lion springs for me, pinning me to the ground. I see confusion in his eyes as he tries to battle against the mind control. Terra was right. He does want to die. I didn't see it at first because of Ra-Mon, but I see he has lost his will to live through his feeble strikes and lethargy. I can make a difference right here, right now.

'Pierce the heart,' cries out Tomas before the lion can strike at me, his claws spread wide.

'Let me go, and I will end it for you,' I whisper into his thick, shaggy mane as it grazes my chin.

His breath warms my face. 'Go,' he says under a low growl.

In a blink, I turn invisible and sprint for the spear. With less than a foot between us, I hear a voice in my head.

Not Amun.

Not Ra-Mon or even Tomas.

But of a girl.

'Terra, is that you?' I say silently.

Stop, she says. *I'll take it from here. I will take out Ra-Mon first. Don't move!*

I couldn't move even if I wanted to.

My energy is at an all time low, my muscles screaming for a rest.

This whole day has been one huge fifty hour workout and my hands shake as I dig deep to hold onto my invisibility.

Ra-Mon obviously cannot hear or see Terra. Neither can I, come to that, and I covertly try to pin point which dark crevice she might be sheltering in.

And then I see her.

Well, I think it's her.

God, I hope so, although I'm not sure what good a scorpion can do.

It scurries closer, sending a chill up my spine. I've never taken to insects too well. There's too many in Australia that can kill you, including scorpions. It scuttles towards Ra-Mon, and I can't begin to wonder what kind of damage a scorpion can do to an immortal. If it was me, I would've turned into a bear at least, that way I could've taken down the lion afterwards.

Ra-Mon seems to notice the scorpion at the same time, and shrinks back, his face a mixture of fear and surprise.

'You will not defeat me, woman,' he screeches at it. The scorpion strikes with lightning speed evaporating Ra-Mon into a cloud of icy blue mist.

'Nicely done,' I sing out my praises to Terra.

With Ra-Mon's presence gone, Othniel retreats enough for me to see the sadness in his eyes. 'Let's be done with this, boy,' he softly growls at me.

Spiking a ferocious lion I have no problems with … killing an overgrown tomcat ready to meet his maker has me deliberating whether I can go through with this.

Same old story for me – good old indecisiveness.

I know what I need to do, and yet it feels wrong. If River were here, he'd know exactly what to do and we'd be on our way out of here with an impressive throw rug draped over his shoulder to hang above his fireplace back home. He'd also be telling me to grow a pair and get on with the job that needs doing.

I return to visibility and draw the spear back. I tighten my grip on the staff, its power radiating down my arm. My hand shakes, heat scorching beneath my skin.

I inhale a breath.

Then another.

Then push aside the sorrowful eyes of the majestic animal in front of me, begging me, pleading with me to ease his pain.

I plunge the tip into the lion's chest, in one clean and forceful thrust. He doesn't put up a fight and surrenders to his fate, dropping to the floor, his heavy head falling between a pair of colossal paws.

I glance over at Longinus, his body becoming more and more translucent by the second until nothing remains other than a swirl of dust.

I turn to see the same happening to Othniel.

'Wow! Did you see that?' I call back to Tomas, spinning around to share in my victory.

He is not there.

Nor is my backpack, with the Crown of Thorns inside. I spin around to look back at where Othniel lay.

The staff is there.

But the spearhead is gone.

What the hell am I going to tell River?

TWENTY-FIVE

I emerge from the Colosseum, shielding my eyes, confused with that jetlag feeling of time passing without knowing it. I go to check my phone to see what time it is, and remember it's flat.

Fuck! I've no plan, other than to make my way back to the windmill. The only thing going for me is that I've got an awesome set of wings to get me there. The shady parklands across the road, looks the perfect place to carry out my magic trick and I'm about to dissolve into thin air, when I hear a familiar bird call.

'Terra?' I call out. I feel stupid, scouring the nearby trees, calling out her name, especially when she's probably looking down at me, laughing. 'If you don't come out in the next five seconds, I'm leaving,' I half-yell into the thick canopy above.

At first, I don't see her standing beneath the low branches of a mature elm tree, her hair wild, her eyes wilder. There's a grin on her face that says nothing about her being happy to see me, and everything about me being right about her spying on me. And so rather than going for the jugular, I adopt a less abrasive approach and brush off her attempt to ridicule me. One of us needs to repair what's left of our relationship.

'That was an awesome little trick back there! You saved my life with that stinger. Did you see Ra-Mon take off like a little girl, pissing his pants?'

Terra frowns. 'What the hell are you talking about?' She pushes off from the tree and walks towards me.

'The scorpion,' I say animatedly, 'that cool, frigging scorpion you turned into.' Her frown deepens. 'I would never have thought of that in a million years. How did you know it would work? I was thinking of a bear, or tiger or …'

'That wasn't me, you moron.' She pushes her inky black hair from her face just in time for me to see her best eyeroll ever. Her head shakes in disbelief. 'I was the beetle, hiding beneath your backpack.'

'*What*?' The word echoes inside my head.

'I was waiting in case you needed my help.'

'If *you* were the beetle, *who* was the scorpion?'

Terra scrapes her hair back into a ponytail and fastens it. Her skin is pale, her eyes barely surviving the horrors she's seen. 'I have a fair idea, but we have more to worry about right now than Isis.'

'*Isis?*'

The soft breeze stalls.

The birds cease to tweet, and silence finds a home amongst the tall timbers around us. For all of five long seconds.

Then she lets me have it. 'Surely, you can't be that dumb? She's been helping us every step of the way. When are you going to wake up and put the pieces together for yourself instead of waiting for me to spoonfeed you all the time?'

I come to my senses. 'I'm not! And, I know it's Isis,' I blurt out. 'She came through for me at Notre Dame, *remember*, but you know what, "*Eve*", not all of us have a cheat sheet with us, twenty-four-seven, with all the answers. So, why don't you cut me some slack, because this "*I'm better than you*" shit is getting old.'

Terra's lips tighten as anger sweeps across her face, her eyes streaked with emerald fire. 'Then stay away from me, if you don't need my help.'

'Fine.'

Terra spins on her heels and marches off, arms pumping.

'Fuck,' I mumble under my breath. And I was really trying to find some common ground with her. Every time I open my mouth, she rips me a new one. God, I wish I knew what kind of heartless bastard I've been for her to hate me this much. The second my thoughts are set adrift, her footsteps abruptly halt in the leafy undergrowth assuring me she's heard every word. Fuck seems to be my word of the day. I look up to see she has stopped several metres away, her shoulders heaving in some kind of defeat.

She turns to face me, enough space between us to qualify for a dual. I grit my teeth, preparing for the next onslaught. Except, it's nothing of the sort. And in the moment between moments, in those perfectly constructed instances when you're allowed to peek behind the veil a little, her gaze drops to the ground, and the frown that was once there has gone, her eyes brimming with apology. 'I don't hate you, Skye. There's just …'

It is the softest she's ever spoken to me and it pulls against my heart. She's struggling and I get it. Now, is not the right time. 'It's cool. Really.' I jog to catch up.

She offers me something that could pass as a smile, bridled with embarrassment rather than warmth. 'When was the last time you heard from River?'

River! Shit. I'd forgotten all about him. 'We got separated.'

'Why doesn't that surprise me?' Terra lowers her eyes. Shakes her head.

Here we go again. I'm about to walk away when I hear her trembled breath.

'I'm sorry, I didn't mean it like that.' I'm suddenly privy to a whole heap of self-loathing going on inside her head. By the sounds of it, when her emotions run riot, the barrier comes down. 'Would you believe me if I said it's a defence mechanism?'

I totally would, after all, I've used humour to mask my feelings most of my life. I understand the knee-jerk reaction to fire off when questions are tough or judgement is staring you down. 'We all have our problems, Terra. Me included.' Even softening my voice, like I need to right now, and still sound genuine, is like pushing a barrel of rocks up a mountain. But it is warranted and definitely something I need more practice in. 'I may seem like an easy target, but I'm not your personal punching bag.'

Her teeth graze her bottom lip, her foot aimlessly toeing through the leaves in front of her. 'I know. I'm trying, I really am. It's how I've survived.' There's a lengthy pause, and I begin to wonder if it might be a cue for me to speak. And then she softly mutters, 'I've never had a friend before.'

Her words catch me unaware.

Stir in my chest.

Bring a lump to my throat that won't go down, no matter how many times I swallow. Again, we are venturing into territory that requires a couple of bottles of cheap wine, or at the very least, a comfy chair with pillows, fluffy blankets and a tub of ice-cream. And it's not that I'm not curious about what makes Terra tick, I am, however, we need to get back to the others.

'I'm hoping they are waiting for us inside the confines of the slave keep.'

'So, how are we going to do this then?'

I click my tongue. 'What about turning yourself into a horse, and I can ride you back?' Her glare is fierce enough

319

to peel paint but eases just as quickly. 'Okay, scratch that idea.' The fire in her eyes simmers. 'Howabout you get your pigeon feathers on and head south-west and I'll holler if you go the wrong way.'

I hear the sound of her teeth grinding. 'Fine. Although don't get too close to my tail feathers, otherwise I might think you're a tourist, and shit on you.' I holster my snigger.

As bold as brass, and without considering our environment or who might be watching, she transforms into a beautiful eagle - all in the space between blinks.

'Just so you know … I'm massively impressed,' I yell out as the magnificent bird takes flight. I flick on my invisibility, ignoring my thirst and grumbling stomach and tack on behind her.

As I soar above the Italian countryside, the mid-morning sun warming my skin, a cool breeze teasing my hair, my heart lighter than it has felt in months, somehow the beauty passing below me is more memorable than I've ever known. Winding country lanes seem to know when to dissect the lush green meadows at the precise place to create a patchwork of perfection, whilst fields of corn and towering sunflowers add a splash of sunshine into Mother Nature's lap. Petite stone cottages with matching stone-pitched walls, gardens bursting with flowers and countless rows of vegetables remind me how full, and yet how simple, life can be.

I spy the slave-keep before Terra, and yell out to her to head that way. She swoops over the busted up windmill and lands on one of the lesser broken sails before dropping to the ground. She is back to her human form before I land and do the same.

My lips break into a smile when I hear Ember's laughter. She rushes at me, her red hair a tangle of fire, her face smeared with dirt. 'I told River you'd come back for us,' she says breathlessly, clinging to me. She pulls back for a few blinks, inspecting every inch of my face, before resuming her embrace.

I catch River's eyes, and he lifts his chin at me. 'You okay?'

I nod. 'Look who I found.'

From the opposite side of the keep, Terra steps out of the shadows.

The relief breaking on River's face isn't hard to miss. 'It's good to see you,' he says, stepping forward then stopping, awkward about the whole *hug* thing.

It doesn't bother Ember in the slightest. She gives me another quick squeeze before throwing herself at Terra. 'I'm so glad to see you both.'

Terra and I exchange glances, the same lines dancing through our heads – *we're happy to be here too.*

'And the lion?' says River.

'Dead,' I say flatly, 'along with Tomas's uncle, Longinus.'

'And I take it from the relief on your face that's a good thing?' says Ember, raising her eyebrows and looking directly at Terra for clarification.

Terra smiles.

And, I mean *really* smiles.

Her face alters in such a way, so totally indescribable, she seems almost approachable, her eyes alive with unexplainable wonder, her skin glowing as though her soul has been touched and ignited for the first time. 'Yes, it's a good thing. They are both free from their miseries, and the Third and Fourth Initiations are now complete.' Listening to Terra speak about being part of something wholesome and righteous, and peaceful, somehow adjusts my wiring, giving me a greater belief in who I am and who I could be. I feel honoured to have been a part of it, and a forty-kilo dumbbell lifts off my chest. 'Justice has been served,' she continues, 'and, don't go and get a big head about it now,' she turns to face me. Bites nervously on her lip, and says, 'and it was all because of this guy.'

Wow! An actual compliment. I'm in shock.

The smile that lights up Ember's face is reward enough without the hearty slap on the back River gives me in his usual emotionless, brotherly way. However, my happy thoughts are blunted as Hayley speaks. Shit, I forgot about her.

She eyes me curiously. 'What happened to your backpack?' she asks, standing a good distance away from everyone else.

'Err, yeah, about that,' I mumble, walking towards her.

She buries her face into my neck. 'Didn't think I'd see you again.' And just like that, the tremor of old habits creeps back in. I can't explain it, other than when she wraps her arms around me, squeezing me with such vigour, I can't shrug off the urge to hug her back just as tightly. I'm happy to see her and relieved she's safe and all that, and yet there's a feeling of disconnection between us.

Terra catches hold of my thoughts, a light frown dusting her brows as if to say, *is everything okay?* I feign a smile, peeved that she can see straight through it.

'And Tomas?' asks River.

I feel my face screwing up. I push back from Hayley, a little relieved to have my own space again. 'Probably in the same place as my backpack.'

River pulls me to one side. Our backs to the girls. 'What are you saying …? Tomas *stole* it?'

I can't see it, somehow. I mean, he simply isn't the type. And yet I have no explanation why he would take off with the Crown of Thorns *and* the Spear of Destiny, and not say anything. 'Honestly, I don't have a clue.' I won't allow myself to think he is double-crossing us. 'Maybe he's keeping it safe,' I say, noticing the girls looking over at us.

I jut my chin towards them, and River catches my drift. 'We should talk about this later,' he whispers before joining the girls again.

It's after nine by the time we make it back to the hotel, and we all agree that a shower, a little room-service and a good night's sleep, are all we have the energy for. River and I are bunk in together as usual, and all three girls share the room next to us due to the hotel being fully booked out. It's unusually quiet in there and I'm tempted, several times, to stick my invisible head through the wall to check up on them.

I don't, instead, I stretch my legs down the bed, balancing my pizza on my lap. I recount my adventure with Tomas and Longinus, not forgetting the role that Ra-Mon and Isis played in it. River takes it all in, although when he's particularly attentive when I tell him about crossing dimensions to speak with Tomas's father. He even puts down his sandwich for a bit. We then get back onto why Tomas would take the backpack and like earlier, I have no answers for him, so he settles on his own idea that Tomas is keeping his cards close to his chest.

'Did you know that Terra can change into any animal form she wants to?'

River looks up from his cheese and tomato toasted sandwich and stops in mid-chew. 'I didn't, for sure, so thanks for the heads up. I thought it might only be birds because Em had mentioned she'd found a heap of assorted feathers in their room in Paris.' He lets out a loud yawn, 'I get the feeling her powers are going to come in real handy.'

Over breakfast the next morning, a new plan begins to form as everyone throws in their ideas. Hayley slides a plate in front of me filled with eggs and bacon, three rounds of toast with baked beans on top, which I hate, mushrooms, spinach and five assorted pastries dotted around the edge.

'You need to keep your strength up,' she whispers to me, smoothing the back of her fingertips along my jawbone. 'You look tired.'

And yet, I feel amazing.

Best sleep ever!

'With the first Four Initiations done, what does the fifth mean, Terra?' asks Ember, buttering her toast.

Terra hasn't said a word to me since we turned in last night, and I know at some point, a conversation is due. For now, she looks directly at me, her mind blank and her eyes full of fire. She directs her attention to Ember. 'The Fifth Initiation is Perses or Persian. It also symbolises a crescent moon and stars, a sling pouch, a sickle or a Phrygian cap, which was a hat traditionally worn by Roman slaves.'

'Do you know which one it is?' asks River.

Terra offers him a tight smile. 'I don't suppose I will be setting off Krakatoa anytime soon by disclosing this, so here goes. It is a man. A Persian man, in fact.'

'Who is he, and where do we find him?' Ember's question is on all of our minds.

Terra's gaze lands on me again. 'Ask Skye. He's spoken to him.'

'*Me*.' I have no idea who she is talking about but then it dawns on me. 'Oh! You mean Tomas's father, Tiberius?'

I hear her silent applause in my mind, and although my instinct is to bite back at her cheap shot, I find I'm over the moon that her mind is no longer off-limits. She sniggers at my new revelation.

'Well, it doesn't take a genius to work it out. He's the only Persian that has anything to do with this.'

She's right. 'We need to go to Falicon, like Tomas said, and search for his father's remains. I'm confident that is where Tomas has gone.'

We finish breakfast and everything is going well, until Ember rushes in to tell us Hayley is sick.

Violently sick.

Too sick to move.

River and I inspect the patient, and there's no denying the pale green colour of her skin and red rings under her eyes, that she's really crook.

'Riv, she can't travel like this. She's grey as … and throwing up every ten minutes. Juggling her around in a car isn't going to help her. Or us!'

'Mmmmm,' is all River says.

'We've still got three weeks left until we have to face Isis. There's plenty of time – and there are only three Initiations to go. Dude … please.'

'This doesn't concern her,' butts in Terra as the girls step outside their room to join us in the corridor. Hayley is tucked up in bed with a rubbish bin beside her. 'We'll come back for her.'

River doesn't look happy about that scenario either. 'We can't leave her stranded, ill, in a strange country. She's our responsibility.'

Relief filters in.

Terra shrugs one shoulder and turns up her lip. 'Whatever,' she snaps. 'But don't expect me to play nursemaid.'

'Wouldn't dream of it,' I snap back in the same sour tone. 'Why don't you make yourself useful and go down to reception and rebook our rooms for the next two nights.' She storms off, leaving Ember looking at River, and me shaking my head.

The following two days are a bit of a blur. I spend most of the time, holding Hayley's hair back and sponging down her face. She insists it's probably something she's eaten as none of us are sick. I have to agree with her. I feel fine. Amazing, actually.

River and Ember had stayed away, in case it was viral, and I'd only caught up with them for meals, River constantly expressing his concern about time running out for us.

Terra has been missing the entire time.

On the third day, over lunch, I notified them that Hayley seemed to be on the mend, and was able to keep a piece of toast down.

'That's good,' says River, flatly. His face is paler than usual, and the whites of his eyes are streaked with blood, like he's been out on an all-night bender. I study his face, listening in on his thoughts. No actual words form, his thoughts a battlefield. He must be holding on tight. 'I'm going to hire a car for tomorrow and we'll drive to Falicon first thing in the morning.' He gets up, smiles at Ember, although it fails to touch his eyes as he leaves the room

Ember waits until he's out of sight, and then looks to me with pleading eyes. 'Can you do me a favour?'

I know what she wants to ask before the words are even past her lips. 'Don't ask me to do that, Em. I told you I would look out for him, and intervene if needed. He is struggling. In pain too. But River is strong. The strongest of us all.'

Ember's lip wobbles. 'He barely speaks anymore. I'm certain it's the reason why he's in such a hurry to finish this.'

I nod. 'I get it. I do. I promise you, it'll be fine.

I'm about to leave, to go check on Hayley and take her a fruit platter, when Terra walks in. Her clothes are filthy.

'Where have you been?' I ask. She turns to me and I gasp. 'What the hell?' One eye is swollen, almost closed and her nostril is clotted with blood. 'What happened?'

She looks right through me for one of those seconds that lasts for ten, before flopping down into the chair. Ember's mouth is open, and she reaches for Terra's hand.

'What happened?' repeats Ember.

Terra snatches up the leftover salad roll from River's plate and shoves it into her mouth, barely chewing, tearing off chunks as though she hasn't eaten in days. My gaze switches from Terra to Ember. Terra then makes a grab for the pitcher, pours a glass of water, sloshing half of it onto the tablecloth, before draining the glass. She refills it, and then slowly drains her second glass.

We're waiting … patiently.

She swallows the last mouthful, grabs the last piece of crumbed fish from my plate and stuffs that down too.

She wipes her mouth. Sits back in her chair.

'I was rock climbing,' she simply says.

She rests her hands on the back of the chair for a beat and looks out of the café window. 'I need a shower.' And she leaves.

Ember, eyes wide, mouth mimicking a goldfish. 'Tell me you read her mind?'

I did try, but her barrier was as resilient as ever. 'She's a vault, what can I say.'

Nothing more is said on the subject.

We bundle into the car the next morning, ready for the seven-hour car journey around the coastline of Italy to the French Riviera. The mood is sombre, to say the least and from the sun glinting through the early morning skyline, I can only hope that we all find something to feel grateful for before the day is out.

Terra is riding shotgun with River, like before, her eye still puffy, a mauve bruise blossoming on her cheek. We're all still in the dark about what happened, and if there's one thing we are in agreeance with, don't go asking questions she has no designs to answer, especially if you want to keep your face intact.

I'm sitting in the middle between Em and Hayley, who thankfully looks much better today. I can't remember how many times she apologised last night for being a nuisance and holding up our plans. I assured her, she wasn't, and there was that familiar meekness about her, like the old Hayley I remember from two weeks ago.

We find the small village of Falicon perched on top of a rocky mound, overlooking the city of Nice. The journey up the side of the mountain, zigzagging back and forth wasn't kind to Ember, who complained that her ears kept popping.

'We're nearly there,' says Terra. 'Just keep swallowing.' I lean forward, surprised to hear her speak. She's been on mute for the last eight hours. Her last words upon leaving Rome were, the quicker we're out of this shithole, the better.

'Thanks,' she answers, pinching her nose and swallowing. 'I need a toilet too, Riv.'

As we arrive in the heart of the village, the road promptly narrows turning into one way streets and lanes. Terracotta and white stone houses have been squashed together, separated by quaint cobbled alleyways. It's like god had decided to fit as many lopsided terrace houses into as tight a space as possible, and then splashed them in similar tones from the same paint pot because he ran out of all the other colours.

It is charming, I'll give it that.

River nods. 'I couldn't find any hotels here, so I got us the next best thing.' He checks his google maps and swings into a tight driveway.

'Whoa!' Are you serious?' I say, as we pull up at a modern-style rustic villa. 'Is this whole place for us?'

'Sure is,' answers River, turning off the car before stretching in his seat. We all pile out, Hayley a little less enthusiastic than the rest of us.

It's like somewhere a famous actor would sneak off to, to avoid the press. The white stone walls are a huge contrast to the restored pastel peaches, pinks and different shades of beige and terracotta from the village, and yet doesn't look out of place with pale green shutters at every window and an arched ancient carved door.

We head inside.

It's light and airy, with a modern kitchen, open fireplace in the lounge area, comfy sofas loaded up with more scatter cushions than I've seen in Target. All four bedrooms have their own private veranda, complete with soft lounges and umbrellas. And, let's not forget the most spectacular panoramic view, seen from just about every window. It's out of this world.

I rush outside to get a better look. Dozens of quaint villas and terracotta residences are dotted amongst the bushy foothills that seem to flow right into the city of

Nice as the terrain levels out. I look beyond, to calmness, to a place my heart belongs.

I loose a sigh.

Beyond that, is the undisturbed view of the ocean. It looks flat, hardly a ripple, no good for surfing, but nevertheless, I surrender to its call. I let myself be consumed by it for a few minutes before I invite reality back in. I cringe at what this must have cost. More money than I'd ever have.

And did I mention the pool? 'Riv, home run dude. *Seriously*,' I yell out to him as he pokes his head out of the patio doors.

'Unpack. Go for a swim or explore. Chill for a couple of hours and then we'll meet up and go from there,' calls out River to nobody in particular.

Ember and River take one of the bedrooms and as much as Hayley and I are seen as a couple, I decide on a room to myself. She doesn't seem overly upset by it, however she does insist that we need to spend some quality time together. There's something on her mind, I can tell. I have a few things I need to say too, one being about the fudge she made with Wally … Tomas wouldn't have mentioned it if it wasn't important, but first, I want to check in with Wal and get his side of the story.

Slinging my bag beside my bed, I take a step outside onto my veranda, and pull up a sun lounger. Although, it's still fairly cool, the mid-afternoon sun has me taking my hoodie off. I check my messages … there's still nothing from Henri. I debate on whether I should send him a follow up text to remind him, but think better of it. Henri won't forget. If I haven't heard anything in a few days, I'll phone him.

Now to Wally.

I punch in the number and he answers almost instantly.

'I was just thinking of you lot. How's life on the Costa del Sol?'

I'm not a hundred percent sure what he means, but I figure it has something to do with being in Europe. 'Yeah, good. Good.' I find myself stalling. For some reason, the answer Wally is about to give, isn't something I want to hear.

'Wal, before we left, did you and Hayley rustle up a batch of fudge?'

Silence.

I can hear my heart beating through the earpiece.

'Wal? Did you hear me?'

'Yes, lad, I did. The strange thing is, I know I meant to tell you I did, but I don't actually recall making any fudge. To be honest, I wouldn't know where to start. I'm more the savoury type.'

'Thanks,' is all I can think of to say.

I hang up.

My mind spins up a gear. Why would she lie? And for what reason would she make it?

TWENTY-SIX

I spin around to the sound of the colonial doors opening behind me. Hayley comes towards me, head down, hands behind her back. She has replaced her dark blue jumper and jeans with a cream shirt and black pants. A long woollen cardigan swamps her petite frame. Her caramel hair is brushed and tied back, and her face looks fresh and clean, a pinch of red tinting her cheeks.

'That feels much better. I needed to freshen up a little,' she says apologetically. 'I hate being stuck in a car all day.'

'Me too,' I reply robotically.

I swing my legs off the sun-lounger to allow her to sit beside me. 'It's been a strange few weeks hasn't it?' she says softly.

'You can say that again.' Although for me, it's been a strange decade.

'Are you having second thoughts about me being here?' I don't want to say no, yet I can't say yes. I settle with, 'I think it's too dangerous for you to be here.' Nervously, her teeth repeatedly graze her lip, nibbling, until her lips are rosy red. Guilt leaks in. I reprimand myself for thinking it was a great idea to bring her with us. I force myself to look at her and then wished I didn't. Rejection radiates out of her. I opt for the cowards way out and switch my gaze to the ocean. Lose myself in the wonder of stillness and tranquility. Here, in the middle of nowhere, on top of the world, and away from a thousand voices, this is my new favourite place to be.

Until ...

'You don't seem too worried about your backpack?' Her question, straight out of left field prompts me to turn and look at her. Her fingers twist and turn the wooden toggles on her cardigan.

Of course I'm concerned about it, and that's the second time she's mentioned it. 'The question is, why are you?'

Hayley laughs. Not just a girlie giggle, but a full on belly laugh.

Something churns in the pit of my stomach. 'What's so funny?'

'Oh, nothing,' she says, 'it's just ...' Worry lines replace her laugh lines.

'*What*?' I can't hold back the hostility.

'I don't know,' she says, her face in her hands. She rises, walks to the edge of the veranda. Doesn't turn around.

Time to find some answers.

'Can I ask you a question?'

She removes her hands from her face and her arms swing idly by her side as she turns around. 'Sure.' The lightness has gone from her eyes.

'Why did you tell me you and Wally made fudge together?' A hint of a smile pulls at her lips. She says nothing. 'I phoned him and asked. He has no memory of you two making fudge.'

Hayley nods her head and keeps nodding, her smile getting wider and fuller with every second.

'You've figured it out, haven't you?'

I continually shift my body weight from one foot to the other and my heart does this double thud thing where I have to cough to catch my breath. 'Figured what out?'

Hayley shakes her hair loose, runs both hands through it. 'Let me tell you this …' She blots the edges of her lips as though she's just applied lipstick. 'Without me, you wouldn't have gotten this far.'

'What does that even mean?'

I hear another door slide shut.

River steps out onto his veranda in a pair of shorts, no t-shirt. There's a striped towel over his shoulder. He stops when he sees us. Takes in our tense situation. 'Everything okay out here?' he asks.

'All good,' replies Hayley. 'Would it be okay if I use the car? I thought I'd nip into town and grab some dinner for tonight.'

'Great,' responds River. 'Keys are on the kitchen bench.'

Hayley smiles at him, ruffles her hair again, and waltz's back inside. A few minutes later, I hear the car tyres squeal out of the driveway.

'What was that about?'

'I'm not sure. But I think Tomas is right. She can't be trusted.'

River raises his eyebrows and shrugs before detouring through the rockery bed, blooming with flowers, to get to the pool. Even though Nereus is no longer inside him, I suppose we all need that downtime, and his is definitely water. And with Isis's blood slowly poisoning him, it's probably the best place he can be right now.

I think about going off for a quick flight myself, but I settle for a shower instead.

I head back inside to see Terra disappearing around the front door. I call out to her, but she either ignores me, which is more likely, or doesn't hear me.

I call out to Em, and she pops her head out of the bedroom door. 'What's up?'

'Where's Terra off to?'

Ember looks up from her phone. 'I'm not sure,' she says, yet her face says she knows. I dive into her thoughts, only for her to scream NOT FAIR at me.

'How did she get that black eye?'

Ember's shoulders roll forward, her posture slackens. 'Please don't ask me, Skye. She begged me not to say anything.'

'I swear on my life I won't say anything.' I hold up my right hand and place it over my heart. 'I swear.'

Her face creases. 'I'm only telling you because I'm worried about her. If she finds out, I'll know it's come from you.'

I cross my heart. Mimic zipping my mouth and throwing away the key.

Ember sighs. Then pauses. 'She's monster hunting.'

'What the …' Words fail me, which doesn't happen very often. 'Is she *nuts*?'

'Maybe … no … I don't know.'

'Why?'

'She says it's a failsafe. She is cleaning out the local area so they don't randomly pick up her scent and follow her back here, thereby putting us all in danger.'

Wow! 'That's admirable of her,' I say, impressed. 'Stupid, but admirable.'

'I know,' says Ember, her brow creasing. 'I wanted to tell you in Paris …'

'*Paris? Christ*! How long has she been doing this for? No wonder she looks wiped out most of the time.'

'Since we busted her out of Nevermore, but more so in the last few weeks. It's why she always wants a room to herself. She's been sneaking out at night for several hours, scoping the area, keeping us safe.'

'Does River know?'

'No.' Her face shuts down immediately. 'And I'll be her next victim if he finds out. She knows he would never allow her to do it.'

'And, I *would*?'

'You're different.' I don't know whether to take that as a compliment or not. Still, she rewards me with one of those warm, heart-stopping smiles I'm sure River dreams about.

'Now that you know, maybe, keep an eye out for her if you see her take off by herself.'

'You mean … like just then.'

She nods, and the message comes through loud and clear. I'm invisible and out the door before she can finish saying, *don't get sprung*.

Flying high above Falicon, the roof tiles forming a collage of a hundred different shades of peach, I begin to realise what a mammoth task I've set for myself. Terra could be anywhere, any animal. She could be watching me.

I have to think like her. Where would a mythical beast hide? Obviously, not around too many houses.

I fly north, past an old quarry and over the next canyon. There are very few houses scattered amongst the dry, scrubby foothills.

The further north I go, the more dramatic the landscape gets. Thick, brushy conifers huddle amongst the many pine and spruce trees, varying the tapestry colours from brown to bottle green. It's moss-like from up here, and grows darker as the mountain range climbs higher.

What I would give for eagle eye vision right now.

I decide to drop a bit lower, when something catches my eye. Through the thickets and scrublands to the west, *something* is being chased by a large black animal, covering immense distances …faster than any land mammal I know.

335

I punch on my thrusters and speed towards them before they disappear into a dense pocket of trees up ahead. The thrill of the chase rushes through my blood, sets my heart off at a million kilometres an hour.

The creature leaps and pounces on its prey.

By the time I drop through the trees, a few feet away, I see them circling, sizing each other up - a panther and a … I actually don't know what it is. It has the head of a gorilla, minus all the hair, and the body of a human man. Now that the initial fright has left me, it looks more like a pig-man. I can deal with the pointed ears, stapled with thick black hoops and studs, and the short dreds that lie in straight rows down its bald head, but the teeth, noticeably the two boarish tusks protruding from the side of its mouth, leave me a little concerned.

My heart is racing.

So hard.

So fast.

I'm sure they can hear me.

The beast snorts loudly as he and Terra face off. I say Terra because how many panthers do you see in the French Riviera these days … my guess is… none!

The Pig-man is clad in olive green leather pants, cut off at the knee, ripped in places and stained with God knows what … blood probably. His chest is covered by a thick leather breastplate, black like its eyes and crisscrossed with silver studs through it. His arms are bare, skin muddied with years of grime, muscles bulging in his neck and shoulders and with biceps a powerlifter would be proud of. In one of its meaty hands, it brandishes a battleaxe.

One tick of the clock and Terra reverts back to her human form. Hunched over, she continues to circle. The beast looses a low, guttural laugh. 'There is your first mistake, Earthchild. Humans are weak. You will be easy to take apart now.'

Part of me wants to yell out to her …to tell her to change into a tiger or a bear, but when the smile on her face widens, it gives me confidence she's got this.

'Really? I'm just getting started.'

The beast stretches his neck from side to side, tossing his axe from hand to hand, limbering up. 'You were easy to find.'

This time, it's Terra's turn to laugh. 'You are the dumbest race …ev-er!' She laughs again. 'Because I *let* you find me, shit-for-brains.' Bearing its teeth again, it snarls viciously at her. 'You fell into *my* trap.'

The beast snorts, hot breath steaming from its nostrils. 'But do you have enough traps for us all?' he growls.

Still taking wide, sideways steps around some imaginary arena they have created, she says, 'you bet I do. And if they all stink as feral as you do, it will be my pleasure wiping you from whatever cesspool of a realm you've crawled out from.'

Large spruce trees surround us, the floor littered with brown pine needles.

'Your scent is known to us all.' The beast opens its mouth and bellows out a thunderous roar.

'Do I look worried, vomit-breath?' she asks confidently.

'My name is Gurtak, and you'd be wise to remember it, because capturing you and taking you to my master will make me famous.'

Terra laughs. 'I don't give a shit who you are. You're not going to be around long enough for anyone to remember that *stupid name*.'

Gurtak glares at her. 'You should be worried. Toroth is coming for you,' he says, grinning, exposing his yellowy teeth.

Her smile disappears.

Her face, deadpan.

Eyes, cold … lifeless.

I take it that the talking part of this battle is over when Gurtak raises his axe to waist height. In three giant strides, he crosses the circle, swinging and chopping as a display of his power. He hits nothing.

In a blink, Terra morphs into a wolf.

A freaking, up-sized, snarling wolf, with thick grey fur except for the underbelly, which is white, and a set of white pointy teeth that would tear through a pork roast in seconds.

She lunges for the beast, making short work of ripping into the flesh on his arm. Gurtak cries out, dropping the axe to the ground.

His thick, heavy arms close around Terra, his fists drumming against the wolf's ribcage until she releases him. Terra doesn't appear to be hurt, but she stalks him more cautiously now, standing fiercely in front of the axe so Gurtak can't pick it up.

'I don't need a weapon, Earthchild,' it spits at her. He swipes a slow fist at the wolf's head, and then another, missing by inches.

Terra throws her head back and lets out a howl before launching into another attack. This time, she aims for the legs, clamping hold of his thigh. His agonising roar rumbles through the airwaves, through the mountains, and to the ocean. My first thought, is to gag him before he brings a whole army of mutts our way. Eyes bulging, Gurtak clenches his mighty hand and thumps down on Terra's head, knocking her away.

She lets out a pitiful whimper as a red patch blooms across her white muzzle. My temper flares and I wonder whether I should step in and help. I hold back … for a few minutes, then wished I didn't as Gurtak grabs the wolf around the neck and squeezes. Squeezes until the wolf's legs kick out, claws splayed, trying to find its target.

I quietly move forward from my position, the soft needles beneath my feet, cushioning my tread. But not silently enough.

Gurtak looks up.

Stares in my direction.

And sniffs.

He's picked up my scent but cannot see me.

In his distraction, Terra morphs from the wolf into a python. She slithers out of his strong grasp and coils her patterned body around his neck, twirling and twirling, until I can't see the beast's head any more.

His body jerks as he fights for survival. Terra seems to sense victory and intensifies her hold, crushing down on him with every breath he takes, the strong muscles in the pythons body flexing and tightening.

Gurtak's legs stop jerking. His body goes limp.

Terra loosens her coils, twisting her body until she is free of him. His body slumps to the ground, his eyes remain open, his mouth agape in a silent scream. She slithers a few feet away before shrugging off her scales and replacing them again with flesh and bone.

She shakes out her hair. 'You lot are so predictable. You all go for the obvious moves.' She pulls out an elastic band from her trouser pocket, and fastens her hair back, laying her thick dark curls over her shoulder.

She then smells her hands, her hair, her red sweater. 'God, you lot reek. I'm never going to get the stench out of these clothes.' She releases the hem of her jumper and groans. 'I know you're there. You can come out.'

I pause, in case another creature has ventured into her web.

'Skye, I'm not waiting all day.'

I could stay hidden.

Fly home, pretend I hadn't been here and then lie to her face when she confronts me about it. But that wouldn't be right.

I flick off my invisibility.

'How was the show?' she asks casually, her head dipping to one side.

I'm positive I have that, *I'm frigging impressed* look on my face. 'For the record, you were awesome.'

A smile tugs at her lips. 'Nah. This mutt was a pushover.'

The questions start piling up in my head. 'Who was that?'

She shrugs. 'Probably a scout. No real threat.'

'No, I mean What. Was. That?'

'My guess, a goblin or a hybrid, or something unnatural like that. I never let them hang around long enough to ask.'

She turns to face me head on. 'You're hurt,' I say, closing the distance between us. Her lip is split, and blood is streaming from her mouth. She blots it with the arm of her jumper, before spitting out a mouthful of red saliva.

'It's nothing,' she says offhandedly. She spits again, staining the tan pine needles red. 'We'll need to bury him.'

'Why?'

'*Why*? Because people come walking up here and he could be found. If we start exposing our existence, and the existence of other realms, the world will become what Ra-Mon has always wanted.' She pauses. 'We mop up our dead.'

I look around. 'I don't have a shovel,' I say in response.

Terra clicks her tongue. 'Who needs a shovel? You clearly haven't heard of the American badger before?'

I shake my head.

'Oh, move out the way.'

In the time it takes to eat a sandwich and make a cup of tea, the hole is dug and Terra is back to being human again. We drag the body over and dump it in the hole. I now understand what she means about the stench – dried sweat, unwashed genitals and urine are what I get. Disgusting enough to make me want to chuck up.

'Why badger?' I ask as we push the dirt over the corpse.

'It's the fastest digger on the planet.'

'Right. Of course it is. I'll remember that for next time.'

It's a nice moment and we both laugh.

We throw a few handfuls of pine needles over the top.

'Good,' she says, inspecting the area.

We get ready to leave. 'Skye, can we keep this between us? I don't want the others to worry.'

'Okay,' is all I say.

We walk for a bit, not speaking, although my questions are still stacking up. I try my luck.

'Is that how you got a black eye? Fighting those …*things*?' I ask.

She's quick to answer. 'Yep. I was having a slow day, that day.'

'Aha.' I don't say anymore – she's being truthful and that's what matters. 'And getting into Le Louvre that time … how did you manage that?'

She laughs out loud. A crack in the shady canopy above sends a beam of sunlight onto her face. Brings a sparkle to her eyes. 'I wondered when you were going to ask me about that?'

I go for a timid face.

'Alright, but only because we have shared a moment here,' she says, still smiling. 'I turned myself into a fly and hitched a ride on the cap of one of the guards. I saw everything. Heard their comments. Listened in on their private conversations.'

I let out a small laugh of my own. 'I thought it must have been something like that.' The air around me feels suddenly lighter. More fragrant, softer, if that's even a thing. We have finally found some common ground. Now is the perfect time to be genuine. 'I'm sorry for trying to kill you all the time.' I glance at her arm, where I shot her with my pellet gun.

She looks across at me as we walk. 'Thanks,' she says shyly. 'You weren't to know.' We both inhale at the same time. 'I was angry for a long time. Angry at my parents. Angry at this *gift*. Angry at everything. And I'm afraid you copped a lot of that.' Something compels me to reach across and take her hand. She flinches at first, then entwines her fingers around mine. 'I'm glad we're finally friends,' she says, giving my hand a squeeze. 'It's something I've always wanted us to be.' My cheeks fill with heat as a tremor flits in and out of my body in a rush of awkwardness. She diffuses the tension with another laugh. 'Now, I'll race you home.'

Before I can reply, she transforms herself into a peregrine falcon and soars into the sky.

I still have a smile on my face as I enter the villa. Terra is sitting at the kitchen bench, alone, grinning and drumming her fingernails on the granite. 'What took you?'

'Ooh, I dunno. Maybe you're the world's biggest cheat.'

Terra wipes the smirk off her face with her palm. 'What can I say … fastest flyer, fastest digger.'

'What about fastest chef?' I say, noticing the bag of shopping on the table. 'I'm starving.' Hayley must be back but there's no sign of her. 'Where are the lovebirds?'

Terra points to the bedroom. 'I heard some interesting noises coming from there, so I thought …' she gets up and goes to the sink, 'thought I'd start on dinner.' She grins sheepishly.

'I'll be in to help shortly, but do you mind if I have a shower first?'

'Go for it,' she says, pulling pasta out of the bag.

I head down the hallway towards the bathroom, noticing through the front windows that the hire car is parked under the majestic olive tree. I tiptoe past Hayley's door, figuring she must be in there, grab some clothes from my room and hightail it into the nearest bathroom. I'm just not ready to go another round with her.

The shower was exactly what I needed and the delicious aroma of home-cooking hits me as I head back into the kitchen.

'Here,' says Terra, sliding a glass of juice towards me. I sit and watch her as she potters around, adding herbs to the sauce and placing chunky slabs of garlic bread into the oven.

'These mini expeditions you go off on …' Terra swings around to face me. I can't tell if she's going to jump down my throat as a wave of irritation makes a fleeting appearance across her face. I switch tracks in an instant and go for a different approach. 'Just so you know, you don't have to do them alone.'

'Smooth,' she says, 'you're definitely learning how to be less of a smart-arse.' I grumble internally at the way she has total access to my thoughts, and yet I am only thrown the occasional crumb to hers. 'And thanks.' She smiles. 'They can get kind of lonely.'

We both turn as we hear Ember and River join us.

'Taking in the view?' I say to River. He shuts me out of his head with an extended middle finger.

'Yeah, something like that,' he says, his skin looking more flushed than it has in a while. River pulls out a stool as Terra spoons the pasta onto the plates. He's following her every move, staring at her split lip. 'What on earth have you been up to this afternoon? Is there some abusive boyfriend I need to have a word with?' He looks directly at me.

'Don't look at me. I didn't do it.'

'Well …?'

Ember cringes as she pulls the stool out next to him. She gives me a pleading look and I offer her a sly wink.

'It's nothing,' says Terra. 'I'm into … ' she pauses, her gaze flitting quickly to me, 'extreme sports.'

I cough into my juice to disguise my laugh.

'Sure. Whatever. Just please be safe. You're next on his list.'

'How can I forget,' she says soberly.

We are in the middle of dinner when Hayley finally graces us with her presence. Em had knocked on her door several times, mentioning her curtains were closed when she snuck onto the veranda, so we assumed she was asleep.

'I'm sorry. I still don't have much of an appetite. I think I'll have a glass of water and go back to bed.'

She does look a bit peaky, a stark contrast to the feisty young woman I saw earlier. 'I'll pop my head in before I turn in,' I tell her as she smiles politely at us before walking back to her room.

We decide on an early night, knowing tomorrow could be a long day investigating the pyramid, and final resting place of Tomas's father.

When I decide to turn in, I notice Hayley's bedside light is on and her door, ajar. She must hear me enter because she rolls over to face me, her cheeks flushed and streaked with tears.

'Are you alright?' I whisper, kneeling by the side of her bed.

'No,' she says and starts crying.

I pull back the covers and crawl in next to her. She clings to me. Sobbing into my chest. I wrap my arms around her and stroke her hair.

'Tell me,' I ask.

Her sobs quieten. 'I didn't *want* to lie to you about the fudge,' she says, burying her head into my neck.

I'm confused. 'Then, why did you?'

I draw her head back so I can see her face. Her eyes are closed.

'Look at me, please.' She pinches her eyes shut even more. 'Hayley?'

After another couple of breaths, she slowly opens them. I stare at her, inspecting every inch of her face. Looking for the lies. Identifying those telltale signs. 'I don't know. I don't know what I'm doing or saying these days.'

Her eyes drop.

'I don't know who I am anymore.'

I don't know why, but my thoughts drift back to Iris and her unconscious ramblings.

TWENTY-SEVEN

THERE's a tap, tap, tap at my window.

It's surprising how quickly my body remembers … how fast I relapse into fright mode.

My body locks into place. Hands gripping the sheets. Legs solid like my skin has been dipped in cement.

I hear it again.

I hold my breath.

Fuck … I thought I was over this!

Slowly, I turn my head towards the veranda doors. After Hayley had fallen asleep, I'd slipped out of her room and fell into my own bed, forgetting to close the curtains. I chance a glimpse at the window. The sun hasn't quite breached the horizon, but that doesn't prevent my heart from ceasing to beat as a dark, shadowy figure stares in at me.

Fear finds a way in, convincing me it's the beast Terra fought yesterday who has somehow sprung back to life and dug himself out of the grave we'd buried it in.

Sanity kicks in.

I breathe out, realising it wouldn't be knocking.

'Skye. Are you awake?'

Terra.

I cross to the window in nothing but a pair of jeans. A few days ago, my first question would be to ask her what she wanted. Not this time. 'Are you okay?'

She gives me a fleeting smile. 'Get dressed. We have some reconnaissance work to do.' I copy her dark attire, adding a black t-shirt and sweater. She tosses the backpack to me that was slung over her shoulder. 'Provisions,' she simply says. 'Just in case.' I peer inside to see a couple of bottles of water, something wrapped in foil, protein bars and a torch.

We slip outside, the air cool and fresh against my face. I'm pumped at the thought of sneaking out but also that we're coming to the end of the Initiations, and I can step out of the limelight and go back to being plain old me that no one gives two shits about.

'Where are we off to?'

'The Falicon Pyramid.' Half of her face is still in shadow although I don't miss her eyebrow lift. 'Are you up for it?'

'What about the others? River said …'

'I know what River said, but I can't risk it.'

The bottom drops out of my stomach. 'Risk *what*, exactly?'

Terra pulls my sleeve to start us walking towards the scrubland behind the house. 'I didn't want to say anything to the others last night, but I spoke with Gaia.'

I can pretty much guarantee her next words aren't going to fill me with joy. 'And …'

'That pig-goblin has blabbed about where I was, and Gaia said she's felt a growing surge of evil around us, so I thought …' her lips twist one way and then the other, 'that we should fly over there and take a look. Make sure it's safe. What do you think?'

I'm thrilled that she wants my opinion on this, and I also know River, and his foul temper. He wouldn't think highly of me for going along with it. 'I'm in,' I say without hesitation. He can scream and holler all he likes when we get back.

'Follow me,' she says. A magnificent brown eagle pushes off from the ground, creating an updraft from its powerful wings.

I tack on behind her as she heads west, back through the town of Falicon. The valley below is bathed in a smoky orange haze as the sun starts to peer across the Mediterranean, bringing just enough light to see the last of the beige villas with their aqua coloured swimming pools disappearing behind us.

The terrain then changes to bushland, not quite as dry as the Aussie bush. Barren and rocky patches take turns between clumps of shrubs and trees, although I wouldn't have a clue what species they are. I'm sure Terra would know even *with* her eyes closed. On the high side of the next ridge I spot a crumbling stone structure. Bike tracks and foot trails spread out from it in every direction like dusty, yellow veins.

Terra begins her descent.

Surely, that can't be it?

She drops down next to the white, stoney ruins, changing to her human form the second her feet impact the earth. 'What do you reckon?' she asks. My confused expression must have prompted the question.

'*This* is the pyramid?'

'Yup. Cool, right?'

I'm not sure how to answer that, having never seen the decaying remnants of a pyramid before. It stands a mere three metres at its highest peak, and in truth, a little underwhelming, with the entire top section missing as though it's been sliced off by a giant machete. Stupid, I know, but I thought it would be more *Egyptian like*.

'Wow,' is all I can say.

She leads the way.

Some of the nearby undergrowth has been cleared away and frequently trodden paths take us around the side of the ramshackle old shell. One side has completely collapsed, leaving a gaping hole.

Surely Tomas must have his wires crossed. *This is his father's final resting place?* The entire area is a hazard zone and needs to be roped off with a warning sign pinned across it to tell people to *Keep Out*.

'There's our doorway,' says Terra, pointing to the hole at the pyramid's base. I stare down into the darkness, contemplating my next move, dreading going into another creepy cave.

A shove in the back startles me. 'Saved ya.'

'Very funny.'

'Are we going in, or are you too chicken?'

'I will if you will.'

Conveniently, there is a make-shift rope ladder fastened to a metal stake. I'm impressed that she's thought about making our entrance a little easier.

Terra shakes her head. 'Nothing to do with me, I'm afraid.' She cocks her head at my wordless question, and I conclude, it must have been Tomas then. Fearlessly, she backs up and steps into the first rung and descends into the cave, like she's done this a thousand times before. I glance behind me, saying a last farewell to fresh air, sunlight and the mass of pink flowering shrubs at my feet.

Five seconds later, I'm standing at her side.

'Do you really think we will find Tiberius's remains down here?'

She flashes the torch under her chin. 'Do I look like someone who knows everything … past, present and future?'

'Yes, you do.'

'I love your confidence, but …so you know, it's not always that clear cut – sometimes the information I get is down to interpretation, meaning … I *might* get it wrong *occasionally*.' She clicks off her torch.

'Look, I'm good with *occasionally*. It's got to be a hell of a lot better than getting it wrong ninety-nine per cent of the time … like I do.'

Terra laughs. 'Problem is,' she says, 'I can't afford to get one per cent wrong, let alone ten. There's too much at stake *not* to be correct. I have to trust the information Gaia gives me otherwise …' She trails off.

A sliver of sunlight cuts through the darkness and finds her face, revealing a little more depth to this girl I hardly know. Dusty mauve shadows let slip how hard she's working, how little sleep she is getting, and yet there's a brightness to her eyes like looking at a new blade of grass through a raindrop. Words I hadn't put next to Terra's name before … excitement and passion find a home in her voice, in her eyes. And I see something new …friendship. I see mystery and honesty in the same smile that curls around her lips. Lips that don't want to snarl at me anymore.

She sniffs and grins at my new summary of her. Bumps her shoulder against mine. 'Come on, Indiana. Let's go dig up some bones.'

I trail behind her, wondering what the hell is with these incessant single-file tunnels that I always seem to find myself in, and why the walls are always sweating with moisture. The pathway is fairly stony with more divots than a polo field, and sloping downwards and mainly to our left, giving the tangled tree roots free rein to tickle my face and get caught in my hair. Along with the musty tang combined with the aroma of sulphur hitting the back of my throat every time I breathe in, making it hard to take in a deep breath. I conclude, being underground is my least favourite place to be.

'You know this is a karstic cave, right?' says Terra, shining her torch about giving me even more glimpses of this god-forsaken place. 'It has been formed from the dissolution of soluble rocks such as limestone and dolomite. They have their own drainage systems down here, which can create sinkholes. Watch that,' she says casually.'

I reach into my pocket for my phone, accidentally running into the back of her. 'Sorry.'

'Stalagmites,' she says. 'There's heaps down here.'

'You're enjoying this, aren't you?'

'It's like being in the belly of nature. What's not to like?'

I could name a lot. Still, it's like being with a walking encyclopedia.

She laughs. 'I'm sorry. I can't help it. The Earth has many memories and a loud voice. Plus, I talk a lot when I'm nervous.'

I glance over her comment about the Earth having a loud voice. I guess she not only has to contend with the thoughts of humans, but animals, trees, *shit* … even rocks. 'What do you have to be nervous about?'

'Oh, you know. The usual stuff.'

To me, she is fearless.

She makes a funny sound in her throat, a bit like a laugh but not quite. 'Anyway, moving on …this is known as The Cave of Bats.'

'It's probably a good idea then, that Ember didn't come. She hates bats.'

'For real? I kinda like them. They have these cute little faces, and their tiny furry bodies remind me of miniature monkeys.'

'Yeah, with sharp teeth,' I say around a grin.

I stop her. Turn her around. Shine my torch at the ceiling between us. 'What does scare you? You can tell me.'

'You *really* wanna know?'

I nod. 'I do.'

She pauses for a moment. Searches my eyes. 'Okay … it's the dark.'

I sniff. 'The *dark?*'

'Yes, *the dark*. What's so odd about *that*?' Her cheeks look pinched and tight.

'Nothing. It's just … that I understand what you mean. For me, it's small spaces. And then ravens come a close second. Or did, until recently.'

Terra's face softens, the ghost of a smile playing with her lips. 'And yet, with your Elementar power you can zap straight out of there. Whereas, the dark …' She steadies her breath. 'Too many bad things happen in the dark.'

I'm learning more about Terra as the layers slowly peel back – the good, and the painful. And yet, I would never have guessed it was something so … so …*normal*. I turn on my chivalry. 'Would you like me to go first?'

Her eyes crinkle at the corners when she smiles. 'Thanks, but I'd rather face whatever is about to happen head-on, rather than have it attack me from behind. I don't like being defenceless.'

Her breath catches in her throat as she accidentally downloads a series of disturbing images of Nevermore into my head. They steal my breath and shut down my heart. I think about extending my ear to her, or offer my counsel for what its worth. Even to be that shoulder to cry on, but from one thing I've learnt about Terra, the victim mentality isn't her thing. Every bad experience has become her source of strength.

'We need to push on,' she says, turning her back on me.

I'm only getting glimpses of the track through the light on Terra's torch, when she lets out an almighty scream. Almost as fearsome as the one I heard her cry back in Nevermore. Her torchlight vanishes.

'TERRA.' My voice echoes through the cold, dark, tunnels.

I freeze.

I am alone.

I am in total blackness.

I click on my phone, fumbling to find the torch. I release a deep breath when I finally locate it and click it on. I shine it about, stunned she is nowhere in sight, despite the fact that we have come to a dead end. 'TERRA!'

I inch closer, the luck of the torch light preventing me from falling into the same gaping black hole at my feet. I shine the light down, but it's too deep. I can't see the bottom. 'Terra? Are you okay?'

Still silence.

I engage my power and float down, expecting my feet to hit the bottom at any moment. The trip takes a good thirty seconds. When my eyes adjust to the dim light, I see two people instead of one.

'Tomas. Boy, am I glad to see you,' I say to him. I'm surprised to see him still wearing his jeans and hoodie. I thought he would've changed back into his cloak and battle armour by now. He is sitting on the ground, back against the wall, one knee up, one leg stretched out long, his sword lying across his lap. A fire torch is slung in a bracket above his head. Terra is standing beside him. 'Are you okay?' I ask her. 'When I heard you scream like that … I thought …'

'I've been waiting for you,' interrupts Tomas, getting to his feet.

I give him the once over, spying a familiar item. 'I see you have my backpack.'

He nods. 'Yes.'

'And that's it? No explanation why you took it?'

'No.' His face is as staunch as ever, the heavy scar running down his cheek seems to ripple in the firelight. 'For the moment, all you need to know is, that I will keep it safe.' I'm not happy with his answer, it doesn't look like I'm going to get anything else out of him.

Terra cocks her head to one side. 'Do you hear that?'

I strain to listen, but hear nothing other than Tomas's heavy breathing. He lifts the torch from the holding and raises it above his head. 'This way.'

He directs us into another massive room, overflowing with tombs.

'Do you have any more of those?' I ask, gesturing to the torch. He zigzags in and out of the tombs and ignites two torches on the far wall.

The room comes to life with the dead, the ethereal energy alive and pumping with century old spooks.

The warmth in my body runs out in a big hurry.

I count twenty-four tombs.

Some have already been opened, evident by the missing stone tops. Some have enormous gaping cracks as though they've been hit with a sledgehammer.

'There it is again,' says Terra. 'Surely you heard it that time.' Again we stop and listen, and again we both turn to each other and shrug. I hear nothing. We don't have time for "crazy nut-house Terra". Her response is a glare that could peel paint.

'This was where you found the book, wasn't it?' I ask Tomas, lifting my chin to the mass burial chamber, eager to change the subject. 'Did you check every tomb for your father?' I casually glance over at him when he doesn't answer. He is standing in front of the only tomb which is completely intact, his face the colour of marble and set the same way. I walk over to see what he is staring at. On the front panel of the tomb, there's an ancient Egyptian painting, dulled with age, of a green-skinned man wearing a pointy hat. There is something about the picture that looks familiar to me.

'I did not open this one,' he says, a grim expression casting shadows over his face.

I frown. It's not like Tomas to be so careless in his investigations. 'How come?'

'I didn't get around to it,' he says. There is a break in his voice. 'I was interrupted.' I feel as though someone is watching me through the cracks in the walls.

'By who?' asks Terra, unzipping my backpack to retrieve a bottle of water. She has a sip before replacing it. I'd also like an answer to her question.

Tomas is still staring at the tomb. 'But no one will stop me this time,' he says forcefully.

'How are you going to open it?' I ask him.

He storms towards it and smashes the hilt of his sword into the stone top.

'WAIT,' screams Terra. This time, I do hear something. A rustling, clicking, chirping sound that is getting louder by the second.

The tomb lid cracks open, half of it falling to the ground in a cloud of white dust, the other half left hanging precariously on the edge. Determination: sledgehammer, not required. Just a powerful Roman Centurion with a big-arse sword.

From out of the top of the tomb, bursts a mass of black. 'Bats,' cries Terra.

Naturally, I duck for cover. Tomas copies me. Terra, of course, does not. She raises her arms above her head and lets out an almighty screech. The bats stop flying erratically and form an orderly huddle, flitting and hovering above her hands, waiting for her command.

From the look on Tomas's face, if he had gum in his mouth, he would've swallowed it.

'Believe me now!' she yells over the top of the chirping. 'The next time I say I hear something, you might as well bloody believe me, or I'll let the next animal devour you.'

She flicks her hands to the right and squeaks something in "bat language" and they take off.

Tomas approaches the tomb and peers in.

I don't need to see the look of disappointment on his face to determine it isn't the result he's after. His massive shoulders heave, his posture in all kinds of misery. 'I was expecting him to be there,' he says wearily.

'Oh, move out the way,' demands Terra. 'He is there, you're just having a "mans look".'

She muscles her way between us and looks in. 'Here … hold this.' She launches into the tomb and drags out a mummified corpse, swaddled in stained muslin. The second the corpse touches me, my hands fly to my sides, sending the bundle of bones to the ground.

It doesn't take long for me to realise these aren't the remains of a Roman soldier – but that of a penniless peasant. 'This has been placed here recently.'

Terra resumes her position, leaning into the tomb. 'Now, this is more like it,' she says, excited.

Tomas and I veer closer and gingerly peek over the edge. Inside lies a Roman soldier, dressed in full battle gear, including helmet, shield and staff. His hands are positioned across his chest, one hand brandishing a leather whip of some kind.

'Not what I was expecting,' admits Tomas. He leans in a bit further. 'I need to check something.' Very carefully, he prises open the jaw. Inside, is a coin. He takes it out and inspects it.

He inhales a sharp breath, and lethargically steps away from the tomb. 'This is my father,' his voice is barely a whisper. His face revealing every long year he has been looking, every disappointment, every dead end, every inch of hope he's held on to.

Tomas grips the coin in his fist, brings it to his lips, eyes pressed so tightly together anyone could easily see how much pain resides in his heart. His search is finally over. 'How did you know he would be there?' Tomas asks Terra.

'The bats,' she says with a casual smile. 'The bats told me they weren't alone, so naturally I had to look. You know, bats are inquisitive creatures, who've copped a bad wrap in the past. They were seen as both good and evil, birth and death, and during Roman times they would tuck a dead bat under the left arm to prevent that person from sleeping.'

'You think a spell had been placed on him so he wouldn't sleep? So he would stay in The Underworld?' Casually, I hop up onto a nearby tomb and sit down.

'Probably,' answers Terra.

'That's all very fascinating, but what's with the whip?' I ask, 'And the coin.'

She shrugs her shoulders. 'Not sure about the coin, but I think I've figured out the whip. All of the objects relating to the Initiations are held by our current belief system.' She hops up on top of the tomb beside me and wiggles in to get comfy.

'How do you mean?'

'The belief we have in our God is strong, right?'

'I guess.'

'That is what makes them powerful, yes?'

I nod.

'Well, think about it. First, the crown worn by Jesus, then the spear which stabbed him, then the lion who punished the soldier who speared Jesus, and now the whip.'

'What's a whip have to do with it?'

'Honestly, do you know anything about history or religion?' She rolls her eyes. 'I would bet money that this was the whip used to flog Jesus thirty-nine times before his execution in order to humiliate him.'

'And you know all this because …'

'You forget, I was cursed with the knowledge of the Akashic records. Gaia sees and hears all, and that is *kindly* downloaded to me in dribs and drabs. I simply joined the dots.'

'Yeah right, that still doesn't explain the coin.'

'Do you remember me saying about the coin that I didn't hand over to prevent falling under the witch's curse?' says Tomas.

'Yes.'

'It appears my father had kept his also.' He rubs it between his thumb and forefinger. 'A coin is placed inside or on the mouth of someone of wealth when they die. This means his spirit was not sent to The Underworld for eternity like I thought, but to a barren wasteland … an *in-between* world created by a spell.' He looks at me as he turns the coin over and over in his hand.

I glance over at Terra, her face dumbfounded. 'Only one way to find out for sure,' I say. 'I can ask him.'

Tomas's eyes widen. He nods his head once. 'You will do that ... for me?'

'It's the least I can do.'

I jump down, and remove my shirt. I kneel on the hard, dusty earth, like before, and stretch out my radar to find Tiberius. The energy is somehow smoother to pass through, like being pulled through crystal waters rather than wading through thick, sticky mud. The atmosphere isn't dense and the sweet tang of daisies hangs in the humid air. Flowered meadows stretch out before me instead of landscapes of bitter nothingness. The sounds of laughter and birds chirping, dance across my senses. Grass, as soft as I've ever felt it, cushions my knees as I brush my fingertips across it. I already know he's in a better place.

'Tiberius, son of Tomas, brother of Longinus.'

Tiberius steps forward immediately.

As far as ghosts go, he looks healthy, if that makes any sense. I know it doesn't, but I can't describe it any other way than his cheeks are flushed and he appears to be well fed. His long white hair is tied back in a leather band and his breastplate and sword have been replaced by a dark tunic that falls to his feet. I'm at a loss for words for once.

'Young'un. You seek me out again so soon?' His voice is clear, light, vibrant.

'What happened?' is all I can say.

'When the darkness lifted, I found myself here.'

Darkness? Aahh, the bats. That makes sense. So it was a spell.

'Is this heaven?' I find myself asking.

'It is peace.'

That's good enough for me.

'I know why you summon me. You seek knowledge on the whip and staff.'

'What staff?' I hadn't even noticed it.

357

'The staff lying next to my body. It was created on the sixth day of creation by God, and has been passed down through major patriarchs. It was the staff that Aaron performed wonders with before the Pharaohs. Jacob used it when he crossed the River Jordan. It is also called the Holy Rod, which Moses used to part the Red Sea, and turn the Nile blood-red. It was passed to David, who slew Goliath. But most of all, it was our Lord Jesus's shepherd crook. It is the most powerful object this world possesses and what Mithras needs, in order to rule over all life forms.'

'Right, so it definitely needs to be thrown onto the next bonfire then?'

'No. It cannot be burnt. First, it must be used to battle Zurvan, the beast who watches over Mithras. Only then, can the staff be used to raise Mithras from the shadows.'

'*What*?' I choke on saliva. 'I don't want to be responsible for raising another maniac who wants to rule the world. We can't get rid of the *other* idiot, let alone an egotistical, Roman deity with a chip on his shoulder.' Oh my God, I can only imagine what River would say if he were here right now.

'Once Mithras rises, he will become mortal, and *can* be killed.'

I see the bigger picture now.

'But use caution. Ra-Mon is planning to use Mithras as a syphon to drain Amun's power, so he can then extract Amun from you without expending any of his own power.' I remember Doc saying how it requires an incredible amount of Ra-Mon's power to keep Nuria and Nereus bound and powerless.

'Got it.'

'You also have an ally.'

'Who?'

'Upon presenting the Son of God's Graces …'

'The *what*?

'The Graces – the Cup of Life, the Crown of Thorns, the Spear of Destiny, the Scourging Whip and the Lord's

Staff also known as the Holy Staff. Upon presenting the Son of God's Graces, your ally will reveal themselves.'

Frustration kicks in. 'Why don't you just tell me now? Why do I have to wait?'

'There is a plan in place, Young'un. Trust me.'

My head feels too heavy to hold and lolls forward. A shudder finds its way over my body. I desperately need to contact Amun, if I'm to get a handle on what the fuck I should or shouldn't be doing.

My concentration is slipping and I sense the connection between us is breaking.

Fatigue sets in.

Nausea washes through me, and I find myself bare-chested, kneeling in between two tombs, Tomas and Terra staring intently at me.

I push my way up to standing, only to see Terra and Tomas, wide-eyed and open-mouthed, at something behind me.

'We shall meet again, my son,' says Tiberius.

His ghostly figure wavers for a moment, like a heatwave in the Aussie desert, before disappearing.

'What's the matter? You two look like you've seen a ghost.' I roar with laughter, and clap Tomas on the shoulder. 'He's good, dude. He's in a really good place.'

Tomas steadies himself against a tomb. It's the first time I've seen him rattled. 'I face my death willingly now,' he says.

I explain to them the extent of my conversation with Tiberius, him being the Fifth Initiation, the whip being the Sixth and the Holy Staff being the Seventh. I told them about the need to present the Son of God's Graces.

'We can't do that,' says Tomas abruptly. He takes my backpack off and opens it. 'These Graces, including the whip and the staff, are the only way out of this immortal life for me. I must present them so I can rejoin my family … my father.'

Seems like everyone has been offered the same deal.

'I need them too,' I say, unable to draw my gaze from him. 'River's soul is at stake here. He is banking on me to get the antidote for the blood he drank.' Also to kill Zurvan, unleash a powerful God, them kill him, and then to expose an ally, but I don't say that out loud.

We stand in silence, realising the magnitude of this problem.

'Look, fellas. Can't you see? Isis is hedging her bets here. She's got both of you doing her dirty work. She doesn't care which one of you gets her these relics. I imagine, whoever presents them, will be the one to earn the reward.'

'Not helpful, Terra,' I say.

'If you let me finish … what I was about to say was …all we have to do, is devise a way to kill two birds with one stone, and I think I know a way.'

'How?' asks Tomas.

'Play one off against the other. You know Ra-Mon and Mithras ended their relationship on bad terms, don't you?'

'No. How would I know that? Dumb idiot here, remember.' I jab my finger at my forehead, but it has no effect on Terra.

She continues on. 'Ra-Mon double-crossed him.'

'Nah, that doesn't sound like him.'

'According to Gaia, he's not likely to trust him again anytime soon, which *has* to work in our favour.'

Terra winks at me. 'You up for a little payback?'

I love her ballsy approach. 'Count me in.'

TWENTY-EIGHT

STILL sitting on a nearby tomb, her knees drawn up, her arms hugging around them, Terra leans over and peers in at the remains of Tomas's father.

'I suppose we should get this over with,' she says, rolling up her sleeves before jumping down. She dives into the tomb to pluck out the Holy Staff, but something stops her. She pins me with a long stare before withdrawing her hand. 'Maybe you should be in charge of the Staff.'

'Alright,' I say, thinking nothing of it.

I pick up The Scourging Whip first, and examine it. The wooden handle is about eight inches long with three long separate thongs of leather attached to it. Each strap is assigned two pebble-sized lead balls threaded onto the ends. I shut out the image of what kind of flesh-tearing pain it could cause being flogged once with it, let alone thirty-nine times.

I coil up the whip and drop it into the backpack next to the thorny crown, a wooden cup and the spearhead. Then, in good faith, I hand the bag back to Tomas for safekeeping. He acknowledges my gesture with a nod.

Now for The Holy Staff.

Again, without too much thought, I reach in to retrieve it. My fingers barely make contact before I sense the low-grade electrical current emanating from it – the kind of charge you might get from standing too close to a cattle fence back home. Clearly, with no sense of self-preservation, I seize the staff, pushing through the tingly feeling. I consider dropping it, at one point, but instead, I squeeze my fist tighter until the buzzing subsides.

I lift it out.

It towers over me by almost half a metre. I've no clue what kind of wood it is other than it's smooth to the touch, surprisingly light and encompasses the natural curvature of the tree it came from. There is a slight curve at one end.

Terra's face is alight with wonder. 'How does it feel?' she asks breathlessly. 'Your eyes … I mean, they're so … so …intense. No, I mean luminous. No, no, that's not it either.' I know exactly what she means. I'm sure as shit my face portrays the same expression River had when he parted the lake a few months back.

I don't have words for how it feels. I imagine the same way you'd feel before getting on a roller coaster except intensified by a thousand per cent. Excited, like nervous knots in your stomach, yet strangely serene and composed. 'Do I look qualified to herd sheep?'

Terra laughs. 'C'mon, oh holy one. Our work is done here.'

Tomas is eager to go, too.

I check my watch, shocked that we've been down here for three hours. River and the girls would be awake by now, and I reckon he's asking a million questions about where we are.

We retrace our steps to the bottom of the proverbial rabbit hole, and I'm about to ask Tomas how he got down here, when he disappears into thin air. Perks of being immortal, I suppose. 'Meet us at the top then,' I shout into the blackness, my voice echoing.

Terra transforms into a bat, I mean, why wouldn't she? At least she can see where she's going. I casually float up, staff in hand.

The sunshine on my face is as welcome as the fresh air is to my lungs, and I manage to enjoy it for a few brief seconds, before it's gone.

Then there is pain, and black, and more pain.

When I finally open my eyes, I discover the reason why. Five reasons, to be exact.

Five creatures of varying grotesqueness.

Panic strikes me in the chest. Terra? Tomas? I make the mistake of swinging around too quickly to locate them, unceremoniously punished by gut-wrenching headspins. Blood roars in my ears.

Fuck! They are nowhere to be seen.

I stumble to my feet as the creatures form a circle around me. Sure, I could fly out of here in a blink or turn invisible. But these scumbags are after Terra, and if I can take them out, it will be five less she has to deal with. Plus, I have the most powerful stick in the entire universe …*somewhere*! I spy it on the ground, no more than twenty paces away.

The short, stubby creature with the horn on its head comes at me first. His skin is green and leathery as though he's been soaked in swamp water and left in a damp corner for too long. He lurches forward, swiping a long-handled scythe at me. 'Give us the Earthchild, and I won't poke a hole in your belly and empty your guts out in front of my comrades,' it snarls. His guttural voice is higher pitched than I thought it'd be.

'How about you and your friends go fuck yourselves.' There is a roar of different pitches of laughter.

'You're a brave boy, aren't you?' says horn-head. 'For someone who's not going to be around long enough to enjoy his next meal.'

'He wants to play hardball,' says a much larger one with a bald head. This deformed mutt's mouth sits too far to one side of his face, exposing a row of fangs that protrude at odd angles. The thick, heavy club he carries could do a lot of damage if the beast had the muscles to wield it, but with a pair of stumpy arms and flabby tummy, it looks more for show. The most concerning element is the string of human toes hanging around his neck.

The other three look very similar, maybe from the same tribe or gene pool, if that's even a thing. Humanlike – yellowish skin with eyes like a cat. Pointy ears and sharp, crooked teeth give them a conventional goblin appearance whilst wisps of long hair trail across their faces in greasy strands, except for one, who has tied it back. Each has a weapon, whether it's an axe, spear or a spikey ball on the end of a chain. Their clothing is primitive too, made from cheap leather or rough animal hides, all clad in knee-high boots lined with fur or tied with leather bands. The bald one is the only one not wearing a vest.

Okay, so I'm not trained in the art of fighting, and even though the staff could be fun to use, if I fuck up, and one does manage to slip away and report there's a new Top Dog in town, I could bring some serious shit down on us.

For all of us.

Especially Terra.

So, sticking with what I know, my first task is to acquire a weapon. And the best way is to steal one of theirs.

I flick on my invisibility, much to the horror of the beasts who voice their disbelief.

'Where'd he go?'

'Do you see him?'

''E was 'ere one minute.'

They spin left and right, noses in the air, trying to pick up my scent. I walk boldly up to horn-head, position myself ready to throw my arm around his neck and then

364

flick off my invisibility. Having never tried to strangle anyone before, I've no idea if it will work, but it catches him off-guard enough for me to tear the scythe out of his grubby mitt.

He lets out a throaty howl as black blood spurts everywhere. The deep slash running the length of his spine is greeted with snorts of rage from his buddies. He falls to his knees, so I ram the heel of my foot into his back, driving him face-first into the dirt. Without hesitation, I plunge the tip of the scythe into his back. The lethal blade goes through his flesh with ease.

My first *real* kill, and strangely enough, I'm okay about it. My only thought is one down, four to go.

The big fucker with the bald head comes at me next. Each swing of his thick bladed axe is slow and awkward, like he's here for show and not to fight. I decide after our first few clashes, he'll require a little more effort to take down. A lucky strike across his belly comes first, not quite deep enough to spill his guts, but painful enough for him to squeal in agony. For a big fella, he's got some moves, more than I gave him credit for, and a shit-tonne more advanced than my movie-inspired fighting manoeuvres that aren't fooling anyone. However, I somehow manage to land a one-in-a-million shot to the back of his thigh, severing his femoral artery, spraying more black gunk all over the joint. He grabs for his leg to staunch the flow, and I dole out the final and fatal blow, a clean easy stab beneath the ribcage. He falls to the ground, gurgling on his own blood.

My confidence soars.

And the three little pigs watching me, know it.

They hesitate, their bodies hunched, eyes darting here, there and everywhere, feet shuffling, scuffing up the pine needles to reveal the dusty soil beneath.

I turn it up a notch and throw in some ninja moves whilst clumsily swinging the sharp bloody scythe. I have no idea what I am doing and it obviously shows.

'He's an amateur,' laughs the one with his hair tied back. 'Get him.'

The three close in, tightening the noose around me. I carve up the air, missing them by inches. I definitely need to level-up my hand-to-hand combat skills and I know just the fella to help … *if I ever get out of this mess.* Thinking of Tomas, I quickly scan the area again, for my friends. Still nothing.

Rookie mistake.

The second I take my eye off my adversaries, one thumps me over the back of the neck.

My bones rattle in my ears, making me cough.

The scythe falls to the ground.

Next minute, I follow it, earning myself a pine needle and dirt sandwich. Realising I'm in real danger here, I pull my ripcord and immediately flick on my invisibility.

They snarl and grumble again. I'm juicing up my power at a steady rate, and if I don't squash this foul-smelling brute-squad soon, it could be all over, red rover.

The closest object to me is The Holy Staff.

What the hell, if I can't figure out how to wield its power, I could always whack them around the head with it and be back at the villa drinking a caramel latte, where I'm positive Tomas and Terra are waiting for me.

I become flesh and bone again and snatch it up.

They slowly back up. 'Yeah, that's right. Pissing in your pants now, aren't you?'

They take several more steps away, their faces frozen in a different kind of horror. Something I haven't seen before. I raise my arms and they scarper into the scrubland. It's not what I'm expecting, and at first, I'm thrilled, but then reality kicks in.

Letting them go is a bad idea.

The staff begins to vibrate in my hand. Raw, celestial power, no doubt supplied by the Big Dog upstairs, surges down my arm and into my chest. My body shudders, trying to contain it. A heaviness creeps into my bones, anchoring me to the hardened ground like the burrowing roots of a mighty oak descending deep into the earth, preventing me from lifting off and finding my way back to heaven.

I feel instantly nauseous.

And if it helped, I'd empty the contents of my stomach if there was anything in there, but there isn't. The chilled air rushing along my skin does nothing to prevent my head from feeling like it's about to explode. It's all too much. 'Stop,' I yell.

By some curious fluke, the three mutts hit an invisible barrier fifteen metres away, landing in a heap of tangled limbs. I was actually talking to the staff, but this works in my favour too. My eyes are drawn to the staff as a compilation of erratic responses spill out of my mouth. 'What the fuck! …That was so cool! …How the hell did I do that?'

I gather my thoughts as the trio of terror try to scramble away. Four bold strides and I am standing over them, the staff raised above my head. Fear finds them quivering in the dirt, fight and flight oozing from their pathetic pleas. 'We will not look for the EarthHealer again,' one says, cowering.

'You have our word,' says another.

I don't know what the word of a mutant goblin is worth these days but I find myself at a crossroads. It doesn't feel right to slaughter them unarmed, yet I can't let them go and report our whereabouts and potentially bring a larger posse of stinking undesirables to the area.

Think, Skye, think.

What I need … is for them to disappear.

The moment the thought is out of my head, they start to dissolve. Panicked cries cut through the silence as they become more and more transparent. Their feet disappear first, the mysterious power gobbling up skin and bone as it races up their legs to their knees and then thighs, erasing them from existence. Their flailing arms frantically grasp at their vanishing stomachs, and then chests. Hands, elbows and shoulders evaporate until all that's left are three screeching heads, eyes ready to pop out of their sockets. It's pretty sick, as far as divine extermination goes, but I have to admit, it's clean, methodical and somewhat humane. Simultaneously, like three balloons popping, one minute they are there, and the next they are gone. The mini fallout of expended power is enough to blow my hair back.

I bark out a sharp laugh. 'Problem solved.'

I turn my attention to the other slain beasts. The horned one is still writhing on the ground. I raise the staff and repeat the process, calling out *disappear*. In a matter of seconds, they both evaporate *balloon-style* like their counterparts.

'That's one way to do it,' says Terra, clapping behind me. 'No more digging for this little badger.' Tomas is with her, a smile stretching the full length of his lips.

I am happy to see them, although my tone hasn't received the memo. 'Where the hell were you?'

'Over there ... behind those trees.'

'And you didn't think to ... ooh I don't know ... help!'

'You seemed to have it under control,' says Tomas, folding his arms across his muscular chest. He looks to Terra, who raises one eyebrow at him, humour playing in her eyes.

'Under control? Are you nuts? Thanks to that feral, I'll have a bruise on my back the size of a dinner plate.'

Tomas looks confused. 'But you are alive?'

'Yes,' is all I can think of to say, blowing out a hearty breath. 'No thanks to you.'

Terra presses her hands into a prayer position, the tips of her fingers touching her nose. 'Would you believe me if I said it was a test, of sorts?'

'Of what? To see how big my balls are? If you want to see them, you only have to ask.'

She skips over my last comment. 'Yeah, kind of. I wanted to see if you'd rat me out.'

'Rat. You. Out.' I feel as though someone has disembowelled me with that monstrous scythe.

Terra throws her hands in the air. Her volume rises a few decibels. 'I needed to be sure you had my back. *Okay*? You haven't exactly been my biggest fan.' I roll my eyes. 'Plus, I wanted to see if you could handle all of them at once.'

'Handle them all at …' I'm downright insulted. 'I've battled a Minotaur, an oversized feline, plus a handful of gargoyles. Doesn't that count for anything?'

'Of course. And don't get crabby about it. It was Tomas's idea not to intervene.'

I look to Tomas. 'Your idea? Well, thanks a bunch, dude. I thought we were on the same page.'

'We are,' he says, frowning. 'I needed to evaluate your skills. In case you didn't know, a battle is coming, and you *all* need to be trained in combat.'

'I also wanted to see the Lord's Staff in action,' admits Terra, hiding her smile behind her hand.

'You *knew* it had REAL powers? And, you didn't say anything?'

Terra's teeth nibble on her lip. 'I wasn't sure. Well, not a hundred per cent. I had a hunch it was powerful, but it's …sort of …*temperamental*.'

'*Temperamental?*'

'Only certain individuals can summon its power, and because you have Amun inside you, I figured, you'd qualify.'

'Which is why you didn't touch it in the tomb, right?'

She nods. 'It was putting out a weird energy to me.' I squint at her. 'After you've been around me a while, you get used to that word *energy*. Everything in the world has an energetic vibration … even a rock, and being plugged into Gaia 24/7, you tend to learn a thing or two – like when *not* to touch things.'

'Right. We still need to work on our communication skills, so perhaps next time, let me know before I pick up some ancient staff that can level the land around us for ten kilometres.'

I simmer down. Look to Terra. 'For the record,' I pause and run my hands through my hair. 'I will *always* be there for you, no matter what.'

She smiles as she faces me, her fingers firmly clasped around both of my biceps. 'I've been waiting a decade to hear those words come out of your mouth.' She then ruffles my hair and lightly pinches my cheek. 'Let's get back to the others.'

We start to make a move.

'Not so fast.' It's a female voice I don't recognise.

I go to take another step, except my legs won't move. My torso, arms and head aren't encumbered – just my legs.

'The son of Sol's witch,' spits out Tomas, the snarl on his lips more menacing than the scar slashing his cheek in two. With feet glued to the ground, I twist the top half of my body around, the same time Terra does, to see Tomas glaring at a woman behind us. I try to fly, turn invisible – nothing works.

'I can't transform,' hisses Terra, that wild and crazy look returning to her emerald eyes.

'You are spelled,' says the woman in a chocolaty, velvet voice that I perhaps dreamt of once. The dream breaks. 'I know you,' I say, the fog lifting. 'You're the chick from Iris's apartment. You're Isis … aren't you?'

'Yes,' she says, elongating the s.

It's hard not to stare at her.

I might be bewitched.

Her eyes, as black as a moonless night, match her blue/black hair - hair straighter than any I've seen. And her olive complexion glows so vibrantly she could have a thousand tiny candles hidden beneath her skin. She is rocking a low-cut burgundy dress, cinched at the waist and hips, the bottom flaring out like a bell jar. The hem of her dress gathers a collection of dry pine needles as she saunters towards us. I am not surprised to see that her feet are bare.

'Just so you know, this *new you* is a huge improvement,' I say, recalling the old duck in green that gave me the runaround at Notre Dame. She feigns a smile at me.

Tomas is fighting to move. 'I will kill you,' he fires at her. 'What you did to my family … my father.'

I haven't made up my mind yet if every move she makes is graceful, deliberate and hypnotic or intimidating, devious and calculating. There is a fine line there, almost too fine to distinguish. 'Technically, that wasn't me,' she says, twirling a strand of hair around her finger before flicking it away.

Terra is also turning this way and that, trying to free herself. 'Let me go and I will show you who has the most power.'

'Silence,' she says. 'We must go. Hold your breath.'

I haven't even processed what she's said before the ground disappears from under my feet in some sort of magical whirlwind, the earth spinning away from me so fast I can barely see … barely breathe.

When the vortex stops, I find myself face-down on a white tiled floor. A second later, Terra and Tomas, show up.

'Are you okay?' The words are getting easier to say to her.

Terra doesn't answer. She jumps to her feet and has that familiar hardened look on her face like she's going to tear someone apart. 'I can't morph. I still can't morph. Try yours again,' she says to me, clearly agitated.

I zone in on my power, any of them, all of them but it's useless.

And that is when I realise – the one miracle I've waited for, hoped for, prayed for …

    For.

        Ten.

            Long.

                Years.

Is finally here … Silence.

I can't hear anyone's thoughts but my own.

No static. The buzz is gone, the low lying hum of voices has vanished. Even of those who have crossed over.

Silence.

Glorious silence.

I close my eyes and breathe into that wonderful, wonderful sound. I can't speak. Don't want to utter or even think of what a word might sound like. My brain is a blank canvas. White space. Totally my own.

'Skye?' snaps Terra.

Reluctantly, I speak. 'Nope. I'm gassed out. Wonder what's going on.'

She shakes her head. Blows out an irritated breath. 'No idea.' Her gaze disappears over my head to a wall of windows cleverly disguised as bi-fold doors, a heavy frown etched into her forehead. It's pitch black outside. 'Where the hell are we?'

I glance around the room, not recognising anything. We appear to be in someone's lounge room – a pretty humongous lounge room and a modern one at that. The furniture is top of the line - a couple of plump, earthy coloured sofas, a big screen TV, a stylish mat of chocolate brown beneath my feet and a coffee table with a plant on top. The walls have a natural curve to them, rustic but tastefully painted, soaring vaulted ceilings with exposed beams, and the room's main feature, standing front and centre, is a double-sided stone fireplace. At the highest point, the room must be twenty-five metres high. No expense has been spared. I follow the wall of glass doors that run the entire length of the room, past the fireplace to a lavish kitchen and dining room. At the far end of the house, I discover four double bedrooms and three bathrooms. And a massive room with no furniture.

I make my way back to Terra, who is still transfixed with the blackness beyond the sliding doors. 'Doesn't make sense,' she mutters to herself.

'How many times have you asked yourself that?'

'Six. Only six.'

She clasps her hands against the back of her head and sighs as Tomas strolls over. 'Some fresh air would be good,' he says, going for the door handle. The next thing he is flying backwards through the air, arms pinwheeling. He lands on his back with a heavy thud, several feet away.

'What the hell,' I yell out.

He groans as he gets to his feet, clenching his fist and shaking the final remnants of electricity from his arm. 'It is also spelled.'

'We're trapped,' says Terra. Even with her power gone, she is flukey enough to steal the next line out of my head.

None of us are game to check the other doors or windows, not after the bolt Tomas just got.

'What next?' I say out loud to nobody in particular. Terra and I take opposite sides of the same sofa, whilst Tomas hobbles over to the cold hearth and rests his back against the stone fireplace.

It's then I think of River and Ember.

'We need to let the others know we're okay.' I get out my phone.

No signal.

'Fuck. This is a prison,' says Terra, leaning over my shoulder, checking her own phone at the same time.

'I could think of worse places to be shut up in,' I add, trying to inject a little optimism.

'It still doesn't account for the timeline though,' says Terra, jutting her chin to the windows and the cloudless night sky.

'What time did we exit the pyramid?'

'The sun had not reached its highest,' answers Tomas.

I look at this man I have come to call friend, with his crazy dialect and curious aloofness to mankind, and smile. 'Not helpful, dude. You need one of these.' I tap on my watch face. 'It was nine-thirty in the morning,' I inform Terra.

My stomach says it should be close to lunchtime, yet the inky blackness outside says we missed supper by a mile. And, although I'm keen to solve Terra's timeline mystery, I'm more interested in chowing down on a good curry. On cue, my belly gurgles. 'Surely, there must be something to eat in this joint.'

I get up and detour around the fireplace to the kitchen, which houses so many cupboards. I'm not sure where to start, so I deliberate for a second before opting for the fridge instead.

'You guys should get in here,' I call out. Tomas and Terra rush in. 'Anyone for salmon patties? … Hold the phone.' I am elbow deep into the fridge. 'I've got something much better.'

'We shouldn't,' says Terra as I drag out a giant cheese board. It is loaded with grapes, strawberries, every kind of cheese you can think of, cold meats, cherry tomatoes, nuts, dried apricots, some creamy dip looking stuff, a glass bowl full of green and black olives, breadsticks and crackers and a shit tonne of blueberries, carrot sticks and pickled cucumbers. 'Skye, this could belong to someone,' says Terra, wincing.

'Yeah, us. Look, the way I see it is, if Isis has dumped us here, intending to keep us *prisoners*, then what's here …is ours.'

Tomas agrees, eyeing the food with delight. 'I haven't eaten in days.'

'Exactly,' I pipe in, 'what kind of *guests* would we be if we let it go to waste.'

'I think we should wait until our host arrives.'

Tomas and I ignore her and tuck in. 'She is not known for her reliability or punctuality,' says Tomas.

Oh. My. God … the best food I've ever tasted.

Terra doesn't hold back after watching us down a couple of handfuls of grapes and strawberries, and drags a barstool out from under the kitchen bench and ploughs in. 'What do you think she wants with us?' she asks, popping a piece of cheese and cucumber into her mouth.

I swirl a carrot stick around in the dip, thinking the exact same thing. 'I figure you might have some idea seeing as you know everything, past, present and future.'

'Well, it doesn't seem so in this case, does it?' There is no sourness in her tone. Just confusion.

Tomas has polished off most of the top corner of the platter, barely coming up for air. 'What do all witches want ...'

'Goddess,' Terra corrects him.

'She makes the rules up as she goes, using her devilish black magic.'

'Earth magic,' Terra amends again.

'And when she said we were spelled, when we couldn't move ... she disabled our powers by using a binding spell on us?' He continues to eat. 'The same way she has confined us to this dwelling, and we won't be able to leave until she says we can.' Tomas rises and walks over to an exterior wall. He runs his hand over the undulating surface, his fingers outlining a rectangular shape. 'This house is made from mud bricks.'

'And ...?

'The witch can spell a house made from mud, keeping all inside safe, but also hidden.'

'Hidden? From who?'

Terra replies promptly. 'There's a fair few beasties out there that want my blood. My guess is to keep them out. Keep us safe.'

I shrug. 'Sounds reasonable enough.'

'Or to slaughter us at the right time,' adds Tomas.

'Or that,' I say sarcastically.

I hop down from the barstool, stomach full, limbs tired, mind deliciously quiet other than a little messy with unanswered questions. My fingers linger on the backrest. 'We've finished the Initiations, *right*? And there's no longer a deadline to hand over the swag to Isis, is there?' Terra half shrugs one shoulder. 'We seem to be here at her *request,* so she knows where to find us if she wants them. Leaving us one choice - wait it out.'

'I suppose,' says Terra. Tomas says nothing. His eyes are lost in darkness.

'Maybe tomorrow will bring the answers,' I say, pushing the stool under the bench.

The cheeseboard has been picked clean and the madness of the *shorter than normal day* is beginning to take its toll. 'I can't eat another thing, and I need to freshen up.' My shirt stinks of gunky mutt blood.

Terra hums in agreement whilst Tomas strolls around to the far side of the fireplace. He puts a match to the kindling already nestled in the hearth and sits back on his haunches. After all these long years, I suppose this one simple action is normality for him. It bursts into flame almost immediately, making me believe there is more of a supernatural element at play here than just paper and kindling. As the flames grow, he throws a couple of larger logs on from the well-stacked logholder and makes himself comfortable on the sofa. He kicks off his sneakers and lumps his feet onto the coffee table.

And stares into the fire.

He looks beat, and normal … like one of us, and not the two thousand year old soldier I know him to be.

I stand at the end of the sofa. 'Is there anything I can get for you before I turn in?'

Tomas stretches his neck to look up at me. It isn't difficult to read him. His eyes reveal he's been without hope for an eon. 'Not unless you can reunite me with my family and restore my father's guiding hand on my shoulder.'

I let out a breath. Rest my own hand on his shoulder. 'Believe me, if I can … I will. You have my word.'

I take a step back when Terra joins us. 'I think I'll call it a night, too,' she says, yawning and stretching her arms out in front. We both turn to leave, when Tomas calls out my name.

'Skye, I want to extend my sincerest thanks to you … to both of you.' His face is soft, grateful, almost peaceful.

'For releasing my father. You did, in a few minutes, what I've spent twenty lifetimes trying to do.'

'It's all good, fella. Let's call it quits, hey? You did save my arse in the labyrinth, after all.' A tight smile cracks through his solemn lips.

It would be good to see him laugh one day.

I pick a bedroom and shrug out of my clothes, realising these might be the only ones I have for a while. I step into the shower and let the hot water run over me. My first thoughts return to River and Ember, and Hayley, of course. They must be panic-stricken, wondering where we are. If only I could get a message to them … somehow.

Also, a shadow has been growing in my thoughts.

Zurvan – a beast of immeasurable power and strength who I'm destined to kill. When and where will this happen and does this have anything to do with the prophecy on my page of Peri Phuseôs tôn Ontôn - *through your own error, death will seek your companion?*

Protecting Amun is going to be a struggle, too.

Then, if we get through all of that, we still have to face Mithras, Isis and then Ra-Mon, all between acquiring the vial from Isis to heal River and break the curse Tomas is under.

Yet despite these ominous encounters waiting in the wings, I can't believe how far we've come. The Seven Degrees of Initiations are done and dusted.

Yay me …

Something I didn't think I was capable of, yet here we are. In all honesty, it was a breeze. Far easier than I thought it would be, which kind of scares me that I might've missed something. Shitty old doubt creeps in and I push it aside like an unfaithful lover.

The reason it went so smoothly, was because of friends. I couldn't have done it without them.

Friends … that word has taken on new meaning for me now. It's been a while since I've had people in my life I can truly rely on. People I would trust with my life. People I would sacrifice my own life for, if needed. All heroes need a side-kick ... I've been blessed with a handful. There is something to be said about strength in numbers versus flying solo, and although we are getting down to the pointy end - down to the wire, there will be a time when I really need to step up and be who I was born to be.

And I think I'm okay with that now.

I throw back the thick puffy doona and crawl into bed. The sheets smell amazing, and I release a soft sigh as I snuggle down.

I close my eyes to the sound of silence.

That glorious silence.

It overwhelms me again.

My eyes grow hot with tears at the immense pleasure of going to sleep without headphones in. No longer required to drown out a town full of people with a million worries on their mind.

That blissful nothingness.

TWENTY-NINE

SPRAWLED out in the middle of a kingsize bed, wearing nothing but my boxers, I wake from a hazy dream of buttered croissants and crisp white tablecloths, wondering where the heck I am.

I close my eyes again, dozy, warm, content. Silence hums lovingly in my ears, the kind of silence you might experience when you're dead, or on a deserted island. No voices. No thoughts. No words. Not even a pesky sparrow chirping about how great and simple life is.

Nothing!

Panic sets in.

I don't recognise this place.

I bolt upright, half-blinded by the sun streaming in through my window, my heart going at an unnatural, frenzied pace.

And, then I remember.

We'd been teleported here, if that's the right word to use, except, none of us have any idea where *here* is. We could be ten feet away from our luxurious villa in Falicon or halfway across the world, for all we know. And we don't have our powers either.

Bummer!

Just for shits and gigs, I have a crack at flicking on my invisibility only to discover psycho-witch Isis is still holding all the cards … meaning we are trapped inside this magical, all-inclusive home, and with no means of contacting anyone.

An echo of laughter disrupts my thoughts. It's a rare occurrence of late; nevertheless, the glorious sound of full-blown belly laughter has my body locking into place, head cocked to one side in curiosity.

Terra!

I rub the sleep from my eyes and drag a t-shirt over my head as I stumble along the hallway in the direction it's coming from, the glossy white tiles cool against my bare feet.

Views of rolling green hills and vineyards greet me from every pane of glass as I enter the kitchen. I slide around the bench and pull up a stool. A fat slice of sunlight, sneaking in through a high window, warms my face as I turn to see what Terra is holding.

'Can you believe this?' she shrieks. The excitement in her voice startles me out of my stupor, and I can't help wonder if her eyes ever sparkled that much on Christmas morning. Terra throws my travel bag at me. 'Mine's here too.'

I have to say, I'm not the slightest bit surprised our bags have magically found us, especially after pondering our potential wardrobe dilemma last night. 'And, I suppose *our* bag of goodies is long gone, right?' I'm cross with myself for not keeping the backpack and staff with me, or at least stashing them under my bed.

'Nope,' she says, taking another bite out of her muffin. Several chocolate chips find their way onto the kitchen bench and she casually picks them up one by one and pops them into her mouth as she speaks. 'It's right where we left it.'

Now that *does* surprise me. 'Hmph! Weird. Don't you think that's weird?'

She shrugs, more interested in her muffin. 'I suppose.'

'I mean, if we can't get out, maybe Isis can't get in.'

Terra raises her eyebrows at me. 'Oh pl-ease, you can't be serious?'

'How do we know? Are you the magic police?'

Of all the people in the world, Terra has the best eyeroll, ever! 'Skye, it's *her* spell. You don't think she wouldn't know how to get around one of her own spells?' I'm staring at the crumb stuck to the corner of her mouth. I reach over to brush it away when she steps back, taking care of it herself.

Now I feel stupid. 'I don't know. I would've snuck in here last night while everyone was asleep and bolted with it, but that's just me.'

'Obviously, it's not the most important thing on her mind right now, is it?' says Terra.

'It doesn't appear so.' But I can't for the life of me figure out what she's up to. 'Is Tomas awake?'

Terra gestures with her chin. 'He's in that enormous room that didn't have any furniture.'

'You said, *didn't*?' I push my chair out at the precise moment I hear the unmistakable sound of steel on steel.

'What the …' I'm intrigued. 'So you know,' she calls out behind me as I hastily weave around the fireplace to the lounge room and beyond, 'he's totally in his element.'

I open the door and can't believe what I'm seeing. Tomas has attached his shield to some kind of mannequin and is thrashing the living daylights out of it with his sword. 'Whoa!'

The room that was bare last night has been transformed into a fully equipped combat training room. Against every wall are racks of spears, swords and shields, all of different styles and sizes, all lethal and all battle-ready. In the middle of the room, placed in strategic fighting positions, is an army of training dummies made from canvas and straw. Some have red bullseyes painted on their chests. And next to Tomas's legs are two baskets of wooden practice swords.

Tomas has shed his twenty-first century attire and looks fierce, impressive and totally invincible in his full Roman Centurion uniform, minus the helmet. His rich, red Roman tunic is trimmed with gold braiding, and the dark brown breastplate has perfectly hand-crafted pecs and abdominal muscles moulded into the leather, emphasising his athletic physique. Dark brown leather guards hug his forearms and shins, and on his feet are a pair of open leather sandals.

'How?' is all my brain will allow me to say.

Tomas continues his training, chopping the air left and right before swinging around with a sweeping action, slicing the air in front of me. The sword stops directly at my neck.

I think I just shit my pants.

'She came to me in a dream.'

'Who?'

'The witch.'

'You mean Isis? She is a goddess.'

'She is, and always will be, a witch to me. After what she and her son did to my family ...' I take a moment and wait for Tomas's jaw to soften, his eyes to lose that brutal, blood-thirsty killer look I've seen a few times before. 'She warned me of a mighty battle.'

'Nothing we weren't expecting, though.'

'Yes, but a battle I am not to be a part of.'

This changes things. 'What does that mean?'

He slices the air a few more times beside me, sunlight catching the surface of the shiny steel. 'She is full of riddles. Do not let your guard down. She cannot be trusted.'

Something about his words doesn't quite ring true for me. 'And yet we are in this crazy, all-you-can-wish-for house that not only knows when I'm hungry but what kind of meal I'm craving. That doesn't sound like someone trying to harm us.' I gesture to the room, 'and she's kitted out this room and helped us with the Initiations. She didn't steal our bargaining chip, which shocked the shit out of me, so sorry if I don't trust my instincts on this. It seems like she might be on our side.'

'It may seem that way ... but remember, I have faced many lifetimes with her.' His face is grim. 'This falseness could be leading you into a trap.' I shake off the creepy image of Hansel and Gretel's candy cane house.

It's a fair point. 'I will keep a vigilant eye on her,' I say with a smile.

This seems to satisfy Tomas enough that he throws a wooden sword at me. 'Your training starts now.'

I look down at my boxer shorts and t-shirt. 'Have you got another skirt I can borrow then?' I refer to his traditional Roman garment of multi-layered strips of leather around his waist.

I let out a sharp laugh but cut it off as Tomas regards himself, his face a mass of confusion and hurt. 'This uniform symbolises strength, commitment and loyalty.'

'No offence, Tom. It was a ...' I stop. There's just no point explaining the joke. 'Never mind, give me five to get some pants on.' I lob the sword back to him. He nods and goes back to his training.

I exit the room and pass Terra curled up on the sofa playing a game on her phone. 'I suppose this is what *normal* feels like,' she says without looking up. 'It's kind of strange not to be watching my back every five minutes.'

I can't imagine a life like that.

I can't imagine having no one to turn to. No one to trust. 'You can come and train with me and a real-life Roman Centurion, if you want normal.'

She laughs. 'Yeah, why not. I suppose there's nothing else to do around here.' She goes back to her phone, and

I think that's the end of our conversation. 'Can I ask a question?'

'Shoot.'

'Are you and Hayley really a *thing*?' There's a slight blush on her cheeks, which makes her glossy emerald eyes even brighter. I stare at her curiously, wondering what is going on in that head of hers, which I believe makes her more nervous as her hands start to fidget. 'Wh-what I mean to say is, I don't see the attraction …' she pauses to tug her lip. 'I don't think you're right for each other. There, I've said it.'

This conversation requires my undivided attention so I slip between the sofa and the coffee table and plonk down next to her. She's a wild one, this girl I hardly know, and yet the energy around her has become so familiar to me like we've been mates since kindergarten. There's passion and recklessness that I haven't seen in any girl I've met before. There is fire and poison in her words, depending on her mood. And yet I've grown to like her. Depend on her. Even look to her for advice … all in a matter of days. How does that even *happen*?

As far as Hayley goes, in the beginning, there was heaps I liked about her, however, something has changed, and I'm not entirely sure I know what that is.

Terra is waiting for my reply.

'If I'm totally honest with you,' I pause. Go over my thoughts one more time. 'I do have feelings for her.'

Her eyes become light and shade, flitting between the two, in blinks that seem desperate to cancel the other out. Her lips tremble and she nips at them nervously. My best guess, being the total amateur that I am for reading people, is she's emotional, although I have no idea why. This is one time I'd pay every dollar in my pocket to know what she is thinking, but Isis's spell has robbed me of that knowledge. Those cat-like eyes, so intense, so probing, seem to blaze at me, wishing they could drop in on my deepest desires, daring me to say more. So I indulge. 'She's a nice girl, with a kind heart, but I can't read the future, like you can. So, if you have something to tell me, you'd better spill it.'

In a snap, her emotion is washed clean and she sits up a little straighter, her protective mask dropping back into place. 'I wish I could. But I can't. There is too much at stake.'

I know she knows something. 'C'mon, you can't leave me hanging like this.' I drop to my knees. Pretend to beg. 'Just one hint.'

A smirk starts at the corner of her mouth and works its way across her face. 'You are the most infuriating little worm when you want to be. Loveable but infuriating.'

'Loveable, hey?' My heart skips a beat.

A faint glow tints her cheeks. 'I mean that in the most non-sexual way, you know, like a baby brother.'

'Oh.' Shot down in flames. Glad no one else was around to hear that.

'Listen, all I can say, is what you have with her isn't real. Can we leave it at that?'

How can I leave it at that? 'Isn't *real*?'

She gets up. 'I need to get some suitable attire on if we're going to be smashing the shit out of each other.'

She starts to walk off to her room. I'm still standing there, mouth open. 'Terra? Isn't real? What does that mean?'

'Come on, loverboy. That's all you're getting out of me.'

Three hours later, bone sore and every inch of my body screaming at me for a rest, for food, for a massage, I slump to the floor in a pile of tired muscles and useless limbs, gasping for breath. The wooden sword in my hand feels like it weighs ten kilos instead of two and I've got a nice collection of blisters on my palm. 'I'm done for the day,' I say, rubbing my forearm for the hundredth time. Terra is a worse shot than I am, and I'd lost count of the times she walloped me on the arm or wrist with her missed aim.

'Don't be a sook,' yells Terra, bouncing on her toes next to Tomas. 'I'll go easy on you, I promise.'

'You said that an hour ago,' I groan. 'Plus, there's something about sparring with a girl that feels wrong.'

Green fire erupts in her eyes. 'I'll pretend I didn't hear that,' she says savagely. Her scowl lasts all of five seconds before her lips press together to curb her laughter. 'Fight with Tomas then.'

No, I definitely don't want to do that. The man has a zero pain threshold and unlimited strength and energy, plus if I spend another hour with him today, I'm fairly certain, I won't be able to walk tomorrow. *Widen your stance. Both hands on the grip. Do not go for the easy strike. Move your hips, and that constant word over and over whenever I landed on my arse – AGAIN.* The tips Tomas had screamed at us are now forever imprinted in my brain.

'Thanks, but no thanks. Anyway, the kitchen is calling.'

I hobble out of the room and head towards my favourite fridge, which naturally has been restocked with all my favourite foods. *Prison … Ppft! I couldn't think of a better place to be than right here.*

I spend the next week - loading up with the best food I've ever tasted, me listening to Terra recount her fun and not-so-fun stories of the last five years, including her darkest moments at Nevermore. And then being pummelled and punished for five to seven hours a day in Tomas's room of hell. Sometimes, Terra would turn up for an hour or two and join in, or watch and laugh, and offer her two cents worth. But mostly, she would sit in the cosy corner chair that turned up one day, like most things in this crazy house, with a stack of pillows and fluffy blankets in tow, reading, the sun glinting over her shoulder. Those long, daydreaming stares out of the window have become a thing of the past, and for the first time ever, she looks relaxed and comfortable in her own skin. There was only one day when she seemed more withdrawn than usual, and so rugby tackling her onto the sofa was a necessary act. I did it in the hope a smile might find its way back to her. And it did. The price: one stolen chocolate coated strawberry that had my name on it.

Every night, we'd cook dinner together, trying to out-do the other with our favourite dishes. She begrudgingly conceded yesterday that I was the hands-down winner, citing she had zero cooking lessons at Nevermore. Every time she brings up that place, it makes me sick to my stomach what they did to her.

She did eventually get her own back on me.

Last night, I came off worse when the washing-up ended in an extreme bubble fight, me being drenched to the skin. The space between us has become warmer, and the days of her biting my head off are long gone. She's opinionated and still likes to boss me around all the time or throw insults at me at least twenty times a day, and yet it doesn't seem to bug me like it used to.

At night, before sleep whisks me away to a place of peace and silence, I think of River and Ember, wondering, hoping, praying they're okay. Hayley barely scratches my thoughts, the pull to be near her has all but gone. And as for Tomas, Terra is right about him being in his element. He is thriving on our training and almost looks happy. The dark circles beneath his eyes have vanished, and he's smiled more in the last three days than since I first met him.

Another day has drawn to a close and I sit across from her on the sofa, her feet tucked up underneath her, black curls tumbling past her shoulders, her nose in another book. As though she senses me watching her, she looks up. 'What?' she asks, a curious smile reaching her eyes.

'Nothing,' I reply, stretching my legs out along the sofa, pretending to yawn.

'I know that look,' she says, raising her eyebrows. 'Something's up. What is it?'

This getting to know someone, without reading their thoughts first, is new and awkward for both of us. And a little frustrating. I feel an ache in my throat. I'm not sure I can say the words.

'Come on. It won't kill you.'

I swallow. Hard. A lump that won't go down.

'Maybe not me … but.'

Her head angles to one side. 'What's going on? It's not like you to hold anything back.'

She really does know me, more than I give her credit for. How do I say it? 'This is different.'

'I don't mean to be evasive, but this is the hardest thing I've ever had to say aloud. This *headache* has been with me for years.'

She puts down her book, gets up, walks over to my sofa, swings my legs off and sits down, crosses her legs, and gives me her undivided attention.

Her hand reaches out.

Touches my arm.

Her fingers are warm, comforting, as she says, 'it can't be that bad. Please.' Her voice breaks a little on that last word. Enough to make me look up. Her eyes search my face, a small pinch of concern above her brows. 'Please,' she says again.

I start out slow, because it's the only way I can encourage the words out of my mouth. 'What did your page say in Peri Phuseôs tôn Ontôn?'

A shadow grows over her eyes. She withdraws her hand instantly. It falls heavily into her lap. 'I … I …'

'I'm sorry.' I'm angry with myself. I shouldn't have asked. I shy away from the turmoil peeking through her skin, guilt stirring a lethal cocktail inside me. There is no doubt in my mind, something is on her page that she doesn't want to discuss – just like with mine.

I end up blurting it out, because holding it in anymore isn't an option. It is poisoning me. Tearing me to shreds – the burden just too heavy. 'Did it have anything to do with someone …' I squeeze the words between my teeth. 'dying?'

That gets her attention. 'Is this what it says on your page?'

I nod, lowering my gaze. A shuddering breath escapes – the one I've held in for what seems like forever. My chest tightens – this feeling vulnerable stuff is shit.

Her hand finds its favourite position on my arm again. 'Skye.'

I haven't the heart to look into her eyes – what if it's her. What if …

Her fingers gently grasp my forearm as though they are desperate to squeeze the life back into me. 'Look at me.'

I can't.

I can't.

How can I…

We've become friends.

Close, even.

How can I tell her I might be the one to end her life?

'Do I need to smack you around the side of the head? Look. At. Me.' She slips her fingers into mine, and holds my hand like a lover might. It works like she hoped it would, and painstakingly slowly, I raise my head.

Green fire blazes in those eyes of hers. She tightens her grip on my fingers. 'Listen to me because I'm only going to say this once.' I'm watching the way her lips move, the way her eyes are drilling into me. 'Skye, it's not me.'

A cloud passes over my eyes and then is gone. 'Not you? How can you be sure?'

The reddest lips I've ever seen push upwards into a smile. 'Trust me. I know everything.'

'You could be mistaken. You might have read the signs wrong?'

'Skye, I know how my life ends.' My frown prompts her to say more. 'I've always known. Now, relax, and please don't ask me anymore. I *really* can't tell you.'

I think it's relief that propels me forward … to throw my arms around her and pull her into my chest. She doesn't resist in any way, and I breathe in the smell of her shampoo.

It doesn't feel weird. No longer awkward.

It feels safe.

Like walking through the door of your family home and having everyone there, making life that little bit more perfect.

'I just want to say …' we part slightly, our arms still clinging to each other. 'I'm here if you need me … for anything … even if you need to crash and burn.' It's all coming out the wrong way. I clamp my teeth, shut my eyes, search for the right words. 'What I want to say is, you're not alone anymore.'

Terra's eyebrow twitches a little, the rest of her face motionless. Her blinks are unhurried, gentle, in slow motion as though someone has pulled on the brakes of her life. Her eyes bubble up, look all shiny and glassy. It is a solitary moment of togetherness, of connection, a bond that can never be broken.

'Skye …' Her breath tumbles from her lips in a quivering, soft moan. She flings her arms around my neck and hugs me like I've never been hugged before, like her life depends on it, like if I let go she would crumble into a million pieces, like she has been starved of moments like these her entire life.

'Ooh, this looks cosy.'

We pull apart like two malfunctioning magnets to see River, Ember and Hayley, staring at us.

We are as shocked to see them, as they are catching us in some kind of romantic embrace, even though it couldn't be further from the truth. 'You're here.' It's all I can think of to say.

No response.

To me, it's the funniest thing ever. I glance over at Terra, who is bursting to keep control of herself. Neither of us can hold back and roar with laughter. 'It's not what you think. Honestly.'

Ember and River regard each other and exchange smiles.

Hayley doesn't. 'Then what is it?' The iciness in her words pull me up straight away.

River recognises the awkwardness of the situation and jumps right in. 'It's good to see you guys. We were so worried.' He comes around the side of the sofa and drags me upright by the front of my hoodie to give him a hug. I have so many questions, the main ones being … how did they find us and how in the hell did they get in the house.

I take a seat back on the sofa, Terra next to me, which shouldn't feel uncomfortable but now does because of Hayley sitting across from us on the coffee table, throwing daggers at us both. Ember and River take the other sofa.

'We had no idea what happened to you … for days,' Em says breathlessly. 'No note. No word of where you'd headed off to, or if you'd been kidnapped. We didn't know where to start looking.'

'A week passed and we were beginning to fear the worst,' chimes in River.

Ember reels in a shaky sigh. 'We thought you were …'

'*Dead*?' I finish for her.

Ember nods solemnly. 'Then, out of the blue, Hayley gets a text message from you, telling us to meet you back in Paris.'

Terra and I turn heads at the same time 'We're in *Paris*?' she says to me. I also want to circle back to how Hayley received a message from me that I never sent.

'A few miles outside of Paris, actually,' chips in Hayley.

'How do you not know where you are?' asks River, frowning.

'We were teleported here. One minute we were outside the pyramid, fighting supernatural creatures, and the next…'

Worry creeps into the eyes of my companions. 'Wait. What?' River launches off the sofa to stand before us whilst Ember's hands fly to her mouth.

'Maybe you should tell them,' I whisper to Terra.

Keeping to the facts, Terra brings them up to speed with Tomas's dad, the Lord's Staff, the completion of the Initiations, my fight outside the pyramid and how we were magically transported here, not once mentioning Isis.

'So, you reckon you've been here *nine* days?' says Ember.

'Yup.' I check in with Terra and she confirms my response with a firm nod.

'That's so odd,' replies Ember. Our three newest housemates regard each other, foreheads frowning, heads shaking. 'It's just … you have been missing for *two* weeks.'

'Two weeks,' Terra and I say together. I flick through the timeline of days. I'm no mathematician but I can add up. 'That's impossible,' I say.

Terra nudges my arm. Looks directly at me. There is a smile in her words. 'When are you going to realise *nothing* in this world is impossible?'

I huff. Smile. 'True.' And for a moment, it feels like it's just me and her again, having another one of those amazing get-to-know-you conversations.

River's voice breaks our eye contact. 'Which means we have three days to locate Isis and get the backpack to her. Please tell me you still have it.'

'Of course we do. And we don't need to locate …' Terra subtly kicks at my feet, making it look like an accident.

Hayley notices and stands. Folds her arms across her chest. I think she's about to unleash on me, but I couldn't be more wrong.

'Isis will come for us.'

'And you know that, *how*?'

She shrugs. 'I don't know. I just know she will.'

'And the message you sent to Skye?' demands Terra. 'What's *that* all about?'

'What? He sent it to me.'

Terra snarls. 'You're a liar.' Venom laces each word.

This time, I don't rush to Hayley's defence. I want to know what she has to say for herself.

'I am not,' she says sulkily. Juicy, fat tears well up in her eyes.

I'm about to ask Terra to ease up, when she says, 'we haven't been able to send messages or receive phone calls since we got here, so how could he have possibly sent it?'

'It … it was before, when you were outside the pyramid.'

Terra hurls her body out of the chair. The two girls are nose to nose. I can't see the fireplace between them. Hayley's face is side on to me, giving me no clues, but I see Terra's eyes. Talk about freaky. Scary, even. The emerald green, so vivid, so fluorescent it's almost non-human.

Terra thumps her hand over her heart. 'By the power instilled in me by our earth mother, Gaia, I command you to speak the truth.'

This is new.

And very unexpected, considering all our powers are languishing on some far-off exotic island. River and Ember look at me. I shrug my shoulders and mouth the words; *I've got no idea.*

Then something happens that soars into my top ten list of all-time weird.

Hayley's body starts glowing.

It's gradual at first, warming up as though someone is slowly turning up the volume until it becomes too bright to look at. Not quite sunlight, but white like starlight. And, just the outline, nothing else. 'What's happening to me,' she cries. Fear finds her face. Scratches panic into her eyes.

I look to Terra. 'Stop this.'

'It's not me,' she says indignantly.

393

'Then who?' asks River.

I shield my eyes as both light and heat billow towards us, the makings of a shimmering human mirage.

'What do we do?' yells Ember.

Composed, neutral, unemotional, Terra looks at each of us in turn. 'Nothing. We sit back and we do nothing.'

I can't believe what is coming out of her mouth. This is so not the vibrant, funny girl I've enjoyed getting to know and curling up next to the fire with to watch movies. I'm starting to ask myself if the looney has returned. She casts her eyes my way as if she's heard me, begging me, pleading with me. *Trust me*, they say.

The energy in the room is suddenly electric. A low rumble through the house gathers momentum, rattling windows in their frames and crockery in the cupboards and drawers. The thick wooden beams running across the centre of the ceiling protest as the house shakes from the foundations up, an earthquake of immense magnitude growing beneath our feet. Except, it is no earthquake. I've witnessed firsthand what an earthquake feels like whilst visiting New Zealand some years back, and this is nothing like that. This is something different. The houses is swaying, yet the view outside is peaceful, the land at rest.

My thoughts come back to Hayley. And just in time, it seems. Her body is stretching – widthways – like she's a piece of warm rubber about to tear in half. A scream rips through the air before the roar of devastation dims.

The house stills.

And, one body *unbelievably* becomes two.

Isis stands next to a very shell-shocked Hayley, who has no idea where she is.

'I knew it all along,' boasts Terra. 'You've been manipulating us the whole time, haven't you?'

Right at that very moment, Tomas walks in from the training room. He doesn't look the least surprised to see Ember and River, or Isis for that fact. 'I felt your magic, witch.'

River and I are on the same page and rush at Tomas as he makes a run for her. Two feeble lads, not long out of school, verses an immortal warrior is a laughable offence, and yet River and I lock arms with Tomas to hold him back. 'Tom, man. If we're to find out what the hell is going on here, we need to let her speak,' I say to him, struggling against his strength.

I turn to Isis.

She doesn't look the slightest bit concerned, but I still say to her, 'we can't hold him back for long, so you'd better start explaining yourself.'

Togged up in a long white dress, no sleeves, her long dark hair hanging down past her waist and eyes as dark as midnight, she clasps her hands in front. 'We both want the same thing, Centurion,' she says, her voice no higher than a whisper.

'And that is?' demands River.

'To destroy Mithras.' Silence and shock take turns with each of us, even Tomas. 'You have the items I requested?'

She knows we do. 'We've had them for a week, *remember* … you saw us at Falicon. So why don't you do us all a favour and give Tomas and River what you owe them, namely their freedom and the antidote, and let's get on with this,' I growl at her.

'We need to wait till the moon is high.' She smooths her hair with the flat of her hand.

'Okay,' I say with an air of sarcasm but mainly because I'm confused.

'I will be at my strongest then.' She takes her time to look upon each of us individually. 'I will come for you in three days.

'And that's it …' says Terra.

'You of all people, Earthchild, should understand. Knowing too much is dangerous.' Her eyes fix on Terra. 'You know the rules. Break them, and the world will become ash and ruin.' With that, she vanishes.

We are now all looking at Hayley. 'I couldn't stop her,' she says defensively. 'I knew something was wrong … *different*, but I couldn't …'

'It's alright,' says Ember, crossing the room to give her a hug.

'I want to go home,' she sobs into Ember's chest.

And that's as real as it gets.

She is a pawn in all this, like the rest of us, although the four of us won't be so lucky to receive a get-out-of-jail-free card. If we fail, then … I can't let myself think of the alternative. We have to win.

Hayley sniffles again. I do feel sorry for her. Isis used her to get to me, to see out her plan, whatever that looks like to her, and will continue to use anyone for her own gain.

A shudder flickers up my spine.

All the times Hayley and I spent together, the intimate moments, oh god, that was Isis.

My stomach clenches.

I pull River over to one side. 'How did you get in here?'

His brow darkens. 'How'd you think we got in. We walked through the front door.'

I flat out run to the entrance, knowing in my heart, it won't be the result I want. Not only is the door closed, it's locked too. And the spell is working just fine.

'Fuck!' I grumble under my breath, getting up off the floor, shaking off the effects of the kick-in-the-arse electric shock. 'We're locked in again.' There goes my idea about getting Hayley home.

THIRTY

I'D never heard of vegetarian nachos until Ember told me it was a thing. They didn't taste too bad either. She'd whipped it up, courtesy of our phenomenal self-stocking fridge, in no time at all, whilst River and I spoke at length about how the last two weeks had been hell for them, not knowing where we were. He wasn't the least bit reserved in telling me what an inconsiderate prick I was for leaving and not telling them where we were going. I apologised profusely, which seemed to ease his naturally irate self, explaining my reasons, or more to the point, *Terra's* reasons. I'm fully aware he sees himself as the big brother and the leader of our gang, and being the eldest, he's taken it upon himself to accept full responsibility for every action we make, the good and the bad, still like I told him … we are all adults here, and individually, we all have a job to do. And, other than Hayley acting a little weird, talking to herself and going off for hours at a time, they'd hung out at the villa in Falicon, in case we returned. Then once Hayley had received the text message, they'd driven the ten hours back to Paris. River was keen to hear more about the staff, and what Tiberius told us from beyond the grave, than what they'd been up to, however, the hand to hand combat training with Tomas interested him the most. So, I invited him to join us tomorrow morning at six sharp; any later than that, and Tomas would be dishing out an extra hour of stick fighting. I learnt quickly to be on time.

I scoop the last of the guacamole from the bowl with a corn-chip and glance around the table at five of the most unlikely people to share a meal with.

What an odd bunch of misfits.

Hayley hasn't said one word since we sat down, and my main priority is to figure out a way to get her home. The last thing I want on my conscience is more guilt. I couldn't bear it if anything happened to her. I glance across at her three or four times. She doesn't look up.

River notices, and comes to my rescue, no mind-reading powers necessary. 'Hayley, we're all trying to come up with a way to help you get home, so please don't worry.'

'Oh, I'm not worried,' she says. She blows her nose with a tissue. 'Isis says as soon as she comes for you, I'll be free to leave.'

This changes things.

'If Isis could zap us here, then maybe she could …'

'No,' Hayley snaps. 'I-I can't. Not that way.'

'It might be the only way home. We can't exactly book a flight with no internet or phone in this place. I can't even order a taxi to come and pick you up, and I'm not letting you walk out of here by yourself.'

'Yes, you will. Because you have no choice. I will book a taxi and a flight after you all leave.' She turns to me. 'I was capable of running my own life before you turned up, Skye.' Hayley pushes out her chair and stands up.

'But …' River clamps hold of my arm to keep me seated. 'Let it go, brother,' he whispers. 'Just for now.'

Hayley scans our little group before heading to the bedroom she'd claimed.

'I feel bad,' I tell him.

'It was her decision to come, remember. You didn't force her.'

'I know, but that wasn't her making those decisions … was it? It was Isis.'

Decisions?

What would life be like without the need to make decisions? I shower and crawl into bed, all under the luxury of silence. It's taken a while to get used to, and every now and then I feel as though I've forgotten something I'm about to do, or say. It's odd, but I love it. I close my eyes to the sounds of cicada's singing me a lullaby.

Ember shakes me from my sleep.

'What is it?' I ask, peeking bleary-eyed at my watch. It's five-thirty.

'She's gone.'

'Who?'

'Hayley.'

Sleep is ripped from me and I'm wide awake.

I scramble out of bed and run to her room. Her bed hasn't been slept in. Her bag is gone.

'She left this.' Ember hands me a note.

First things first.

I race for the front door, guessing it'll be locked, hoping it won't be. I deliberate for a second about whether to touch the handle. I choose option two and peer out of the window instead. The driveway is clear, apart from River's hire car. Beyond that, the world is still engulfed by darkness. She is long gone.

I go back to the note.

I open it to see a second smaller note inside, with my name on it. I slip it under my armpit.

The note to all of us reads:

My dear friends

I didn't want to make a big drama out of all of this, so I thought it was best if I leave without any fuss or awkward goodbyes. I have enough money to get home, so please don't worry.

You all have been so wonderful in accepting me, and I can see you have much on your plates right now.

I never wanted to be an addition to that burden.

I hope you find a way to win this for all our sakes.

I will be praying for you.

Hayley xx

P.S. Terra: I'm sorry for giving you such a hard time. I really am a nice person.

I read it twice.

A lump balloons in my throat, making it hard to swallow. Hard to breathe. Even hard to think. Ember circles her arms around my waist and leans her head against my back.

'I'm sorry, Skye. She's a nice girl. She doesn't deserve this. None of us do.' She's right, she doesn't, but it is what it is, and all I can do, is suck it up and get through the day. Right now though, it's too early to deal with this shit and I use that excuse to sneak away.

'I'm going back to bed.' Ember kisses my cheek before heading back into River's room.

The note personally addressed to me seems to burn against my skin, demanding to be read.

I hop back into bed and flick on the bedside light, releasing a slow, steady breath.

I open the note to find it is a list, of all things.

I smirk when I see everything she's sorry for and an explanation of her actions.

1. I'm sorry about the eggs I made you. It was a spell to make you stay.
2. I'm sorry for throwing my shoe at Terra – that was all me – I have a natural fear of black birds.
3. I'm sorry for lying about the fudge and feeding it to you. Isis had placed another spell on them, making you want to be with me.
4. Our moment in the plane toilets wasn't me. I would never do that. I'm sorry – that was Isis.
5. I'm sorry I lied about the souvenir shop. Isis had organised a meeting with a woman, an English Private Investigator, who gave me the original Spear of Destiny. It's the real deal, like I said it was. The woman then placed a wooden cup in my bag and told me to make sure you got it. I'd never seen her before in my life.
6. I'm sorry I got sick. It was Isis, slowing us down.
7. Isis possessing my body meant I could hear and see things going on around me and yet couldn't do a damn thing about it.
8. I'm sorry about snapping at you, being rude or downright childish – again the words came from Isis. She told me I was a pivotal part of a bigger plan.

She finishes with ...

I believe the only time I saw you with my own eyes was when you passed out in the carpark of Nevermore. That was the real me. She signs off with her name and a kiss.

My brain fires up, and I lay there, unable to go back to sleep. I decide to get up, and wander into the kitchen, to see Terra leaning over a cup of coffee. 'Kettle's just boiled.' A hot chocolate would go down well.

I fuss about, getting what I need and join Terra at the kitchen bench. I pull up a stool, even though she's not sitting.

I gaze out at the grey morning.

It has rained overnight and my first wish would be to open a window and inhale that sweet scent. My second wish, to hear the rain against the glass like a thousand tiny feet that will never know the earth. The grassy area, sprinkled with tiny white flowers is sodden and the paved pathway leading up to a rose-covered gazebo is underwater in places.

'I miss being outside, don't you?' says Terra. I turn to see her staring at me before her eyes revisit our waterlogged backdrop. She takes a sip of her coffee.

'Especially when it rains,' I add. 'I love the smell.'

She hums. 'It's called petrichor.'

I frown.

'The scent of rain – it comes from the Greek word petra, meaning stone, and ichor, meaning blood of the gods. Well, the aroma actually comes from the oil within the stone that is released when rain is pending…' She stops talking and looks up at me. 'I'm sorry, I don't know when to stop sometimes.'

'It's okay.' Her little info sessions have a way of snapping me out of my lows. 'Did you ever have raindrop races when you were little?' I ask her as I slip down from my seat and approach the window. She draws closer, her shoulder nudging my arm.

When she doesn't answer straight away, I cast a sideways glance at her, noticing her own raindrop has wet her lashes. She quickly blinks it away. 'No. I never did that,' she mutters.

Now it's my turn to apologise. 'I'm sorry. I should've known …'

'Don't be.' She paints on a smile. Touches her fingers to mine. 'We're good, aren't we?' I hear the lilt in her voice.

'Course we are. Besties,' I say, nudging her back with a playful grin.

'And *Besties* tell each other the truth, right?' I wonder where she's going with his, and reply with a dubious, yes.

'I'm wondering, with all these unbelievable, yet temporary abilities we've been burdened with, yours especially …' She pauses to place her empty mug on the kitchen bench. Stalling … anyone can see she is stalling. 'Why you haven't contacted your parents?'

My heart stutters.

My lungs refusing to pull the air in.

'You miss them, right?' she continues, 'and I know how much you're struggling with it.' Somebody's been snooping into my thoughts more than I realise.

Fat rain droplets rolling off the leaf of a large maple tree, before free-falling into a puddle captures me in its spell. I can't withdraw my gaze. 'You have the chance to set things straight with them.' I hear her words, and know she's right, and yet the glass in my throat, the raw, emotion stabbing my heart, is just too damn painful to deal with.

I pull away. Arms fold across my chest. 'No.'

Terra hangs her head.

We don't speak … for what seems like ages. A thousand rain drops race down the window before she faces me and says. 'Will you have a raindrop race with me.'

I turn and smile at her, push the deep ache in my chest down as far as I dare, and brush my fingers against hers. 'Love to.'

I know I told River to meet at six for the training with Tomas but a breakfast meeting is warranted. I scramble a dozen eggs, toast up a loaf of bread, and summon the troops. They sit across the table from me, silence rippling towards me. It's time to bring everyone up to speed.

403

'I've *decided* to let Tomas hand over the crown, spearhead, whip and staff to Isis, so he can go home to his family.'

The silence is ripped from the air as a million questions start - 'Have you thought this through? Why are you the one to decide? Are you serious? When were you going to tell us?' to name a few. I'm prepared for the round of shocked responses.

Tomas, however, says nothing.

The lightness that touches his face and the relief leaving his chest in a big hurry, isn't hard to miss and assures me, I've made the right decision.

'What about River?' barks Ember. 'Have you forgotten about him?' Fear enters her gaze. I stretch across the table and lay my hand ontop of her clenched fists.

'Let's rewind a bit,' I say in a calm voice.

Whilst I retrieve the backpack, there is a flurry of action happening with spooning eggs and toast onto plates. I resume my seat and take out the crown, spearhead and whip, and position them in front of me. The Lord's Staff I rest beside my chair.

'I need to recap for you. The First Initiation is Corax, right? Whether I was meant to break the curse or not, to bring Terra to us, is irrelevant - the First Initiation is complete. The Second, Nymphus, which Terra informed us is the Crown of Thorns, is right here.' I slide it towards them. 'The next is Miles, which represented the Spear of Destiny which we are also in possession of.' I slide exhibit number two forward. 'Next came Leo, or Othniel as I came to know him. The objection here was to break another curse and the only way was to kill him with the Spear of Destiny. The Fifth Initiation is Perses, the Persian, who happened to be Longinus – a two for the price of one Initiation deal, and who is now finally laying to rest. Another curse.' I pause, offering a quick eyebrow raise. 'The Sixth Initiation is Sun-runner or Heliodromus, which is symbolised by the whip, which we retrieved from Tomas's father.' I push the last item towards them. 'And finally, the Seventh Initiation is Pater, meaning father, aka Tiberius. Again another bargain. I believe Tiberius knew about the Lord's Staff and hid it from Mithras. I imagine it was the reason he was murdered and his soul never laid to rest.' I point to lot number four. Which leaves this.'

I retrieve the wooden cup from the backpack. 'This turned up in my bag when Hayley casually dropped the spearhead in there. She said an English Private Investigator gave it her.'

River's eyes widen all of a sudden. 'Iris,' he mutters in disbelief.

'Yes, and we all know how sneaky Isis is at possessing bodies.'

'Actually, Nephthys, Isis's sister, helped out in that department too' chimes in Terra, a little embarrassed. Terra's cheeks deepen in colour as we all stare at her, mouths open. '*What*? I have a gag order on me. Cut me some slack.'

We all fold at her request. 'Now, I believe this is no ordinary cup. Tiberius mentioned the Cup of Life being one of the Lord's Graces. I'm sure this is *that* cup. I'm going to trade the cup for the antidote.'

A satisfied smile makes its way to Ember's lips.

'I figure it's another ace up our sleeves, if we need it.'

There is a look on River's face that I haven't seen too many times before, especially regarding me – he's quietly impressed. If only I could read his mind right now.

Em pushes her empty plate away. 'When this is all over, I'm going to stay in bed for a whole week.'

River, Tomas and I train until about three-thirty, stopping for a quick sandwich before getting straight back into it. A small part of me enjoyed River getting a good pummelling, with him swearing he'd be black and blue by morning. Ember came in for a bit and sparred with Tomas. She's quite handy with a spear, a natural Tomas had said, pleased by her footwork and effortless technique. She casually played it down stating it was due to being in the school's javelin team. Terra took up her usual spot in the corner, reading, and occasionally gazing out of the window at the lush gardens, all shiny and clean from the rain. A typical day, really. Then dinner rolls around, and another day bites the dust. We're coming down to the wire now. One day to go.

We wake the next morning to find a note pinned to the fridge from Isis. It simply says: Be ready to leave at midnight.

I'd be lying if I said, I wasn't nervous about what's to come. After all …

Tomorrow is the full moon.

Tomorrow, I have to dual a beast I've never seen fight before.

Tomorrow, Tomas could be left in limbo for eternity or free to join his family.

Tomorrow, River may lose his soul forever.

Tomorrow, Amun could be ripped from my body, giving Ra-Mon one more stripe before he becomes master, ruler and creator of our world.

Fuck … tomorrow is going to be the most important day of my life, and the life of every living creature in this world. And, although I don't drink whiskey, the thought of downing a bottle and riding out tomorrow in complete ignorance is appealing. Instead, I grit my teeth, give myself a little peptalk as I pour cereal into my bowl and focus on today.

Tomas and I keep our training session to a measly two hours. Afterwards, we chat about Zurvan, and what I might expect from his fighting skills. His advice, is not to go for the easy strike, respect his size and power, regardless if his blows are slow and clumsy, and to lead with my left foot. I should have Amun's powers once we split from this joint, so I will have flight and invisibility to fall back on if my sword skills fail me. I hope I remember how it all works. I then join Terra on the sofa and watch back to back movies. River and Ember have been behind closed doors most of the day, no guesses what they're up to, but I suppose, if the end of the world was just around the corner, laying in the arms of the person you love most would be the only place I'd want to be too.

We eat early, pack our bags, have a light supper around ten-thirty, and sit out the next hour. Apart from being free of this place, I can't wait to have my phone again. Two weeks is ample time for Henri to email through those pages. It'll be the first thing I check for once we're out of here.

On the stroke of midnight, there's a knock at the front door. River, with us all huddled behind him, puts his hand on the doorknob.

We wait.

The moment of truth comes.

River twists the doorknob, and miraculously, it swings open. A rush of fresh, clean air sweeps in. I smell wet earth and pine trees, roses and car fumes and some cheap, funky smelling aftershave. 'I'm in heaven,' I say, relishing the light breeze on my face, not the slightest bit interested in the man standing before us.

'Me too,' says Terra. Her eyes close, her head tilts back slightly.

It is a taxi driver. 'Tu as commande un taxi?' the man asks.

River nods. 'Oui. We ordered a taxi.'

I'm aware the spell has been lifted from the house the second the swarming buzz of voices reaches my ears. The taxi driver is mulling something over in his mind in French. Ember and River are on the same track, desperate to know what is going on. Terra and Tomas have their modes switched to silent, thank god, so the initial introduction of hearing people's thoughts isn't thrust down my throat, which I'm thankful for. The array of melodies from our phones, beeping and trilling, also confirms the spell has been lifted.

I concentrate on blocking out the mind-chatter and scroll through my messages.

There it is, the text from Henri.

I open the message and scroll down to see how long it is.

I let out a sigh of relief.

There are three pages, which I will read once we're on the road.

There is also a message from Hayley. I pause before I open it. It simply says – made it home okay. Good luck.

Another relief.

Everything else can wait.

We throw our luggage into the boot of the car, no idea where we're heading. River gives a fleeting glance at the hire car they drove up in and tells me, he'll have someone come and pick it up.

Tomas gets in the front, and the rest of us squeeze in the back seat. Ember hasn't left River's side most of the day, and even though she hasn't said much, the barrage of inner monologue, going off in her head right now is actually making me dizzy.

I rest my head in my hands and take a moment to regroup. By all indications, we are on route to the heart of Paris.

I flick my phone back on and scroll to Henri's message. Not quite the appropriate time to be doing this, but I'm not sure when or if I'll get another chance. I sit quietly, reading through the translation of Iris's diary. My heart is in my mouth.

'What's wrong?' Ember asks several times. I want to say nothing, but it isn't nothing. The timing couldn't possibly be any worse, and we all need to have a clear head. My lips manage to scrape together a thin smile. 'You worry too much,' I say to her. Her thoughts don't buy it and she considers calling me out on it. Instead, she tucks herself into River's shoulder. He kisses her head and whispers he loves her. It's exactly what I need to hear and puts my mind at ease that I've made the right decision in keeping those pages to myself for a while longer.

Twenty minutes later, we pull up next to a light beige apartment block, too flashy for even River's monthly allowance.

We all bail out.

Bushy plane trees have found a home between black, ornate lampposts that run the entire length of the street. A cool wind picks ups, scented with late night coffee and the faint traces of saline. The *almost* full moon emits enough light to see the lush public gardens across the street, stationary cars cued up along the kerb, and a couple walking away from us, hand in hand.

I look to River.

He shrugs.

'Apartment 1111,' says the taxi driver.

I chuckle to myself. That's the same time we were all born.

We find the apartment without too much trouble, on the top floor, of course, and nothing like the dogbox I used to live in. These are luxury to the max. A crazy-paved pathway runs along the front of the building, there's flowers in full bloom, whilst tall, slender saplings sway in the warm breeze, adding an extra softness to the concrete environment. A vast difference from my usual haunts. The only flowers close to my front door were the faded, hand-painted daisies courtesy of some hippie. Not one sign of graffiti. And definitely no vomit.

River raises his hand to knock on the glossy white door, when it opens of its own accord. It should freak me out, and yet my heart barely notices the weirdness anymore, especially when it automatically shuts behind us. Strangely enough, Isis's digs are similar to how I imagined them – dark, mysterious, modern and with no expense spared. She's gone with a black, white and gold theme, and the place screams chic and stylish from the moment we step into her spacious split-level living room. Four wide stairs take us down to a highly polished wooden floor, stretching out towards three long skinny windows on the other side of the room, partially hidden behind pairs of black sheers. Every item of furniture tastefully compliments the piece next to it. I mean, the thirty foot ceilings alone, clad in black marble and flecked with gold, is a show-stopper in itself, let alone the assortment of intimate downlights contributing to that perfect romantic dinner moment … not that I think she'd be having too many of those.

A light flicks on, and wow, what a light it is. A cluster of thirty or so small circular lights, each hanging from a strand of black wire, all of varying lengths, dangles from the ceiling like a rainstorm caught in slow motion. It distracts me momentarily from the woman sitting in a high backed, white leather armchair. The armrests and legs are decorated with bands of gold, giving it a throne-like appearance. I catch a glimpse of River, who seems to be a deer in headlights for it, too.

Isis's black hair is coiled up in some kind of plaited bun, woven with gold threads, as opposed to flowing over her shoulders like she normally has it. She is wearing a plain white dress edged with gold around the neck and hem, her arms and shoulders, bare. Her rich olive skin has all the flawlessness of a diamond. A choker style necklace of tiny tightly-meshed gold rings, tasteful in its design and probably more expensive than all of River's cars put together fits snugly around her neck. Her ears are adorned with smaller versions of her necklace. A gold cuff fits snugly to each wrist.

Now I see the Goddess.

She doesn't get up. 'Come in,' she says and waves us closer. 'Do not be afraid.' We slowly drift over and sit across from her on one of the long black lounges hugging a glass-topped coffee table. Floor to ceiling bookcases line the wall behind her, crammed to the max with black and white bound books. The entire top shelf is dedicated to scrolls that I can't even begin to guess what kind of secrets they possess.

Tomas doesn't budge.

'Come now,' she says to Tomas, her voice as silky as the dress she wears. 'When you see the bigger picture you will realise your part in all this.'

Boldly, he walks towards her, his head high, still dressed in his traditional attire. In the time it takes me to blink, he has drawn his sword, pivoted and swung the mighty weapon in the direction of Isis's throat.

Although his sword never makes its mark.

It stops short, the same way I can control gravity.

'Your powers are useless here, Centurion. Like all of your powers.' This time she looks at us.

She's right. This room of over-sharing minds is now a ghost town.

'Ra-Mon cannot touch or see you in my temple. So relax. Please.' It doesn't look much like a temple, more like a penthouse suite.

'We don't know you. We only know of you, and what you've done,' says River. His frown is back and there is an angry, gravelly tone to his voice.

'Again, you only know half the story.'

'Then why don't you fill us in,' I say forcefully.

She encourages Tomas to take a seat, so he opts for a black armchair. She waits for him to settle before she begins. 'To set the record straight, I am first and foremost, the Divine Mother.' She flicks her eyes to Terra, 'after Gaia, of course.'

'That's true,' says Terra, her gaze wandering about the room. 'Maybe once upon a time, but what do you stand for now?'

'I stand for balance. I protect the balance of life and death.'

'Your son murdered my family because I would not serve you,' Tomas spits out.

'He had a job to do,' says Isis. Her tone, forever soft, forever soothing. Just like a mother.

'You know how this all plays out, don't you?' blurts out Ember.

She smiles but not wide enough to ripple the porcelain texture of her skin. 'Knowing everything comes with its difficulties … sometimes you have to sacrifice a few for the greater good.' It reminds me of something Doc once said. Now, she looks directly at Tomas. 'Your children were not slain.'

'I saw it with my own eyes, witch,' replies Tomas, his face full of fury, his breathing coming in fast hisses.

'Nor was your wife.'

He stands and points his finger at her. 'Do not try to bewitch me again. I saw what your son did to her … to them.' Agony pours out of his body, in his voice.

'What you saw … was an illusion.'

THIRTY-ONE

TOMAS says nothing.

His hand finds his sword.

The tightness of his jaw and the whites of his knuckles say everything about what is going on inside him.

'I cast a spell upon your eyes so that you would serve me and see what I wanted you to see. You were the strongest, bravest warrior of that time with heart and vision, and I needed you to be the shield for these four misguided souls.'

'What about my family? Did they not count?'

'Your family lived a long and happy life, fully aware of your sacrifice, knowing you were destined to help your future descendants.' She looks directly into my eyes. 'And, what better place to hide a god, than in the same family tree of the blood-slave working in my service. Who would suspect that?'

I regard Tomas.

His face pales, the blood draining from his legs. He teeters backwards, his calves colliding with the chair. He sits, his brow creasing, eyes flitting this way and that, piecing together history's oldest jigsaw puzzle. A thick vein pulsates in his throat.

It takes me a few heartbeats to register what she's saying too … until realisation dropkicks me in the gut.

'We are …' I begin to say, and yet, Tomas isn't entirely convinced.

Terra gets up. Kneels in front of him. Takes his hands in hers. 'You know I can only speak the truth?' He nods. 'You know the past is also the truth, right?' He nods. 'Then let me show you.'

Tomas flinches when she places her palm against his cheek. His eyelids become a series of rapid blinks as though caught up in some frightful dream.

When it stops, he opens his eyes.

They are full … searching.

In awe, he examines me. My hair. The contour of my ears. Registering that we have the same shaped lips. My shoulders. The length of my fingers. Picking up on small similarities, here and there, he'd never noticed before. 'You are the son of my son,' he says, his voice thick with emotion.

It brings a lump to my throat. 'We … are … *family*?' The words stumble out.

In the time it takes me to rise from the sofa, he has already taken two giant steps towards me.

He hugs me.

Really hugs me.

Like a brother ought to.

Like it's the most natural act in the world. Only when I feel his body relax does he finally release me.

'You are strong, Skye. We come from a long line of warriors, brother. Trust. Believe. You have my blood running through your veins. I know you will succeed.' Ember and River are sitting there, mouths agape, a mask of sheer disbelief on their faces.

'You wish to go home?' Isis says to Tomas.

He turns. There is heartbreak in his voice. 'It is all I've ever wanted.'

I feel the emotion slice at my throat. Swallowing is next to impossible.

'You still have your coin?' asks Isis.

He retrieves it from under his shoulder plate. 'The old man from the marketplace said not to give it to you.'

'And he was right to say that, back then,' Isis replies. 'He is a wise and mysterious man, *Empedocles*.'

'*Empedocles*?' I gasp. 'You mean Doc? He was the old dude in the marketplace?' The truth falls into place. That crafty old codger. 'I can't believe the two of you are in cahoots all this time.'

A soft smile touches her lips. 'You know him as Empedocles. I know him by another name,' states Isis, folding her hands into her lap. 'The ultimate goal is, we both want the same thing.'

'Which is?' asks River.

'To restore balance.'

'Ha!' I can't believe this. 'We thought you were the baddie,' I say without thinking.

This time her smile shines from her eyes. They sparkle like sunlight over water. 'Not everything is as it seems, young one. Remember that.'

She returns her attention back to Tomas. 'Hand me your coin.'

Tomas's jaw clenches three times as he attempts to swallow ... struggling to compose himself. His eyes find me, his mind with a million wise words to share, if only we had more time. He takes one step away and heartily shakes River's hand. The two exchange their final goodbyes. Tomas then bows his head gracefully to Em and holds a smile with Terra. He comes back to me, his hand finding my shoulder. I mimic his action with my opposite arm. His hand clasps the back of my neck. 'I will miss our training sessions,' he whispers, leaning towards me so our heads touch.

'Me too,' I tell him, choking on words I'll never get to say to him. A golf ball wedges in my throat.

Tomas drags me into a hug. 'Your father would be proud.' My eyes squeeze tight, blocking out the world around me. Blocking out the judgements of others but mostly of the judgement, I inflict on myself. 'I wish we had more time,' I tell him.

'Farewell, my friend, my kin, my brother.' Tears bubble at my eyes, and I blink them away.

He releases me and stands before Isis.

He drops to one knee and hands over his coin. Isis rises tall, the silky fabric of her white dress pooling at her feet like a pot of spilt cream. 'You have been a loyal subject and have fulfilled your destiny with honour. Rest now. Be at peace.' His solid form grows thinner and thinner until his body becomes nothing more than the air we breathe.

'Somebody's playing both sides of the fence,' I add as she resumes her seat.

'This plan has been in progress for two thousand years.' She pauses to brush back a curl of hair. 'But it rests on a knife's edge. Anything can happen … one turn of events could change our course.'

'Like what?' Ember asks.

'Human actions, for one …emotions and decisions are out of my control. Our failsafe plan could crumble if one thing should go wrong, if one decision is reversed …' River looks to me and raises his eyebrows. I know what he's referring to – my going off half-cocked attitude and making it up as I go along agenda. 'The only way I have complete control is when I inhabit a human body.'

'Like you did with Hayley,' I say.

'And Iris,' chips in River. It's obvious why Iris was having nightmares the last time I broke into her apartment. She was living a half-life, exactly like Hayley.

'Precisely. Except the more bodies I occupy, the quicker it drains my power. Tomorrow night is the full moon. I am at my strongest then, which is why it was necessary to slow you down and keep you safe in my temple.'

'You mean captive?'

Isis rolls her eyes. An actual Goddess rolled her eyes at me. 'Did your mother ever tell you that just because you think something, it doesn't mean you should say it?' Stifled laughter erupts from the three friends I've come to love and respect. They know me well. I also know better now and take it on the chin.

Isis continues. 'Tomorrow, I will present you to Ra-Mon as my prisoner.' She aims her gaze directly at me.

'Whoa, there a minute,' says River, rising to his feet. 'There is no way in hell I'm letting him go in there without us.' A swell of warmth fills my chest.

'It will be dangerous, and I cannot assure your safety.'

'Let *us* worry about that,' says Terra. 'Some of us might not have the full charge of an Elementar, but we can handle ourselves.'

Isis takes a breath. Closes her eyes. Places her hands into a prayer position. Her breathing slows into a meditative state. I wonder if she's checking in with the Big Boss. A heartbeat later, she opens her eyes and spreads her hands apart as though she's reading a book. 'It's a huge risk … you all going. Especially for you, Terra.'

'He won't come for me yet. Of that, I'm confident of. He'll follow the same protocol as he did with the other Elementars. The kind of power it takes to bind three immortals means I've got a good three months headstart before he'll come for me.' She lifts a curious eyebrow. 'That's not to say he won't send a truckload of monsters my way before he turns up on my doorstep.'

Isis purses her lips.

'It's not up for debate,' adds Ember. 'We're all going.'

'Alright. But you must promise to do as I say.'

I watch the three of them nod. I take Ember at her word … River, maybe. Terra …not in a million years. 'Great!' I add.

'For ev-ery-thing.' Isis switches her focus to me.

'You got it.'

'You will be flying blind in there. Ra-Mon will expect me to cast a spell over my temple, to render you powerless.'

'But you won't, will you?'

'Yes and no.' Why did I even consider that this was going to be anything other than simple. 'He will sense it, if I don't. I will then have to pick the perfect moment to lift it.'

'We could have a secret hand signal then?'

'Can you be serious for once?' Ember reprimands me.

I laugh. 'Sorry. Not in my nature.'

'You will know when the time is right,' adds Isis.

'Okay.' Doubt trickles into my voice.

'Your only objective is to kill Zurvan. Do you understand? Nothing else.' I don't see her rise or walk over to me. She tugs my chin towards her. I see it in her eyes that she means every word. And yet, I can't escape the wondrous aroma of waffles with maple syrup and dove soap hijacking the air around her, reminding me of mum.

I take one last breath in before she steps away. 'Too easy,' I chip in.

'Only then can Mithras be resurrected.'

'A plan,' I say with a sigh. At least I'm not going in totally blind.

'I promised Mithras the four items you bought to me in return for his allegiance. Ra-Mon believes, he has my allegiance and that I am to hand the Lord's Graces over to him, so that *he* can bargain with Mithras.'

'So, you're a bad-ass double double-agent,' I say grinning.

Her face is dead-pan with no hint of a smile. 'Secrets are necessary.'

Terra winks at me from the end of the sofa. 'Told ya.' A sly smirk slides out of the corner of her mouth.

'Where are we meeting him?' River asks.

'My temple in Egypt.'

I bark out a laugh. 'And you're going to piggyback us there, one by one?'

'No, we will go through the Gateway.'

I don't know how, but the room seems to darken suddenly, the air becoming heavy and stale. River seems to notice too and looks about warily. The Gateway doesn't sound like any place I want to go in a hurry.

'And you'd be right,' says Isis, reading my thoughts, 'except it will be quick. It's more like the backdoor to Hell than walking through the barren lands of fire and brimstone.'

'Hell?'

The colour drops out of Ember's face. 'Em, you can stay here if you want,' I hear River say to her.

She presses her lips tightly and throws her shoulders back. 'No way. I'm going.' Terra grips her hands, and the girls exchange a friendly glance.

'Where will we find this backdoor? I mean, the entry to Hell isn't likely to be in plain view.'

A tight smile creeps across Isis's lips. 'And that's where you'd be wrong. Most of the evil in this world is in plain sight.' I sniff, and she carries on. 'You will need to be at the Luxor Obelisk by eleven minutes past eleven, the time you were all born, and use the code Skye has. You do still have the pages in your phone from Iris's diary, don't you?' she asks me.

Busted!

I cringe back into the sofa. Damn ...*where is my invisibility power when I need it?* River and Ember swing around to face me, their brows knotted in confusion.

'You have more pages?' asks River.

'Yes,' I say timidly.

'About me?' barks Ember.

I nod my head again. 'Yes.'

'And you've had them translated?'

I hang my head and mumble another yes into my lap. When I finally lift my head, a fiery tornado has erupted in

419

Ember's eyes. My throat goes dry. 'When … when were you going to tell me? Have you read them? How long have you known?'

I feel my face screwing up as I speak. 'Since our taxi ride here, and yes, I've read them. I had Henri translate them.'

'You saw Henri?' River shouts, now on his feet.

I close my eyes. Clench my teeth. Breathe – because that's all I know how to do – that, and spill my guts. 'Yep. He said to say hi.'

River is still shaking his head. I'm waiting for the hurricane. He turns his back on me to face Ember and doesn't say a word to either of us. His back ribs inflate as he works on controlling his temper. The shock is gone from his eyes when he turns and says, 'Dude, when will you get it through your thick skull, we're in this together.'

I hang my head, and go over and over whether keeping it from them was a good idea, and I still come up with the same answer … yes it was, and I would do it again.

In.

A.

Heartbeat.

I was thinking of them … to avoid giving Em false hope … of the shit roaring down on us right now taking centre stage. We all need to be in the right headspace, but more so, I need River to be focused and not worried about Ember's state of mind. Upon reading it in the taxi, I made an executive decision to tell Ember after we get home.

I glance up just as Terra flicks me a commiserating smile, although sadness isn't the emotion bubbling to the surface right now. I'm a little cranky. 'Sue me,' I blurt out, frustration getting the better of me. 'You don't think I haven't felt like a complete prick for holding onto this. Well, forgive me for waiting for an appropriate time.'

'Like now?' demands Ember. Her voice is pitchy and broken. 'Because you've been caught redhanded?' Em momentarily closes her eyes. Swallows. 'You didn't even tell us you had them, let alone ask Henri to translate them.'

'Like I said, I wanted to tell you, I really did. I just thought we had too much on our plate at the moment.' I run my hand across my chin.

'That wasn't your decision to make, Skye,' Ember says, cheeks flushed, fingers knotted.

Their faces blur as guilt floods my body. I drop my head in my hands.

To hide from the world.

From my friends.

I realise they deserve an explanation, but that means exposing myself. Laying myself open to shame, to disappointment, possibly loneliness. All of the shitty emotions I've tried so hard to bury are out on display. The words fight against me … tired … ready to be spoken.

I relinquish my hold.

'I did what I thought was right, and believe me, I'm paying the price for it.' I pause. The guilt is suffocating. 'The thought of letting you all down again. It's … It's …'

'What?' asks River frowning.

'I'm a total screw-up. Okay? There I've said it. A disappointment to all who dare put hope in me.' I get up to leave. 'You have no idea how much this guilt wears away at my soul. Every day it consumes more and more of me. My insensitive lack of judgement. My inability to trust or tell the truth. The death of my parents.' Air fails me, no longer wishing to fill my lungs or fan my face. I force back the sadness finding its way to my eyes, my throat. 'I'm no longer swimming in guilt. I am drowning in it.'

I have my back to them so they can't see me.

'Please take a seat,' says Isis calmly.

My face feels like it's on fire as I resume my seat, yet all I can think of is how thankful I am I can't hear their thoughts. Those hateful, mocking thoughts. Maybe that's why Isis chose this moment to dob me in, to spare me the torment.

'Let's reset for a moment,' says Terra, getting up and stepping over our bags. She squishes herself between me and the arm of the sofa, dumping two fluffy cushions on the floor as she links her arm through mine. She leans her head on my shoulder and rubs my arm. 'It's okay,' she whispers to me. 'I know you're feeling like shit right now, but please trust me. This is the beginning of something good.'

I take a breath. Feel her hair tickle my cheek. 'You're the best thing about my life, you know that?'

Her cheek smooths against my arm several times until her eyes find me. 'I don't believe that. And neither do you.' She's right, to a certain degree, although my life has brightened since we became friends.

I dig a large hole inside myself, dump my truckload of acknowledged guilt into it and cover it over with a fake smile. I take a chance that my next words will delay the diary pages for a bit. 'So, what's this obelisk *thing*?'

It works.

Isis jumps straight in. 'An obelisk is a four-sided column, made from a single piece of stone or granite, and tapered at the top like a pyramid. There are twenty-one located across the globe, bought, bartered or stolen through the ages by the US, England, Europe and Ethiopia to name a few, with only five remaining in Egypt. The Luxor Obelisks were built as a pair and were erected during the reign of Rameses II to guard the entrance to the Luxor Temple over three thousand years ago.' Isis's eyes drift off to some place else. 'The right one was shipped to Paris in 1833, and is located not far away at the Place de la Concorde. The other still resides in Egypt.'

'Thanks for the history lesson. What do I need the code for?'

'There are a series of hieroglyphs etched into the stonework. When pressed in the correct order, a doorway will open.'

'Sounds simple enough,' I say, trying to sound more upbeat.

'However, you will need to use Amun's gifts of invisibility and flight. The obelisk is thirty-five metres high.'

Terra laughs. 'Can't exactly have you floating in mid-air in front of hundreds of Parisians now, can we?'

'But his power doesn't allow me to physically touch anything without exposing a body part. How am I going to get around that?'

'Stretch out your hands,' Isis says to me. I do as I'm told, palms up. She then places her hands over mine. A massive jolt throws my heart out of rhythm as some kind of energy force enters my body. The taste of sulphur floods my mouth, my fingers burning as though I have them too close to an open fire. In a blink, it stops. 'That should eliminate the problem,' she says, her voice soothing away any discomfort. I have no idea what she has done to me, therefore I'm unsure if its something I want to thank her for. 'I have to leave now, but I will meet you on the other side of the entrance to the Obelisk. There is plenty of food in the fridge. Get a good night's sleep.' Isis beckons me over. 'Ensure you arrive in plenty of time, so you can locate the different hieroglyphs. You will need to activate the first symbol at eleven minutes past eleven, and not a second before. The last one before the clock strikes twelve minutes past eleven.'

'Roger,' I say, giving her a thumbs up.

Isis disappears, leaving behind a vapour of white.

I turn to see the others looking at me. 'Hand it over,' says Ember, gesturing to my phone.

I don't hesitate. I click on the first page and pass my phone to her. It reads:

3 June 2018

On 4 December 2017, an anonymous email arrived in my inbox asking me to investigate a man called Darryl

Burberry. He is a lawyer. After several days of observation, I reported back via email that I suspected him of paedophilia and from my findings is currently stalking a young girl, by the name of Ember Riley. Up until now, the whole case has been very mysterious. Today, I received a second email from the same client, again not wishing to supply their name. The message was to observe and report all predatory activities surrounding Ember Riley.

NB: He's a disgusting slug.

16 June 2018

This disgusting slug still haunts this girl's steps. I've been warned not to notify the authorities because all is being taken care of.

30 July 2018

This man is the epitome of vile. I am watching him now. Watching him, watching her, a smile on his lips. She is with a blonde girl, by the name of Rachel Winters, enjoying a beverage at the Choccy Box café. I want to smash his face in, but again, I have been warned to keep my distance.

22 Aug 2018

A most terrible accident has happened. Ember Riley has been involved in a fatal car crash. She survived, but both parents were killed. The poor child is the victim of a comfortable life, with no knowledge of who was out there to get her.

9 Jan 2019

I'm not sure why I am writing these words, but it seems my hand has a mind of its own. Here are the words I need to say: (Isis) I have had to intervene – I have implanted her name into the mind of the next in line. I have made a startling discovery. That disgusting slug made an agreement with Ra-Mon – kill the parents and you can have the girl for one year. Then you are to hand her over to me.

15 Jan 2020

Nuria is released. My plan is failing.

17 Feb 2020
Nereus is released. No more hiding in the shadows.

Below the diary entry is a bunch of hieroglyphs.

River and Terra are peering over Ember's shoulders as she reads. Simultaneously, they lift their heads when they've finished.

Ember's face loses all trace of life. She breaks into a sob and River scoops her up, bringing her in to his chest. 'He told me he had his eye on me long before I was fostered by them, but I didn't believe him.' She bites back her tears and sniffs. 'He said that the day my parents were killed, that I was meant to be his, and now I know … all along, it was him that killed them … killed them so he could have me.' She buries her head into his shirt, her body trembling as wave after wave of grief hits her. We give Em what she needs, to get it out of her system, as Mum would say. When her sobs finally subside, River gently smooths her hair away from her wet cheeks. 'I promise you; I will pay him a visit when we are done with all of this.'

'Count me in,' I add.

'No. I want him to be looking over his shoulder for the rest of his life, wondering if I will follow through with my threat.' She takes a deep breath, straightens her spine, and throws her shoulders back. The pain is still reflecting in her eyes although now, her jaw is strong, her resolve stepping forward. No more tears fall. 'I'm good. I can't change what's happened, but I can change how I feel about it. I am not going to let that … what did Iris call him?'

'A disgusting slug,' I say.

'I am not going to let that *disgusting slug* take up one more minute of my life.'

'Good for you,' says Terra, feeling for her hand before squeezing it.

River hugs her again. 'I'm so proud of you.' A smirk crosses his lips. 'Can you actually believe it was Isis who

425

told me your name,' he says, an incredulous look on his face. 'All along, it was her.'

It is hard to believe.

Terra leans back into a comfy chair, a knowing smile teasing her lips. It must be equally challenging to know the truth and not being able to reveal it. I never realised until just now, how much strain this must add to her already complicated and damaged life. A newfound respect emerges for her.

Later, as I lay my head on the pillow, I pray to whoever is listening, that this isn't the last night's sleep I ever have.

The next morning, breakfast is quiet, like I expect it to be. I can't eat, even under the repeated attempts of Ember pushing plates of fruit and muesli under my nose. My brain is busier than ever, which is totally nuts considering it's just me upstairs to contend with. After carrying out multiple stocktakes of my backpack, I fidget like a nervous schoolgirl on the sofa, unable to stop my legs bouncing or fingers fiddling with anything I can find.

The minutes drag by.

Terra suggests a walk to stretch our legs, although she retracts her offer almost immediately when she gets a mental download of the future – an ambush of six or so burly assassins waiting for us on the other side of the park. She assures me they will be gone by the time we leave and when I ask how she knows that she simply says Gaia would evacuate the area. I suppose a flash of white earth-energy, covering a five-kilometre radius, vanquishing all non-human entities, would be the way I'd do it. Terra merely shrugs when I share my thoughts with her.

We leave dead on the dot of ten thirty, giving us ample time to get there and prepare. I feel kind of stupid walking out the house with a seven-foot staff in my hand, but there's nowhere else to put it. I do keep a watchful eye for any beasts that may have slipped through Gaia's net, but other than it rained during the night, leaving behind a damp, dreary feeling of doom, we are orc-free. Thankfully, it's not too cold and the gentle wind is doing little to blow away the heavy clouds. The air quality is good enough to see right across the river to the Eiffel Tower, some three kilometres away. But after today, Paris's weather will be somebody else's problem because we'll be in sunny Egypt.

The Luxor Obelisk ends up being a six-minute walk from Isis's apartment and not hard to miss. Encased within a metal fence, nearly two-metres high, this giant needle's resting place isn't that different from the dry desert sand of Egypt. It now resides on an island of concrete, seemingly abandoned in the middle of a busy Paris intersection with nothing but the company of a few dozen black ornate lampposts, exact replicas as those on Isis's street, and two oversized fountains one at each end. The obelisk stands resolute, cars whizzing by as we dodge our way through the traffic to stand at her base. Terra mentions how certain religious and historical structures seem to form particular shapes, either triangles or straight lines, like that of the Arc De Triomphe that passes through the Luxor Obelisk to form a direct line with Le Louvre.

Coincidental positioning?

I think not.

From what I know of the world we live in; these *so-called* tourist attractions are a cover for something more mysterious. Something evil.

I nudge River's elbow.

A bus load of tourists has pulled up as we stand at the base of the obelisk. 'That could be a problem.'

Ember laughs. 'Oh my god, Skye. When are you going to realise any human problem, is no problem for us? I can easily create a diversion,' she says, sparking a flame with the click of her fingers. I chuckle.

'Or I could flood those fountains over there,' says River. 'Shouldn't be too hard.' We end up going with

Terra's idea - a massive flock of pigeons could be easily gathered and used as cover if needed.

I punch on my invisibility and float upwards, passing the main pedestal on which the obelisk is placed. There isn't time to read the tribute to King Louis Phillip or study the detailed gold diagrams of how the obelisk was raised and transported either. Another time … maybe if I survive this?

I stop about halfway up the column and inspect the hundreds of symbols etched into the stone. There are crosses, ankhs and squiggly lines, an assortment of birds, and then random objects like eyes, pharaoh's, bulls, and strange ancient markings I have never seen before.

I take out my phone and open my photos to reveal the page from Iris's diary. Enlarging the picture, the first symbol off the rank is none other than a bird, strangely resembling a raven.

What are the odds?

The only problem is, there are four faces on the obelisk and each face has three vertical columns of hieroglyphs … all etched with ravens.

Fuck!

I have no idea which one to start with?

THIRTY-TWO

CALM, *dude*, I repeat over in my mind.

     Just.

          Keep.

               Your.

                    Head.

I check my watch. I still have ten minutes to figure this out. I examine the photo on my phone again, trying to work out if there is some form of pattern. The next symbol is a duck, and then an owl. Then, a lion, three wavy lines and a stork, followed by an ankh. I zip around each side of the monument, checking my phone against the different possible combinations. On the face of the column that has no inscription or diagrams on the base, I discover all the hieroglyphs are within relative reach of each other.

Could it really be that simple?

I take it as a sign.

429

'I think I've found it,' I call down to them. *God, I hope I have*, otherwise all of this will be for nothing. When no reply comes, I concede that they probably can't hear me. I can, however, bank on River downloading his thoughts to me. He lets me know they're all in position, each taking a side, waiting for the entrance to reveal itself. I glance down to see them casually leaning on the metal railings as though they're transfixed on the gold inscriptions.

I check my watch again.

Three minutes to go.

I extend my fingers out to touch the stone column, praying Isis is true to her word and has downloaded a magical upgrade to Amun's standard powers. The second I feel the rough granite, I heave a sigh of relief. I could've done with this a few months back.

The group of tourists have now exited the bus and are standing around.

Two minutes is all I need.

With my eye on my watch, ready for it to tick over to eleven minutes past eleven, I hover in front of the raven.

Tick!

I tap the first hieroglyph.

Nothing happens. Fuck!

There are several ravens above and below the first one I chose, and I frantically start tapping each one, praying for a miracle. I've already used up thirty seconds and my heart leaps into my throat as I press the last one. Instantly, it turns a shade darker as though it's been rained on.

I almost piss my pants in excitement.

I've got this.

Like a sniffer dog on speed, I repeat the same process for the rest of the hieroglyphs, waiting for each symbol to change colour.

'Get ready,' I yell down to them. Terra is the only one who looks up. She sticks her thumb out at me.

We're ready, River says into my head.

A rush of energy comes at me as I face the Ankh. A humming sound vibrates across the airwaves, the same time I see a wisp of dark cloud racing towards us.

Except it isn't a cloud. It's Terra's exit plan … a massive flock of pigeons.

I press the last symbol as the pigeons engulf us.

The sound of stone grinding upon stone reaches me before River shouts, "*this side. Over here.*" He scales the fence. Em and Terra scramble over the railing as a blizzard of pigeon's swarm in circles around us. A panel of paving drops away beneath the base of the obelisk, presenting a stone staircase.

I fire up the old thrusters, suddenly aware the doorway is about to close. My arse skims the coldness of the stone steps, automatically flicking off my invisibility as the panel slides back into place behind me.

We're back in the darkness.

Again.

'Cutting it a little fine,' remarks Ember, appearing in the glare of River's phone torch, a cynical smile on her lips. Terra is in front of her, and down a few more steps is River.

'Watch your step,' he says, his voice echoing. 'They're a little steep.'

'We should be used to this by now,' laughs Terra, directing her torch at her feet, continuing downwards into the belly of our planet. I decide to flick my phone light on when I misplace my footing, flooding my body with another seemingly endless supply of adrenaline. The last thing we need is a disastrous domino effect.

And down we go … into the abyss.

Deeper and deeper into the earth. No twists or turns. Just a straightforward, everyday staircase … to Hell! The first one hundred steps go past in a blink, the next hundred, and I'm starting to feel the burn in my legs. I'm thankful when River stops us for a breather on some kind of make-shift landing. I take the opportunity to shine my torch around, except there is nothing but blackness. No light or shade. Only a dark nothingness.

I lose count after the next two hundred steps, and time ceases to tick as we push on again, the burn in my legs becoming more of a tremble.

'I wonder how much further,' I ask the darkness.

'Nearly there,' responds Terra. 'I can smell the brimstone.'

I take a deep breath in. I smell nothing. It takes another fifty steps before a strong aroma hits my senses. 'River, did you fart?'

He laughs.

'It's brimstone, you dummy,' says Terra.

'All I can smell is rotten eggs. Are you sure it wasn't you, Riv?' says Em, giggling.

'No, it definitely wasn't me. But, hey, watch that ...' The stairs are changing – becoming wider, the riser no longer as steep. 'I think we're almost there.'

Another thirty treads later, and River declares we're at the bottom.

I bend over and stretch, my hamstrings tighter than a pair of highly-strung guide ropes. Em and Terra follow suit, although River seems okay – it must be all that swimming.

'Look. Fire torches,' says Ember, breathing onto one. It jumps to life in an instant, revealing a familiar figure.

'Good. You're here,' says Isis, stepping out of the shadows. Her white dress is replaced with a sleeveless black jumpsuit, feet are still bare. 'This way.'

We walk in silence for a while, me ...as used to finding my way in the dark these days than breathing. We ditch our phones for fire torches which are more practical for light, but exacerbate the heat. I expected it to be hot down here, but flaming active volcano hot, isn't something I have much experience with, even living in Australia. I can't imagine how the Poms are holding up. I take shallow sips, like Isis recommends.

A steady stream of sweat has forged a gully down my forehead and cheeks that seems resistant to any amount of mopping. My t-shirt is soaked through too, becoming a second skin against my back. I drag my hoodie over my head, and wipe my face with it before tying it around my waist. What is more concerning is the fiery breath of Hell that swirls around my chest, trying to corrupt me, and invade my heart. How do I know … nasty little whispers chant their intentions on the airwaves around us. I decide to keep this little piece of info to myself. Ember looks petrified enough.

We head down another tunnel, another rocky pathway, all looking exactly like the last one we were in, and I begin to wonder if we're going around in circles. My question is answered a few steps later as the tunnel suddenly turns out onto a vast cavernous space … with a plunging headfirst drop into oblivion on one side.

My stomach jumps into my throat as I peer over the edge, the blackness not quite so black anymore. Shades of dark grey and chocolate brown replace that silent inkiness, no different than being inside the house with a pair of dark sunnies on.

Isis stops us. 'Stay close to the wall,' she advises. The same wall resembling one of those flashy water features you might find in a posh shopping mall, the black rock all glossy and shiny with water. I run the back of my fingertips along it as we walk. And walk. And walk. Which seems to go on forever.

Isis has a pretty impressive CV. She informs us that she is the giver of life, the mother of all gods, the patron of magic, nature and healing, and is the protector of the dead. She goes on to say that going via the back door of Hell shouldn't present any issues as she's also the queen of The Underworld. 'Why do you think Ra-Mon wants me working for him?' she calls over her shoulder.

I sniff. 'I'm super glad you're on our side,' I reply, bringing up the rear.

She turns to address us. 'I will need to bind your hands and powers now. We are very close to my temple, and Ra-Mon will be able to sense Amun and Gaia very soon.'

Wisps of silvery smoke circle our wrists like an imaginary thread, cutting off our powers. The chatter in my brain from everyone's thoughts ceases immediately and the steady pulse of fear pumping in my neck is saying *shit is about to get real*.

We trail behind her until we come to a flight of steps. My legs haven't recovered from the last lot, and wearily, I begin the mighty climb. Thankfully, there aren't as many as before, or maybe there are, but the journey out doesn't seem half as long. When I clear the top step we find ourselves in a wide hallway, bigger and longer than any cathedral I've ever been in, and with a ceiling twice as high. The temperature has gone from near boiling to subzero in a matter of minutes and I dive back into my hoodie. I see River doing the same, Ember sliding her arms into her denim jacket.

Thick, square slabs of turmeric coloured sandstone lay before us, corners crumbling, worn away by fifty billion footsteps. Small fire torches light our way as we follow behind Isis, the walls no different in colour to the floor, although more gouged and primitive in their design. It's near impossible to believe this place was ever alive with people instead of the forgotten tomb it has now become. Monstrous square pillars line both sides of the hallway and I raise my fire torch closer to get a better look at the Egyptian soldiers carved into the stone. The images depict battle scenes and soldiers holding spears, faces side on. I imagine this place would have been guarded by the very men now immortalised in these columns. There are more hieroglyphs too, just like the obelisk. And, of course, there are plenty of ravens to go around. It's no wonder they've haunted me for so long because some part of me recognises this place.

'We're almost there,' says Isis, interrupting my thoughts. 'You can leave your torches here.'

We cross the room, and ditch the torches as we approach a magnificent arched entrance. It could be the mouth of a mighty cave. Now, all that stands between me and the cool, albeit dusty air is a final set of twenty or so stairs.

'Welcome to my temple,' says Isis as we clear the last step.

Heaven!

Not in the literal sense, it just feels good to breathe in deeply again and swap out the taste of sulphur for warm, gritty air. I close my eyes, throw my head back and let it waft over my face. I take several breaths before I realise where I am and what awaits us.

I slowly open my eyes and gaze up at the clear night sky, sprinkled with a handful of shiny white diamonds. The moon is full, so buttery yellow, and hanging so low in a sea of darkness, that if I stretch out far enough, I believe I could touch it.

Wait … *full moon*? 'Riv,' I say softly, 'It hasn't been more than a couple of hours since we left Paris and now it's nighttime? How do you think that's possible?'

'S'pose it's another of those need to know *magic* things.' He rakes his fingers through his hair. 'There's water close by, too,' he says, swinging his head around to check out our surroundings. I follow his gaze to a body of flat, still water. 'That'll come in handy when I get my powers back.'

'You mean *if* we get them back.'

River raises his eyebrows at me.

'Guys. Sorry to interrupt, but I need a moment,' says Terra, fidgeting.

There's a strange tremor in her voice. 'Not really the time for sightseeing,' I add, confused by her sudden need to delay the inevitable, considering she'd pretty much set the marathon-like pace past Hell.

'I need to go,' she says, more urgently now.

'Go where? We've got monsters to slay,' I add, throwing my arms up in the air.

'For Christ's sake, Skye. I've gotta take a piss. I can't do anything on a full bladder.'

'Oh!' My cheeks burn.

Whilst Terra makes her way to the water's edge, in search of some nearby bushes, dragging Ember along with her, Isis tells us her temple used to be on the Island of Philae but had been moved due to the dam flooding a hundred years ago. I get the feeling she disapproves of the new location, especially when her last line ended with … *humans? Why can't they leave things alone that don't concern them?* I suggest she smite the lot of them and be done with it, but she simply pats my arm and offers me one of those condescending smiles.

The girls rejoin us, and we make a beeline for the sandstone courtyard directly ahead of us.

'Wow!' I can't help being impressed. Ember lets out a sigh of appreciation too.

Side by side, we march straight up the middle, dodging massive chunks of sandstone boulders that are randomly scattered across the forecourt. Perhaps a storm blew them down, or more likely they've been picked up and dropped by a couple of giants playing marbles. However they got there, nothing in this world is going to shift them. Other than our shuffling footsteps, the night is silent, amplifying the sound of my heart thumping in my chest, in my ears. It's so damn loud, it could wake the dead. In fact, I'm kinda glad my powers are off – there is no doubt in my mind that this place would be crawling with spooks. It's eerie though, not to hear a single chirp from a cicada or the hollow cry of an owl.

The soft glow of moonlight makes it difficult to appreciate the carved images and hieroglyphs, not that we have the time or desire to admire them right now. However, that isn't what is holding my attention. Ominous dark passageways to my left and right, created by two vertical rows of circular pillars, steal my focus, increase my pulse. Ragged sandstone blocks connecting all the columns together, like some kind of top plate, are responsible for both roof and shadow.

The perfect setting for an ambush.

And, yet Terra is all over this. A real pro. Examining every rock. Every shady corner. She catches my two second gaze in her direction, extends a middle finger, flutters me a jovial wink, all beneath a wry smile. Even Em isn't hiding under River's armpit, which surprises me. Her posture says alert, brave, capable, her eyes searching every which way. A new level of confidence takes hold of me. Just the medicine I need.

At the far end of the courtyard, silhouetted against the midnight sky, is an H shaped structure. Like everything here, it's also built from sandstone blocks and covered from top to bottom with hieroglyphs. Isis informs us this is called the Monumental Gate. Slap bang in the centre of that H is a spooky black entrance that leads to Isis's temple. From the way we're all looking at it, it might as well be the doorway to Hell.

'Ra-Mon is waiting,' she whispers to us, prompting one of us to go first.

I step up to the plate. It is blacker than the inkiness above us, and the perfect location for a surprise attack. I inhale deeply, calming myself as I pass two granite lions standing to attention. Shadow and blackness engulf us momentarily until the passageway spits us out on the other side. My eyes slowly adjust as we enter another courtyard, not as big as the first, but definitely big enough to play a game of footy on. Flat, shallow steps lead up to Isis's temple.

And there, seated on a black marble throne, like it has no place to be there, is Ra-Mon. He doesn't sit like a king at all, in fact he's almost sliding off the seat. One leg is stretched out long, his elbow resting on the arm, hand propping up his chin. He looks bored.

My eyes flick left, sensing Em tense up next to me as we walk towards him, River clenching his jaw. What I would give right now to be able to read their minds.

We make it halfway across the courtyard when he raises his hand. A hundred fire torches burst into life, scaring away the darkest of shadows. Ra-Mon appears semi-human in his black trousers and shirt, and could double as Dracula if it wasn't for his long grey hair hanging over his shoulders, or the royal-blue satin lining in his cloak that should be red.

With the staff firmly in my grasp, hands crossed over at the wrist, feigning imaginary handcuffs like Isis commanded, we stand before the fiendish god who wants control of our world.

'Welcome, welcome,' he says as though we're all old friends. Cobalt-blue flames flicker in those sinister eyes of his, before spreading to that same eerie grin Em says, still keep her up at night. He rises from his seat and approaches the top step. His eyes wander from me to Ember, onto River and then Terra. His smile widens when his gaze falls upon Isis. 'You've done well,' he says to her. She acknowledges with a slight nod of her head. His eyes zero back to me. 'I see you have the Lord's Staff.'

'Suppose I do,' I spit through my teeth. I get a nudge on the arm from Em.

Isis joins Ra-Mon. Stands at his side.

'Let the games begin,' shouts Ra-Mon, flicking out the back of his cloak and taking his seat.

Nothing happens for a minute.

Like … Nothing.

My eyes pass over every rock, over every stone pillar.

More minutes tick by.

The gnawing in my gut, growing.

Then from out of the darkest shadow, beyond the furthest stone pillar, I see him emerging.

Terra steps out of line to stand beside me. 'Zurvan,' she gasps. Her body tenses. River tries to drag Ember behind him, but she protests, wanting to stand her ground.

Out of the blackness, Zurvan strides towards us. The body of a man, and I can see what Terra meant about the likeness of a lion –a lion that died a hundred years ago.

His face is a deathly shade of grey and is well decayed in places, with ragged flaps of skin hanging from his neck and forehead. His eyes have sunk into his head and the fat has been stripped from his cheeks. His mouth is full of broken, yellowing teeth. My gut curdles just from looking at him.

The rest of him is frigging *huge*.

I swallow even though my mouth is dry.

'Release the challenger,' boasts Ra-Mon.

I drop my hands to my side and remove my backpack. I stand it near River's legs. 'Don't lose that,' I whisper to him.

'Skye …'

'It's okay, brother. I've got this.'

The pain and fear he has for me flashes in his eyes. Makes them water. So many things he wanted to say. So many things he wished he hadn't said. I offer him a grim smile, turn my back on him, and walk confidently into our make-shift arena.

Standing a whopping two feet taller than me, rippling from shoulders to calf in muscle, Zurvan is dressed in a pair of dark shorts, cut off at the knees. In his hand, he holds a two metre long spear.

'Not exactly a fair fight,' I shout out to my host. 'I have no weapon.'

Ra-Mon laughs loud and boisterously. 'You have the Lord's Staff …' he bellows.

'And yet no power to wield it.' I raise it above my head and threaten Zurvan with it. The beast flinches, and for a second I see fear growing in his eyes. 'Your witch stripped us of our powers.' Zurvan gathers himself … puffs out his chest, white clouds steaming from his nostrils.

'Don't poke the pussy cat,' calls out Terra. Her words irritate Zurvan, and he crouches into a fighting stance.

Ra-Mon turns to Isis. She bows graciously to him. 'Very well.'

A sword appears at my feet. 'Hold this,' I say, lobbing the staff to River.

He catches it and then promptly drops it. 'Fuck.' He shoves his hand under his armpit for a few seconds before inspecting it.

'Interesting,' I hear Ra-Mon murmur, not taking his eyes off River for a moment.

I bend over to pick up the sword, only Terra kicks it away. 'This is not your fight,' she says, her green eyes blazing, warning me not to challenge her.

I turn to Isis. Anger boils in her eyes, urging me to take control. Fuck is becoming my word of the week, yet nothing else comes close. I'd choose to be stuck between a rock and a hard place than between two goddesses … any day of the week. I grumble out my frustration before twisting around to argue the point. 'It's not yours either. I've got this.'

'You don't understand,' she says, her voice pitchy … breaking. ' You might have this. But I *need* this.'

Terra steps into the arena and releases her hands from their imaginary bonds. Isis fakes a stumble, making a panicked grab for the throne. 'My lord, she is too powerful for me to control. I cannot hold them all.'

'YOU!' barks Zurvan, rotating his deformed head to look at Terra. He bows subserviently to Ra-Mon. 'I choose the Earthchild as my challenger.'

Ra-Mon raises a hand. 'So be it.' The throaty growl of approval from Zurvan launches mammoth-sized shivers up my spine. Indecision pays me a visit. I contemplate ignoring Isis when a familiar voice churns inside me … *pick up the sword.*

Amun … you legend!

Strength returns to my muscles. Clears my head. Boosts my confidence. With adrenaline coursing through my veins, fear clenching tightly around my heart, I reach for the sword. By the time I look up, Terra has transformed into a pissed-off grizzly bear.

She charges Zurvan, and he fends her off with the tip of his spear. I have nothing to fear, I keep telling myself. Terra isn't the one to die. She told me that herself. She promised.

Her thick, sharp claws are no match for Zurvan's gut-ripping talons and yet she still swings at him with fast, deathly blows. One finds its mark, and I hear the snort of victory from Terra's muzzle.

Fury explodes in Zurvan's eyes as he cries out, blood spraying from the four red ribbons across his chest. He swipes at the wound and licks the blood off his fingers. 'Is that all you have? I expected more from you.'

Life can happen, or it can be taken away, all in the blink of an eye. One minute Terra is stalking Zurvan, mouth frothing with every breath … the next, the spear is sailing through the air with one target in mind. His aim is so fast, so accurate, I don't even have chance to warn her before it hits with a thunk into her hindquarter.

Her shriek of pain brings me out of my shock coma.

'Terra,' I yell out.

Now it's my turn.

I go in swinging my sword, doing everything Tomas warned me not to do, but I can't see anything but Terra desperately trying to bite the spear out of her leg.

My impulsive nature catches Zurvan off-guard. The keen edge of my sword opens up a gash across his taut abdomen, instantly spilling out his blood.

I smirk at my good luck because that's all it is. A lucky strike.

I leap forward again and drive the sword towards him, aiming for the same injury. He swats it away with his meaty forearm, sending me reeling forward, awarding me precious seconds to take stock of the situation. I recall my training. Hear Tomas's voice in my head. I adjust my feet, widen my stance as Zurvan thunders toward me. At ten feet tall, he has to stoop to get close to me, and I use it to my advantage. I duck under his arm as his fist comes my way, pivot and thrust the sword upwards. This time, I slash at his shoulder, a hit that Tomas would be proud of.

Zurvan howls again as the blade comes away, coated in crimson. A river of blood flows down his left arm to his elbow. He has no weapon, but the size of him, and those lethal talons, he really doesn't need one.

Like the warrior he is, he waits for my rookie mistake. With a grunt, he knocks the sword clean out of my hand on my next strike, and then thumps me around the face for good measure. I see stars and black, and my brain feels like it's become a new home for a family of bees. I try to shake it off as I stand, blood gushing down my cheek and from my nose, into my mouth. I spit it out. The light is fading from one eye as it starts to swell, and I manage to get to my knees. The ground, somehow unstable, tilts with every movement I make.

I throw up.

Laughter echoes around the courtyard. I'm unsure why it's getting louder and louder until I feel a kick to the stomach.

I gasp for air.

Air that has been my comrade in arms for so many years and yet cannot find me when I need it most. I try to plant one foot on the ground when a skull crunching uppercut, sends me airborne. I land on my back, unsure whether I'm alive or dead. My brain is ringing. I think I'm in that semi-unconscious space where I'm on the verge of passing out and yet all I hear are the words from Tomas shouting … AGAIN.

Numb.

Delirious.

Through bleary vision, I see two people walking towards me. '*Mum? Dad?*'

It can't be. I must be dead.

'*We believe in you,*' they say.

Mum bends down and whispers in my ear. 'You are here for an extraordinary reason. I knew it the moment I held you in my arms. We have no regrets, and you shouldn't either. Now, go and protect your friends.'

I have a vague recollection of being picked up by the scruff of my hoodie and thrown to the ground.

Life thumps back into me with a jolt.

A surge of energy takes over me, and I sit up. I'd like to think it's Amun because my reserves bottomed out a while ago. Whatever it is, I'm grateful for it.

I yank my hoodie over my head.

It is restricting my movement, not to mention acting as an easy purchase for Zurvan's next manoeuvre. Blood gushes into my mouth again and I lean to one side and spit it out. At the edges of my vision, I see Zurvan stalk over to Terra and fearlessly wrench the spear free before thrusting it into her torso.

'No,' I scream out.

Her mighty roar sparks me into gear, and in the time it takes him to raise the spear above his head for the final blow, I don't know how, but I am sprinting straight for him.

I slam into him.

It's like hitting a steel pylon at a hundred kilometres an hour. But I can't let go. I grip tighter around his torso and drive him into the ground, giving Terra enough time to drag herself to safety.

Except she doesn't.

She stands on her hind legs and lets out a growl that would make anyone shit their pants and run. Blood and saliva are dripping off her teeth, her hot breath disappearing into the cold air. She presses down firmly on her abdomen, the dark brown fur matted and soaked with her blood.

Zurvan is back on his feet, quicker than I am, spear in hand. I roll to one side in the nick of time to prevent myself from becoming a chicken skewer.

Terra rushes at Zurvan, distracting him, allowing me to get to my feet. The beast snarls. 'You are no match for me,' he growls.

'Maybe not, but she is.' My eye has almost closed and yet I can see well enough to dive through Zurvan's legs as Terra takes another colossal swipe at his head. It gives me enough time to jump onto his back. This would be so much easier if I could use my invisibility.

I manage to get him in a choke-hold but Zurvan is no flea-bitten orc, and I am no match for his strength. I am the child on the back of a gorilla. Effortlessly, he throws me over his head, digging his sharp talons through my t-shirt and into my skin.

I cry out in pain.

My face slides along the gritty sandstone as I hit the deck, the back of my t-shirt clinging to my skin, wet and sticky with blood.

I hear River scream my name and look through blurred vision as he and Ember battle to break their restraints. Looks like they truly are bound.

Zurvan stalks towards me, unsheathing a knife from the leather pouch attached to his calf. He thrusts down, and I close my eyes to …

Nothing.

Nothing happens.

I open one eye.

There's a raucous behind me.

Terra has transformed again – this time into a silverback gorilla, like the one that flashed through my head only moments ago.

This is now a battle of strength.

They tread in wide circles, looking for an invitation, looking for a way in. Terra throws herself into him, and they both go crashing to the earth. He manages to get a cheap blow to the back of her neck with the hilt of his dagger, but he drops it as she gouges his eyes. She pounds her powerful fists against his head and chest, over and over until he rolls out of her reach. Unarmed, he pivots, quicker than I think possible for a creature of his size, and clamps his powerful mitt around her neck, forcing downward pressure. He smashes her face into a nearby boulder before backhanding her, causing her to stagger backwards. 'How do you like that?'

Terra recovers quickly, shaking off the pain in her head.

I see his plan. Terra sees it too.

He is after my sword.

She makes a break for it, the same time he does.

The race is on.

Thumping colossal footsteps hammering upon the ancient stones beneath their feet could easily be mistaken for thunder. Their primal battle cry like something out of a movie. I have to keep telling myself this is real.

This.

Is.

Real.

With less than a few steps to go, Zurvan intercepts her, knocking her sideways, his weight crushing down on her leathery chest. He sits over her, locking his clawed hands around her throat whilst she bashes the shit out of his back ribs.

I glance around for the spear.

I spot it on the other side of the courtyard, red-tipped where it had been ripped from Terra's flesh.

I realise it's come down to a decision. Another damn decision … the spear or Terra.

For a moment, I am frozen. I can't think. Can't rationalise. Can't even determine the possible outcomes. I squeeze my one good eye shut to block out the world. *For fucks sake, Skye. This isn't the time to waver.* I take a breath, try to settle myself. Relax my thoughts. I need to consider the bigger plan here and not rely on the fly-by-the-seat-of-my-pants playbook by Skye Buchannan.

Decisions?

I hope I never have to make a decision like this again. My thoughts continue to ramble until one sentence stands out amongst the lot. Terra, although in a life-threatening predicament, convinced me she isn't the poor bastard on my page to kark it, so it comes down to one thing - I need the spear to kill Zurvan.

Decision made.

A cut-off gurgled sigh jars me from my thoughts. Terra's clobbering fists suddenly stop, altering the decision for me.

I have nothing but myself to launch at him.

I weigh up the odds. I'm probably going to be killed.

It's worth it.

I sprint at full speed, launching myself at his back. My arms circle his shoulders, gripping onto him with every ounce of strength I have, my fingers scratching his face.

He releases his hands from Terra's throat and grabs me by the back of my neck, dragging me over his head for a second time. Only this time, he has me by the throat, his arm stretched out in front of him. The bones in my neck begin to crackle, my airway closing off. My body goes limp, the sensations in my arms and legs, ebbing away. The blackness is coming for me again, and I hear Ember sobbing uncontrollably, River screaming his lungs out, Ra-Mon clapping enthusiastically. Nothing from Isis. Nothing from Amun.

And then I'm flying.

Soaring through the air, the warm breath caresses my skin, and for a second I wonder if I've died all over again … until I slam into a stone pillar. The crunch my bones make, ricochets in my ears. I slump to the ground, coughing. I try to roll over only to cry out as something in my side grips tightly, sharp and yet dull at the same time. My body hurts in so many different places I don't know where to begin. The pain is all around me, blurring my vision, killing my senses.

I push the pain aside, brace my ribs with one arm as Zurvan struts victoriously in my direction, sword in hand. I prop myself against the pillar, accepting my fate.

My time has come – it is me who dies, not my companions. I realise that now.

The warrior stands tall, a triumphant grin parting his lips, daring me to get up. But I am done. He has won. He lifts the sword over his head and I half shut my eyes, waiting for the end.

A muffled cough, followed by a sharp breath.

Confusion flits across his brow as his eyes grow cold and dull. It is the realisation that his own death is imminent.

Zurvan lands heavily on one knee, his hand fumbling for the spear protruding through his chest.

THIRTY-THREE

'**YOU** still alive?' asks Terra, crouching at my head, her fingers sweeping my hair from my eyes. 'You look like shit,' she says and laughs. 'And thanks for the gorilla tip. Great idea.'

'Thanks.' I groan. 'And what can I say, you're my hero.' Clutching my ribs, she tugs me to my feet. I look at her through the slit of my swollen eye, blood pissing out of my mouth and nose. 'Loved the grizzly bear too.'

Her brow creases. 'It was a Kodiak Bear. Next to the polar bear, it's the largest and strongest bear in the world.'

'I'll remember that,' I say, suddenly aware that, although mortally wounded, Zurvan is still with us.

'And you, you ugly piece of shit,' she turns to Zurvan. His muscular chest is stained red. He coughs, spraying blood out of his mouth. 'It's time to put you down. No more nightmares. No more threats. You are dead.' She steps around him, grabs the spear in both hands and forces it further through the beast's chest. Its eyes roll back before face-planting onto the rough sandstone. A dark cherry puddle of blood pools around his torso. 'And just for good measure,' she says, picking up the sword. She swings down in one powerful blow and hacks off the beast's head.

She then loops her arms around my neck. 'Thanks for being there for me.' She quickly kisses my cheek. 'And don't get any funny ideas.'

I flick her a mischievous wink. 'Anytime.'

The sound of a solitary person clapping, steals the moment from us.

'An outstanding performance from both of you,' shouts Ra-Mon. Blue flames lick at his lips as his sadistic grin erupts into laughter.

I lean heavily into Terra, limping worse than a cripple, totally forgetting she has wounds ten times worse than mine.

'Are you two okay?' Em whispers softly into my shoulder as we fall into line next to them.

'Don't worry. This will be over soon.'

'Will you bring forward the Lord's Graces,' Isis asks, her gaze upon me.

I ease the backpack over my shoulder and hobble towards her, picking the Lord's Staff up on the way.

'Open the bag,' she asks me when I stop in front of her.

I do as she commands.

'Place the spearhead at your feet.' I grimace as I bend down and carefully pick through the bag, cautious of the Crown of Thorns. I find the spearhead and lay it at my feet.

'Now The Scourging Whip.'

Again, I follow her orders to the letter.

I dive back into the bag, my fingers skimming over the rim of the cup until I find the whip.

'Now place the bag at my feet, and let me summon the Crown of Thorns.' Her hand hovers above the open bag, drawing a bright light from inside. The crown rises and she sets it down next to the other items, making no mention of the cup, and floats my bag back to me before magically zipping it up. She regards The Lord's Staff already at my feet.

Isis closes her eyes, her hands, palm to palm, as a soft chant begins. I can't understand a bloody word she's saying. I don't think I'm meant to.

'It's in Egyptian,' says Terra, reading my mind. 'She's summoning Mithras.'

We wait.

The process takes longer than I thought it would, and long minutes tick past by the dozen. My posture starts to wilt, my knees buckle. Terra threads her arm through mine, keeping me upright. 'Not much longer,' she whispers.

And true to her word, one more minute passes before Isis stops.

To my right, behind Ra-Mon's throne, a haze-like mirage cuts through the backdrop of Isis's temple, the fuzzy edges of a man's shoulders becoming more solid after every blink. Tight blonde curls frame his face, the rest is trapped beneath a cap, like a Christmas elf might wear. He's wearing a light brown tunic, gathered at the waist. A short red cape attaches at the shoulders with a brass pin. On his feet, a simple pair of leather sandals.

'Welcome, my friend,' says Ra-Mon, rising. The two *men*, if you can call them that, clasp forearms as was the old way of greeting. Ra-Mon looks pleased to see him. Mithras, not so much. The spook-like god, or whatever he classifies himself as, doesn't have a clue where he is, and he eyes his surroundings with suspicion.

He stares beyond us, his gaze abruptly stopping when he sees Zurvan in the arena, motionless. 'Who is responsible for defeating my champion?'

Terra steps forward, releasing my arm. 'It was me,' she says, her voice strong and steady.

He looks her up and down. '*You*?' There is laughter in his voice. 'You are a child?'

I let out a laugh, and Mithras turns his piercing gaze to me. I brace up, breathe slowly and wait to speak.

He opens his mouth … then stops, spies the Lord's Graces in front of us.

'So, it is true,' he says. The look of adulation on his face follows the clenching of his square jaw. 'Finally, I have been resurrected to replace that false god. That Christian who took my rightful place as most loved and worshipped.' He spots the Lord's Staff laying in front of me.

'Hand me that staff.'

'No,' I say, flatly.

He turns to Isis first, and then to Ra-Mon. 'Are you going to stand for this insolence?'

'No,' replies Ra-Mon. He snarls at me as he rises from his throne. His eyes turn the same shade of cobalt blue as the flash exploding out of his hands. A jagged shard of lightning crackles out of his fingers … with one target in mind … River.

It hits him square in the chest.

He doesn't have chance to scream.

He doesn't have chance to tell Ember he loves her.

He falls to the ground.

Gaze ...staring blankly at the velvet sky.

Dead.

'Noooooooooo,' screams out Ember. 'Nooooooo.'

She falls to her knees and cradles his head in her lap, rocking the life back into him, her hands brushing his hair. 'Rivvvvver,' she cries out. She looks up at me, eyes streaming, heart tearing into a million pieces. 'Help, Skye. Pleeease,' she wails. 'Noooooooo. Please, nooooooo.'

Terra circles her arms around Ember, crying into her neck.

All that talk about me being the one to die was false. All along. It was River. The prophecy of my page has come true.

All the horrors in my life … realised.

It's my fault … again.

I've killed him.

He is dead because of my error. Because I don't know when to shut my big, fat mouth.

I can't think.

I don't know what to do.

What to say.

Tears burst forth, and I wipe them away in anger. In frustration. In total despair.

I've screwed up.

I'm a screw-up.

Over and over, the words echo inside my head.

'You prick,' I yell back at Ra-Mon, my jaw so tight I can barely force the words out. 'He had nothing to do with this. It's me you want.'

Ra-Mon laughs so loud, the ground tremors beneath my feet. 'I told you before. You are all expendable. I say when your time is up.' There isn't a glimmer of emotion on his face. 'Will you bring forth the staff?' he repeats, 'Or would you like to say goodbye to another one of your friends.'

Why me?

Why me?

Why me?

I can't think of anything else except those two words.

Trust …

Trust in your ability.

You are worthy enough to be a hero.

My companion – Amun.

I want to tell him he's left it too late to help, and that I want him out of my body NOW!

My legs tingle as power surges up from my feet. Confidence rises into my chest, but it is not of my own doing. It is all HIM.

452

You must take him out, Amun says inside my head. *Use the staff. Only you can wield it. Only you have the power to finish this. Mithras is evil through to the core. None of you will survive if he attains The Lord's Staff. Terra will be kept prisoner until Ra-Mon has gathered enough strength to take her down, and with Mithras at his side, he will destroy your world. Destroy everything you hold dear.*

I glance over at Terra, who is aware I'm watching her. Her eyes plead with me to do something.

Isis speaks, drawing my attention. 'Why don't you try the crown on, my lord,' she says to Mithras. 'Only then will you be as infamous.' He spins around to face her. 'Only then will you be revered … and truly respected.'

He breathes in, his chest ballooning with pride. He snatches up the crown and positions it upon his head. She personally hands him the whip and the spearhead, and bows lowly to him.

We are done for.

Everything we've worked for is lost.

But then, a line of worry touches Mithras's forehead, touches his eyes. The unhuman glow he possessed has become dimmer, in fact, it isn't there at all.

'Something has changed,' he says as he scans the length of his body.

He is human, Amun says. *The Lord's Graces have made him human. Only a human male may possess the power of the Lord's Graces.*

TRUST!

This has to be my cue. Isis said I would know, and this is it.

I flick the staff up with my toes and snatch it out of the air before anyone can stop me. I point the staff at his chest and think of nothing else but squashing his human heart with my bare hands.

The staff emits a white light, like a million diamonds gazing up at the sun, so bright I can barely open my eyes

453

to it … just like outside the Falicon Pyramid. The pulse of power rushing through my arm is a tidal wave of energy, stealing my breath, shaking me through to my core.

Mithras shields his eyes.

His piercing scream fills the courtyard … the skies. Loud enough to hear across vast cities, countries. I need no convincing that the life is being emptied out of him.

It's over in less than sixty seconds. The light dulls as he falls backwards, blood oozing from his ears and eyes.

Ra-Mon leaps out of his throne.

His gaze of fire and pure hatred, first twists to Mithras in confusion and utter disbelief, and then to me. 'What have you done?' he spits at me.

I wave the staff at him. 'Stay back, or you're next.'

He laughs at my empty threat. 'We both know, you don't have the strength to go up against me, boy. With or without your little magic wand.'

Trust, I hear again. This time, the tone is deeper … more like Tomas.

A cloak of ice surrounds me, the air freezing, becoming thinner like I'm hardly breathing at all. White clouds form with every breath I take.

My feet are rooted to the spot.

Time is slowing down.

Slower … slower … and, slower … until …

Everyone around me, including Ra-Mon, are marble and stone.

Just like at Chartres.

The shadowy figure of Tomas appears. 'How are you here?' I ask him, shocked and stoked at the same time.

'Your mother and father are here.'

Seeing them wasn't a dream.

Wasn't a hallucination.

They emerge from behind Tomas, wearing the same clothes they were buried in – I don't know why that pops into my head.

454

'A choice stands before you,' says my father, resting his ghostly hand on my shoulder.

'Tell me something I don't know,' I say, stifling a laugh. 'When haven't I had to make a life-altering decision recently?'

Mum smiles. 'It's all part of the preparation, lovey. All leading up to this one moment.'

'Great! That makes me feel heaps better. So …' I say, letting out a breath, wanting to hug them both so hard. 'Which choice do I go for?'

'You will know.'

'Spectacular,' I say, lifting my brows. 'Glad I asked.'

Mum slips her fingers in Dad's hand, and they both look down at their union. 'You don't need to hold onto the guilt anymore, son,' says Dad. Tears bubble up in my eyes. 'We knew what we were in for. On the day you were born, an old man came to the hospital and said he was a doctor. Before he blessed you, he told us your life's purpose.'

'*Old man? Doctor?* Oh my god. DOC? Doc came to see you?'

They both just smile. 'We are so proud of you.'

Tomas places his arms around my parents and disappears into the stoney face of the temple.

Time starts ticking.

My mind, clearer than it has ever been. My heart light, unhindered. Free.

As though I haven't been missed, I turn my attention back to Ra-Mon.

I put my knee into the middle of the staff and yank hard on each end. I quickly glance over at River. 'Bring him back, or I will snap this like a twig.'

Ra-Mon laughs. 'Not even you are capable of that.'

I force it a little harder. 'You wouldn't dare.'

'Try me.'

His head snaps up as the wood begins to creak.

'STOP.'

I yield a little, maintaining my position.

'It is not in my power to give life.' He turns to Isis. She has gone.

She was there only a second ago. I saw her.

During our little dick-measuring competition, she disappeared and took Mithras's bloody corpse with her. It doesn't take a genius to see how pissed off Ra-Mon is, his face an open book of rage and revenge.

He catches me off guard. No hand movements. No shards of lightning. With a flick of his hand, I go hurtling through the air, the staff out of my reach.. as my back hits the solid ground remembering the pain.

A fireball is hurled at him.

Ember!

Which means one thing … our powers are back. Isis must have given us half a chance when she took off with Mithras.

A second fireball and then a third come buzzing passed him.

Ember is standing over River's still body, her hair full of flames, face of fiery determination, churning out gigantic wheels of fire. Ra-Mon deflects them easily enough, but that's not what it's for. I hear her yell inside my head – GET THE STAFF.

It's a distraction.

I hear Amun in my head again: *If Ra-Mon takes possession of the Lord's Staff, it will be the undoing for us all. With the four elements at his side, it will transform into the Staff of Amun-Ra – a weapon that has no equal and which cannot be destroyed.*

So, I do what I do best … I think without acting.

I vanish.

The aggravated roar from Ra-Mon tells me I don't have long before he unleashes hell on all of us. I lunge for the staff, wrap my fist around it so tightly, my knuckles ache, and in the blink between blinks, those crucial seconds before I think about it too much, when life hangs in the balance …

I tear across the courtyard, my flight in full rocket mode, to drop down behind him.

Ember is tiring.

Her fireballs becoming smaller and less in number. HURRY, she screams at me.

I grit my teeth and pray to whoever is listening. *Please let this work.*

I switch to visible mode and aim the staff at Ra-Mon's back – a little cowardly, I know, but we are talking about the end of the world here, and the rules of engagement don't apply.

The second he senses me, he spins around. White light shoots out of the staff, encasing Ra-Mon in a bubble of some kind.

'How are you doing that?' asks Ember.

I shake my head. 'No idea.'

'Whatever you do, don't stop.' I don't intend to.

Terra skates across to the throne and grabs my backpack. 'I think I know a way we can help River.' She dives through the bag and pulls out the cup. 'We need water.'

'The dam,' says Ember, resuming her spot next to River.

'None of you move. Especially, not you,' Terra says to me with a smile.

I focus on Ra-Mon, the staff doing *its thing*. I don't sense a drop in power at all, which worries me. Yes, it's the most formidable weapon ever, so where is it drawing its charge from?

And then I realise.

Amun.

Dude, how long can you keep this up for?

There is no response.

Fear finds me.

Shakes my legs and hands and sends a wobbly welcome message to my stomach. If Amun is weakened, he won't have the strength to fight off Ra-Mon.

I need to find another way.

457

Just as I am about to pull up on the staff's almighty power, Isis reappears.

Alone.

She stretches out her arm, her fingers pointing directly at my chest. 'This might hurt a little, Air-child,' she says around a wicked grin.

My body goes taut. Jolting, like I'm touching the wrong end of a freshly charged cattle prod. The light force around Ra-Mon collapses immediately.

'My lord,' gasps Isis, 'how has this happened?'

'Bind them,' Ra-Mon yells at her. 'NOW!'

Isis raises her hands first at Ember, then at me. Terra hasn't returned from getting water, so I'm not sure if she still retains hers. I hope so. 'It is done,' she says.

'How could you have been so foolish?' The fury in his voice echoes around the barren courtyard. 'Their powers returned when you left?' he snaps, looking at me as though he wants to tear my throat out … tear anyone's throat out.

Isis bows her head. 'I had to take Mithras to The Underworld, my lord. For safe keeping. I feared he would seek revenge for tricking him, and making him mortal, so I placed him somewhere he can never escape from. He will stay there for all eternity.'

This seems to calm him a little at least to the point he isn't going to burn down the entire city.

'I NEED THAT STAFF,' he snarls.

'You will need Amun before you can place your hands on the staff, my lord,' says Isis, almost apologetically.

I glare at her, but say nothing. I get that she's supposed to be on our side, but there's that tiny element of doubt that she could be selling us out. I play along with it … for now.

'*You must let him take Amun.*' I hear Terra's voice in my head. '*I have seen his mind. Ra-Mon means to kill Ember, and then you. Then he will come for me. I cannot do this without you. I am not self-healing. You must release Amun, and we shall live to fight another day.*'

458

Her words are insects scratching and biting inside my head. She's right.

I close my eyes. The one thing I am hopeless at … decisions. *You are running out of time*, says Amun. *Release me now.*

'Alright,' I growl, hating that I have to roll over so easily and without a fight.

I take a deep breath.

And then another.

More than ever, I sense Amun at the forefront of my consciousness. There's no digging or begging for him to make himself known to me. He could be standing beside me.

'My lord, Amun will join us,' assures Isis.

Ra-Mon joyfully claps his hands. 'Come, my old friend. Let us be reunited. I'm sure Nereus will be overjoyed to see you.'

My body tears like paper as Amun pushes through my bones, ripping through my muscles, through my blood, to get to my skin. I cry out as the white, hot pain sears through me, erratically taking control of my body, throwing my head backwards, chest to the heavens, arms splayed wide in a gesture of surrender.

And then stillness.

And silence.

I drop to my knees as a transparent figure, tall and handsome, stands before me, stunning me with his brilliance. His shoulder length golden hair almost acts as a halo over his sharp, angular jaw and cheeks. His sun-kissed skin glows beneath his white tunic.

He waits until our eyes meet. 'We shall see each other again,' he whispers to me.

Ra-Mon looks to Isis. 'Keep them here. I will deal with them on my return.'

'Yes, my lord,' says Isis obediently. She bows once more.

Amun regards me, with a fleeting glance over his shoulder before fading into nothingness, right alongside Ra-Mon.

Isis's spell falls away and my body is back to being sore and swollen and bashed to a pulp. There's an ache that hums inside my bones.

'Hurry,' says Isis. 'We don't have much time. Ra-Mon will return for the staff.'

'What about River?' I ask.

'The cup of life can save him,' says Isis, 'but first I need to get you all to a safe place.'

'Take Ember and River first. I will wait here for Terra.'

A moment later, River and Ember disappear in a shimmer of light. I heave a sigh of relief.

Minutes pass before Terra hobbles towards me, full cup in hand and looks at the empty space where River lay. 'Isis has taken them?' she asks.

'Yep.'

She tips out the water and drops the cup into my backpack. 'And Amun?'

'Gone,' I say in a gruff tone.

'Good. Glad you got my message.' She wiggles her fingers into my palm, shivering next to me. I'm sure she was wearing more clothes.

'You go next,' I say to her, her arms sprinkled with goosebumps. In the light of the torches, I see for myself the full extent of her injuries. She's ripped the arm off a flannelette shirt and made a tourniquet of it, binding it tightly around the top of her leg to stem the blood. Her pants are soaked in red. The rest of the shirt is stuffed down her t-shirt to pack the wound on her stomach. The light cardigan she'd removed, as we passed through Hell, has been knotted and fastened over the top to keep the whole thing in place. I regard her First Aid technique again - the flannelette shirt, I notice, is actually my flanny hoodie I couldn't find before we left Isis's place.

'No can do,' she says. 'We've run out of time.' She reaches up and kisses me on the cheek. Thanks for being my friend. It means a lot.'

She barely gets the words out before Ra-Mon returns.

He looks around for Isis. 'She's taken them to Hell, you mutt,' hisses Terra.

Ra-Mon squints his eyes at her. Looks to me. 'Give me the staff, or I will crush your girlfriend too.'

'*Girlfriend*?' is my first response.

'Don't you dare, Skye. I can take care of myself.
'But …'

'You promised. You promised me. Trust me.'

'Enough,' snaps Ra-Mon, roping an invisible bond around Terra's throat and pulling it tight. She claws at her neck, gasping for breath. He swings her around to face me. Her eyes beg me one last time. Her fingers lightly brush the back of my hand before she disappears.

My heart plummets.

Skips too many beats.

'I told you not to test me, boy. Now, give me the staff.'

This one time, I trust.

I trust in everything I know, and everything I have been taught. I trust in the love I have for my family, my friends and the promises I have sworn to them.

But most of all, I trust in the decision I'm about to make.

Backpack slung over my shoulder, I grip the rod of the staff with all my might.

And vanish.

ACKNOWLEDGEMENTS

Thanks to Natasha @ natashasnowdesigns.com for another fantastic cover. You have immortalised my characters forever.

Thanks to you, my readers, for without you, I would have no one to share my crazy creativeness with.

To my family

You all spend many hours without me in your life so that I can do what I love doing … writing.

And for that I want to tell you

I love you

I love you

I love you

BOOKS BY LORRAINE ELJUGA

The Elementar series

FlameMaker
WaterLover
AirWhisperer

Ω

COMING SOON
(last in the series)

EarthHealer